SLEEP NO MORE

ALSO BY IRIS JOHANSEN

SLEEP NO MORE

IRIS JOHANSEN

**Doubleday Large Print
Home Library Edition**

ST. MARTIN'S PRESS ⚇ NEW YORK

SLEEP NO MORE. Copyright © 2012 by Johansen Publishing LLLP. All rights reserved. Printed in the United States of America. For information, address St. Martin's Press, 175 Fifth Avenue, New York, N.Y. 10010.

ISBN 978-1-62090-479-4

**This Large Print Book carries the
Seal of Approval of N.A.V.H.**

ACKNOWLEDGMENTS

Many, many thanks to my son, Roy, for all his help with creating our very special Kendra. She is difficult, complex, and definitely a challenge, and yet he handled her with cleverness and originality. Working with him to meet that challenge was one of the great joys of writing this book.

SLEEP NO MORE

CHAPTER

1

The kill should be ridiculously easy.

Not really worthy of his talents, Drogan thought as he moved silently down the hall. It was all a question of timing. The nurse who was usually on duty at the desk of this private wing had left on her break three minutes ago and would not return for another seventeen minutes. Another nurse from the ward on the third floor, who was scheduled to cover her absence, was due to make a routine check in about ten minutes. No other coverage was considered necessary since the patient was always heavily sedated. He'd have to be out of here by then. The nurses at Seahaven were always as punctual and routine-oriented as everyone in the plush mental hospital. They had good jobs and wanted to keep them.

Too bad. The private nurse's job taking care of the woman in that suite down the hall was about to come to an abrupt end.

He stopped before Beth Avery's room and carefully, silently, opened the door. The lights were out in the room, but Drogan could see her heaped beneath the covers on the bed across the room. She should be sleeping well; he'd been told they always gave her extra drugs at night.

Including this night, her last night.

He took the hypodermic out of his jacket pocket.

Yes, it was too easy, he thought. Any of her doctors or nurses could have given her the fatal injection. She was drugged and helpless. Why pay a hit man to do the job?

Because they had no guts, he thought contemptuously. Because Dr. Harry Pierce, with all his fancy degrees in psychiatry, was a coward who wouldn't risk his fine career and put his neck on the chopping block. That took nerve and skill and the ability to take the final step. Drogan possessed all three qualities, and that made him a giant far above these ineffectual assholes.

Ten minutes. Make the kill and get out of here.

He glided toward the bed.

What did you do, Beth Avery? Why do they want you dead? Are they tired of dealing with you? Not that it mattered. As long as he got his money, that was his only concern. Still, it was curious . . .

He had reached the bed. He put out his hand to shift the blanket so that he could make the injection. Then he would wait until he was sure that the stuff had worked. A less professional man would just take off, but he was proud of his work ethic.

It would take several seconds, but he'd be able to tell when she died. He knew death. It was an old friend.

He flipped back the cover.

Shit.

No Beth Avery. Pillows. Three pillows.

Pain.

He staggered back as he was struck from behind with the base of a lamp.

He fell to his knees as the room whirled around him.

A woman . . .

Tall, slim, dark brown hair, in her thirties . . . Beth Avery. He'd been given a photo of her. The target.

She had the lamp lifted to strike him again.

"No way, bitch." He lunged forward and brought her down. He had dropped the hypodermic when he fell and he lunged for it.

She brought her heel down on the syringe, smashing it. Then she pushed him away and rolled away from him.

God, she was strong, he realized dimly. Avery was supposed to be weak and drugged, but she was as sleek and muscular as a young lioness.

But a lioness can be taken down like any other cat. His hands closed on her throat. Die, bitch.

She butted her head against his nose as hard as she could.

Damn her. He could feel the blood spurt from his nostrils as his hands loosened from her throat.

She tore away and jumped to her feet. She grabbed the lamp and swung it again.

It connected, and he fell backwards.

She ran out the door.

Gone. She was gone.

Rage and humiliation tore through him as he struggled to his feet.

"No you don't." He reached the hall in seconds and caught sight of her turning the corner. She was obviously heading for the emergency exit. He'd chase her down the flights of stairs and grab her before she reached the lobby exit. She didn't realize how well the privacy of that stairwell would work for him. The kill was supposed to look like a natural death, but he'd worry about that later. It wasn't his fault that Beth Avery wasn't what they'd told him and had taken him off guard. That damn Pierce could just rig something that would keep all their asses out of trouble. He couldn't worry about that right now. The bitch had made a fool of him. She had hurt him physically and stung his pride. He wasn't going to stop until she was dead.

Find her.

Catch her.

Kill her.

• • •

Beth opened the door of the linen closet a tiny crack, watching him jerk open the emergency door down the hall and start down the stairs.

Him. She didn't even know who he was. He had tried to kill her, and she didn't know his name.

Crazy. As crazy as the doctors here sometimes called her. Not to her face, they were always gentle and kind to her face. But she had heard Pierce laugh and whisper behind her back.

She wasn't crazy, and she wouldn't let them put her to death like some rabid dog.

The man who had tried to kill her must have reached the second flight of stairs by now. She opened the linen-closet door and flew to the freight elevator around the corner. She punched the button for the basement.

Slow . . . The elevator was so slow. What if he found she wasn't in the stairwell or the lobby and ran down to the basement? He could be waiting for her when the elevator door opened.

The elevator stopped.

She held her breath, bracing herself.

No one. The parking garage was brightly

lit, but there were no security guards or parking attendants. Billy had told her that the area closed down at ten at night, and she should be safe.

Still, relief flooded her as she punched the elevator button to send it to the top floor before she left the elevator. She hadn't been sure about anything. She ran down the concrete walk toward the door that led upstairs to the parking lot.

Unlocked, as Billy had told her it would be. One flight upstairs, then another un-locked door that opened to the rear grounds of the hospital. The hospital was built on the edge of a cliff above the sea, and she could hear the sound of the surf on the rocks below. Freedom was beckoning. Why not try to just keep on running?

No, Billy had told her that they would catch her if she took this way out.

Red herring, he had said. Be clever. Trust me.

But she was so afraid. Her hand instinc-tively reached up to clasp the gold key on her necklace. Help me . . .

But the key was only a symbol, and Billy was the only one who could help her now. Do exactly what he said.

She turned away from the cliff and back toward the corridor leading to the elevators. She deliberately left the door cracked open so that they would think she'd already left the hospital. Then she ran back toward the elevators.

Red herring. Go back upstairs to the third floor, where Billy would meet her. Billy would help her. Trust him . . .

Run.

Billy had worked his magic. He had not asked questions, had not even let her speak. He had just grabbed her hand and pulled her from the corridor into the room. He had told her exactly what they would have to do to get her away, and they had done it. She had been too frantic to even be afraid. A few minutes after she entered the room, she was outside the gates of the hospital.

Then she was running across the manicured green lawns toward the woods.

Her heart was beating hard as she reached the shelter of the trees. No one was behind her. No one had seen her.

Free. Am I free? Will I ever be free? What the hell is free?

But she had to do everything Billy had

told her to do. Make the call. She reached into her jacket pocket and drew out the pre-paid phone Billy had given her and dialed the number he had given her. "I'm in the woods, Billy. I'm making my way toward that motel you told me about, where the Greyhound bus stops. I don't think I was followed." She drew a long breath. "You didn't let me tell you, Billy. You were right. There was a man . . . he was going to kill me."

"I told you that I thought it would be tonight after I overheard that last phone call. You should have believed me."

"It was . . . hard. It didn't make sense. But I did what you said about the pillows and everything."

"But instead of running to me right away, you had to stick around and see for yourself. Thank God, you were at least ready for him." He muttered a curse beneath his breath. "I could have gotten you out of there a lot easier if you'd trusted me before this."

"It didn't make sense," she repeated shakily. "Why, Billy? I never hurt anyone. Why would they want to kill me? And why now? I've been here at the hospital for years. What did I do that made them want to get rid of me now?"

"I don't know, Beth. I only found out bits and pieces of what's going on. Stop asking questions and concentrate on just getting away. But you've got to remember everything I told you. They'll be hunting you down. From now on, don't trust anyone." He paused. "Not even me."

"Of course I trust you." If she didn't trust Billy, then she was absolutely alone, and the thought frightened her. "You always told me to trust you."

"That's over. You can't trust me any longer. I won't let them catch you by using me. You're safer if you realize you can't depend on anyone but yourself. I gave you the tools to save yourself, now do it. You don't need anyone."

"Then why do I feel as if I need you, Billy? Dammit, I don't *know* anything. It's as if I've been lost at sea for all these years, and now that I've come back to port, everything I knew is gone, and I'm lost again."

"Then change it to suit yourself. You can do it. I've seen how you meet a challenge. Are you at the motel yet? There should be a bus leaving there in ten minutes."

"I think I see the neon sign."

"Hurry. You have to get out of the area

right away. They'll be searching the grounds for you for quite a while. They won't expect you to have a plan."

No, why expect a plan from a crazy woman, she thought bitterly. "I am hurrying." She was almost running. "I'll call you when I reach—"

"Don't call me. I won't answer. You're on your own." He hung up.

On her own. The words sent panic racing through her. She suddenly felt terribly alone. Billy had tried to warn her he couldn't be there for her, but she hadn't wanted to believe him. He was the only one at the hospital who cared anything about her. He had helped her shake off the drugs, talked to her, made her aware of what they were doing to her. He had been her friend. If she didn't have Billy, she had no one.

Calm down. What was different? She couldn't remember when she hadn't felt alone. No, when they'd used the heavy sedatives on her, she hadn't felt anything but a blurred sense of contentment. She hadn't felt loneliness or sadness or fear. It was only when they started lessening the doses that she'd begun to feel the emotions that everyone else felt, the emotions that made them human beings instead of mindless robots.

She felt a wild burst of anger as she remembered the little cups of pills handed her by the nurses. The shots administered to calm her when she was calmer than anyone on the medical team who'd clustered around her, smothering her.

Now she could see the Greyhound bus drawn up before the motel entrance. Her hand in her pocket closed on the scrap of paper with the address scrawled on it. She started toward the bus at a dead run. She was not going to miss that bus. It was going to take her to a new life, a new start.

She was *not* mindless. She was *not* crazy.

And she would not let those bastards rob her of either her mind or her life.

Lake Cottage
Atlanta, Georgia

Running.
Panic.
The trees were all around her, tall shapes in the darkness. Eve could hear the sea

crashing against the rocks though she couldn't see it from here. But she had seen it from the hospital every day for all those years. Sometimes, she'd even been permitted to go down to the shore. But there was always a price.

Always something she had to give up in return.

No one behind her yet.

But how did she know?

Run faster.

Her breath was coming in gasps.

Did she hear someone? A crackling of leaves under a heavy footstep. He'd been a big man. She'd barely managed to get away from him. Could she get away from him again if he caught her? She didn't want to die.

She wouldn't die.

Just run faster.

Fight them. Don't let him kill her.

That bus was right ahead.

Get on it. Lose herself. But she was already lost. She'd been lost as long as she could remember.

Run!

"Eve, wake up!"

A hand grasping her shoulder.

He'd caught her! Fight him.

"Eve, dammit, wake up."

Joe.

She opened her eyes to see him leaning over her. "Joe?"

Joe. Not the man with the syringe.

The lake cottage, not the hospital by the sea.

No one chasing her through the woods.

"Shh." Joe was holding her close. "Just a dream, Eve." He kissed her temple. "But it must have been one hell of a violent one. It took me a couple minutes to bring you out of it. And you almost knocked me out."

Her arms clung to him with all her strength. Safe. Joe would keep her safe.

"Hey, it's okay now." He brushed back her hair from her face with a gentle hand. "I've never seen you like this after a nightmare."

She had never felt like this. "I hit you?" She shook her head to clear it of the last vestiges of sleep. "Lord, I'm sorry, Joe. It was so real . . ." She sat up in bed and ran her fingers through her tousled hair. Her scalp was as damp as if she'd really been running through those woods. "It still seems that way." She drew a deep breath. "I think I need to get a drink of water and some fresh air. Go on back to sleep." She swung her feet to the floor. "It's almost dawn, and you have to be at headquarters in a few hours. I'm sorry I woke you."

"Don't be silly," he said curtly as he sat up in bed. "What does that matter? You're upset. You're still shaking. I'm not about to go peacefully back to sleep. What kind of nightmare was it?" He paused. "Bonnie?"

It was natural that he'd jump to that conclusion. Her daughter, Bonnie, had been kidnapped and murdered many years ago when she was only seven years old, and it had been the tragedy of Eve's life. She and Joe had searched all those years they'd been together for both Bonnie's killer and her body, and they had only recently been found. There had been many nightmares during those first years after Bonnie had been taken from Eve. Later, there had been other dreams of her very special child that had been sad but strangely comforting. And then, crazy as it seemed, she and Joe had become convinced that those were not dreams at all but visits from the spirit of her Bonnie. Dear God, how long it had taken her to accept that impossible concept. "Not Bonnie." She slipped on her robe. "I've not dreamed of Bonnie since we found her body a few months ago." She tried to smile. "I miss her, Joe."

"She knows," he said quietly. "She'll come back to you, Eve."

"Well, she's taking her time about it. I think she's trying to cut me loose. She's always worried that I think too much about her and not enough about you and Jane. She says ghosts should never have top priority." She shook her head. "It's not true. I know how lucky I am to have you in my life. I just want it all."

"Perfectly natural." He tossed the sheet aside. "Go out on the porch. I'll get your water."

"Joe, I don't need you to wait on me," she said in exasperation. "You're treating me like a kid. It was only a nightmare."

"Shoo." He gently swatted her behind as he passed her on the way to the bathroom. "Get moving. And don't stop at your worktable on the way to the porch and do a few more touches to that reconstruction."

He wasn't going to pay any attention to

her. No one could be more stubborn than Joe. Particularly when it came to guarding and caring for her.

She left the bedroom and headed down the hall toward the porch. She slowed as she glanced at the forensic reconstruction on the dais on her worktable. It was the skull of a little unknown girl Eve had named Janelle when she had begun to work on it two days ago. When she had first started her career as a forensic sculptor after Bonnie had been taken, she had begun giving the skulls names as a gesture of respect, and she had never stopped. Janelle's skeleton had been found scattered in a quarry in Indiana, and the Indianapolis police had no idea of her identity and sent the skull to Eve for help. So far, the only thing that Eve could determine was that she was Asian and approximately nine years old. But it had only been two days, and the depth measurements had just begun. When they were completed, she would start the actual sculpting with the clay, and soon she would have a face whose features resembled those of the child before she had been murdered and thrown into that quarry.

"We'll get there, Janelle," she murmured. "You're important. No one had the right to throw you away. I'll bring you home."

"Out." Joe had caught up with her, and his hand was beneath her elbow. "Another minute, and you'll be over there working." He opened the front door. "You'll probably do it anyway, but I'm going to make sure you're okay first."

"I'm okay. For heaven's sake, it was only a nightmare. I'd probably be better off working and forgetting about it." She took the glass of water he handed her and went out on the porch. The air was clear and cool, and the waning moon cast silver paths on the lake. She immediately felt the sense of serenity that she always did when she looked out at the familiar woods bordering the lake.

Run.

Through the woods.

The sound of the sea on the rocks.

No, that was the nightmare. Forget it. She was being foolish to let it bother her. She took a long drink of water. "You don't have to stay out here with me. I'm okay now, Joe."

"Liar." His arms slid around her from behind and he pressed his cheek against her hair. "I can see the pulse pounding in your temple. You're still jumpy. Just relax and stop trying to cheat me of being with you. Moments like this are good."

Being with him was always good, she thought as she leaned back against him. She could feel the warmth of his lean, muscular body through his brown terry robe, and that warmth was flowing into her, bringing the contentment and love it always did. They had gone through tough times during the years they had been together. Joe was a brilliant detective with the Atlanta Police Department, and she had her own career as a forensic sculptor. Along with demanding careers, they were two people struggling against death and loss and trying to grow and make it through the storms to a brighter life together. But the love had always been there. Love and passion and humor, and all the things that made the battle and the life together worthwhile. "Okay, have it your own way."

He chuckled. "And your way."

She nodded. "My way." She turned and went into his arms. She loved the feel of him. He was strong and warm and good.

When they were like this, she felt as if he was flowing into her and filling every emptiness in her heart and soul. All was right with her world.

Alone.
Always alone.
So hard to hide when there's no one to care if you live or die.

Why couldn't she shake off the memory of that damn dream? she thought impatiently. That terrible loneliness had nothing to do with her or her life.

"You're tensing again." He pushed her back away from him, and his hands cupped her face. "I think it's time you talked it out." He was studying her expression. "Yes, definitely tense. This isn't like you. You're sure it wasn't Bonnie?"

She shook her head. "I wouldn't lie to you, Joe."

"Or Jane? You're not worried about Jane?"

She grimaced. "I'm always worried about Jane." Jane MacGuire, an artist, was their adopted daughter and had been working in Scotland for months. It was sometimes difficult remembering that Jane was an adult and no longer the street kid they'd taken into their home all those years ago. "But that goes with the territory when you love someone. I know Jane can take care of herself." She smiled. "Are you going to go down the list of family and friends? Stop analyzing, Joe. There wasn't some mysterious trigger that caused that dream. It was just one of those nutty chase-and-pursuit nightmares."

"Someone was chasing you?"

"Yes." She frowned. "No."

"Well, that's clear."

"I told you it was nutty. I'm not sure it was me that was running." She shrugged. "But it must have been me because I was so afraid."

"Why?"

"Joe, drop it."

"No, I don't like you to be afraid even of things that go bump in the night. It's not like you. In fact, it's damn weird. Talk it out. We'll get rid of it."

That was just like Joe, she thought. Face it, solve it, then send it on its way. It was how he'd become a great police detective: it was how he lived his life. Except he'd never sent her on her way, thank God. He'd kept her close to his heart, and she was grateful every day of her life that she spent with him.

"Okay, I'll talk it out. But there's nothing that really makes any sense. I was running through the woods, and I—"

He nodded at the trees along the lakeshore. "Those woods?"

She shook her head. "And no lake. There was an ocean . . ."

"What ocean?"

"I don't know. Stop interrogating me. I was being chased, and I was trying to catch a bus. It was . . . bizarre."

"What was bizarre?"

"Stuff I was thinking. Most of it didn't make any sense. Except for the fear. I knew I had a reason to be afraid. That's all I can remember. See, just a string of disconnected thoughts and emotions." She gave him a quick, hard kiss. "There, I've talked it out, and I'm much better. Now let's go to bed and see if you can go back to sleep."

He shook his head. "No, I'm not sleepy. Let's sit over there and cuddle for a while."

He was leading her toward the porch swing. "Don't worry, I'm through cross-examining you. I just thought it might help. We'll talk about Bonnie and Jane and you and me." He pulled her down beside him and drew her into the curve of his arm, with her head in the hollow of his shoulder. "Or maybe not talk at all. We've both been pretty busy lately, and I've missed this."

So had Eve. She could hear the beating of his heart, and it seemed to be beating within her, too. She always felt closer to Joe in special moments like this.

She had always been alone.
She was more alone now than ever.

That poignant thought from the nightmare again. It just proved how disjointed and foolish it had been. Eve had never been less alone in her life. She had Joe and family and friends she loved around her. Life was never perfect, but loneliness was no longer one of her problems. She pushed the memory away, firmly blocking it.

She cuddled closer to Joe, her gaze on the moonlight on the lake.

No panic. No danger. No wrenching loneliness.

Not here with Joe.

"I've lost her," Drogan said, when Dr. Harry Pierce picked up the phone. "It's your fault, Pierce. She wasn't what I expected. I would have handled it entirely differently if I'd realized that she wasn't what you told me."

"Excuses, Drogan?" Pierce asked softly. "What a tough guy you are when you can't even handle a woman who's spent almost two decades in an institution. You were recommended very highly, but I suppose they were wrong."

"I'll handle her, but I'll handle her my way. I shouldn't have trusted a man who doesn't have the guts to follow through on a job. You've probably been collecting from the Avery family for years, and you still have to come to me when they want to pull the plug on sweet Beth."

"Why should I trust you? You failed me. I'd do better hiring someone else."

"Go ahead. But I'll still go after her and cut her throat. I'm not going to take you or anyone else telling me how that crazy drug addict got the best of me." He paused.

"And after that, I may go after you, Pierce. Did it occur to you that the Avery family might be tired of dealing with you? After the woman is dead, you'll be useless to them. Yes, I think I may contact them and see if they need me to tie up a loose end."

"Stay away from them," Pierce said harshly. "None of this must touch them. Do you think they won't take both of us down if they see a threat? Do you know the kind of power they have?" He drew a deep breath. "Maybe I was hasty. We can work together. I've already had that mess in her room cleared, and I've put out the word that she's run away from the hospital. It shouldn't take you long to find her. She won't be able to think straight with all the drugs we pumped into her. You probably scared her, and she panicked. I don't even know how she managed to get away from the hospital without someone's seeing her."

"Bullshit. She didn't act scared."

"As I said, panic. She's like a child, and she'll have no idea how to hide from you. But when you find her, no violence, no slitting her throat. It has to be a tragic accident brought on by her mental condition.

One that could be expected from a woman who has delusions and could suffer disorientation when faced with having to cope with the outside world."

"Tragic accidents can be violent . . . and painful. You're a doctor. You can make it look like anything you want it to be."

Pierce didn't like the sound of that. He had heard some strange things about Drogan when he had hired him. "Look, I won't tolerate any of that voodoo stuff I was told you like to pull on occasion. That's not what I hired you to do. It has to look natural, dammit."

"And it will if she doesn't make me any angrier than I am right now. If she does, then I may have to introduce her to the Snake God. I'll tell you when I get close to her." He hung up.

Problems. I don't need these problems, Pierce thought with irritation as he pressed the disconnect. He liked his comfortable life and the generous favors thrown his way by the Avery family. He couldn't see why Nelda Avery had decided that Beth Avery had to die. He'd had Beth under control all these years, and she hadn't bothered anyone. He had even tentatively suggested that they keep the present arrangement in place.

"Have you told the old bitch yet?" Stella Lenslow stood in the doorway. In her nurse's uniform, she should have looked crisp and businesslike, but the white made her red hair blaze in contrast, and she exuded an overpowering sexuality. "No, I can see you haven't. You still have your head on your shoulders." She closed the door behind her. "I told you that you should do the job yourself."

"Or give it to you." His lips twisted. "I can't see you taking a risk that could cause you to end up on death row. You have a very good sense of self-preservation. So don't tell me what to do, Stella."

"But you like me to tell you what to do." She crossed the room and stood before his desk. "When it pleases you."

And most of the time, everything she did pleased him. They had been together for six years, and he'd found her sexual appetite as voracious as her greed. She'd been his "patient" since her parents had brought her to him for private therapy after a run-in with the law for prostitution. She'd only been seventeen at the time and totally out of control as far as her parents were concerned. Upright, churchgoing people, they had been frightened and bewildered by their daughter, who had been a bad seed all her life. Even as a small child, she had been totally remorseless and without conscience, and, lately, she had begun to terrorize them. The Lenslowes didn't know how to deal with someone who had no sense of right or wrong and could not be taught. They had come to the point that they had only wanted to get rid of her and salvage the remainder of their lives. They had eagerly accepted Pierce's suggestions as to how to do it and were probably lucky they'd washed their hands of her. Pierce had diagnosed her as an incurable sociopath during the first month of therapy. But he had no problem with that when she provided him with such intense and extreme entertainment. "Well, you're not pleasing me at the moment. I told you to give Beth enough pills to put her out. You didn't do it."

"I gave her plenty." She dropped down onto the chair beside his desk. "Don't blame me, Harry. Just tell me when you're going to get her back. I don't like the idea of her running around out there. It could cause trouble if anyone connects me with her. They'll find out I'm not a real nurse. I'm still on probation, and they could send me to prison. I like it just fine here."

Because he took such good care of her, he thought dryly. He bought her whatever she wanted. He'd even given her the perfect job for her temperament. She dealt out medicines and gave the shots. She liked the feeling of power over the patients.

She liked the feeling of power, period.

"I'll get her back. But you'd better keep a low profile for a little while. I'm trying to keep the media from finding out that we've lost her, but I had to tell the staff when we were searching for her. Someone may talk." He smiled. "And you never bothered to make any friends among the other employees. You'll probably be a target."

"Low profile?" She shook her head. "Not me. I won't fade away for anyone. That's for other people. That's for that mousey, plain excuse for a woman who you're trying to run to ground." She wrinkled her nose. "I never did like her."

"You never like anyone. You don't know what it means." He raised his brows. "But that usually means you did something that wasn't quite ethical. What did you do, Stella?"

She shrugged. "I cut down her drugs a little."

"In hopes that it would cause her to go into withdrawal and experience severe pain. You are a complete bitch, my darling."

"She's nothing. She was like a dummy. She annoyed me. I wanted to see her hurt." She added quickly, "But she had a full dose last night, just as you told me."

"That had better be true."

"I got tired of everyone tiptoeing around and treating her like a princess. She was only a zombie." She met his gaze. "You should know that's all she was. You're the one who made her like that."

But she had never confronted him with that fact. She was proving unpredictable and therefore dangerous. He might have to do something about Stella. "Stay away from the media. Don't answer any questions." He reached for the phone. "And get out of here while I call Nelda Avery."

"I want to stay."

"I know. You'd enjoy seeing me uncomfortable. I won't let you have that pleasure." He stared her in the eye. "Go upstairs to my apartment and take off your clothes. Lie down naked on the bed and wait for me. After I get through talking to the Grand Dame, I'm going to need a release. I'm going to screw you until you won't be able to crawl out of that bed. I'm going to make you scream, Stella."

She moistened her lips. "Is that a threat? I can always go you one better. Why not do it on the desk while you're talking to her? I could strip down now if you weren't afraid someone would walk in on us."

She would do it, and he was tempted. "Get out of here. Do what I told you."

"Whatever." She stood up and sauntered toward the door. "Good luck, Harry. Don't be too long, or I might get bored and leave."

That wasn't going to happen. She understood the rules. Sex anytime, any way he wanted it. "You won't leave." He reached for his phone. "You like it here, remember?"

He watched the door close behind her before he began to dial the number. He was already feeling the tension that usually gripped him when he spoke to Nelda Avery. She always made him remember that she controlled almost every aspect of his life. Over the years, she had gradually become the puppetmaster who pulled the strings. He could visualize her sitting in her elegant house in Charleston, dressed in a designer business suit, her carefully coifed brown hair with only a few threads of gray. She was in her seventies but looked much younger, and her gray eyes were the coldest he had ever seen. She didn't tolerate mistakes, and those eyes were going to be icy before he was done with her that day.

It was going to be a hellish call.

Keep the feeling of dominance and lust he felt toward Stella in the forefront of his mind. Think about what he was going to make her do. She was a woman like this ice queen to whom he was going to have to submit for the next few minutes. Substitution. Release. He would get through this.

Nelda Avery was on the line.

"Nelda, I'm afraid there's been something of a glitch. Nothing irreparable, but it will be a little . . ."

CHAPTER

2

Eve's phone was ringing.

She ignored it. Not now, she thought impatiently. It couldn't be Joe; she had spoken to him an hour ago, and he had told her he was going to be in a meeting at the mayor's office. Anyone else could wait. She had to get two more depth measurements on Janelle's midtherum area. The reconstruction was going exceptionally well. The skull was not broken, and all the pieces were—

The ringing stopped, then immediately began again.

Okay, dammit, she had to answer it. You

didn't ignore anyone that urgent. She crossed the room to where her phone was lying on the coffee table by the couch and checked the ID.

Sandra Duncan.

Her mother, Sandra. Maybe it wasn't all that urgent. Sandra believed everything she did or experienced was vitally important and urgent. Eve was tempted to wait and call her back. Their relationship hadn't been warm in years, though Eve had made every attempt after Sandra's latest divorce to bridge their differences. Sandra hadn't phoned her for months and had been either cool or entirely ignored Eve's monthly duty calls to check on her at her condo.

No, Eve would only feel guilty if she found out anything was really wrong. She picked up the call.

"Hello, Sandra. How may I help you?"

"It took you long enough to answer." Sandra's Southern drawl had a distinct edge. "You can't help me. I want to talk to Joe."

"Joe's not here. Do you need something?" She and Joe had paid off the mortgage on Sandra's condo years ago and saw that she had a generous allowance. But Sandra had never been good with money, and it wasn't unusual for her to come to Joe and ask for an "advance."

"Of course I need something. Why else would I be calling you? Joe has to help me. I've been trying to reach him, and his phone is turned off."

Why else indeed would Sandra be calling? "Joe is in a meeting. He won't be home for another couple hours. I'll ask him to call you." This was ridiculous. Why saddle Joe with a potential problem? "But that's not necessary. I can take care of anything that you need. Joe is always glad to help you, but, after all, you're my mother, Sandra. Now what can I do for you? Do you need money?"

"No, I don't need money," Sandra said curtly. "And you can't help me. I need Joe for this. He's the detective. I'm in my car on the way to your place. I'll be there in fifteen minutes." She hung up.

So much for getting any more work done on the reconstruction, Eve thought ruefully as she pressed the disconnect. Her mother had always been self-absorbed and had a tendency to blow up small problems into gigantic ones. She had probably received another traffic ticket and thought Joe should fight it for her.

She went back to her worktable and carefully placed one more depth marker before she stepped back and wiped her hands on the towel. "Sorry, Janelle, I have to take care of this first. I'll get back to you later." She heard a car on the road leading to the cottage. "She usually doesn't take long. Joe and I are too boring for her." Eve was grateful that Sandra led a busy life, with lessons and card parties and trips out of town with her different social groups. At least she was off the drugs that had plagued her while Eve was growing up. She hadn't touched them since Eve had given birth to Bonnie. Those seven years before Bonnie had been killed had been the only period when Eve and her mother had been truly close and bound in the common bond of their love for the child. After Bonnie's death, both Eve and Sandra had tried desperately to survive in their own individual ways and just drifted apart. Sandra had suffered another tragedy years later, when her adopted son, Mike, had been killed at college, and she had bitterly blamed Jane MacGuire,

Eve's adopted daughter, for not taking better care of him. Jane had always acted as a big sister to Mike and had pulled him out of jams since they had been kids. But that was one jam she hadn't been able to fix for him. No amount of arguing could convince Sandra that Jane had done everything she could for the boy. Since then, Sandra had withdrawn from contact with any of the family except when she needed something.

Like now.

Eve forced a smile as she threw open the front door. "Ten minutes. You must have been closer than you thought."

"I was in a hurry." She strode into room. "And, no, I didn't get another ticket. Though I don't see what good it does to have someone working for the police department if he's not willing to take care of little things like that."

"That's called corruption, Sandra. And Joe is never corrupt. He told you that you were out of luck when you asked him the last time."

"It's just a little thing." She went to the automatic coffeemaker on the counter and put in a K-cup. "It's not as if I were dealing drugs or something."

"Is that why you want to talk to Joe?" Her lips tightened. "No way, Sandra. I won't let you put him on the spot like that."

"No, that's not why I need him." She took her cup of coffee and wandered over to the reconstruction on the worktable across the room. "Another one, Eve?" She made a face as she looked at the skull that looked like a voodoo doll with the red markers piercing it like swords. "Ugly. I'd think you'd get tired of this job. So depressing."

And Sandra had shied away from anything depressing all her life. That rejection was evident in every aspect of her appearance. She must be seen as young and beautiful no matter what her age. That's why she had asked Eve to call her by her first name from the time Eve was only a child. She had always been Sandra to her daughter. She was smaller than Eve and very pretty, with stylishly layered red-brown hair that flattered a face that had undergone at least two face-lifts, to Eve's knowledge. Very good face-lifts—she looked almost as young as Eve these days and was far better dressed. She was wearing a short beige skirt, high heels, and a cream-colored hip-length sweater with a glittering gold multistrand necklace.

"Yes, I do get depressed occasionally," Eve said quietly. "How can I help it? But what I'm doing can bring resolution to parents who have lost their children to monsters. You know that, Sandra. I'd have been grateful if someone had been able to do the same for me when Bonnie was taken." She looked her in the eye. "We both went through hell not knowing, remember?"

Her eyes slid away. "I try not to remember. I'm not like you, Eve. You're stronger than I am. You always work and try to change the world. Well, I don't care about the rest of the world. I care about me." She lifted her chin defiantly. "And why not? I grew up in the slums and kept getting beaten down. I never hurt anyone. All I ever wanted was a good time. I deserve the right to forget about all that ugliness."

"I grew up in those same slums, Sandra."

"It was different for you." She walked away from the reconstruction. "You made it different. I was weaker; I couldn't fight them. But that doesn't mean I was wrong. I had to do what they told me."

Eve frowned. What was Sandra talking about? The drugs she'd been on all those years ago? "I'm not condemning you for anything, Sandra."

"You'd better not. I did the best I could. My mother wanted me to have an abortion when I got pregnant with you. I kept you."

"This is all past history. Why are you bringing it up now?"

"I don't know." She gestured toward the skull. "Maybe it's that ugly thing. It made me think about— Where's Joe? Shouldn't he be home by now?"

"Soon." Sandra was definitely upset. Her hands were shaking, there was color in her cheeks that wasn't rouge, and she was moving around the room like a bird afraid to land. Joe didn't need to have to deal with her in this state. "Maybe. It could be longer. Why don't you talk to me? Joe will tell me anyway. We don't keep secrets from each other, Sandra. Why do you need a police detective?"

"I don't *need* a detective. I just want to have someone check into something for me." She amended quickly, "Well, not for me. It's for a friend in my casino club. Jackie Mestrad." She frowned. "But I don't want to talk to you, Eve. That's not what I planned. I don't want you involved."

"What you ask Joe involves me. So we'll wait for Joe, and you can tell us both."

"Oh, very well," she said, annoyed. "But it's practically obscene that you're so close. You'd think that two people would want to live their own lives."

"Jackie Mestrad," Eve prompted.

"It's just a favor. Jackie's concerned about a cousin, a young woman in a mental hospital in California who seems to have disappeared, and I told her I'd have Joe check it out."

"California?"

"Santa Barbara. Well, it's not as if he'd have to fly out there. I wouldn't ask him to do that."

"I wouldn't think that you would," Eve said dryly. "Since California is a little out of his jurisdiction. Has your friend contacted the police out there? What does the hospital say?"

"Nothing. They say there's nothing to worry about. The woman wandered away from the hospital, but she's no threat to herself or anyone else. They've asked the police to conduct a discreet investigation so that it won't embarrass the patient's family."

"And they agreed? I'd say a mental patient wandering around the city offers a multitude of problems, and embarrassment to the family is the least of them."

"They agreed," Sandra said flatly. "The family is a huge donor to the hospital and also has a lot of influence in the city. The police were happy to cooperate."

"And when did this woman wander away?"

"Two nights ago."

"At night? A strange time to wander. Does she sleepwalk?"

"How do I know?" She moistened her lips. "Jackie didn't tell me. It's not something I'd ask."

No, Sandra was seldom interested in other people's problems. "And why didn't one of the nurses or doctors stop her? And there had to be security if it's a mental hosp—"

"I don't know. Stop asking me questions. Have Joe find out what happened. That's why I came here. He has to find her."

"I'm sure he'll be glad to communicate

with the Santa Barbara Police Department. But that's really all he can do."

"No, he mustn't do that." Sandra's tone was suddenly panicked. "That will stir things up, and I don't want to cause trouble. All I want is for him to find her. I mean, that's all that Jackie would want."

"Then do what I do with my reconstructions. Go to the media and publish a picture. Let the public search for her."

"Don't be stupid. I can't do that. I told you that any search has to be discreet."

"To protect her precious family? Screw that, Sandra. It's the patient who is important. Why would it matter if she was in the newspapers or not?"

"Because she was in a mental hospital. She's crazy, dammit."

"And there's a stigma surrounding mental illness? Well, it's time that stigma was put away. You can't cure something if you don't accept and understand it."

"Well, I don't understand it. It scares me, and it probably scares other people, too. I don't blame the Averys for not wanting anyone to know about her."

"Avery?"

She was silent, then said, reluctantly, "Beth Avery. She's some distant relation to the South Carolina Averys. Maybe you've heard of them."

"Who hasn't heard of them? There hasn't been a more powerful political family since the Kennedys." George and Nelda Avery were the head of an immensely wealthy dynasty who owned factories, mines, and a good portion of the lumber in the state of South Carolina. It was also rumored that they owned a good many of the Democratic senators in Congress and were aiming to catapult their son into the Oval Office. "They're reputed to be kingmakers. No wonder the police are proving so cooperative if the Averys own a big part of California, too." She frowned, trying to remember anything else she'd heard about the family. "But I don't recall hearing anything about this Beth Avery. The spotlight is on everything the Averys say or do. Why don't I know anything about her?"

"A distant relative. No one important," Sandra said quickly. "And she's been in that hospital for a long time. If the media were interested, they've probably forgotten about her by now."

"And the Averys don't want her to be remembered," Eve said. "Maybe they regard mental illness as a stigma, too." She grimaced. "Though I don't think even a crazy woman would scare George and Nelda Avery. It's more likely that they regard her as an inconvenience."

"Why do you say that?" Sandra asked indignantly. "They took care of her, didn't they? It's a nice hospital. Seahaven Behavioral Health Center, they call it. And it looks like a luxury hotel. They did everything they could for her."

"Then why did she wander away?"

"You can't blame—" She stopped. "I told you that I didn't know anything about that."

The entire business was very strange and completely unlike Sandra. "Perhaps I'd better ask Jackie. What's her phone number?"

"No, don't call—" Sandra's eyes were suddenly glittering with anger. "Stop interfering. All I wanted was for Joe to check and make sure that she was safe. That's not much to ask." She whirled and headed for the door. "I'll wait for him outside. I'm going to take a walk."

"In those high heels? You'll break your ankles."

But the door had slammed behind her.

Eve followed her and stood on the porch, looking at her as she stomped down the porch steps, then wobbled in her high heels down the uneven dirt path toward the trees. Should she follow her? Sandra had been angry but also upset. Perhaps Eve should have been more diplomatic instead of acting like Joe giving a third degree.

But, dammit, she didn't know how or why to be diplomatic in this situation. Sandra's behavior was completely different from that of the woman she knew.

And she had been lying to Eve. Nothing could have been more obvious.

Why?

Her phone rang. Joe.

"Is Sandra there?" he asked when she picked up. "I've just come out of the meeting, but we still have a few things to tie up. She left three messages, and the last one said that she was on her way to the cottage. She sounded . . . impatient. I thought I'd touch base with you to see if I need to hurry home."

"She'd say you do." Eve was silent a moment. "No, there's no reason for you to rush home. Do what you have to do. I'll take care of her."

"That sounds familiar. It's what you've done all your life. She's never been a real mother to you." He paused. "I suppose I shouldn't have said that. I'm just surprised you've never resented it."

"I did resent it when I was a kid. I got tired of blaming it on the drugs, and I wanted her to be the kind of mother that my friends had." She wrinkled her nose. "Not that a lot of them weren't just as neglectful. Dysfunctional families were pretty common in my housing development."

"They weren't unusual where I grew up either."

"But you were a rich kid, and you only got sent to some fancy school instead of getting kicked out on your ass." She added, "But Sandra never threw me out. Between her welfare payments and an occasional job, we made it until I was old enough to get a job myself to help out. Look, some people never grow up. I think Sandra may be one of them. But beneath all that vanity and self-absorption, she has a good heart. I was better off than a lot of kids." She looked at Sandra, who was nearly out of sight. "And she was good to my Bonnie. She might not have been a good mother, but she was one hell of a good grandmother. That was more important."

"To you. I'm afraid I feel differently. You're the one who is important in my world." He went on before she could speak, "But that doesn't mean I'm not willing to take responsibility for her. Does she need money?"

Joe was always ready to take responsibility, bear the burdens, fight her battles. Which was the reason she had to protect him from his own instincts. He had appeared in her life after Bonnie had been taken, and it would have been easy for her to go into a cocoon and lean on him, but she had been careful to maintain her own independence. And taking care of her mother was part of that independence. "No money. Not this time. And if she did, I'd manage. But if you could make a phone call or two before you start home, it might smooth the way to easing her off our doorstep."

"Another traffic ticket?" he asked warily.

"I'd never ask you to do that. What the hell are you thinking?"

"I'm thinking that you seem to be feeling softer and more lenient than usual toward Sandra. Who am I supposed to be calling?"

"Santa Barbara Police Department. Maybe the local mental hospital. According to Sandra, Jackie, one of her friends, has a cousin in a mental hospital out there. The woman wandered off two nights ago from Seahaven Behavioral Health Center, and she hasn't been found. Sandra is worried and wants you to do something to get her back."

"Sandra is worried?"

"I know, it's not like Sandra to empathize. And I think the friend is phony. But I don't know what the hell connection Sandra has to all of this."

"What's the name of the patient?"

"Beth Avery. And she's a member of the South Carolina Avery family. Low on the totem pole, but enough clout to cause everyone to keep the media at bay until they can find her."

"Mental patient. What's her diagnosis?"

"I don't know. Sandra is pretty vague about everything. You'll have to find out."

"I'll do what I can." He was silent. "Strange. None of this is making sense. I wonder what's going on with Sandra. You're sure I shouldn't come right home?"

"I'll take care of her," she repeated. "If you'll make those calls. That's all you could do if you were here. I'll see you when you get home." She hung up.

The sun was almost down, and trees were casting long, dark silhouettes on the lake.

Where the hell was Sandra? She was nowhere in sight.

Sandra was prone to melodramatic gestures, like stalking off into the sunset, but the moods never lasted long. Particularly if she was subject to discomfort like this chill that was sharpening the air.

And she had seemed genuinely upset when she had left the cottage.

Okay, go after her. She might still be irritated with Eve, but she could just deal with it. Eve wanted all the outbursts and the main problems brought out into the open before Joe got home. Joe might think he was responsible for everything in Eve's life, but she wouldn't let it include her mother. She and Sandra had gone through experiences and traumas that she would never confide to Joe. He would only become an-

gry and protective and want to shut Sandra out of her life. Eve couldn't do that.
These days, Sandra was more difficult than
pleasant, more selfish than giving, but you
had to accept the cards you were given.

She started down the porch steps, her
gaze searching the trail.

And the cards Eve was being given at
that moment was the task of going after
Sandra, bringing her back to the cottage,
and getting her to tell the truth about this
Avery business.

She found her mother leaning against a
pine tree a half mile down the lake path.

"I didn't think you were going to come."
Sandra was limping toward her. "I fell down
and hurt my foot."

Eve hurried forward and put Sandra's
arm around her shoulders. "Those damn
high heels."

"Don't you tell me that you told me so,"
Sandra said. "You said I'd break my ankles. I only hurt my foot."

"Big difference."

"And it's your fault. I wouldn't have had
to leave the cottage if you hadn't been
nagging at me." She leaned heavily against

Eve. "But you're always like that. You never believe me."

"I was only asking questions." Now that she was closer, she could see that Sandra's face was tear-streaked, her stockings torn at the knees, and one heel had broken off her shoe. "Are you hurt? You don't look so good."

"I'm fine." She was shivering. "A little cool. How do you expect me to be? I'm a city woman. I don't like the outdoors. I don't know why you'd move out here anyway."

"We like it. It was Joe's house before we started living together. But it's our home now. You should come out more often. You might get to like it."

She shook her head. "There's nothing for me here."

"You never can tell." Five minutes later, they had reached the porch stairs, and Eve was gently helping her climb them. "You weren't sure you'd like to help me take care of Bonnie after she was born, but it worked out fine."

"And what did it get me? I got to love her, then she died. It's better not to get too close. You always get hurt."

"Sometimes." They had reached the front door, and Eve helped her into the house and over to the couch. "Sit down here. I'll go get some water and salve. Can you manage to get those hose off?"

"Yes. I'm not helpless, Eve."

No, but Sandra looked weak and shaken, and her eyes were glittering with unshed tears. "I know you're not," Eve said quietly. "But you took a fall, and if I can help you, I want to do it. You'd do the same for me. I'll be right back."

When she came back carrying the basin of water, Sandra was leaning back against the couch, her eyes closed. "I have to talk to Joe," she whispered. "When is he coming?"

"It will be a little while. But you need some time to pull yourself together." She began to gently bathe Sandra's scraped knees. "You're a bit tousled. You looked so pretty when you got here. You don't want Joe to see you when you're not at your best, do you?"

"I did look nice, didn't I? This is a new sweater." She opened her eyes. "I looked in the mirror this morning, and I thought that I didn't look too much older than I did when I gave birth to you, Eve. Was I lying to myself?"

"Everyone says that you look much younger than you are."

"That's important. A woman like me has to look nice. Sometimes it's all you have."

"Nonsense. It's important that you look good if it pleases you. But it doesn't weigh in very heavily in the scheme of things. It's what you are inside that matters." She was wiping Sandra's face with the damp cloth. "You were crying. The fall must have hurt you."

"I was crying before I fell." She smiled shakily. "This reminds me of the time when you cleaned me up after that terrible man beat me up in that hotel room. You were only sixteen. Do you remember?"

"Yes, I didn't think you did. That was a long time ago."

"It just came back to me . . . You were always there when I needed you. Sometimes you didn't want to be, but if I called, you'd come." A ripple of pain crossed her face. "It should have been the other way, shouldn't it? But I was never good at being a mother. I only had you because I felt angry and cheated. I wanted to get back at them."

Eve stiffened. "Cheated?"

"You're getting angry with me. I knew you would. That's why I have to talk to Joe." She reached out and grabbed Eve's hand. "It's not my fault. None of it is my fault, Eve. Don't be angry with me."

"Calm down." Sandra's grip was nearly bruising, and her face was pale. "I'm not angry. I'm just trying to get to the bottom of this. You said you were crying before you fell. Why, Sandra?"

"I wanted to *do* something, but I didn't know what to do. I knew you'd make me tell you. If Joe had been here, it would have—"

"Joe isn't here," Eve interrupted. "I want to help you. I *will* help you. But you can't tell me any more lies. What the hell is happening? How much of that story you told me about that woman in the mental hospital is true?"

She didn't speak for a moment. "Most of it. I didn't lie much. Only about Beth Avery being Jackie's cousin."

"Then why did you make up that story? Why not just be honest with me? Who is this Beth Avery to you, Sandra?"

She didn't answer.

"Sandra, you were right. I'm going to keep after you until I find out what's wrong. Now answer me."

"I knew you'd be like this." The tears were running down Sandra's cheeks. "But you've got to promise not to be angry with me."

Eve drew a deep breath. Patience. "I told you, I'm not going to be angry. For heaven's sake, stop crying. All I want to do is help you. Who is Beth Avery, and what is she to you?"

"I didn't want anything bad to happen. I have to do something to make it right, Eve."

"Tell me."

"I'm getting there." She moistened her lips, then said in a rush, "I'm her mother, Eve. I'm Beth Avery's mother."

Shock. Eve felt as if she'd been punched in the stomach. "What?"

Sandra lifted her chin defensively though the tears were still running down her cheeks. "I didn't want to tell you. You made me."

"Sandra." Eve spoke very slowly. "Would you repeat what you just said?"

"You heard me. You've got to do something. Beth Avery is your sister."

CHAPTER

3

"Sister?" Eve asked hoarsely. Her throat was so tight, she could barely speak. "Sandra, what are you saying? This is crazy."

"No, it's not. It just happened, okay? It wasn't my fault. I was only fourteen, and I just wanted to have a good time. There's nothing wrong with that." She pushed Eve away and sat up straighter on the couch. "Stop looking at me like that. You should understand. Your Bonnie was illegitimate. These things happen."

Eve was trying to feel her way through this maze. "And how did this . . . happen?" She sat back on her heels, trying to think.

"You always told me that I was born when you were fifteen. I have a sister?"

"Oh, you weren't a twin or anything like that, thank God. I was sick all through the pregnancy carrying just one baby." She paused. "Beth was born when I was fourteen. I fibbed a little about when I had you. It was a couple years later."

Her head was spinning. "Why would you lie?"

"It was . . . easier. No one could know about Beth."

"Why not?"

"I was scared. I'd signed papers. They told me they'd put me in jail."

"You were a minor. Nothing you signed would be legal."

"I didn't know. I wasn't very smart about stuff like that. My mother told me that I had to do whatever they said."

Eve drew a deep breath. "Who is 'they'?"

"Rick's family." Her eyes filled with tears. "They were so ugly to me, Eve."

"Rick? Who is Rick?" She stiffened as it hit home to her. "Richard Avery? He's Beth's father?"

"Yes, Rick." She took the washcloth from Eve and dabbed at her eyes. "Though they tried to call me a liar. They said I was trying to trap him. Why would I lie about a thing like that?"

Eve could see why the Averys would want to deny any involvement between Sandra and their son, Richard. Good God, Nelda and George Avery's son, their pride and joy.

Their hope for a shot at the White House.

But she had to get this straight. She was having trouble comprehending it. But the mere reluctance Sandra had displayed about telling her about Beth Avery was leading her to tentatively believe it. But she had to make sure this outrageous story was true. "How did it happen? How did you even meet him? You certainly didn't travel in the same circles."

"I was pretty," she said simply. "Maybe even prettier than I am now. Guys like pretty girls around. It makes them look good to other guys to be able to provide girls at their parties."

"You were only fourteen yourself, almost a baby."

"That didn't matter. I just didn't tell anyone, and I always had a good time. I looked older." She shrugged. "And some guys like

young girls. Rick did. I wasn't usually in-
vited to many of the fraternity parties at
Georgia Tech, but that night, Cal Drake
called me and asked me to come to one
and meet his friend, Rick. Rick was going
to Harvard Law and had come down to
Atlanta to visit Cal." She paused. "Cal said
I didn't have to pretend to be older. Rick
liked girls my age . . . or younger."

"Shit. How old was he?"

"Twenty or so." She frowned. "I think. I
didn't care. He was good-looking, and he
liked me."

"I bet he did," Eve said grimly. "How
soon did you go to bed with him?"

"That night. He was fun. He made me
feel special. We went to bed lots of times
that weekend." She shook her head. "Why
are you looking at me like that? It wasn't as
if I was a virgin. I told you, I was pretty. All
the guys wanted to screw me from the time
I was in middle school. I liked Rick, so why
not?"

"You were fourteen."

"He liked me," she said defiantly. "He
didn't try to rape me. We smoked some
pot, then we went to bed and had a damn
good time."

"And he didn't protect you and got you pregnant."

"Not that night. He came back a couple times in the next few months, and I think it was one of those nights."

"Didn't anyone tell you how to protect yourself?"

"Sure, but he didn't like to use anything. He said it wasn't fun for him."

And a young girl's life changed forever because of that self-indulgence. Smother the anger. "What did he say when you told him you were pregnant?"

"I didn't tell him right away. I didn't tell anyone." She moistened her lips. "I didn't want to believe it. I wanted it to go away."

Eve remembered the day she had found out that she was pregnant with Bonnie. The disbelief, the panic. And Sandra had helped her through that nightmare period. She reached out and covered Sandra's hand with her own. "Who did you tell?"

"My mother. But not for more than four months. I was beginning to show, and I couldn't hide it any longer. She was angry. She said that she wasn't going to take care of a kid, that I had to get rid of it."

"Charming." Eve had never known

Sandra's mother. Her grandmother had never been in her life, and Sandra had just said vaguely that her mother had gone away and lived in another state. "But you obviously didn't do it."

"I was going to do it. I didn't mean to cause trouble. But then my mother started asking me questions about the baby and who the father was and stuff like that. She said that we should get something for my whoring." Her lips tightened. "I wasn't a whore. I never asked Rick for anything. All I wanted was a good time."

"But your mother decided the Averys should pay when she found out that Richard Avery was the father."

She nodded. "It was nasty. His parents said I was a tramp and a liar, and they wouldn't pay anything. They sent detectives around asking questions about me. But my mother wouldn't stop and said she'd have Rick arrested for rape."

"She should have done it."

"But then they wouldn't have given us any money. And I keep telling you, it wasn't Rick's fault. He was good to me. I didn't want to call in the police." She paused. "He finally told his parents the baby was his, and they had to pay for an abortion."

"Finally?"

"He was scared of his parents. It was hard for him to confess to doing something they wouldn't like. But he did it." She shrugged. "But I was six months pregnant by then, and the doctor wouldn't do an abortion. I had to have the baby. My mother said that was just as well so that we could prove Rick was the father. We'd keep the kid and hit the family for a monthly allowance. It would be a bonanza. But Nelda Avery wasn't having it. There was no way that she was going to be blackmailed for years because of Rick's mistake. She paid my mother a lot of money as a settlement and told her that the family was to get custody of the baby the minute it was born. She made both of us sign those releases and denials that Rick was at fault and guarantee that we would never have any contact with Beth once I gave her up. They were to be in total control."

"And you just went along with your mother and let your child go to them?"

"Why not? I didn't want her. What could

I do with a baby? Rick came down to see me and told me that he'd make sure that the kid was well taken care of."

"And you believed him?"

"Of course. Why would he lie? He was like me. He just wanted the situation to go away. I signed the papers, my mother got the money, and I thought that would be the end of it."

"But it wasn't?"

She shook her head. "I didn't know I would— Why should I feel like that for a kid? It was all wrong . . ."

"You didn't want to give her up." Eve knew how powerful that maternal feeling could be. She hadn't been able to give Bonnie up, though she'd thought it would be best for her. Sandra had been surprisingly understanding during that time, and now Eve realized why.

"They didn't come to get her for three days. I saw her all the time at the hospital. She was so . . . beautiful. She looked like me, only with Rick's dark hair. I told my mother to give back the money."

"But she wouldn't do it?"

"She called the Averys and told them to come and get the baby quick. That afternoon, my baby was gone from the hospital. I was angry. I felt cheated. My mother didn't pay any attention. She packed me up and took me down to Miami. We stayed at a real fancy hotel, and she told me how lucky I was she'd been able to get me out of that fix. I didn't feel lucky. I was mad. I wanted to punish her. I wanted my baby." She shrugged. "But I knew I wasn't going to be able to get Beth back. That Nelda woman scared me, and I'd signed those papers . . ."

Eve was trembling, and she crossed her arms across her chest. "Let me fill in this particular gap. You couldn't have Beth, but what was to stop you from getting pregnant again? You'd be punishing your mother by doing something that would prove inconvenient for her."

"I didn't really think about it. I just started to party again and having a good time." She smiled. "I was pregnant a year later. I told my mother that I wasn't going to have an abortion, and she had to give me enough money to take care of me and my kid. She was furious." Her smile faded. "But she didn't give me any money. After I gave birth to you, the nurse gave me a note from her that said that she was done with me and leaving town. That wasn't right. She shouldn't have left me there with no money and a newborn kid. After all, it was my money. How was I supposed to take care of myself?"

"The way you did. Though I can see how it must have proved a shock to you. I gather that you didn't have the same flush of maternal yearning over me that you experienced with Beth."

"How could I? I was too worried." She added quickly, "It wasn't that you weren't a very pretty baby, but I didn't know I'd feel something different. Not that I didn't like you. I just didn't know what to do with you. I was alone, and I didn't have any money. She shouldn't have done that to me."

"And you shouldn't have done that to me." She had to control her anger. "No child should be brought into the world because of anger."

"It all came out okay," Sandra said defensively. "You have a good life. You should be grateful I didn't get an abortion."

"You've used that card all my life," Eve said. "That I had a duty to you because you brought me into the world in spite of all the problems that meant for you. And I bought what you said because you're my mother, and I care about you." She turned on her heel. "God knows why."

"Where are you going?"

"I want to shake you. I have to get away from you for a few minutes."

"I knew you'd be angry that I didn't tell you about Beth."

"Beth? I can't even think about her right now." She glared back over her shoulder. "You know, Sandra, all my life I thought I was just an accident, and I could accept that. I'm having a little more trouble with the concept that I was a weapon for you to get back at your mother. That's a little cold for me." The front door slammed behind her.

She drew in a deep breath of cool air. Why had she gotten so angry? She was a mature woman, and she knew Sandra. They had never had a relationship on which to build. It was all past history.

But the history had changed a little. As a child, there had always been the hurt, the fear that her mother didn't love her, and she had been thrown back to that time with those few words Sandra had uttered. She hadn't realized she'd had two strikes against her even before she was born. She was a substitute for the daughter her mother had wanted, the daughter she couldn't have.

And it hurt, dammit.

Screw maturity and understanding—it hurt.

"Eve." Sandra was standing in the doorway with a cup in her hands, her gaze fixed apprehensively on Eve. "Don't be mad at me." She came toward her. "I brought you a cup of coffee."

Like a little girl trying to bribe her way into forgiveness for a transgression. Sandra was a little girl in many ways, Eve thought wearily. Mentally and emotionally, she had stayed a child even though she had been allowed to grow up too soon. That dichotomy, Eve found, was one of the toughest things she had to deal with in her mother. Sandra probably didn't even understand why Eve was upset. She couldn't see beyond the boundaries of her personal sphere. What the hell. Accept the bribe. She took the cup of coffee. "Thank you."

Sandra looked relieved. "And I forgive you for stomping out here even though it was rude."

"Don't push it, Sandra."

"After all, this isn't about you."

She took a sip of coffee. "Isn't it? For a minute, it felt like it was. You've always discouraged me from asking anything about the time when you had me, and I went along with you." Her lips twisted. "I didn't want to be insensitive. But considering what you've told me, I'd like to ask you a question or two. We know Beth's father was Richard Avery. Who is my father, Sandra?"

She was silent.

"You don't know?"

"I'm not exactly sure. I think he might have been the artist I met at a beach party at Fort Lauderdale."

"His name."

"Gary . . . something." She trailed off. "I don't remember. He was an artist and going to Haiti the next day. What did it matter?"

"It matters to me." But it obviously didn't matter to Sandra. "So you were left alone with no money and a baby you found you didn't really want after all. Why didn't you just put me up for adoption?"

"I thought about it. But like you said, I didn't have any money, and the people at the hospital said I could apply for more welfare if I had a kid."

"Oh, yes, by all means, you had to be practical. That was in Miami. How did you end up back here in Atlanta?"

"I thought maybe my mother would come back here. I needed my money. She shouldn't have taken it. But she wasn't in Atlanta, and none of the people we knew had seen her. I never saw her or my father again. She meant it when she said that she was through with me. I had to get by on my own. It wasn't easy." She added defiantly, "I know I wasn't what most people would call a good mother, but I did what I could. Don't you blame me, Eve."

"I'm not blaming you," she said wearily. It was too late to condemn Sandra or hold her accountable. Too many years had passed, too much water under the bridge of life. This new knowledge might hurt, but she couldn't change human nature. Sandra was what she was, and those traits and frailties had been formed by the life she had led. "I'm just trying to understand. You've thrown me a curve, Sandra."

"I don't know why. This isn't really about you. It's about Beth."

And Sandra couldn't see the domino effect learning about Beth Avery had caused in Eve's life. "I guess that for you, that's all it's about." She took a sip of coffee and tried to gather her thoughts. "Okay, let's talk about Beth. You said she was a mental patient in Santa Barbara. How do you know? You told me that you'd signed papers giving her up, that they had total control of her."

"And I did the right thing," she said quickly. "When she had the accident, I would never have been able to give her the kind of care the Averys did."

"Accident?"

"She had a skiing accident when she was seventeen and had a severe concussion that caused brain damage. That's why they had to put her in that mental hospital to try to get her better."

"Seventeen . . ." Eve was having trouble not only accepting her relationship to Beth Avery, but bringing into focus their separate pasts. "That would have been about the time I gave birth to Bonnie, wouldn't it?"

Sandra nodded. "But I didn't know much about her then. It was after Bonnie was killed that I decided I had to find out if my Beth was doing well." She added in a whisper, "I missed Bonnie so much, Eve. I did love her. After I gave up Beth, I thought I'd never feel like that again, but Bonnie was special."

"Yes, she was wonderful." She looked out at the lake, remembering just how special and wonderful her daughter had been. "And when we lost Bonnie, you felt you had to reach out to Beth?"

Sandra nodded. "Not really reach out. It was too late. She was already in that hospital. But it made me feel kind of nice to find out things about her. Like she was really mine. I hired a detective to tell me all he could about her."

"And what did he find out? I can't imagine the Avery family accepting her."

She shook her head. "They placed her with a couple, Laura and Robert Avery, who were distant cousins of Rick's father and lived in a small town in Virginia. They were the poor relations of the family and were very grateful to be paid so well to take care of Beth. Nelda didn't want anyone to connect Rick to her, so Laura Avery told everyone that Beth was the daughter of Nelda's uncle who lived in Switzerland.

That way they had an excuse to send her to different schools in Geneva and Rome. They didn't want her in this country and have to answer questions about her. It was much easier to keep her in Europe as much as possible."

"Why not all the time? Why that house in Virginia?"

"Well, after she was five, she was always at boarding school. But Rick wanted to go see her sometimes when she was little. He liked her."

"What?"

"Why are you surprised? I told you he was a good guy. Why wouldn't he care about my daughter?"

Eve wasn't going to argue how that "good guy" had carelessly impregnated a girl who was little more than a child. "How do you know that was the reason?"

"He told me so. After I found out about the accident, I went to see him, and he told me all about her. I thought he'd be mad because I wasn't supposed to get in touch with any of them after I signed those papers." She smiled. "But he was real nice, just like I remembered him. He told me I was just as young and pretty as the day he met me."

"And what did he tell you about Beth?"

"What I told you. He said that his mother wanted to keep her totally out of sight, but he'd fought her. She would have preferred to have Beth put out for adoption to a family halfway across the world, but Rick wouldn't have it." She shrugged. "So the relatives in Virginia were a compromise. He visited her whenever he could until they sent her to Switzerland, then he'd drop in at least a couple times a year wherever she was at school. Naturally, since he was in politics, he had to keep the visits low-profile, but he'd bring her presents, and he got to know her real well." She added, "He said she was so smart. Good grades all the time. And she won trophies for skiing and swimming. She loved to ski."

Her smile faded. "But she had that accident when she was skiing. Rick said she'd never be the same. The family sent her to that hospital in California, to some fancy psychiatrist, but she's never gotten any better. He said that if she ever did recover, he'd let me know and take me to see her. That was years and years ago . . ."

And the seventeen-year-old girl who had entered that California hospital was now a little older than Eve. All the laughter and tears and experiences of those years had been smothered within the walls of an institution. She shuddered at the hideous picture that thought brought to mind.

"How did you find out that Beth had wandered away from the hospital?"

"The detective I hired told me."

"The detective who gave you the initial report on Beth? He's been working for you all these years?"

"Of course not. Don't be silly. I couldn't afford to do that. But Hermie said he'd make a couple contacts at the hospital and occasionally let me know how she was doing." She moistened her lips. "There wasn't much to tell me. She must be real bad. Hermie said they kept her on pretty heavy drugs. But a few days ago, he called me and told me that she might be in trouble. She'd left the hospital, and no one could find her. I gave it another twenty-four hours, but they still haven't found her. So I came to tell Joe he had to help. He's smart, and he'll be able to locate her." She let out a relieved breath. "There. I've told you everything. I hope you're satisfied. Now call Joe and tell him that he has to help me."

"I don't have to call him. We'll talk when he gets home. Who is this Hermie? The detective?"

She nodded. "Herman Dalker. He likes me. He said he understood how I had to give up Beth and that I was a wonderful woman to be so concerned about her even though she's sick in the head."

Eve flinched. "Give me his telephone number. And the name of Beth Avery's school and anything else you can remember. Joe will need it."

"Hermie's number is in my purse. The school is some Catholic academy. St. Cecilia or something like that. Yes, that was it. St. Cecilia. I'll scrawl it down when we go back inside," Sandra added eagerly. "You'll tell Joe to help her?"

"I don't tell Joe anything. I ask him. You should know that by now, Sandra. Is there anything else I should know about this?"

"That's all." She hesitated. "I don't really know much at all about Beth, do I? Just what Rick told me and the detective . . . I should probably not worry about her. The Averys have taken such good care of her.

They've sent her to all those neat foreign places and schools. And after that accident, they spent all that money trying to get her well. I'm sure that they'll find her and take her safely back to the hospital."

"But you're not sure, or you wouldn't have come to me and Joe."

"As sure as I can be." She shrugged. "Maybe it's just that I've never been able to give Beth anything, and this is a way that I can do that."

Eve shook her head in disbelief. "So you're going to make a gift of Joe and me," she said dryly. "That's my choice, Sandra."

"But you'll do it. You have to do it. She's your sister, Eve."

"Blood may be thicker than water, but it's difficult to embrace that concept when I've just discovered that she exists." She waved a hand as Sandra opened her lips to speak. "Don't talk to me any longer. Not right now. Just get in your car and go home. I promise I'll discuss this with Joe."

"Discuss? No, I want your promise to do it."

"Go home, Sandra."

Sandra stood there, gazing at her for a long moment. Then she smiled confidently.

"You'll do it. I know you, Eve. You won't be able to help yourself. You can't even keep yourself from working on those ugly skulls because you think it's your duty. How could you refuse to help your sister?" She turned and headed for the door. "I'll go in and get my purse and that telephone number and the name of Beth's school. I feel much better about her now." She suddenly glanced over her shoulder and the smile had disappeared. "I should have loved you more, shouldn't I? You've done everything for me, and Beth is almost a stranger. I *do* care about you, Eve."

"I know you care as deeply as you're capable."

"It's just . . . she was first, Eve. I guess some people only have so much to give. Maybe I'm one of them."

"Maybe you are." She turned away and looked back at the lake. "I'll take care of your Beth, Sandra. I can't speak for Joe, but I'll do everything I can."

"Then it will all work out. I knew it would. Because she's your Beth, too, Eve." She disappeared into the house.

Her Beth? It was going to be strange thinking of Beth Avery as belonging to her.

A sister? She had always been on her own as far as family was concerned. As a child, she'd had to fend for herself because of Sandra's drug habit and general lack of responsibility. Then when she'd given birth to Bonnie, her daughter was her family. Jane MacGuire, her adopted daughter, had come into her life when the girl was only ten years old, but she was mature far beyond her years. They had been friends, not mother and daughter.

She sat down on the porch swing to wait for Joe. She'd have to try to absorb both Sandra's story and the surprise and emotional upheaval that it had brought before she would be able to share it with Joe. Because she did not wish to share the pain, he had gone through too much already during the years of searching for her Bonnie's killer.

A sister . . .

"So what do you want me to do?" Joe asked quietly, when Eve had fallen silent after telling him Sandra's story. "If it were anyone but Sandra, I'd be a lot more shocked. But I can actually connect the dots."

"So can I. Particularly if I think of Sandra

as more of a child than an adult. She was wild and self-indulgent, but she was also a victim." She grimaced. "Not that she's not still a child in many ways, but I have to remember that she probably likes it better than being an adult."

"And how do you feel about Beth Avery?"

"I've been trying to figure that out. Curious, surprised, sad for her condition . . . maybe a little cheated."

"Cheated?"

"That I didn't know her when I was growing up. Sisters are supposed to be . . . close." She shook her head in bewilderment. "But I've never experienced that, so it might be a bunch of bull. How do I know?"

"You can't." His arm tightened around her shoulders. "You have to accept the relationship as it is now."

"There is no relationship. And if there was any hope of one, it probably was destroyed when she had that accident." She nibbled at her lower lip. "I don't know anyone with mental trouble, and I don't have a clue what kind of problems she has to deal with. Was it a physical brain injury? Or was it a mental illness caused by an injury? Or did she have the mental illness before, and it caused an accident? Does she have a chance of being cured? I can't turn my back and walk away. I have to find out, Joe. I have to find her."

"Then I have my answer, don't I?"

"I said I have to find her. I won't ask you to go along with me."

"But you know that I can't do anything else. We're in this together for the long haul." He gave her a quick, hard kiss. "So shut up. I'll catch the next flight I can get out to Santa Barbara. I was thinking that I might have to do it anyway, after I finished those phone calls to the police department and the hospital."

"You made the calls?"

"You asked me, didn't you? I would have told you right away, but I could see that it was more important that you tell me what Sandra had been up to." He shrugged. "I didn't find out much. The local police made me jump through hoops to prove I was a detective with ATLPD, then they were brief as hell about any progress they'd made on finding Beth Avery. According to them, zilch. Then I was transferred to the captain, and he started asking me questions about where I'd received information about Beth Avery's escape from the hospital."

"'Escape'?" Eve frowned. "That sounds . . . odd. It brings to mind padded cells and bars on windows. Sandra said she just wandered off. I got the impression it was very light restraint."

"The word was 'escape.'" He paused. "And I got the same word when I talked to Joseph Piltot, the human resources manager at Seahaven Behavioral Health Center. Only there it was accompanied by panic and a denial that there had been any escape from the hospital. He said I'd been misinformed, and I'd be wise not to spread rumors to that effect."

"I don't like that," she said slowly.

"Neither did I. Of course, it could be that the Averys are trying to keep media coverage of a deranged relative to a minimum. If Richard Avery is going to run for president, a family mental-health issue could be awkward. There's still a stigma out there that's hard to overcome."

Her lips tightened. "And if the media started digging, they might unearth the fact that Avery is a pedophile who impregnated a fourteen-year-old girl."

Joe nodded. "That would be even more awkward." He kissed her again and got to his feet. "But something that you told me is making me uneasy. I believe I'll do some digging myself."

"What?"

"It may be nothing. It's just that all the years Beth Avery was growing up, the Avery family went to a hell of a lot of trouble keeping her out of view and away from anyone who might ask questions. She even spent most of her life in Europe."

"So?"

"There's nothing farther out of view than a mental hospital. Sandra said she was under heavy sedation."

Eve inhaled sharply. "My God." She felt sick as she saw where he was going. "They'd have to be monsters."

"Yes, but we both know there are monsters out there."

"She had an accident. Brain damage."

"I'd like to see the accident report, talk to witnesses, and see the X-rays."

"You're jumping to conclusions."

"I didn't say I was going to do that yet. I'll just put out feelers to see where I can put my hands on them." He smiled recklessly. "You know what a suspicious bastard I am."

Yes, she knew. Joe had been a cop too long to take anything at face value. He was always instinctively searching below the surface, probing, brushing away the lies until he glimpsed the truth. "I hope you're wrong this time. I can't imagine who could be that cruel, to condemn a woman for no reason to exist in a living hell like that for all those years." She shuddered. "She was seventeen, Joe."

"And everything Sandra was told might be true. I'll fly out to Santa Barbara and see what I can find out. If it still doesn't feel right to me, I'll take the next step."

"I'm going with you." She got to her feet. "I'll go pack."

He shook his head. "I'm going to have to bulldoze my way on this one. It's clear no one without police ID and title is going to be allowed at the hospital or the police headquarters. You'd just have to stay in a hotel room and wait." He brushed her nose with his lips. "Stay here, work on Janelle, and I'll let you know what's happening and if there's any reason for you to come out. It may end up with me asking you to man the phones and the computer to track down the details of how Beth Avery was injured." He wrinkled his nose. "And stop looking at me like that. I'm not trying to protect you. I'm telling you the truth."

"She's not your problem. I've no intention of staying here while you do my job. She's my sister, Joe." Lord, it felt strange saying that. "I promised Sandra I'd take care of it. There has to be something I can do out there."

"There may be something if I don't get what I want. I have an idea that might pan out. But not if you're going to be seen or identified with me. You'd blow it." He tossed over his shoulder as he opened the door, "Hell, maybe we'll get lucky, and by the time I get off the plane in Santa Barbara, the police will have found Beth Avery, and she'll be safely back at the hospital. Then the job will be easy. I'll just have to make sure she is safe and where she should be."

"Why are you being so insistent about this?"

"Because you need some time to ab-sorb everything that Sandra told you. I don't believe you know how you feel yourself. Your instinct is to dive in and set everything right, but I don't want you facing a situation that will tear you up more than you are right now, when it may not be necessary." He smiled faintly. "Okay, maybe I'm protecting you a little bit. But I'm not lying about its being better if you come in later rather than sooner."

"I'm not torn up. Naturally, I'm surprised and—" She stopped as she saw the way he was looking at her. Joe knew her far too well, she thought ruefully. He had obviously seen right through her attempt to appear undisturbed. Why defend herself from him when he would be on her side no matter how she was feeling? "Things aren't exactly as I thought they were. That doesn't mean I can't function while I become accustomed to all this."

"I know that. As I said, I may need you as a backup. Give me a little time." He went into the house.

She stood up from the swing as the door closed behind him. Joe, as usual, had taken charge and was formulating possible scenarios, making plans and going full steam ahead. Should she argue and take over the agenda? If it had been a mere issue of his trying to protect her, there would have been no question. But she could see no danger hovering, and he'd said he had a plan that might demand she not be connected to him. Joe was smart, and they had worked together for many years. She was not going to be stubborn if it meant destroying that plan. She could give him the time he said he needed. She could be patient . . . barely.

She went into the cottage and moved across the room to the reconstruction on her worktable. She wasn't going to be able to sleep, so she might as well work. Her mind was full of the thought of Beth Avery, a woman of her blood, near her own age, and yet Eve had no idea what she looked like or what kind of experiences had made her what she was. So much had happened since she had stopped working on the skull when Sandra had arrived. Better to block it out than let those thoughts consume her. Janelle would help her do that, and in turn she would help this broken child.

"Hi, Janelle, it looks like we're going to be able to work a little longer before we get interrupted," she murmured as she reached for a marker. "Sandra called you ugly. It's all those markers sticking out all over. She doesn't understand that you're not ugly at all. All children are beautiful. When we go into the final smoothing phase, you'll be beautiful again." She carefully placed the tissue-depth marker above one eye cavity. "And then we'll find a way to bring you home . . ."

CHAPTER

4

"Why didn't you pick up?" Piltot snapped when Pierce answered. "I've been calling you for the last four hours."

"I was busy." Pierce pushed away from Stella and sat up in bed. "And I believe you should be a little more courteous, Piltot. You can be replaced."

"No, I can't. You wouldn't like it if someone else was handling your patient records, would you? And I'm tired of your bullshit. You're not leaving me to handle this mess alone."

Piltot was genuinely upset, and that didn't bode well, Pierce thought. Piltot was usually subservient and easily handled. "I didn't mean that as a threat. I was joking. You're right, we're in this together." He gave Stella a poisonous glance as she laughed. "Now, what's the problem?"

"I received a call from a Detective Joe Quinn with the Atlanta Police Department asking questions about Beth Avery's disappearance from the hospital. Atlanta? How the hell did they even know about her?"

Pierce muttered a curse as he swung his legs to the floor. "How do I know? What did he say?"

"That they'd received a report that an inmate had wandered off, and they were asked to follow up."

"Report from whom?"

"Quinn said it was confidential. But he was damn persistent. I think we'll hear from him again."

"That's not an emergency. Troublesome, but not a danger. I'll take care of it in the morning."

"The only way you'll be able to take care of it is to find that damn woman and bring her back here. It's been three days. Why haven't the police been able to do it? It's not as if it should be that difficult. I've seen her, and she's almost a vegetable."

"I said I'd take care of it." He tried to keep the edge out of his voice. "Keep calm and let me know if you hear from him again." He hung up, then dialed Drogan. "We've got a problem. How close are you to finding her?"

"She took a bus from Santa Barbara and got off in San Francisco."

"Great," Pierce said sarcastically. "Since San Francisco is such a tiny city, you should be able to locate her with no problem at all."

"She took another bus from the same station south again. She's doubling back for some reason." He paused. "And where did she get the money for that bus? Could she have stolen it?"

"Maybe from one of the nurses. No one is careful around her. She's harmless."

"She's not harmless. Find out where she got the money. If it wasn't stolen, then someone had to have given it to her. If that's the case, then we may be in luck if you can zero in on her source."

"Don't count on it."

"I never count on anything. Just furnish

me with a list of the people who had the opportunity to help her, and I'll do the rest."

"I'll see about getting it for you. But you said you'd find her yourself, do it." He added, "Keep in touch. I may have another job for you. Things are coming apart here at the hospital."

"And you want me to fix it for you. Why doesn't that surprise me?" He hung up.

Son of a bitch.

"Trouble?" Stella was smiling maliciously. "You always seem to be having trouble with Drogan. You can't handle him, can you? I'd like to meet him. I bet I could handle him."

"I might send for him and let you try. I couldn't lose either way." He was thinking. "Tomorrow, drift around and see if any of the nurses have been missing any money from their purses or the petty-cash drawer in the desk. Be tactful." He grimaced at the thought of "tactful" and "Stella" in the same description. "Or at least don't throw up any red flags."

She nodded. "Are you going to tell Nelda about the call from this cop?"

"Not if I can help it." He was beginning

to feel the same panic he had heard in Pil-tot's voice. They had kept the story of Beth Avery's escape very quiet, with absolutely no media coverage. How had the story leaked to a cop in Atlanta? Keep cool. He'd manage to do damage control. "Tomorrow I think I'll pull one of the women patients out of the ward and put her in a solitary room. I'll tell the police it's Beth Avery, and she came back on her own."

"And you'll have me taking care of her and covering for you. Boring."

"You'll do what you're told." He frowned. "I'll tell Nelda the same thing I'll tell the police until I actually find Beth Avery. Though I may still have to break down and tell her that the situation isn't contained. It may be necessary to have Nelda check into who filed that report in Atlanta. She has the political clout to do it."

"But that would annoy her, and she's already angry with you." She lay back down on the bed and stretched lazily. "Maybe she'll hire Drogan to take care of you, too. I think I envy her. I've often wondered how it would feel to be able just to lift a finger, and someone dies."

"Well, you don't have that power," he

said roughly as he came over her. "I'm the one who is in control."

"And you want to show me right now," she said. "Go ahead, I don't mind. Screw me. Hurt me. But no matter how many times you do it, I'll still know I'm the one who is really in control." She smiled up at him. "Someday, you'll realize that, Harry. If you live long enough . . ."

8:15 A.M.
Charleston, South Carolina

"Pierce." Nelda Avery's lips tightened as she hung up the phone. "He said they've found Beth, but the situation is too volatile to take any final action now. He was assuring me that he had everything under control." She threw her napkin down on the breakfast table and stood up. "Fool. He's probably lying to me. Does he think I don't have my hand on the pulse of the situation out there?"

Her husband, George, looked up from his newspaper. "I'm sure that Pierce won't make any more mistakes. He'll be careful. He has too much to lose."

"Not as much as we do." She gave her husband a contemptuous glance as she headed for the French doors. He was as much a fool as Pierce. Lazy and foolish and unable to function properly in a world where every step was watched and criticized. Why couldn't she have married a man who had brains as well as money? "I'm going to the carriage house to see Rick. Remember that we have an appointment with the campaign publicity manager at ten."

"I know." He was reading his paper again. "You reminded me an hour ago."

Because she had to be the one to keep all their ducks in a row. They were close, united in purpose, but she wouldn't allow him to pull her down after all her hard work. "We need this campaign manager. He's the best in the business. Be charming."

"Tell that to Rick. That's not my job." He glanced up at her. "I'm the moneyman."

There was a distinct coolness in his expression that made her hesitate. Had she pushed him too far? She forced a smile. "You can be charming. Why else would I have married you? And Rick may be totally charismatic, but you have a steadiness

and sophistication that he'll never possess."
She opened one French door. "If you don't
want to be involved in the campaign, I'll
take care of it. You're such an asset that I
wanted to show you off."

"Don't bullshit me, Nelda," George said.
"I've never felt good about this, but I just
let you do what you wanted because I love
my son. But it's getting dirtier and dirtier,
and I don't like being in this deep."

Because he was a coward and couldn't
see that you had to risk everything if you
wanted to reach your goals. "You say you
love Rick. We have to fight for him, don't
we? He can climb so high. That's what we
both want for him. How many parents can
give the Oval Office to their sons? But we
have to protect him."

George wearily nodded his head. "Yes,
I guess we do. I'll meet with this campaign
person."

"I knew you would." She gave him a brilliant smile. "Don't worry, I'll do most of the
talking. You'll only have to deal with him on
a minor level." She left the room and headed
for the carriage house.

Ken Spoder, Rick's bodyguard, was lying in a lounge chair by the pool and smiled

at Nelda as she approached. Muscular, tanned, and completely assured. "Good morning. You don't look as if it's a good day for you, Mrs. Avery. Maybe I can brighten it up for you. The town-hall meeting went great last night. Everyone loved Rick."

"Everyone always loves Rick," Nelda said. "That's not one of his problems." She paused. "How has he been, Ken?"

"Good. I told you that I could take care of it. I don't let him make any missteps."

Because she paid him a small fortune to make sure that he watched Rick like the proverbial hawk. "You'd better not. I wouldn't like that. I haven't come this far to have him brought down now." She met his gaze. "I'm not pleased about a situation in California. I may need someone I can trust to take care of it."

"Trust. You? I'm flattered. But I can't watch Rick from California. Since his wife took off for Florida a few weeks ago, I'm the only one who can keep him . . . stable. And we both know that it would only take a few hours to blow everything."

He was right. Rick was the most important part of the entire equation. She thought about it. "It might not take long, and I can control Rick if I'm with him. I'll have to see if I think—"

"Mother, what are you doing here?" Rick strolled out of the carriage house. He was dressed in bathing trunks and looked fit and handsome, and his smile was as bright and warm as the sunlight. She felt a surge of love as strong as it was fierce as she gazed at him. He had been the center of her life since the minute he had been born. And George was quibbling about everything they had to do to realize the potential that Rick possessed? "I thought I wasn't going to see you until dinner tonight." He gave her a kiss on the cheek. "You look wonderful. That suit has to be from Paris."

"New York." Nelda smiled. "We have to have everything made in the U.S.A. The time of Jackie Kennedy and her Camelot doesn't resound in this climate." She took his arm and drew him a few yards away from Ken Spoder. "I just wanted to tell you that everything is going well with poor Beth. She's safely back at the hospital."

Rick smiled with relief. "That's good. I was worried."

"But you let me take care of everything." She added meaningfully, "And that's why things turned out as they should. If you'd gone out there as you wanted, it would have ruined everything. After all, there was no reason. You haven't even seen Beth since the accident."

"You told me that she wouldn't even know me."

"That's right, and it would have upset her." She put her hand on his arm. "And she's much worse now, Rick."

"I know." He shook his head. "Sad . . . she means so much to me, Mother. I didn't get to see her very much when she was little but later I grew to know and love her. And I think she loved me, too."

"And we're going to take care of her just as we always have." She kissed him on the cheek. "Now go in for your swim. Ken tells me you were wonderful last night. You're so good with handling people."

"It's fun. The speeches are almost the same every time, but most of the people who attend those rallies are pretty cool." He was still not smiling. "I've been thinking about Beth a lot lately. I'm glad that she's safe."

"I know you are. But you have to forget about her now. We have too much to do."

She stepped back. "Bye, Rick. Have a good day."

She was halfway back to the house when she heard a splash as he dove into the pool. A moment later, she heard him laugh and say something to Ken. Hopefully, she had stopped him from dwelling on the Beth problem. Thank God he was usually easy to distract. Though he had been very stubborn about Beth, and she hadn't been able to budge him, dammit.

Beth had been a problem for years, and Nelda had always known she could be a threat to her plans for Rick.

She wouldn't allow it.

If Pierce had bungled it, she would take care of eliminating that threat herself.

Seventeen Mile Drive
11:40 P.M.

It was raining again.

She was wet to the bone, Beth realized as she ran down the beach toward the big house. It had been raining hard all day, and that wasn't bad as far as she was concerned. This was California, where rain was probably not that common, and people tended to stay inside, not tempted to ask questions if they saw her on the road or beach.

She liked the rain on her face. It felt good. She had never been permitted to go outside when the weather was nasty or threatening. The doctors had to keep her well and free from germs or disease. Why? Why be so careful to keep her well, then try to kill her?

Don't think. Just keep moving. She could puzzle everything out later.

Now she was climbing the dunes toward the house on the hill. All she had to do was reach the front door and enter the security code. Billy had given her the code, and there weren't supposed to be any guards on the beach side of the property at this hour. She'd go inside and dry off and be safe for a little while.

But only for a little while. Billy had told her that she couldn't trust anyone, that she had to figure out things for herself once he got her away from the hospital.

She felt a tingle of fear. Figure out things for herself? No one had let her think at all during these years. It was like a cripple learning to walk with no one standing beside her to hold her up if she fell.

But she wasn't a cripple. She would not fall. Memories were coming back to her all the time about her life before the hospital. She had not been weak then, and she would not be weak now. Billy had told her she was to take this time to remember and find the answers he couldn't give her.

"Hey, there! This is private property. You're trespassing."

A man in a security uniform was coming toward her! Dammit, Billy had told her there would be a guard, but she'd forgotten.

She whirled and stumbled back down the dune toward the beach. Go away and hide and come back later.

She heard his shout behind her. "Wait. What are you doing here? I want to talk to you."

He was skidding down the dune behind her.

No!

Run.

Keep on running.

He was cursing.

Was he gaining on her?

Run . . .

Run.

The phone on Eve's nightstand was ringing as she struggled out of the depths of sleep and the tentacles of the dream . . .

Joe. She had been expecting him to call all evening. "What's happening, Joe?" She tried to control the harshness of her breathing. "I thought you were going to call me before I went to bed."

"Sorry. I've been on the phone most of the afternoon and evening. I wanted to know more before I filled you in." He paused. "You okay? You sound kind of blurry."

Rain and sand and a security guard chasing her down the beach.

"I'm fine. You woke me. Why have you been on the phone?"

He was silent. "Because I don't like what's going on here. When I went to the local police station this morning, I was told that the case was closed. Beth Avery had wandered back to the hospital last night during a rainstorm and was now safe in the hands of Dr. Pierce and his staff."

"Just what you said you hoped would happen. But it's a curious coincidence. Beth wandered away and just wandered back?" She added dryly, "That's a lot of 'wandering.'"

"It could have happened. But I went to the hospital to check it out and see Beth Avery. I saw Piltot, the human resources manager, I saw Dr. Pierce, but I didn't see Beth Avery."

"Why not?"

"According to Pierce, she was exhausted and disturbed and was to be kept in seclusion for the next few days until she recovered."

"They wouldn't let you see her?"

"They showed me a woman huddled in a bed, obviously drugged and out of it. They said to come back on Friday, and they'd see about letting me talk to her." He paused. "But that wasn't Beth Avery unless she's changed beyond imagining. When I got back to the hotel, I called the records office of the private school she'd attended in Geneva and got them to send me a photo of her. I'll forward it to you. Yes, she was younger and vibrant back then, but other than the dark hair, I couldn't see any resemblance to the woman in that hospital bed. I've been calling that detective, Herman Dalker, but I haven't been getting an answer. I'm trying to track him down."

"And I'm going to call the school and see what I can find out about Beth. I want to talk to someone who knew her before she went into that hospital." She added grimly, "And I want to know what happened that led her to run away from it."

"I'm going to give you the answer that the hospital or a psychiatrist would give you: imaginary fears, schizophrenic delusions, or some other mental problem. And we couldn't argue, Eve. We don't have the facts."

Heart pounding, sand beneath her shoes, rain on her face. Don't let them catch me. Figure it out. Why . . .

"Speak for yourself. I can argue," Eve said fiercely. She hadn't even known the words were tumbling out until they were said. "You may have to have the facts because it's your practical nature. I think she ran away because she was afraid. And not imaginary fear, Joe. She doesn't know why, but she knows they want to kill her."

He was silent. "Would you care to explain?"

"I don't have an explanation. Not a reasonable one. I just think . . ." She drew a deep breath. "That dream the other night? I think it was Beth. It was the night she ran away from the hospital. I think I was running away with her. There was an ocean, a hospital . . . I was a part of her, feeling what she felt. I know it doesn't make sense. Or maybe it does. I didn't even know Beth existed when I had that dream. But perhaps she wasn't meant to be alone any longer. Maybe God or fate or someone else decided that Beth deserved a break and needed a little help."

"Someone else?" He paused. "Bonnie?"

"It's possible." Even probable. She could see the loving spirit of her Bonnie trying to arrange Eve's life to suit herself. "Bonnie's come to me in dreams before."

"I know she has. From about a year after you lost her."

Yes, Joe knew and accepted the fact that the ghost of Bonnie was still with Eve, which was a blessing beyond price. "It could be she just gave me a little push in Beth's direction. Oh, I don't know, dammit."

Her hand tightened on the phone. "But I was dreaming about Beth again when you called tonight. She was still running, but she was on the beach. There was a big house where she thought she'd be safe . . ."

"You're sure it was Beth?"

"Yes, it was much clearer than the other dream. I know all this is weird as hell, Joe."

"A little. But we've gone down that road before and survived. I trust you. If you believe it, then I'll go along with you."

"I believe it. Beth was thinking about someone named Billy. Billy had given her the security code to the house." She was thinking. "So this Billy will know where we can find her. Someone at the hospital?"

"If I can get the password, I can check the personnel records on the computer without letting the staff know."

"Which won't be easy."

"Not for us. But I know someone who might be able to get it for me."

"If they can get into the personnel office."

"That goes without saying. But if I can convince her to take the job, I'll worry about access later. She can be stubborn as hell."

"She?"

"Kendra Michaels."

"A detective?"

"No. Yes. Sort of," he said. "She kind of writes her own ticket."

"But we need her?"

"We need her. She's unique."

"Then we'll get her," she said grimly. "I'm taking the next flight out."

"I thought that would be your reaction. But take that flight to San Diego. That's where she lives and works. I'll meet you there."

"San Diego," she repeated. "I'll let you know which flight. Bye, Joe." She hung up and, a moment later, heard the ping as the photo Joe had promised her was transmitted. She accessed the photo of Beth Avery.

She felt a ripple of surprise.

"Vibrant," Joe had called her. That was an understatement, the face of the girl in the photo was glowing and eager and so alive that it was like an electric shock. A thin, triangular face with full lips and brown eyes beneath winged dark brows. Her shoulder-length hair was also dark brown and wildly curly.

Like my Bonnie's hair, she thought. Not red-brown, like her daughter's tousled curls, but it looked to have the same shining texture and wild buoyancy. For some reason, she had not expected to see any family resemblance in Beth Avery. Eve still couldn't think of Beth in that context. She saw no likeness to either Sandra or herself, but that cap of curly hair had given her a start.

And that vibrance and sheer love of life in Beth's expression had touched . . . and angered her. No one who loved life that much should have it taken away from her.

Cool it. She was jumping to conclusions. She couldn't be absolutely sure that Beth had been a victim of anything but a terrible accident. Because Eve had believed she'd shared the thoughts of that woman in those crazy dreams didn't mean that those thoughts were sane and coherent.

Bullshit. Don't back away now. There had to be some reason that she'd had that first dream of Beth. Some reason that Sandra had come to them with her confession about Beth at just this time. Life wasn't always fair or kind, but she'd learned from Bonnie that there was an order to it that couldn't be denied.

"I'm glad you learned that much, Mama."
Bonnie.

She was sitting in the rocking chair by the window, dressed, as usual, in her Bugs Bunny T-shirt, with her leg tucked beneath her. The moonbeams streaming through the window were touching her curly hair with light.

Eve felt a rush of pure love as she gazed at her. "Well, it's about time you came around. I thought you'd abandoned me."

"No, you didn't. You know better." Her smile lit her small face. "I told you that I wasn't going to be around as often as I was before. You don't need me as much now."

"The hell I don't. I always need you."

"You love me, you don't need me. You're free of me now that you know where I am and who was to blame for my death. Now we can just enjoy the love."

All that wisdom and maturity in one small spirit. Bonnie had told her a long time ago that she couldn't remain the seven-year-old little girl she had been before she died. Souls matured and became what they were meant to be. But Eve wasn't about to let Bonnie talk her into letting her drift away from Eve. *"That doesn't mean you can't come around more often."*

Bonnie threw back her head and laughed. "Mama, you never give up. Admit that you didn't miss me as much as you did before."

"I will not." She added grudgingly, "Okay, I didn't feel as sad and hollow, but that didn't mean I didn't miss you. I was just thinking of you a minute ago."

"I know. Me and Beth."

She stiffened. "What do you know about Beth?"

"Not a lot. I know she's afraid. I know she's strong like you. So strong."

"Even now? In her photo, she looked very strong, but that was when she was a teenager."

"She's stronger now. She's had to fight, and that makes you develop all kinds of inner strength. You don't know how hard it was for her."

"I can imagine." She paused. "I've been dreaming about Beth. Was it—" Bonnie was shaking her head. "No?"

"I can't do that kind of thing. Dreams

aren't easy. I have a hard enough time contacting anyone myself in a dream state. I sure can't link anyone else up."

"Then what happened?" Her lips tightened. "I didn't imagine it, Bonnie."

"Don't be defensive. I'm not the only one around who cares about you . . . and Beth."

"But that's why you came, isn't it? It's Beth."

"No, it's you," she said gently. "You need her. I want to build a wall around you of people you love and who love you. That way you won't want to come to me too soon, Mama."

"I don't love Beth. I don't even know her."

"It will come. All the more reason to go help her."

"I was going to do that anyway. I promised Sandra."

Bonnie tilted her head and smiled.

"Okay, there's something wrong going on," Eve said. "It needs to be fixed. But I can't promise I'll love this woman just because she's my sister. It doesn't work that way." She frowned. "And I don't need any walls of people around me. I have Joe." She had a sudden rush of panic at a sudden thought. "I do have Joe, don't I? Nothing's going to happen to Joe."

"Shh, it's okay. I can't promise, but I think Joe is going to be fine."

"What do you mean, you can't promise? You scare me and tell me about surrounding me with people so I won't try to come to you, then you won't guarantee—" She stopped. "I know. I know. No guarantees."

"That's right." Bonnie leaned back in the rocking chair. "All I can guarantee is that we have a little while together right now, and that feels very good to me. Do you really think that Beth has hair like mine?"

"Sort of. It's darker, of course." Eve slowly curled up against the headboard, her gaze fastened on Bonnie. Any time with Bonnie was good time. "I like yours better."

"She's my aunt, isn't she? How strange . . ."

The words took Eve off guard. "Yes."

Yet the idea of Beth having a bond to her Bonnie was even more jarring than the knowledge of her own relationship.

Beth and Bonnie . . . together.

"Are you trying to make me more aware of the family connection?"

Bonnie smiled. "Yes, it worked, didn't it?"

"Maybe." She smiled back at her and shook her head. "We'll have to see, won't we? You're not at all dumb, baby."

"Neither is Beth, Mama. She's just lost . . ."

Eve's plane landed in San Diego at 12:17 P.M. the next day, and Joe met her at baggage claim ten minutes later.

"You look rested." His gaze was searching her face as he took her bag. "You managed to get some sleep?"

"Enough." She followed him through the doors to the parking lot. "Where are we going?"

"To the studio of Dr. Kendra Michaels."

"Studio? She's an artist?"

"Definitely an artist at what she does. Though she doesn't paint, she's a musician. I understand during her wild days she traveled the country singing and playing her guitar to earn her living in coffeehouses, on street corners, wherever."

"'Wild days,'" she repeated as she got into the passenger seat of the rental car. "Okay, talk to me. Who is this Kendra and how can she help us find out what happened to Beth at that hospital? She sounds like a colorful character, but we don't need color, we need efficiency."

"I'll let you judge whether she can produce after you meet her." He drove out of the parking lot. "But I'll fill you in on her background. And, yes, she's definitely colorful. She was totally blind until she underwent an operation when she was twenty. She had a number of years after that operation in which she tried to make up for lost time in ways that were sometimes not socially accepted."

"The wild years?"

He nodded. "When she got tired of sowing wild oats, she settled down and completed two advanced degrees. She has a doctorate in psychology and a master's in music theory. From what I understand, she's done a lot of important research in the field of music therapy. She also sees clients, mostly special kids, at her studio."

"Well, that's a switch. I can't see any connection between a wild-ass street entertainer and the educator she's become."

"Evidently, Kendra made one." He shrugged. "Sometimes, you can't tell what drives her. You have to go along for the ride."

"And how far is that ride going to take us to finding Beth?" She frowned. "I still don't see her value, Joe. And how did you come across her?"

"Do you remember I was out here a couple years ago trying to track that serial killer, Tim Vick? The local police were cooperating, but we were coming up with zilch. One of the detectives had used Kendra on another case the previous year and suggested I try to get her to help."

"Oh, for God's sake, she's not a psychic or something?"

"No." He chuckled. "Though your horror is a little misplaced, don't you think? It's not as if you don't believe that there are legitimate psychics."

"But they're very rare, and phonies

abound. If Kendra wasn't a psychic, why did the police call on her for help?"

"She has a rare talent. She was born blind due to a degenerative corneal disease in the womb. She's totally brilliant and developed all of her other senses to a phenomenal degree. She compensated by using her hearing, smell, touch, every sense she had. Then, when she was twenty, a stem-cell procedure gave her sight. She applied that same discipline she had learned when blind to everything that crossed her field of vision. Now, nothing gets past her. She can walk into a crime scene or indeed any other scene and pick up on things no one else can see. Often, she can put together those impressions and come up with answers. An agent at the FBI San Diego field office told me that she once cracked a case by walking into a room and hearing that its echo had a different quality than the rooms next to it."

"It sounds kind of spooky." She grimaced. "Shades of Sherlock Holmes."

"Exactly." He grinned. "I knew you'd be skeptical. I was, too. You have to meet her."

"Which we're obviously going to do. I'll

have to decide if I think we should use her after I talk to her."

"Use her?" His smile widened. "That may not be the way it works out. We'll have to ask her nicely, then try to persuade her when she tells us to go to hell."

"What?"

"Kendra doesn't like being taken away from teaching her kids. Or her research. Every now and then, she'll do a job for the police or FBI, but it's rare. She turns them away all the time."

"But you said she took the Tim Vick case?"

"Not at first. She turned down the local police when they asked her."

"But she didn't turn you down?"

"I was more persistent. After I decided that maybe she could help, I analyzed her refusal and went back to see her and attacked her weakness."

"And what was her weakness?"

"The kids. She was devoted to teaching special kids. She's one tough lady, and I don't think she lets many people under her guard. But Tim Vick killed six children during his rampage in Atlanta. I just brought it to her attention that if we didn't catch him, he might kill more in San Diego."

Clever, Eve thought. Joe was always thinking, always searching for the answers, and he usually found them. "She gave in?"

"Grudgingly. She likes her own way and doesn't like to be involved in police work. She wasn't pleased that I'd found a way to manipulate her against her will."

"Was it worth your trouble?" She was trying to remember the details of the case. "Did you get Vick?"

He nodded. "And, yes, Kendra was definitely worth the trouble. She's fairly incredible. I wouldn't have brought you here if I hadn't thought she could get us the information we need."

"Then we'll find a way to get her to go along with us." She wrinkled her nose. "But this time, we have no children in danger to dangle before her to get her to help us at that hospital. Is she really that difficult?"

He pulled into a strip mall. "In a few minutes, you'll be able to judge for yourself. I called her from the airport, and she said she didn't want to see me, but she'd give me thirty minutes so that I wouldn't keep bothering her."

"Did you tell her I was coming with you?"

"No, she knows nothing about you. She saw to it that we didn't get chummy enough for confidences while we were working on the Vick case. She did her job, but she definitely resented my pulling her into it."

"That doesn't sound promising."

He shrugged. "She's tough." He checked his watch. "She's probably still busy with an appointment. She told me that I'd have to wait in the viewing room until she was finished."

"Viewing room?"

"Some of Kendra's students are autistic or have big-time emotional problems, and she likes to work with them alone and without interference. But she gives the parents the opportunity to watch the lessons from an observation room with one-way glass if they prefer." He nodded at a small brick building. "Her office is right over there on the left."

CHAPTER
5

Joe must be wrong, Eve thought as she studied Kendra Michaels's expression through the one-way window. She was sitting beside a little six-year-old boy while he played the xylophone. Joe had called her a tough lady, but this woman's face was alight with eagerness, intelligence, and understanding as she focused all her attention on the child's complete intentness as he played the instrument. She was of medium height and slim but far from fragile-looking. Pale brown hair was shoulder-length and sun-streaked and framed a strong face that reflected control and discipline. Large hazel eyes set far apart shone with intelligence and humor as she watched the boy. Kendra wasn't a beautiful woman, but her smile was beautiful.

Kendra finally put a gentle hand out to stop the boy. "It's time for you to go, Justin. Your mama is outside waiting."

He ignored her, still pounding the keys. She held out her hand and took the stick. He started to fight her, then was still, staring up into her face. "Pretty?"

She nodded. "Very pretty, Justin. Beautiful. Next time, it will be even more beautiful because while you're at home, you'll hear the sound and the notes in your mind. Then when we get together, you'll let me hear them, too." Her finger reached out and traced the outline of his mouth. "A smile can be beautiful, too. It can be like a song that goes on and on and echoes inside you and around you. Maybe you'll let me hear that song, too?"

His intent expression didn't change.

She smiled. "No?" She took his hand. "Think about it." She put his fingers on her lips. "I'll give you my song. Here it is. I'll be waiting for you to give me yours."

He didn't move, his gaze on her face. Then he jerked away and ran toward the door across the room.

Kendra stayed by the xylophone. "Good-bye, Justin. I'll see you in two days."

He stopped at the door and looked back at her. Then he was suddenly running back to her.

Kendra smiled as he stopped before her. "Yes?"

He reached out a tentative finger and slowly traced the outline of her smile. "Pretty . . . song . . ." Then he whirled and was running back to the door and out of the studio.

The smile remained for an instant while her gaze lingered on the door. Then it faded as she stood up and began to tidy the studio. "You might as well come in, Quinn. You're on the clock. I have another student in thirty minutes, and I won't keep her waiting."

Kendra's tone was completely different from the way she had spoken to the little boy. It was crisp, cool, and there was a distinct edge. Her demeanor had the same coolness, and that warm, affectionate magnetism that had been present when she'd been interacting with little Justin had disappeared.

Joe wasn't wrong. Kendra was, indeed, one tough lady.

"You heard her," Joe murmured as he got to his feet and headed to the door that led from the booth to Kendra's main studio. "We're on the clock. Let's get moving."

Eve followed him into the studio. "By all means."

"Hello, Quinn." Kendra looked beyond him to Eve. "Who is she? My appointment was with you."

"But the job that we're asking you to do is for her. Eve Duncan, Dr. Kendra Michaels."

"I'm very glad to meet you," Eve said. "Joe seems to think that you can help us. I'd be very grateful if you'd try."

"No, it's not going to happen," Kendra said. "Quinn knew the answer before he even brought you here. In our last encounter, he backed me into a corner and manipulated me to get what he wanted. In the end, it was for a good cause, but it's not going to happen again."

"You haven't heard what we want," Eve

said. "And if Joe manipulated you, he had good reason." She met her gaze. "You must have thought the same thing, or you wouldn't have allowed it to happen. Joe said you're tough, but you weren't tough enough to let a serial killer be free to kill and kill again. I watched you with that little boy, and I don't think that you're as hard as you're pretending. Joe seems to believe you can do what we need, but I have my doubts. It all sounds pretty bizarre. Now listen, and I'll tell you the situation and what we want from you."

Kendra held Eve's gaze for an instant, then she glanced at her watch. "You have twenty minutes. I'll hear you out but I'm sure my answer won't change. I'm incredibly busy with my work."

She wasn't budging, Eve thought with frustration. "In the end, that's your decision." She briefly and concisely outlined Sandra's story and what they'd found out about the hospital and Beth's mental impairment and the Avery connection.

Kendra looked at Eve without expression after she'd fallen silent. "That's everything?"

"Yes." Eve wasn't about to bring up the

dreams she'd had about Beth running for her life. It would just be another reason for Kendra to refuse. "And it should be enough for you."

"It's enough for me to see why you're so concerned. But you don't really have much to go on." She glanced at Joe. "You're not talking much. I'm surprised you're leaving it all up to her."

He smiled at Eve. "She can handle it."

"Can she?" Her glance shifted back to Eve. "The answer is still no. Sorry."

Eve felt a rush of irritation mixed with pure anger at the woman's stubbornness. "Why not, dammit? Listen, we just want you to go with us to the hospital and take a look around. If Joe is right about you, you could be a big help up there, especially if we can manage to see her room. No big deal. It shouldn't take you long just to try."

"It would be a day away from my students, and that can seem a lifetime to some of these kids. I'm near a breakthrough with two of them. Justin's very close." She added fiercely, "Do you know that he hasn't smiled or cried in three years? He's been locked in an emotional vacuum. I'm not going to let him take a step back just because you want me to play your game."

"Your game," Joe corrected. "You set the rules, Kendra. Most of the time, I can't even see through your hijinks to where you're going."

"It's not hijinks. It's just observation," Kendra said impatiently. "And I don't have time for it. I have a passion in life, and it's the work I do here. I never wanted to play at being a detective. That's your passion in life, Quinn, not mine."

Eve was getting impatient. "Joe, this is ridiculous. I refuse to beg her to do something I don't even have faith she can do. Is she really worth it?"

Joe nodded. "She's worth it."

She was silent a moment before turning back to Kendra. "Okay, then you've got to do it."

Kendra's brows rose. "Really? And how are you going to ensure that?"

"You'll do it because you have no choice. Everyone responds to their own personal drummer. You may be as tough as Joe says you are, but you did what was right about helping him track down that killer because he struck the right note. You couldn't stand the thought of helpless children being possible victims. And you have a career that enables you to protect helpless children from their own disabilities."

"And your point is?"

"You can't resist fighting for those who are young or helpless, it's part of your DNA."

"Interesting analysis. But Beth Avery is no child and may not even be a victim."

"But what if she is a victim?" She took a step closer to Kendra, and her voice vibrated with intensity. "Yes, you're drawn to children, but I believe that fighting for Beth Avery may be just as appealing to you. Because if she was kept prisoner all those years, it would be a hideous crime. Can you imagine it? Joe told me that you went a little wild after you gained your sight. Tell me, did it seem like getting out of prison not to be blind any longer?"

She didn't speak for a moment. "You're very good, Eve Duncan. While I was blind I tried to do everything, hone every sense, so that it wouldn't be a prison. I didn't realize I hadn't succeeded until that surgeon took off my bandages."

"Beth Avery has been in that hospital

since she was seventeen. The drugs she was given didn't allow her to even try to keep it from being a prison. Don't you think she should have someone just check to see if she deserves to be in that place? Joe thinks something shady is going on. That surgeon set you free. You could help us do the same for Beth Avery, dammit."

Kendra shook her head. "I don't want to do this."

Eve could see the beginning of a crack in her resistance. "I can understand that you have priorities. We can work it out."

Kendra was silent for a long moment. "What exactly do you want from me?"

"As Eve said, we want you to go there with us," Joe said quickly. "To see the hospital, her room, and the staff. We want your impressions."

Kendra's expression didn't change, Eve noticed. Was she actually considering it?

"In the meantime, we'll also be looking for a way to access the computer medical records on Beth Avery. We want to see if she had a reason to run away from that hospital. We want to verify that the patient they've produced that they claim is Beth Avery is a ringer. We want to know everything we can find out about her in the quickest amount of time."

"You're not going to find all that in her medical records."

"Exactly," Joe said. "That's why we need you."

Kendra smiled, and, for the first time, Eve glimpsed the faintest hint of the warmth she had shown her student. But only a flash; and then it was gone. "I'm glad I impressed you on our last case, Quinn, but I'm not a miracle worker. I can't see what's not there."

"If you tell me there's nothing, then I'll believe there's nothing. But I'll only believe it if you give it a shot and tell me that."

She was silent. "It better not take long. I don't have time to waste on this."

"You'll do it?" Eve asked.

"I didn't say that. I'll consider it. I'll let you know." She turned away. "Now please get out of here. I have to study my notes on my next patient."

"You need to let us know soon," Eve said. "There may not be much time to—"

"If you're pushing me for an immediate answer, then it's no," Kendra said sharply. "I said I'd think about it, which is more consideration than I give 90 percent of the people who want me to leave my work to help out on their cases. I'm more aware of time constraints than you are. I have an appointment with Justin day after tomorrow that I've got to keep. I'm not even sure going to that hospital isn't a complete waste of time."

"And I'm not sure that bringing you in to help isn't a complete waste of time," Eve said with equal sharpness. "You'll have to show me. But if we're going to do it, let's do it right. Stop dithering." She turned toward the door. "Come on, Joe."

"I don't *dither*." Kendra's hands were clenched at her sides. "And I'm never a waste of time. Show you? Where the hell do you get the nerve to demand that I perform like some Vegas acrobat?"

"I didn't demand anything," Eve said as she opened the door. "I just displayed some good old American skepticism. Call us when you get around to making up your mind."

"Wait." Kendra was glaring at Eve. "If that was your attempt to goad me, don't bother. Hardly a day goes by that some detective or federal agent doesn't interrupt my workday to beg for my help, then insult me by saying I probably couldn't have helped them anyway. As if that will somehow make me desperate to prove myself." Kendra leaned against the table. "But you . . . You've annoyed me just enough so that I'm going to get the last word even though it's quite clear to me that's something you're not accustomed to." She paused. "Just as it's clear to me you two are sleeping together."

Eve tried not to let the surprise register on her face.

Kendra crossed her arms across her chest. "Although I don't believe you slept together last night. You were in Atlanta, weren't you, Eve? You flew here this morning, but Quinn wasn't with you. I'm guessing he picked you up at the airport just a short while ago. Don't you live together?"

"We do, but I've been here in California for a couple days," Joe said.

"Ah, that explains it. You're a little out of your element on this case, aren't you, Eve? You're much more accustomed to talking to the dead. Or, I suppose, letting the dead talk to you."

Eve inhaled sharply. How in hell . . . The

dead? Bonnie? Was she talking about Bonnie? Her gaze flew to Joe's face. "You told her about—"

He was shaking his head and mouthing a silent "no."

"You're a forensic sculptor," Kendra said. "With your help, the dead tell you all their secrets, don't they?"

Eve let out the breath she hadn't realized she had been holding. Not Bonnie. But Kendra's meaning was only a little less startling than the alternative.

"I've always admired people who can do that," Kendra said. "You must be very talented."

"Right back at you," Eve said, trying not to sound as dazed as she felt. "Are you sure you're not psychic?"

"Positive." Kendra turned away. "Now leave me alone. I'll let you know what I decide. I still have your cell number, Quinn. Or would you prefer I call you at the Docket Cove Hotel?"

Eve turned to Joe. "Is that where we're staying?"

Joe nodded. "But I didn't tell her. And there are at least five hotels between there and here."

"More like a dozen," Kendra said.

Eve didn't move and slowly shook her head. "I'm not leaving until you tell me how you knew all that." She thought about it. "You probably found out Joe was coming, and you researched us or asked around. Is that it?"

Kendra smiled. "I value my time a lot more than that, Eve. Until you walked through that door, I wasn't even aware that you existed. But I did know Quinn, and I remembered that he was always somewhat guarded with his personal space. Especially with women. He always kept his face a good six to eight inches farther away from women than he did with men."

"What?" Joe said. "Seriously?"

"I'm sure you're not even aware you do it. I don't think you're afraid of women, but subconsciously you may be wary of leading them on. A handsome man like you, it's probably happened a time or two. But with Eve, I saw you crash through every barrier I ever saw you set for yourself. And instead of backing away slightly, as most colleagues or even friends tend to do, Eve leaned forward. Even though the two of you haven't so much as touched hands since you've been here, it's pretty obvious what's going on between you."

"How do you know we weren't together last night?" Eve asked.

"You're not going to like this."

"How?"

"Because I'm afraid that you smell, Eve."

Eve's eyes widened. "I beg your pardon?"

"Have you ever stepped onto an airplane and breathed in that awful stale odor of recycled air?"

Eve nodded. "Of course."

"That's how you smell to me right now. A lot of that air actually comes through the engines, then is recycled throughout the cabin. Depending on the aircraft, it can sometimes smell like a mixture of jet fuel and bad breath."

"And that's how I smell?" She grimaced. "How very unpleasant."

"Don't worry, you won't offend anyone. It's so faint that no one but me would even be aware of it. But Quinn has no trace of that odor."

"Go on. What else?"

Kendra pointed down at Eve's shoes. "There's the slightest trace of red Georgia earth on the sides of your shoes and spattering the cuff of your pant leg. It could have come from Tennessee or Alabama, I suppose, but knowing that Quinn is from Georgia, it wasn't much of a stretch to think you'd also come from there. The earth is still fairly fresh, not too dry or cracked, suggesting it was just put there this morning. Quinn's shoes, though, are spotless. And unless he's in a crime scene, I know for a fact that he's not too careful where he walks. He strides through the world as if he owns it. Even before I caught a whiff of your scent, I figured he came from someplace else this morning."

"Impressive," Eve murmured.

"What else? Oh, yes, your profession." Kendra walked over to Eve, took her hands, and spread her palms open. "You have faint stains on both of your hands. Dye from a polymer-based sculpting clay."

"How do you know I'm not a rising star of the art world?"

Kendra studied Eve's hands for a moment longer with an intensity that was vaguely unsettling to Eve. She was a private person, and she didn't like feeling this transparent to another individual. What else was this woman going to find out about her? Yet she couldn't deny that the revelations were totally fascinating. And so was Kendra Michaels.

"At first glance, I considered the possibility," Kendra said. "But I rejected it when I saw that you almost exclusively use flesh-colored clay. That fact tilts the scales quite a bit. But I also noticed the tiny callused nubs, on each hand near the tips of your thumb and forefinger. Too small for pen, stylus, or almost any other tool. But just the right size and placement for those spherical-headed spacer pins you'd use in facial reconstruction. I once worked a case with a forensic sculptor here in San Diego whose hands looked very similar, Patrick Chicoin."

"I've met him," Eve said. "He's very good."

"So I've been told." Kendra dropped Eve's hands and her gaze slid away from her. "That's all. We're done."

Eve stiffened. "No, we're not. There's something else besides calluses and clay stains, isn't there?"

Kendra raised her gaze to Eve's face. "Yes, sometimes you have to go beyond the purely physical evidence. There's a

darkness inside you that's visible for anyone to see. It all fits together." She shrugged.
"I didn't expect you to be perceptive enough
to catch that particular nuance. No offense.
You asked."

"Yes, I did." Eve smiled with an effort.
"And I beg to differ. I don't believe I'm that
transparent to everyone. You're fairly incredible." She turned to Joe. "You were
right."

"Of course I was."

"My student will be here any minute,"
Kendra said. "I've wasted enough time.
Will you just leave me to my work?"

Eve turned back to Kendra. "Okay, we're
going. But there's no way I'll leave you
alone now. You're amazing, and you can
be useful."

"If I change my mind—and I don't think
I will—I know where to find you."

"Yes, you do," Joe said. "How did you
know about the Docket Cove Hotel? I
stayed there last night, but I know I didn't
tell you."

Kendra walked across her studio and
opened the door for them. "It's the only
hotel in the area that insists on giving their
guests those long brass door keys. Some

of my clients have stayed there. I'm sure the hotel thinks those keys are more charming than plastic keycards, but they're much less secure." She pointed to Joe's pants pocket. "The key is clipped on your rental-car key ring, which I saw you put away as you walked in here."

Eve smiled faintly. "Now you're just showing off."

"Maybe a little."

Eve stared her directly in the eye. "I can be as determined and stubborn as you are, you know. You'll get tired of saying no to me. We'll work it out." She turned and walked out of the studio before Kendra could answer.

"I feel as if I've gone through a tornado." Joe was chuckling as he fell into step with her as they went out to the car. "Though I should have expected it when I brought two strong women together and set them against each other."

"And then stepped back and let me handle the battle," she said dryly. "Why?"

"I thought you had a better chance with her. She was already antagonistic toward me." He opened the car door for her. "And you did well."

"Sparks. Lots of sparks." She added thoughtfully, "But she's astonishing. She could help us, Joe."

"That's what I told you. And that was a minor demonstration. I've seen her do things that were positively stunning."

"And she'll be difficult." She gestured impatiently. "But that doesn't matter. You're right, Joe, she's worth it." She looked back at the studio. "Look, we have some time. I'm going to go to the hotel to shower and wash my hair. Then we'll—stop laughing, Joe."

"It's amusing. I knew that you wouldn't be able to keep from washing her criticism away." He sniffed teasingly. "Even though it's totally unnecessary. I can't smell even the faintest hint of jet fuel about you."

"But she could, so it must be there. I'll just make sure to get rid of it." She added thoughtfully, "And I've been wondering what it must be like to be surrounded by obnoxious scents that no one else even notices."

"It could work the other way, too. Some scents are wonderful." He kissed her cheek. "And you smell just fine."

"You're biased. I'll still take that shower.

Then we'll go to lunch and give her four hours to call us. That should be enough time. She wants her part in this over quickly. She has a deadline with her Justin."

"And if she doesn't call us?"

That was a distinct possibility. Eve had annoyed Kendra, pushed her and guilted her into taking on a job that she didn't want. But Eve had an idea that the comparison she had drawn between Beth's prison and the life Kendra had led when blind would weigh heavily on her. Heavily enough to swing Kendra into their camp?

What would they do if Eve had guessed wrong?

"Why, then we'll just have to go after her, Joe."

Kendra called Joe three hours later. "Come and get me at the studio. I'm leaving my car here."

"You're going to help us?"

"Don't pretend you're surprised. You brought Eve Duncan here to draw me into the web. She did it." She paused. "I don't like the fact that she read me that well."

"You should talk. The pot calling the kettle black."

"Maybe. But I still feel uneasy. You're good at manipulation, Quinn, but she goes deeper beneath the surface. That can be dangerous. What is she to you?"

Joe looked at Eve in the seat next to him. "Everything," he said simply. "So you'd better give her what she wants, Kendra."

"Is she listening?"

"Yes, you're on speaker."

"Good, then I won't have to repeat myself. I don't care what she wants. I don't care what you want. I've spent time helping patients in mental institutions. If it's possible that there are abuses happening at this one, it needs to be looked into. I just don't want this Beth Avery to be a victim. There are too many victims in this world." She continued brusquely. "Look, I have to be through with this job by day after tomorrow. I don't have time for you to find a way to get into that hospital. Since they know you, it would be too risky. So you're out of it. I've arranged to do it myself."

"Really? And how did you accomplish that?"

"I called my mother two hours ago and told her that I needed a favor." She added bitterly, "You don't know what a sacrifice that was. My mother always demands a payback."

"Your mother?"

"She's Professor Deanna Michaels with UC San Diego. She's a noted historical authority but she has mega influence with every political, medical, and educational board in the state. I told her I needed a valid reason to be given free access at that hospital tomorrow morning. She just called back and told me it was set up, and they'd welcome me with open arms."

"Your mother appears to be very efficient. How did she manage that?"

"She had the lieutenant governor contact Harry Pierce, the chief administrator, and tell him that they were sending a music therapist to examine the facilities and records to see if the hospital would be a candidate for a state grant to help the treatment of the inmates."

"State grant? California is almost broke."

"So? That wouldn't stop a liberal government from funding mental-health initiatives. Believe me, no one will question it. Once I'm accepted inside, I'll find a way to get rid of the escort they give me and get the information you need. I'll be ready to leave here in an hour to drive to Santa Barbara. We'll check into a motel for the night, and I'll be ready to storm the gates at eight in the morning."

"*We'll* be ready to storm the gates," Eve corrected. "You're right, Joe can't come, but there's no reason for me not to go with you. You can get me in as your assistant."

"You don't look like an assistant."

"I can be unobtrusive. I'm going."

Silence. "We'll talk about it tomorrow morning. Come and get me." She hung up.

Eve smiled faintly as Joe pressed the disconnect. "It appears she's jumped into the fray with both feet."

"She doesn't know any other way." He started the car. "But she's right, you don't appear subordinate in the least. Even when you're trying to be unobtrusive, you can't turn off what you are."

She shrugged. "Then that's her problem. She obviously wants to run things. Let her find a way to get me in under the radar."

He smiled. "I'd like to go along and watch. It would be a hell of a lot more amusing for me than staying at the hotel and researching Pierce and all of the hospital personnel."

"Somehow, I don't believe tomorrow is going to be in the least amusing," she said dryly. "But it will definitely be challenging."

Kendra Michaels was waiting outside the door of her studio with a duffel and a guitar case beside her when they pulled up an hour later. "Right on time." She opened the rear door and got into the car. "I just finished and locked up."

"A guitar? I don't really think that will be necessary," Eve said.

"It is for me. It relaxes me to play when I'm in a strange place."

"And do you always have extra luggage at your studio?" Eve's gaze was on the duffel Kendra had thrown on the seat beside her.

"Yes, I do make house calls if my students need me." She met Joe's gaze in the rearview mirror as he drove out of the parking lot. "And I can never tell when I'll need to take off on one of these missions impossible the authorities throw at me."

Joe smiled. "But they're not impossible for you, Kendra."

"I wasn't referring to myself," she said bluntly. "And they shouldn't be impossible for the police or FBI if they'd just block out everything around them and concentrate on what's before them. Then I wouldn't have to be involved. And that goes for you, too, Quinn. You're very perceptive and smart as a whip. You should apply yourself."

"I'll keep that in mind, but I have an idea that I'd have to go around blindfolded a year or two to even approach your skill. Frankly, I don't have the time."

"Not when you can call on me," she said dryly.

"Exactly," he murmured.

"Don't get cocky. You brought in reinforcements. Your Eve is the one who got me on board." Her gaze shifted to Eve. "And I'll do better on my own. Change your mind about going in with me."

Eve shook her head. "Beth Avery is my responsibility. Besides, two can be better than one. I won't get in your way."

"No, you won't," Kendra said coolly. "If you do, I'll run right over you." She turned back to Joe. "What can you tell me about Beth Avery's quarters at the hospital? I suppose you checked everything out when you went to question the people there."

"Right now, the woman they're calling Beth Avery is being held in solitary in a room on the first floor. She's being taken care of by Pierce, and she's not being allowed any visitors and has only a private nurse in attendance." He added, "The room from which she escaped is on the third floor in a deluxe suite where she's supposedly been living since she came there at seventeen. That floor is designated only for rich or famous clients who have been committed for varying lengths of time. There are only two other suites on that floor. Only one is occupied at the moment. Beth's suite was Room 305."

"Very good. Where is the human resources office?"

"First floor, second hallway off the reception area. I downloaded a complete floor plan of the hospital from the Internet and it's on my iPhone. I'll send it to you when we get to the motel."

"And what do we know about Harry Pierce?" Eve asked. "If he's Beth's personal doctor, he has to be involved in whatever is going on with her. How long has he been her psychiatrist?"

"Since she came to Santa Barbara. He

accompanied her from the hospital in Boston, where she stayed when she was first injured. The Avery family insisted he be taken on the staff as her doctor. He was young, and his credentials were only fair and not up to the hospitals standards. But the administrator caved because the Averys were such heavy donors."

"But you said Pierce was the administrator now," Eve said.

"He had over a decade to insinuate himself into a very comfortable niche. With the Averys backing him, it's not surprising he was able to establish his own little kingdom."

Eve's lips twisted. "With Beth as the crown jewel."

"Anyone else we should know about?" Kendra asked.

Joe shook his head. "Give me a break. I only had one visit and the info I could gather on the Internet."

"You didn't give me a break," Kendra said. "I'll give you what you need but I want—" She broke off as her cell rang. "Oh, shit. It's my mother." She hesitated, then reluctantly answered the phone.

"Hello, Mother. I can't talk right now. I'll call you later. No, I'm not with a student. I'm on my way to Santa Barbara." She listened again, then said slowly and distinctly, "No, I do not want you to come to Santa Barbara and help. You've done everything I needed you to do. I have everything under control. Nothing is going to happen to me. It's not as if I'm going to do anything dangerous. I just have to go in and absorb a few impressions. Stop worrying."

Evidently, Kendra's relationship with her mother is as complicated as mine with Sandra, Eve thought. Kendra was so confident that it was strange to see her this soothing and apologetic.

"No, it won't be like that," Kendra said. "Do you think I'd let myself in for that kind of punishment again? I'm not a fool, Mother." She drew a deep breath. "I have to go now. I'll call you tomorrow night. It's going to be fine." She hung up and leaned back in the seat. "Dammit, I didn't want to ask her to pull those strings to get us into the hospital. I was afraid that she'd be on my case once she had time to think."

"It's natural that a mother would be

concerned about her daughter," Eve said quietly. "It's understandable that she's protective."

"You think you understand?" Kendra asked fiercely. "Not unless you grew up with my mother. She's stronger than almost anyone I know. Protective? Hell, yes, she wanted to be protective of me. I was blind, for God's sake. But she wanted me to be as strong and independent as I could be, so she kept herself from sheltering me and made me face the world and find ways to cope."

"But she changed once you gained your vision?"

"She tried to let me go." She shrugged. "Something happened to me on an FBI case I worked on. It scared her. She doesn't like my taking chances. I had to reassure her." She met Eve's gaze. "Sorry I jumped on you. You're right, it's a natural maternal instinct." Her lips twisted. "I guess you recognize the signs. You told me it was really your mother who sent you to look for Beth Avery. She appears to be cut from the same cloth as my mother."

Except that there was nothing strong

about Sandra, and the only maternal affection she possessed had been for Beth.

"No?" Kendra's gaze was narrowed on Eve's expression.

Eve forced a smile. "Not exactly." Kendra's vision might not have had the same fine-tuning as her other senses, but she was entirely too sharp. "Mothers are different. Just as people are different. But I'm glad that you had a woman like that in your life to raise you."

"So am I." Kendra's gaze was still on her face. "But mothers can be a challenge, can't they?"

Change the subject. Eve was feeling as if Kendra were seeing right through her. "What about your father?"

"My mother divorced him. She said it was because of his other affairs, but I think it was really that he wasn't a cheerleader for me. She wanted him to be as supportive as she was." She tilted her head. "You?"

"My father?" She was startled. She hadn't expected the subject to be turned back to her. "I never knew him. I'm illegitimate. So you see, we're nothing alike."

Kendra was silent. "I'm not so sure.

Maybe not on the surface." She looked down at her iPhone. "Quinn, it's hours before we get to Santa Barbara. I can't sit here with nothing to do. Will you give Eve your phone and have her send that floor plan of the hospital to me? I should be able to memorize it before we get to the hotel."

"Big task unless you have total recall," Joe said as he handed Eve his phone. "I don't recall that as one of your gifts."

"It's not," she said absently as she retrieved the e-mail from her phone. "But I had to train my memory from childhood, and I'm pretty good. Braille doesn't really cut it when you're a blind musician. It can be terribly frustrating . . ."

"I think I like this place," Eve said, as they parked in front of the long, rectangular, stone motel that hovered on a cliff over the beach. Its paned windows reflected the rays of the setting sun, and it looked clean and bright and sturdy. "Did you stay here before, Joe?"

"No, I was in and out of town too quickly." Joe got out of the car in front of the front entrance. "I'll go check in for us." He nodded at a large white building high on a hill across the harbor. "That's the mental hospital. It will take about ten minutes to reach there tomorrow morning." He disappeared into the motel.

"Very impressive." Kendra got out of the car and stared up at Seahaven Behavioral Health Center. "But not threatening."

"Did you expect Frankenstein's castle?" Eve asked.

"No, just a comment. I know that bad things sometimes come in pretty packages." She took her duffel out of the car and turned to Joe as he came back out of the motel. "Room service?"

"Minimal. Sandwiches and drinks." He handed her a key. "Your room is around the corner and two doors down."

"Minimal is all I need. I've got to call my mother back, then try to sleep. I'll see you both in the morning." She moved down the walk, wheeling her duffel behind her.

"I believe we've been dismissed," Joe said. "Do you want to go find a restaurant?"

"No." She cast one more glance at the hospital before she turned away. It wasn't Frankenstein's castle, but it was beginning to loom large in her imagination. Had Beth been able to look out those windows and see all this freedom around her? "Minimal is enough for me, too. Let's just shower and get to bed."

"Sounds good. But I have a few follow-up calls I have to make, too." He took out the bags. "I'll shower first and make them while you take yours."

CHAPTER

6

"You're on edge. I can almost feel it. What can I do?" Joe asked quietly as he paused in the bathroom doorway to look at her standing by the window. He was towel-drying his hair as he came out of the bathroom. He had another towel draped around his waist, and with his bare chest and powerful, naked thighs, he reminded Eve of a gladiator. "You don't have to work with Kendra if you don't want to. We can find another way. I just thought this would be easier."

"Easier? I don't think Kendra Michaels could ever be termed easier," Eve said.

"It's fine, Joe. I'd tell you if it wasn't. You know I'm not shy about voicing opinions." She was gazing out the window at the surf crashing on the beach several hundred feet below the motel. She couldn't see the hospital from that window, but she knew it was there, and the knowledge was hanging over like a heavy fog. "Yes, I'm on edge. What do you expect? What if we're wrong? What if that woman you saw in that hospital bed is Beth Avery? It's such a fragile fabric of evidence. We're operating on instinct and dreams and hope."

"So what's new?" He took her in his arms. "And what's wrong with it? It usually works for us."

She buried her face in the wiry hair on his chest. He smelled of clean soap and the faint musk that was distinctly his own. Even if she were as blind as Kendra had been, she knew she'd know Joe by the scent of him. She closed her eyes and breathed deep. "I love the smell of you. Have I ever told you that?"

He chuckled. "Not that I recall. It must be Kendra's influence." He kissed her long and hard. "Perhaps we'd better explore that concept. I'm ready . . ."

"I know you are. It's very obvious in that skimpy towel." And so was she. It only took a touch, a look, and the heat started to climb. They had been together for so long that it shouldn't have been that way, passion was supposed to fade or become comfortable. It was a miracle that their passion was as strong and ever-changing as when they had first come together. Her arms slid around his neck, and her nails bit into the muscles of his shoulders. "You should really take it off. It's not doing you any good."

"You take it off." His hands were cupping her breasts. "I'm busy. Why the hell are you still dressed? It's inconvenient as hell. I should have—" His cell phone rang on the coffee table in front of the couch. "Shit. Not now."

Her feeling exactly. "Ignore it. Let them call back." Then she had a thought. "Were you expecting a call?"

"It doesn't matter," he muttered, his lips buried in the hollow of her throat.

The phone rang again.

"Who . . ."

"The doctor's office at the ski resort in Maine where Beth had her accident. They said they'd call me back. Forget it."

It was what she wanted to do, dammit. But she pushed herself away from him and hurried across the room before she changed her mind. "It's three hours later in Maine than we are here. You may not be able to get in touch with them." She pressed the access button on his phone and took it to him. "Talk to them. Make sure you get everything out of them that you need so they won't call back." She headed for the door. "I'm going outside to cool off."

"Not too much."

She grinned at him. "No way." She followed up with a mock Schwarzenegger imitation. "I'll be back."

"You'd better." Joe was already talking on the phone as the door closed behind her.

She drew a deep breath of the cool, salt-laden air as she paused on the walk outside the motel room. She was shaking, she realized. Trembling and hot and ready. Calm down. It was only a postponement. She was acting like a teenager whose eagerness was as explosive and uncontrolled as a lightning bolt. Just take a break, then go back to him. That was the way it

always was with them. Separation and re-
union but always ending together.

She moved toward the deck chairs on
the verandah overlooking the ocean. It
appeared to be unoccupied. No surprise.
The wind was too strong and cool for it to
be inviting, in spite of the view. Just as
well. She didn't feel like being sociable,
and she needed that coolness at the moment.

She dropped down in the blue-and-white
lounge chair and gazed down at the beach.
Beach . . .

Run.

**The security man cursing as he
stumbled down the dune after her.**

The memory of the dream was suddenly there before Eve.

Had Beth gotten away from him that
night?

And why in hell was Eve so sure that
dream was more than a wisp of fantasy?

"Where's Quinn?"

Eve stiffened and turned to see Kendra
standing a few yards away. She was
dressed in slacks and a navy Windbreaker,
her hair pulled back in a ponytail. She

dropped down in the chair next to Eve. "I'm surprised he lets you out of his sight."

"What?" Eve frowned. "Don't be ridiculous. We're two mature people, and we've been together a long time."

Kendra raised her brows but didn't comment.

"Why are you out here?" Eve asked. "I thought you were going to call your mother, then go to bed."

"I'm restless."

"Playing your guitar didn't help?"

Kendra shook her head. "Not tonight. I finally gave it up and came out here. I always have to get used to new places before I can sleep. I get bombarded."

"Bombarded?"

"Sensory overload. My mind is always automatically trying to absorb, isolate, and identify. After I settle into a place, I can usually accept and block the parts I don't need from the mix." She looked at the sea. "But there's so much life out there that it's hard to do. Listen . . ."

Eve tilted her head, concentrating. "Seagulls, the surf . . . That's all I hear. Is there something else?"

Kendra nodded. "There are two dolphins

jumping and playing just offshore, and the fish . . . so many fish . . . And I was watching the crabs in the sand there on the beach. A little distance down the way, there's a hot dog stand and the smells of the sausage dogs and onions are wonderful. Do you want me to go on?"

"Good God, I had no idea," Eve said, staring at her. "I can see how distracting that would be." She had another thought. "Joe said that right after your operation, you traveled all over the world like a gypsy. If you're that sensitive, going from place to place must have been a nightmare."

She shook her head. "It was magnificent. It was the first time I was able to combine all my senses. I loved every minute of it. I felt drunk on life." She made a face. "But I liked it too much. I was dizzy, and I lost my balance quite a bit. You tend to do that when every moment is a new adventure. I stretched my boundaries way beyond the rules. I'm lucky to still be alive and out of jail." She smiled. "Not that I regret it. I tried never to hurt anyone but myself. And I had to accept that every experience made me what I am." She looked back at Eve. "Bad or good. Just as your experiences made you what you are. But you didn't get off as lucky as I did."

"You mean my 'darkness'?" Eve's lips twisted. "You may be ultrasensitive, but I think you've been doing more than talking to your mother this evening. A little computer research on me?"

"I was curious," Kendra said. "As I told you, forensic sculpting interested me, but I was more interested in the actual technical process or I would have known who you are. I found out you're quite famous." She added, "And the reason that it doesn't mean a damn to you. I'm sorry for your loss, Eve."

"So am I. But my work means more to me than you could imagine."

"Oh, I can imagine." She looked back at the surf. "And I can see why you're so desperate to find your sister. You've lost too much already."

"I'm not desperate. I don't even know her. It's just a question of what is right."

"If you say so." She was silent a moment. "I'll give you what you need from me, Eve. You'll find your Beth."

"You're damn right I will." Then she added

haltingly, "But thank you for your coopera-tion. I appreciate it."

"That was hard for you." Kendra was suddenly chuckling. "You like to handle everything on your own. And you say you're not desperate? I think you protest too much."

Eve opened her lips to protest again, then said grudgingly, "Maybe I'm a little assertive. But, then, so are you."

"True." Kendra leaned back in her chair. "But it shows up on you like a red flag. We have to tamp that down tomorrow. Put your hair up in a chignon and wear those glasses I saw you with in some of the newspaper articles on the Net. Stay in the background. No confrontation."

"I'm not usually confrontational." She smiled faintly. "You were one of the excep-tions."

"Oh, I'm an exception all right," she said wryly. "It's the story of my life."

"Do you regret it?"

"People trying to use me? Occasionally. The ability to use every sense to the max? Not for a minute. After all these years, I'm still drunk with the sensation. I wish I could share it, but it doesn't work that way. You have to concentrate and let the senses come alive. You should try it sometime."

"Maybe I will."

"And maybe you'll get busy and think it's not worthwhile. But that will be your loss." She drew her jacket closer around her. "It's getting cooler. I'm going to stay out here a while longer, but you'd better go on in. Quinn's probably going crazy with frustration by now."

"What?" Eve was startled. "Frustration? How do you—" She broke off as she saw Kendra's expression that contained both slyness and a touch of mischief. She wasn't sure that she wanted to probe how Kendra had known about the passion that was driving Joe and Eve that night. It could be simple guesswork or that damnable highly tuned sensitivity that was anything but simple. If it was the latter, she didn't want to be told what physical or psychological signs had made that sexuality so transparent. She got to her feet. "It is chilly." She started across the verandah. "Good night, Kendra. I'll see you in the morning."

"Good night." Then Kendra called after her, "Why did he stop? Were you interrupted? Is it something I should know about?"

Eve gazed back over her shoulder in exasperation. "Do you have to know everything?" Then she reined in her temper. This wasn't only about Joe and her. Of course, Kendra should know everything concerning Beth Avery. She was going to help them, and they should share information. "Joe had to take a call from the ski resort where Beth had her accident. I'll give you a report in the morning if he found out anything important."

"Thanks," Kendra called as Eve left the verandah. "I was . . . out of line. I'm sorry."

"Yes, you were."

"Well, it wasn't that bad. I've been worse. Have a nice time."

Eve wanted to shake her, but she had an idea Kendra's puckish humor would cause her to enjoy the reaction. Just face her down. "Oh, I will." She found that her annoyance was fading as she strolled back toward the room. It was clear that she was going to have to learn to deal with Kendra Michaels on her own terms. For a short time back there, she had actually felt in tune with the woman. No, admit it, she had genuinely liked her. It was only when Kendra had invaded her space that she had become defensive. How many people in her life had Kendra turned away because she had been able to unable to resist letting them know that she could see far beyond their comfort level? If Kendra was as intuitive and sensitive as Eve was beginning to believe, she must have tremendous restraint that she had learned at great cost over the years.

But she had also enjoyed life to the max. Eve recalled her shining eyes, her lips slightly parted.

I'm still drunk with the sensation.

You have to concentrate and let the senses come alive. You should try it sometime.

Joe was lying naked in bed when she opened the door of the room. "It's about time. What kept you?"

"I ran into Kendra. We talked a little."

"Too long." He held out his hand. "Come here."

"In a moment." She started to undo the buttons on her blouse. But only a moment. She could feel the tension mounting every second. They had waited too long already. "What did you find out from the resort?"

"That Beth had gone skiing alone and the resort sent a team out to investigate when she didn't come back to the lodge. They found her unconscious at the bottom of a hill next to a tree and assumed she'd hit her head. They airlifted her to a clinic near Boston for treatment."

"Clinic? Not the local hospital?"

"Family request. Later, the personnel at the resort heard that she was in a coma and had been sent to California for more tests."

"So there was a serious legitimate injury."

"There was an injury," Joe said. "We still don't know how serious." He paused. "Or how legitimate. The rescue team said that the head wound was to the back of the head. If she crashed into that tree, wouldn't the injury have been to the front of the skull?"

An attack from behind? "Strange things happen in accidents. I suppose a back skull wound is possible." But it was another red flag. "What about the clinic?"

"I checked. It went out of business ten years ago. All records on Beth Avery were sent out to Santa Barbara. Everything seems to be centered around that hospital on the hill."

"Then it's good that we brought Kendra to help make some sense of what happened here." She was naked now and walking toward him across the carpet. "I think we may be lucky to have her, Joe."

"I wasn't lucky to have her keep you away from me so long tonight." He made a face. "Evidently, you may be on board, but I'm beginning to think that she may not be as valuable as I first thought."

"Oh, she's valuable. There may be a lot we can learn from her."

You have to concentrate and let the senses come alive.

Joe's eyes were suddenly narrowed on her face. "Such as?"

Concentrate. Heighten every sense, the scent of him, the sound of his breathing. She reached out and touched his shoulder, the warmth of his skin, the play of muscles beneath her fingers. The sensation was almost too intense.

He inhaled sharply as he sensed something new, something different. "What are you doing?"

"Concentrating . . ."

She climbed on top of him and slowly rubbed her breasts against his chest. She tried to isolate every separate sensation, the warmth, the faint roughness of his hair against her nipples, the tensing of his muscles. She felt an explosion of heat. More. Give more. Take more. "Slowly. Think about it. *Feel*."

He shuddered as his hands grasped her shoulders.

Don't ignore one motion, one feeling, build on it, share it.

Maybe you'll get busy and think it's not worthwhile. But that will be your loss.

No way, Kendra . . .

"You look very subdued, Eve," Kendra said as she strolled toward the car at eight the next morning. "And those glasses are a good touch. I knew they would be." She tossed her duffel and guitar in the backseat of the car and got into the passenger seat. "I'll try to keep attention off you, but stay in the background."

"I'm hardly a riveting personality," Eve said dryly as she started the car. "It's not as if I was flamboyant before."

"But people look at you, then look again." She was studying her face. "Particularly this morning. There's a glow . . ."

Eve gave her a forbidding glance. "Don't go there."

She grinned. "I wasn't. I'm more subtle than that." Her gaze shifted to the hospital in the hills, and her smile faded. "And, besides, it's time I got down to business."

"And start to concentrate?"

Kendra nodded soberly. "That's the name of the game."

Eve smiled faintly. "Oh, I definitely agree."

"Dr. Michaels, delighted to meet you." Harry Pierce's smile was a flash of white in his tanned face as he crossed the marble foyer at the hospital to shake her hand. Late forties or early fifties, he had a shock of excellently barbered thick gray hair, gray eyes, and slightly heavy but regular features. "Such a pleasant surprise. We had no idea we were under consideration for a grant. We do our best, but mental health always seems to be at the bottom of the list."

"Not this time," Kendra said with a smile as bright as Pierce's. "Evidently someone thinks that your hospital deserves help, and musical therapy is the wave of the future."

Pierce nodded. "I understand you're responsible for much of the research in this field, Dr. Michaels. I have to admit I've always been a bit skeptical of its effectiveness since most of the success stories have been anecdotal. But I'm impressed with your evidence-based approach."

"I'm not a believer in woo-woo. Music therapy is a scientific discipline even if some of its practitioners don't look at it that way." She waved a casual hand toward Eve. "My assistant, Lucy Coran." She stepped in front of Eve before he could greet her or get a good look at her. "She'll take my notes and give questionnaires to your staff. Could you assign someone to show us around right away? We'd really like to finish this job before the end of the day. We have another inspection in San Francisco tomorrow."

"Joseph Piltot can do it." Pierce waved at a thin man in a sleek navy suit who was getting off the elevator. "He'll be able to show you the most likely candidates for your therapy. He has all their records on tap."

"Excellent. But I also want to see the entire facility and the grounds. And I don't expect to be limited to the dog-and-pony show you give families. I trust that won't be a problem."

"Of course not." He smiled again, but this time it appeared pasted on his face. "If you need anything at all, please call on me. I'm at your disposal."

"Thank you, but I doubt that will be necessary. As I said, this is just the first inspection. We only want to get a feel for the facility and your long-term patients." She turned to Piltot after he was introduced. "Let's start outside, shall we?"

"Certainly." Piltot led them out the glass doors.

As they strolled through the beautiful, well-manicured lawns, Eve and Kendra only half listened to Piltot's overly rehearsed spiel. He pointed out the faculty's sleek structures, then stopped so they could watch a croquet match supervised by the predominantly youthful staff.

Eve and Kendra casually moved several yards away from Piltot, well out of earshot. "So what did you think of Pierce?" Eve asked quietly, her gaze on the croquet players.

"A total sleazebag," Kendra said. "And a phony all the way. How much plastic surgery do you think he's had? I'd bet at least an eye job and work on that chin."

Eve smothered a smile. "You're the expert on observation. My only impression was that I didn't like him. But you were very tactful. I was surprised."

"I can be diplomatic. Not often. It's not worth the effort."

Piltot walked over to them, smiling. "Ready to go inside?"

"Not just yet," Kendra said. "I want to go around to the other side of the complex."

"Not much to see there, I'm afraid. Loading dock, staff entrance, garbage Dumpsters . . . Surely your time would be better spent."

"Just a quick look around," Kendra said. "Then we can go inside."

Piltot shrugged. "This way."

He led them around the facility's north side, where a keycard opened a tall iron gate. The concrete walkways, skillfully hidden from the nearby roads by bushes and tall trees, possessed a barren, institutional quality. Eve glanced at Kendra and saw the woman's eyes flicking from the windows to the roofline, then down the entire length of the main building. What had that amazing mind latched onto now?

They continued toward the rear of the white stucco building where Kendra leaned over the railing to look at the hillside just ten feet below.

Piltot was frowning. "Is everything okay?"

"Yes." Kendra looked up at the windows above. "I trust that patients get the ocean views and not the staff?"

"Absolutely. There are a few administrative offices facing this way, but those are mostly group areas and recreation rooms up there."

"Very nice. It's beautiful."

They continued on their way, and true to Piltot's word, they walked past a row of Dumpsters. "It smells," Kendra said. "When is trash pickup?"

Piltot hesitated, probably wondering how in the hell this could affect the dispensation of a state grant. "Uh, Mondays and Thursdays, I think."

Beth had disappeared from the facility

on a Wednesday, which almost ruled out one method of escape. Neither night would have been for Beth's escape, Eve thought, which was obviously Kendra's motive for asking the question in the first place. And as they stepped closer to the Dumpsters, she noticed that each lid was secured by a large padlock.

Kendra obviously noticed it, too, and she shot Eve a look. No refuge for Beth there.

Piltot pointed to the employee entrance. "We can go inside here."

"Actually, I'd like to continue around and go back through the front," Kendra said.

"Well . . . sure." He was obviously mystified by her insistence.

They completed the circle and reentered the complex through the main entrance.

"I'll need to examine all the wards and private accommodations," Kendra said brusquely. "Where do you suggest we begin?"

"The wards?" Piltot made a face. "That will be a bit chaotic. You may prefer to focus on the private patients. I'm sure they'll be much more receptive to cultural stimulus."

"People are people, and music bridges all gaps."

"Just a moment, and I'll see what the schedule is for group-therapy sessions. There are probably some going on now."

"Take your time."

Kendra lowered her voice as she spoke to Eve. "The private rooms are on the second and third floors. Beth Avery was on the third floor in Room 305. As soon as Piltot takes us up to the third floor, we're going to need a distraction to get rid of him."

"I'll take care of it." Eve was already taking out her phone. Actually, she was glad to have something positive to do. It was beginning to annoy her having to stay in the background and letting Kendra handle everything. She would just have to bite the bullet and look and listen and see if she could find a way to contribute. "I'll tell Joe to call Piltot when I buzz him and start questioning him again. That should give us time." She looked at Kendra. "But how much time will you need?"

"How do I know? It depends on how well the room has been cleaned. What kind of trace evidence has been left." She grimaced.

"For all we know, the room might have a new occupant."

"True." Eve hadn't thought of that. "We'll play it by ear." She smiled slyly. "Or at least you will. You're more qualified in that area." She ignored Kendra's disgusted groan as Joe came on the line. "Joe, we may need some help."

As luck would have it, Piltot took them to the second floor first, and they spent over three hours meeting patients and checking over their medicines and prognosis. It was early afternoon when Piltot took them up to the third floor.

Eve's gaze flew down the corridor as they got off the elevator. Clearly the hospital luxury quarters, she thought. Wide halls, modern paintings on the walls, and a nursing station at the far end of the corridor. The nurse at the cherry desk was on the phone, and she was smiling and chatting. Good, a distraction. They could only hope that she stayed absorbed in her conversation.

"At present there's only one occupied suite on this floor. Room 302," Piltot said.

"The patient is a young actress who suffered a nervous breakdown two months ago. Patient confidentiality prohibits me from telling you who she is, but—"

"Lara Tagnon," Kendra said absently.

Piltot blinked. "How—I can't really confirm that—"

"On the nurse's desk downstairs on the second floor, there were two DVD cases of Laura Tagnon's most popular movies, along with a thin, silver inked Sharpie pen that one uses for an autograph on the case's dark background."

"Very perceptive, Dr. Michaels," Piltot said.

Maybe *too* perceptive, Eve thought. But Kendra's display didn't seem to arouse any special concern on his part.

However, evidently Kendra was aware that she'd slipped up because she added quickly to distract him, "Not the most professional request for a nurse on duty to make, but I suppose there's really no harm."

Piltot smiled. "As long as you didn't hear it from me."

"I had no idea she was a patient here," Kendra said. "The paparazzi have been scouring the country for her."

"Privacy is important when you're dealing with celebrities. I'm not sure that I can get permission from either her or her manager to have you evaluate her. Surely you don't want to see her."

"Surely I do," Kendra said with a determined smile. "She'd be a valuable addition to the hospital profile. Why don't you go and ask her? We'll wait here."

Piltot hesitated, then turned away impatiently. "Oh, very well. If you insist. But it's a waste of time." He strode down the hall and into a room near the end of the corridor.

Eve was instantly on the phone and beeping Joe. She jammed the phone in her pocket. "Joe is good, but I don't believe we can count on more than ten minutes stalling, tops." She glanced at the nurse's station. The nurse was leaning back in her chair, still absorbed in her phone call. "Let's go. Room 305 is two doors down."

They had taken no more than two steps toward the room when Eve heard a male voice behind them.

"Excuse me, but I don't believe you're supposed to be here."

Dammit, caught.

Eve stiffened and turned around.

A tall orderly had appeared in the hall-way near the bank of elevators.

"You two look lost," he said. "May I help you?"

"No, we're just waiting for Mr. Piltot," Kendra said. "He had to take a phone call."

The orderly hesitated, casting a quick glance at their visitor badges to confirm that they weren't wayward patients. Eve could see the suspicion gradually vanishing. He was a tall, young man with broad shoulders and close-cropped brown hair. He wore the same tight white jeans and T-shirt that the rest of the male orderlies wore.

Kendra extended her left hand. "Dr. Kendra Michaels. Nice to meet you."

"Oh, you're a doctor? Sorry for the questions. Nobody told me we were having visitors on this floor. We're supposed to keep an eye out for reporters." He awkwardly took Kendra's hand and shook it. "Jessie Newell. The pleasure's all mine. Are you sure there's nothing I can do for you?"

"Absolutely not. We won't hold you up."

"Yes, ma'am. Thank you."

They watched as the orderly continued

on his way and disappeared into the elevator.

"Close. We're lucky he didn't see us going into the room." Kendra was moving quickly toward Room 305. "Come on."

Eve was right behind her, and, a minute later, the heavy room door was swinging closed behind them.

"Shit." Eve murmured as she glanced around. "We're out of luck. This place looks spotless."

"Maybe," Kendra said absently. "But there are still a few faint lingering medical odors. Smell that sulfur? If they only went over the room once, we still have a chance."

"What can I do?" Eve asked.

"Be quiet so I can concentrate. And keep an eye on the corridor."

Eve turned to be able to glance out of the rectangular glass inset in the door to the hall. "Right."

Kendra dropped to her knees in the small room, looking underneath the bed and chair. Both pieces of furniture were bolted to the floor, and to Eve there seemed to be nothing distinctive about either of them. Kendra yanked up the fitted sheet and scanned the side panels of the exposed mattress. She had begun to stretch the sheet back into place when she stiffened and gave a low whistle. She quickly ran her hand between the mattress and the wall.

"What is it?" Eve asked.

Kendra pulled the mattress end toward them, curling it up from the wall. "Look."

Eve leaned over to see a tiny slit, not more than a quarter inch long on the mattress panel. "It's a tear."

"It's more than that. Look closer."

As Kendra moved the mattress to the light, Eve could then see the faint oval, and rectangular impressions next to the slit. "Pills!"

Kendra ran her finger over the impressions. "They're not here now, but they were. The patient in this room wasn't taking her meds. She may have hidden them in her mouth, then stashed them here until she could safely dispose of them. When they were here, the weight of the patient would pull this mattress taut against the pills, creating the impression."

"This could have been made years ago," Eve said.

Kendra shook her head. "Look at the frayed edges of the slit. See how much brighter they are than the rest of the mattress? If they had been exposed for any great length of time, they would be much closer in tone to the rest. This is recent."

Kendra let go of the mattress and stood facing the wall.

"Anything else?" Eve asked.

Kendra hesitated, then slowly nodded. "Something pretty nasty. Poison."

"What?"

"You heard me. I think they tried to poison your Beth Avery." She frowned, working it out. "And it had to be within the past few days. They tried, but they didn't succeed."

Eve shook her head in disbelief. Kendra was speaking as matter-of-factly as if she were commenting on the color of the sky. "Dammit, how do you know?"

Kendra pointed high on the wall she was facing. "See that thin line?"

Eve squinted, then shook her head. "No."

"It's perfectly clear, but it reflects the light. Move your head back and forth until you—"

"I see it!" Eve took a step closer. It was an extremely thin line, almost invisible, that arced high on the wall behind the bed. Evidently the spray of liquid had dried on the wall and was nearly undetectable. "But what is it?"

"Conium, I'm pretty sure. It's quite deadly, and has a distinctive odor. It hit me as soon as we stepped close to the bed." Kendra stood on the bed and moved her face within inches of the clear line.

"And I suppose you have a mental catalog of what every poison smells like?"

"Don't be sarcastic. No, but I am good with plants. When you spend the first twenty years of your life without sight, scents are very important. Conium is an extract of hemlock, which grows almost everywhere. It retains both the plant's poisonous properties and its rather unpleasant smell." Kendra pulled a handkerchief from her pocket and rubbed it along the line. "We'll see if we can test a sample off this, but I'm sure that's what it is."

"Hemlock poisoning," Eve said. "That's how Socrates was killed . . ."

"And it would have killed Beth Avery,

but for some reason it ended up sprayed against this wall."

Eve felt sick as she stared around the room. Pills in the mattress hidden by a desperate woman fighting for her freedom. Poison . . . "Someone actually tried to kill her." She looked back up at the lethal streak on the wall. "And even if this didn't work, there's no certainty that they didn't manage to kill her in another way."

"No certainty. But I believe your sister is still alive." She met her gaze. "And I think you do, too. Isn't this what all this is about?"

Eve nodded. "But I have nothing concrete on which to base it. Do you?"

"I don't deal in concrete, but I have an idea or two." She turned away. "I want to take one last look around in the bathroom. Keep watch. You haven't done a good job so far."

Because what Kendra did had a tendency to blow Eve away. She couldn't argue with her that she hadn't been doing her part. "Can't you hurry?" Eve cast another quick glance through the small window in the door. "It's already been ten minutes. Joe can't keep him on the line for much longer."

"I'm done." Kendra glided across the room from the bathroom. "Where's that nurse?"

"She got up and went down the hall toward the waiting room a few minutes ago. Since there don't appear to be any visitors on this floor, I'd bet on her hitting the coffee machine." She swung the door open, glanced at Room 302 before gesturing for Kendra to leave. "Out."

Kendra strode out of the room and down the hall with Eve following. "I'm out. Stop being so nervous. We made it."

Eve drew a deep breath, slowed down, and stopped. Kendra was right. The immediate danger was over. She just didn't like to cut things so close. "Then let's find a place to sit down and be impatient when Piltot shows up. After all, he's been very rude to keep us waiting." She dropped down on a bench across from the nurse's station. "Did you find anything else in the bathroom, Kendra?"

Kendra shook her head. "Nothing that's made an impression. But someone had to have helped her if she got out of here. Maybe we'll know more when we check the file records on Beth Avery tonight and see who has been in attendance or at least in close proximity."

"Tonight?"

"Well, we can hardly march into personnel and tap their records during regular business hours. It will have to be tonight."

"And how are we supposed to get into personnel? It's an administrative office. The chances are that it will be locked up tight as a drum."

"What's locked can be unlocked."

"You're saying we're going to burgle the place?"

"Of course we are. You said you needed information. You must have known there wouldn't be any other way when you brought me here."

Eve nodded. "I suspected that would be the only way. I'm not objecting, just clarifying." Her lips tightened. "Will I do it? You're damn right I will. Conium. I wasn't sure until you identified that drug that there actually was a threat to Beth."

"And are you sure now?" Kendra asked quietly. "You have only my word based on a very freaky talent. A lot of people wouldn't be willing to trust me."

Eve was silent. It was a freaky talent,

and she had known Kendra Michaels for less than twenty-four hours. Why was she so certain that the clues Kendra had found and identified in that room were real? Instinct? She just didn't know. But the certainty was there. "I'm sure." She smiled with an effort. "I've been known to believe in a few freaky things in my life. What's one more?" She added, "So I suppose we should start planning a way to get into that locked office. As a matter of fact, I believe I may have the keys to that particular kingdom."

"You do?" Kendra asked, startled. "What the hell are you talking about? Keys? I was going to call a man who—" She broke off as she saw Piltot coming out of Room 302. "Later." She frowned, turned on him, and said sharply, "May we see your prize movie star or not? What kept you?"

Piltot flushed. "I had a phone call. I apologize. I couldn't get rid of him."

"Did you try hanging up?" Kendra asked coldly. "What's the verdict? Do I get a personal interview with your patient or just examine her records?"

"Neither. I'm afraid that her manager has said that she's not to be disturbed."

"Great." Kendra turned away. "Then shall we continue? You kept us waiting so long that we're behind schedule, and we'll have to get a move on to finish our appraisal by the end of the day."

"Certainly." Piltot was ushering them toward the elevators. "But there are only the two wards left. I'm sure that I can facilitate your work with the patients and make sure you can turn in your report on time."

CHAPTER

7

It was close to seven in the evening when Eve and Kendra left the hospital. In spite of Piltot's marked annoyance, Kendra had gone over all the records of the eighty-seven patients in the two wards. She had interviewed twelve of that number, and Eve had been surprised at the thoroughness and intensity of those interviews. She had questioned, taken notes, and even played bits of music on the small iPod she had with her. If she had wanted to appear authentic, there was no doubt in Eve's mind that she'd accomplished her goal.

"So what do you think, Kendra?" Eve

asked. "Are those patients getting good treatment? Everyone seemed very caring and efficient to me."

"As far as I can tell without in-depth investigation. I'm no psychoanalyst. I wouldn't expect anything else. Pierce wants to be a shining star of the community, and he wouldn't do anything to damage his image. He had one ugly skeleton in his closet, and he couldn't afford any more."

"You were very good," Eve said, as they walked toward the rental car. "Even I was convinced that you intended to accept those patients as students."

"You should have been convinced," Kendra said. "I'll probably accept eight out of the twelve. I don't believe the other four are ready yet. I can't help them." She smiled crookedly as she saw Eve's expression. "I don't cheat, Eve. Life has already cheated those poor souls. I'm not about to compound it. I can fly up here every other week and help them. Usually, I prefer dealing with patients before they reach the point where they have to be confined, but I won't raise hopes, then walk away."

Eve's gaze narrowed on her face. "That's why you didn't want to take this job. You knew that it would mean a long-term commitment for you."

Kendra laughed and shook her head. "I'm not that noble. I told you the truth. I would have turned the job down anyway. Yes, I knew I might get caught, but I wasn't thinking about anyone but Justin." She got into the passenger seat. "And he's still my main focus. We need to get this business over with tonight, so I can keep my appointment with him tomorrow." She turned to face Eve. "Now talk. What do you mean 'keys to the kingdom'?"

Eve fished in her pocket and pulled out an off-white keychain fob. "While you were taking stock of the DVDs on that nurse's desk on the second floor, I unclipped this from a dietician's lab jacket hanging on a chair back."

Kendra's eyes widened. "Damn. I didn't even see you do that."

Eve chuckled. "Is that chagrin? I take that as a great compliment. Not much gets past you." She brandished the fob. "I saw a nurse swipe one of these over a reader at a computer workstation. It gave her access to a patient's medication list."

"That I did see," Kendra said. "But we

also need to get back inside the building. Are you going to get Joe to help you?"

She shook her head.

"Somehow I didn't think so."

"He's a detective. Breaking and entering could destroy his career. Beth is my sister. This is my job."

"I should point out that we could report our suspicions to the local police," Kendra said. "But then they'd come and wave badges around, and whatever useful records there are in that office will be wiped clean if they haven't been already. It makes sense for us to go in and get them right away. Okay, you've been able to get us access into the computer. Now how do we get into the office?"

"I haven't gotten that far. Do you have any ideas?"

Kendra was silent for a moment, and Eve could almost see the wheels turning, rapidly processing all the information she had assimilated that afternoon. What must it be like to experience the world as Kendra did?

Kendra finally said, "We'll walk in through the side gates."

Eve raised an eyebrow. "Just like that?"

"Two members of the kitchen staff come in at 3:30 A.M." Before Eve could ask, she added, "The schedule is posted in the office of the food services director that we passed. We'll be waiting in the trees that line the driveway. When the gate opens for one of their cars, we'll scramble in under the cover of darkness."

"That doesn't get us inside the building."

"No. But we know that the early-morning kitchen staff takes frequent smoke breaks and is fond of propping the outside door open."

"Oh, we know that?" Eve asked, deadpan.

"Sorry, I got ahead of myself. The concrete walkway outside of the kitchen entrance is heavily stained by tobacco ash, like no place else in the entire complex. Even if the kitchen workers try flicking their ashes over the railing, the offshore breeze no doubt blows them right back. Early-morning condensation also causes the ash to stick and stain more easily than it would later in the day, when it would tend to blow around even more. And there's a wood-wedge doorstop on the walkway, meaning that they probably prop the door open to take advantage of those cool, morning sea breezes."

Eve nodded. "So we wait around the corner and slip in through the open door while they're standing outside smoking?"

"At least while one of them is out there. Even if the other employee is inside working, we don't have to cross through the kitchen to get to the food services office."

"Food services? We need to get to personnel."

"Not necessarily. Food service has a computer. If you have someone skilled enough at accessing the info, they might be able to get what we need if the system is linked."

"But won't that office be locked?"

"Doubtful. It looked like it doubles as a kitchen storage area for cleaning and paper products. The staff needs ready access. Once we make our way there, there's a computer that we can use to try to access your sister's file."

Eve held up the fob and shook her head. "This will get me into the system, but it might not give me the kind of deep access I'm looking for, into her confidential patient records, psychiatrist's session notes, that kind of stuff."

"You're probably right." Kendra thought for a moment. "But I think I know some-one who can help us. I was mulling pos-sibilities over while we were touring the hospital." She took out her phone and ac-cessed the directory. "I tried to squeeze a moment to make a call earlier in the after-noon, but Piltot was sticking to us like glue. I'll be lucky to get hold of Sam now."

"And who is this Sam you're going to call?" Eve asked.

"Our way into those computer files. I was also considering using him to get us back into the hospital, but I believe we've got that covered." She made a face. "Voice mail. Sam, this is Kendra Michaels. I'm in Santa Barbara, and I need your help tonight. Pack up your tools and head my way. If I don't hear from you in two hours, I'll try to find someone else." She hung up. "We might as well grab something to eat while we wait and see if I can use Sam. I have a couple other prospects, but they're second-best."

"And this Sam is tops on your list?"

"He's tops on everyone's list. Just ask him."

"It would be difficult since I don't even know his last name," she said dryly as she drove out of the parking lot. "How would he be able to get us into the hospital? Is he some kind of thief?"

"Don't be crude. Sam Zackoff is an expert at entry and exit."

"A cat burglar?"

"Closer. I've never seen a lock or security system he couldn't get around. But he doesn't do it for a living any longer. That was during his misspent twenties. He's the shining sun of Silicon Valley."

"Computers?"

"He's a genius." She shrugged. "And a nerd. He's involved with defense against cyberwarfare now. It suits him just fine. He gets to invent ways to get beyond all the firewalls, then close them up so no one else can." She grimaced. "My only problem is that he's so valuable to the Pentagon that they have him guarded night and day. We don't want him followed here."

"Wait a minute," Eve said. "You think he'd leave a job like that to break into the hospital and tap sensitive records for you? Not likely."

"Not for me. For himself. Sam gets bored occasionally and has to step beyond that gold-lined fence they try to keep around him."

"And risk landing in jail?"

"It's only a slight risk. Unless he burgled the White House, his bosses would find a way to get him off. He'll be a lot safer than we are."

"That's comforting."

"We don't have to do this, Eve."

An almost invisible deadly streak on the wall.

"Yes, we do. There have to be answers in those files in the office." She pulled into the parking lot of an Applebee's restaurant. "I'm just having a few second thoughts about whether I should call Joe and get him out here. I hate leaving him out of this. He's going to be royally pissed."

"If you're wondering, I don't think you're going to do it," Kendra said shrewdly. "As you said, you consider Beth Avery your responsibility, and you wouldn't want to involve Quinn in something that would possibly be detrimental to his career as a police detective. I agree that his police captain would not consider breaking and entering particularly cool."

Neither did Eve, and even though Joe had indicated that it might be necessary, he shouldn't be the one to take the risk. "No, when we were looking for the body of my daughter, I ignored everything but my obsession to find her. I risked Joe then, but I'm not starting back down that trail." She added soberly, "I should make that same rule apply to you, Kendra."

"My choice. I'm not a cop, and if I break the rules, I can find a way to talk my way out of it." Her lips tightened. "And I don't like the idea of Beth Avery helpless, tied to that bed by those damn pills and just waiting to die. It pisses me off." She got out of the car. "Come on, let's grab a burger and a cup of coffee and wait and see if Sam is going to come to our rescue. I want to be—" Her cell phone rang, and she smiled. "Sam." She answered it. "It's the personnel office of a mental hospital. We'll need to copy computer files, possibly break into file drawers, then get out without anyone's knowing we were there. Yes or no." She listened. "What do you mean I'll owe you? You'll owe me. I can tell when you're bored out of your mind. The Chinese haven't been inventive enough for you lately, have they?" She smiled. "We're at the Applebee's restaurant on Sunrise Drive. We'll be waiting." She hung up. "Sam's on his way. He'll be here in a little over an hour."

"He sounds . . . extraordinary. And you must know him very well," Eve said as she opened the glass doors of the entrance. "How did you meet him?"

"I was playing keyboard in a cheap little club in San Francisco about a year after my operation. Sam would come in after hours and play clarinet with the band."

"He's a musician, too?"

"Not a very good one. But you don't have to be good, you just have to love it. He loved it. But I couldn't stand him to be quite that bad, so I gave him a few lessons. We got to know each other pretty well."

"How well?"

She smiled. "Now that's another tale." She smiled at the hostess who was approaching. "Two for dinner, and we'll have someone joining us later."

Sam Zackoff arrived at the restaurant fifty-five minutes later.

"There he is." Kendra waved at the man in jeans, a black T-shirt on which something was written in bold white letters, and black-and-white tennis shoes who had just strolled into the restaurant. "He made good time. Too good. All we'd need was for him to be stopped by a traffic cop when we're trying to be low-profile."

"He doesn't look like he'd care," Eve murmured.

Zackoff was probably in his middle thirties, but he appeared younger. A little above middle height and very muscular, his hair was dark, curly, and cut close to his head. Blue eyes lit a square face that was more interesting than handsome. He swaggered with confidence as if he owned the restaurant. No, Eve corrected her impression, as if he owned the universe. "Interesting. But can you control him?"

"For short periods of time." She got up from the booth as he reached them. "Hi,

Sam." She gave him a quick, hard kiss and pushed him down in the booth. "This is Eve Duncan. Sam Zackoff. Sam and I are old friends."

"Delighted." Sam didn't take his gaze off Kendra. "I've missed you. Why do you only call me when you need me?" He added mockingly, "I feel so used."

"Stop it. We've discussed this before, and I don't want Eve to feel awkward." She gazed directly into his eyes. "You can't take too much of me. I scare the hell out of you. You can't figure me out, and it drives you crazy."

He smiled crookedly. "You're right, you drive me crazy. You always have, and you always will." He turned to Eve. "Sorry. She's right, I'm being rude. I have a tendency to go after what I want and toss everything else aside."

"You're forgiven." She found herself smiling as she was finally able to discern the words written on his black T-shirt.

The geek shall inherit the earth.

It appeared she had mentally overestimated him. He was claiming to own only the earth, not the universe.

"Thanks." He gazed at her curiously. "And how do you figure in the game?"

"It's not a game." Eve's smile disappeared. "I have a sister who may have been a prisoner and a victim for over a decade in that hospital. I have to know who is responsible and how I can find her."

"She's not in the hospital?"

"No, though they're trying to tell me that she is."

He glanced at Kendra. "What do you think?"

"I think she escaped, and if they ever catch up with her that she won't last a day. Here's the layout of the hospital. I have an idea how we can get in. I don't think we should try to get in until after three in the morning." Kendra drew up the layout of the hospital on her phone. "Can you do any prep work to find out what you'll need to access their computers?"

"I've already done most of it on the way down here. I've— It will only take a little while longer." He took his computer out of his bag. "Order me a pot of coffee." He glanced up at Kendra with sudden mischief. "You should say, 'Yes, sir.' Don't I deserve a little ego stroking? It's only in a situation like this that you'd ever take orders from me."

Kendra's lips turned up at the corners. "Yes, sir." She lifted her hand to summon the waitress. "Anything else?"

"Just sit there and let me look at you while I'm working."

She snorted. "As if you'd pay any attention to anything once you're in the zone."

"Subliminal." His gaze was on the computer screen. "You know about things like that . . ."

"I seem to be de trop." Eve got to her feet. "I'm going outside to call Joe. He'll worry if this is going to go on into the wee hours. I'll see you later."

"I was rude again, wasn't I?" Sam made a face. "She'll make me pay."

"No, she won't. I don't care if you're rude. Not if you can get me what I need. Get to work."

"Yes, Sam, do what she says." Kendra was chuckling as she leaned back in the booth. "Get to work."

Eve stepped outside the restaurant and sat down on the wrought-iron bench at the curb. She was glad to get away from Kendra and Sam for a few moments. They were both clever, quick-witted, and trying their best to help her, but Eve had been trying to suppress the shock and sickness she was feeling ever since she realized that suspicion had become fact. She drew a few deep breaths of cool air before she pulled out her phone. She was dreading this call. Joe wasn't going to be pleased about being excluded from the action. And she didn't like going forward without him.

Too bad. Beth Avery was her sister and her responsibility, and she wouldn't involve Joe in something that was potentially illegal. Potentially? Definitely, illegal. But what then was attempted murder? Just make the call, tell Joe everything that Kendra had found and deduced, then take it on the chin when Joe displayed his displeasure.

She quickly dialed his number. "Joe, here's what's happening."

He was very quiet, asking no questions until she had finished. "So it was poison? No wonder she ran for her life." He paused. "But I wouldn't imagine that conium would be used by any of the doctors or staff at the hospital. I'd think that if they were trying to kill her, they'd use a medical derivative to simulate an overdose. Conium is a little exotic."

"A hit man?"

"Possibly. If Pierce didn't want to get his hands dirty. He impressed me as a man who always covered his ass."

Eve had gotten the same impression. "Kendra thinks she had to have someone help her get away that night. And to start her drying out from those drugs."

"Then we'll have to see who was around her during the last months."

"Yes."

He was silent. "You're hesitating. Does that mean what I think it means?"

"I have Kendra and Sam. You don't have to go along." That sounded wimpy as hell. She added firmly, "You're not going, Joe. I'm not having you risk your job breaking into that place. Forget it."

He was cursing softly.

"It's going to be fine. This Sam evidently knows what he's doing."

"And I'm supposed to be comforted by the fact that one of Kendra's old buddies is a professional thief?"

"He not a thief now. He's reformed."

"Except that he jumped at the chance of delving into the old life. No, Eve."

"I'm not asking, Joe," she said quietly. "I'll call you when we leave the hospital. As I said, it will be fine. Sam's not going to let anything happen to Kendra. Good-bye, Joe." She hung up and leaned back on the bench, trying to relax the tension that was gripping her muscles.

"I take it he's not happy." Kendra sat down beside her on the bench. "Are you still going to go for it?"

"Of course." Eve stuffed her phone in her pocket. "I have to find her. This isn't about Joe."

"You could have fooled me," Kendra said. "I believe he thinks everything concerning you is about him, too. You're like two halves of a whole."

She shook her head. "That sounds sappy. We're two individuals who happen to love each other so much that it causes us to worry."

Kendra shrugged. "Describe it how you like. I'm just a simple woman, and I prefer to be sappy."

"Simple? You?" Eve chuckled. "Not likely."

"Well, inexperienced in that particular area. I don't like to dive into deep waters."

"What about Sam?"

"Oh, we made a few mistakes together. I've learned better, but Sam still likes to skate on thin ice. It's the male thing. But most of the time, we can maintain a decent friendship." She got to her feet. "Sam's going to take another hour or so. Don't stay out here. Come in and have a cup of coffee with me."

Eve smiled. "Are you being protective now? I assure you that I wasn't feeling deserted."

"Why should I be protective? You're a grown-up. Maybe I want company to ward off Sam."

"And maybe not." Kendra was complicated and strange, and Eve couldn't quite read her. She had an idea that it had been a desire to protect and help that had drawn Kendra out here in spite of her denial. An idea but she wasn't sure. Yet there was no doubt that talking with Kendra had relieved a little of the tension that had gripped Eve. She was feeling less upset than when she had disconnected from Joe. So accept the good and ignore the uncertainties.

She started toward the glass doors. "At any rate, I could use a cup of coffee."

Seahaven Behavioral Health Center

Eve checked her watch—3:22 A.M. She glanced at Kendra and Sam kneeling beside her, huddled behind the row of trees lining the service driveway. No sign yet of the kitchen workers arriving for their three-thirty shift.

"Anytime now," Kendra whispered.

Eve nodded. She could tell that Kendra was as tense and alert as she was, but Sam looked perfectly at ease. If anything, he appeared a little absentminded. He was probably performing mental gymnastics to prepare for his assault on the hospital computer system. He had spent much of the hours after they had left the restaurant in the backseat of the car, trying to hack the system from his laptop. But he eventually realized that the most confidential records would only be accessible within the complex itself.

Dammit.

"Are you good to go?" Kendra asked Sam.

"Yeah, I have a good idea what software package they're using." He grimaced. "But I'd feel better if we could access the computer in the personnel office."

"Too risky. I have faith in you, Sam."

"Then I can change the rules of time and space if I have to do it." He added in a low voice, "And I may have to do it. The food services computer may not even be linked. But I'll do my best."

Kendra chuckled. "If the Pentagon trusts you to foil the Chinese, who am I to—" She broke off as a pair of headlights speared from the road and swept across the trees in front of them. "Here we go."

A dark sedan stopped only yards away as the motorized security gate groaned and slowly swung open. The car moved through the gate and turned the corner that would take it to the complex's subterranean parking garage.

The gate started to swing closed.

"Now!" Eve whispered.

She, Kendra, and Sam bolted for the entrance and slipped through just as the gate clanged shut behind them. They sprinted down the dark driveway and climbed the narrow set of stairs that would take them to the upper-level sidewalk.

"There," Kendra mouthed as she waved them around the corner to a dark alcove on the side of the building. They ducked into the shadows as they heard the gate opening below them and saw another set of headlights turn into the garage.

"That's the other kitchen worker," Kendra said. "The next one will be here in ninety minutes. When he opens that gate, we need to be ready to get ourselves on the other side of it."

"No pressure or anything," Eve said to Sam.

"Oh, of course not." He turned to Kendra. "What now?"

"We wait for that first smoke break. Or for that door to be propped open, whichever comes first."

Kendra kept watch on the door while Eve and Sam scouted around for any sign of a security patrol. "Security camera down the walkway," Sam murmured as he spotted the glowing red eye fastened to a tree. "I'll take care of it."

He was gone only a few minutes, the

red light went out, and Sam was back with them. "All clear."

Less than thirty minutes later, the door swung open, and a heavyset man dressed in white lumbered toward the outdoor railing. He pulled a pack of cigarettes from his pocket, tapped one out, and lit up.

"He didn't prop the door open," Eve whispered.

Kendra shook her head. "Plan B."

"Right." Eve bent over and tightened the laces on her tennis shoes. "How much time will I have?"

"About seven seconds once the door starts to close."

Eve smiled and shook her head. Of course Kendra had thought to time the door's closing when the man stepped outside.

After a couple minutes, the kitchen worker stamped out his cigarette, picked up the butt, and turned back toward the door. He pulled out a keycard, waved it over the sensor, and pulled open the door.

It would have been a hell of a lot more convenient for all of them if he'd propped the damn thing open, Eve thought. Why wasn't anything ever easy?

As the kitchen worker stepped inside, Eve quietly bolted toward the door as it swung closed. Shit, she thought in panic. She couldn't make it. The door was just—

Got it!

She gripped the edge of the door and froze, waiting to see if either of the kitchen workers had heard her or noticed that the door hadn't entirely closed.

They hadn't. She heard a door close across the kitchen, and the room appeared empty.

She hoped.

Kendra and Sam were directly behind her. Eve peered through the crack between the door and the frame and saw nothing but a short, dim hallway. From the left she heard running water and clanging pots. From the right, in the direction of the office, there was total silence.

She turned back toward Kendra and Sam, nodded, and crept through the doorway. Kendra and Sam were right behind her. They quickly moved down the hall and ducked into the open office. Kendra silently closed the door and lowered a roll-down shade that covered the door's large glass pane. They switched on their tiny xenon-bulb flashlights as Sam moved toward the computer and punched the spacebar to wake it up.

"What do you think?" Eve asked.

Sam studied the monitor. "Well, it's the system I thought they were using. I hoped this user would still be logged in, but he's not."

"Is that a problem?" Kendra asked.

Sam pulled a USB thumb drive from his pocket and inserted it into the computer tower next to the desk. "This may coax some of the user history out of this baby."

While he worked, Eve shined her flashlight around the office. As Kendra had noticed, it doubled as a storage room, with tall metal shelves holding supplies, paper products, and linens. "If the kitchen staff needs something, they might pop in here at any time."

"I locked the door," Kendra said. "But I'm sure at least one of those men has a key."

"More pressure," Sam murmured. "Hand me that fob, Eve."

Eve gave him the cream-colored fob she had lifted earlier. He swiped it across the reader, and the computer responded with an approving beep.

"I'm over the wall," he said, his gaze intent on the screen. "Now let's see how far I can get."

His fingers moved furiously over the keyboard as Eve saw scores of user menus and graphical representations of the complex. "Any sign of the patient histories?" she asked.

He shook his head. "Not yet. It looks like I can access everything else in this place except what we want. I'm really afraid it may be on a separate—" His eyes lit up. "Wait a second."

Kendra leaned closer. "What is it?"

"This is it!" His fingers worked even faster over the keyboard. "It's not where I thought it would be, but it's here."

Kendra suddenly tensed. "Shit." She backed away from the computer.

"What is it?" Eve asked. But after another second, she heard it, too.

Footsteps in the hallway.

"Quiet," Kendra whispered.

They held their breaths as the footsteps grew louder outside.

The doorknob jiggled.

Eve saw a shadow appear under the door.

A voice in the hallway called back to the kitchen. "Steve, I need your keys. The damn door is locked."

Eve looked frantically around the office. There was absolutely nowhere to run, to hide in the small area.

"Sam." Kendra whispered as she thrust herself back in front of the computer monitor. "Can you control all the systems we just saw here?"

"Yeah, of course I can."

"Call up two menus. Now."

He frantically typed while trying to keep the keys from clicking too loudly. "What am I doing?"

Kendra pointed to the screen. "Turn on the sprinklers in the kitchen zone. Can you do that?"

As if in response, the sound of spraying water echoed down the hallway, followed by the shouts of the other worker down in the kitchen. The shadow under the door vanished, and the footsteps pounded away.

Kendra pointed to another part of the

screen. "Now cut the lights in this entire zone."

A second later, the light under the door disappeared.

"Let's go," Kendra said. "No flashlights." She threw open the office door and raced down the completely dark hallway.

Eve struggled to keep up, straining to hear Kendra's footsteps over the sound of the sprinklers. Kendra was moving through the dark quickly and with complete ease. Almost as if—

As if the woman had been blind for the first twenty years of her life, Eve thought with self-disgust.

Kendra opened the back door and held it open long enough for Eve and Sam to join her on the walkway outside. They sprinted down the stairs and ran alongside the driveway, once again hiding behind the row of trees.

Eve inhaled sharply as she saw the gate looming ahead of them. "It's open!"

Sam smiled. "I did that, too. Didn't feel like waiting for the next shift to get here. It will close behind us. I'm known to be a little impatient."

"In this case, impatience is definitely a virtue," Eve said as she ran through the opening.

Seventeen Mile Drive

Safe!

Or maybe not, Beth thought as she tossed and turned on the couch. She should be safe. The lights of the kitchen had gone out. Water was pouring down inside the kitchen of the hospital.

Water? Not rain?

And how had she gotten back to the hospital when she had thought she was free?

She was still free. She was running down the hill toward the rental car. Her heart was beating wildly, and she could hardly breathe. They had gotten out of that place, and she only hoped Sam had managed to get the records before he had set off the sprinklers.

Sam? Who was Sam? Beth didn't know any Sam. Maybe he was one of the security guards from the hospital.

No!

Beth's eyes flew open in panic, and she jerked upright on the couch. She wasn't back at the hospital, she realized with relief. It had only been a nightmare.

She was in this spacious, beautiful study, lying on a brown leather couch and covered with a soft throw. There was a portrait of a woman and a dog over the fireplace. She had been afraid to use one of the bedrooms. They had seemed too large and intimidating.

She drew a deep, shaky breath, and slowly lay back down. She supposed she was lucky that she hadn't had any nightmares about the hospital since she'd been on the run. She wasn't used to bad dreams. The pills made her sleep too deeply for dreams. Or maybe she had dreamed, then not been able to remember. Perhaps that was another thing she had lost.

Go to sleep. She was safe here. Billy had said that she would be given a chance to heal and make her plans at this deserted house.

But evidently she was not safe from dreams.

She had been so afraid . . .

No, the fear had been there, but it had

not been Beth's, she realized drowsily. She had been dreaming of someone else, feeling someone else's fear . . .

Who?

It didn't matter. After all, it was only a dream.

But the name came to her just before she drifted back asleep, perhaps to prove just how much it didn't matter. Because it was a name she didn't know, a stranger she had never met.

Eve . . .

Seahaven Behavioral Health Center

Eve could hear the gates clang shut behind Kendra and Sam as they all hugged the shadows and ran down the hillside road to where Eve's rental car was parked. They deliberately parked some distance away, and they were all breathing heavily as they climbed in the car.

As soon as she caught her breath, Eve turned toward the backseat and looked at the USB thumb drive still in Sam's hand. "Please. For God's sake, tell me you were able to get Beth's patient files on that thing."

"Sorry, Eve, no time. There was just too much. A couple gigs at least. It looks like they have interview notes, hours of audio and video of her sessions, maybe some photos . . ."

"Dammit." Eve's fist pounded the steering wheel in frustration. "All this for nothing?"

Sam smiled. "Hey, remember who you're talking to here. I took care of you."

"Took care of her how?" Kendra asked.

Sam pulled a pen from his pocket and scribbled something on a fast-food hamburger wrapper. "Your sister's entire file is uploading as we speak. It'll take an hour or two, but it's all going to a secure Web site that I set up. You can access it and download the whole kit and caboodle anytime you want. And after it's done, my program will delete itself. No one will ever know. Here's the Web site's address and password." He tore a piece from the bag, handed it to Eve, then leaned back in his seat. "Hey, all this spiking adrenaline is making me hungry. Anyone in the mood for pancakes?"

CHAPTER

8

"Pecan pancakes," Sam sighed blissfully as he took the first bite of the stack of pancakes at the IHOP at the edge of town. "Almost as good as sex on the right occasion." Then he made a face. "What did I just say? Crazy. I must be working too hard."

"You certainly worked hard enough tonight," Eve said quietly. "And I'm very grateful, Sam."

"I enjoyed it." He lifted his cup of coffee in a mock salute to Eve and Kendra. "We make a good team. Call me anytime."

"I hope that won't be necessary. If we

can find out enough from those records, we might be able to find out everything we need to know about Beth. As soon as I get back to the hotel, Joe and I will start plowing through them."

"Plow is right," Kendra said. "It may take a long time to pull everything together."

"We'll begin by trying to find out how she escaped from the hospital," Eve said. "And if someone helped her. That could be a lead for us to locate her."

Kendra nodded. "But you don't have to waste a lot of time on that. You have Sam."

"She does?" Sam put down his fork. "More work?"

"You're the expert. It won't take you any time. Your pancakes won't even get cold. Boot up your computer and tap into the list of people who surrounded Beth Avery during the last few weeks."

He shrugged and slipped his computer from its case. A few moments later, he turned the laptop around so that it faced Kendra and Eve. "There's the list. About twenty people."

"But only one of any importance," Kendra said softly, her gaze focused on the list. "Bingo. I thought it would be there, but

I had to be sure I was right about how Beth got away that night."

Eve's gaze flew to Kendra's face. "You knew?"

"I told you, I didn't have all the pieces of the puzzle. I needed confirmation. We were too busy today to get it earlier."

Eve's gaze shifted back to the computer list. "Who?"

Kendra pointed to the twelfth name on the list.

Jessie William Newell.

Eve frowned. "Who is—" Then the memory came back to her. "The orderly?"

Kendra nodded. "That nice young man who was conveniently on the same floor as we were while Piltot was showing us around."

"That doesn't have to mean anything."

"No, but your sister had to have help from someone. You've seen the security measures there."

"It would be hard even with help."

"Yes, I saw only two outdoor areas that weren't covered by security cameras, both out back. It would take someone who could have scouted the entire facility—as we did—to know that. Both of these areas have long drops to the hillside below, which is probably why cameras aren't covering them."

"You think Beth jumped from one of them?"

"She was lowered from the north side of the rear walkway. There are tiny pieces of white stucco on the hillside below that spot. Nowhere else. The pieces probably came off when she braced her feet against the wall as she was lowered."

"Lowered? You believe someone lowered her down?"

"Not someone. Jessie William Newell. He had light abrasions on his knuckles and upper arms, all of the size and character consistent with the sharp stucco on that wall. They're especially apparent on his left hand."

Eve had a sudden memory of the orderly reaching out to shake Kendra's hand. "You used your left hand. I thought it was awkward at the time."

"It was awkward, but I had to get a better look. I'm sure he leaned over the walkway with a rope and helped lower her. If you'd bothered to look up there, you would have seen places where the stucco wall was obviously marked from a rope with a weight on it."

"I did glance up there," Eve said dryly. "But I obviously wasn't *seeing.*"

"Concentration." Kendra was smiling. "It has many applications. Some less pleasant than others."

"Are you through with me?" Sam asked. "Are you satisfied that Kendra is right about this dude, Eve?"

Eve looked at the list of names again.

Jessie William Newell.

Billy had given her the security code for the house.

William. Billy?

"Yes, I'm satisfied," she said slowly. "But I'm not through with you. I need everything you can pull up on this orderly. Will you send it to my phone?"

The sun was beginning to come up over the dark sea when they left the IHOP forty minutes later.

Eve stopped as they reached Sam's car. "I'm not going to say thank you again. But I owe you, Sam."

"That's always a plus." Sam shook her hand. "I'll remember and use that IOU if I need it." He turned to Kendra. "How about you?"

"Am I grateful?" Kendra thought about it. "No, I gave you an entertaining experience. If anything, you owe me." She turned back to Eve. "I'll get my bag from your car. Sam can take me to the airport and drop me off." She checked her watch. "I should get back in plenty of time for my appointment with Justin."

"Just as you planned," Eve said as she unlocked her car and took Kendra's case from the trunk. "I'm glad you were able to fit me into your schedule." Such polite, almost stilted words, and yet they meant so much. Kendra would resent thanks, but she had opened new doors for Eve in so many ways. She handed the duffel and guitar case to Sam. "Take care of her."

He shrugged. "As if she'd let me." He strolled toward his car.

Eve turned back to Kendra. "Good luck with Justin."

"Thank you, I'll need it. *He'll* need it." She frowned. "I don't like leaving you like this. It feels . . . unfinished."

"You've done everything we asked of you."

"I certainly did. And more."

Eve chuckled. "And more," she agreed. "So why does it feel unfinished?"

"I guess I'm afraid that you'll lose everything we've won if I'm not there to help. Though I admit that you were pretty good tonight."

"Thank you," she said gravely. "I'm honored by your opinion."

"No, you're not." She stood looking at her. "I do admire you, Eve Duncan. I hope you find your sister alive and well." She paused. "If you get stuck and need to talk through something, you have my number. I can't guarantee I'll be available, but I'll do whatever I can to help." She smiled slightly. "You can never tell, I might even be persuaded to help you and Quinn wrap up this mess." She turned and walked toward Sam's car. "But not until I finish working through this breakthrough with Justin . . ."

Joe was standing alone on the verandah overlooking the beach when Eve reached the motel.

He did not look pleased.

Well, what could she expect? She would

have been angry, too, if he had closed her out.

"Are you communing with the seagulls?"

He didn't look at her. "For lack of better company. Did you take Kendra to the airport?"

"No, Sam did." She came to stand beside him and looked down at the blinding bright sunlight on the sea. "I called you and told you I was safe as soon as we left the hospital. I did what I thought was right, Joe."

"I know you did. It doesn't help. It's going to take a while to forget sitting here twiddling my thumbs all night worrying about you. I was tempted to go in and stage a little raid of my own. And I wouldn't give a damn about losing my badge." He glanced at her. "Do this again, and I just might do it."

He meant what he said. Joe never bluffed. "I'll keep that in mind. Anything else?"

"Yes." He pulled her into his arms and kissed her. It was hard, passionate, and completely sensual. Then he let her go and turned away. "I've been thinking about doing that all the time I've been wondering if you were going to get your head blown off by a security guard." He moved down the verandah steps to the walk. "Now let's go to the room, and you can get me up to speed. Then you can go to bed until at least noon since you haven't slept all night, while I download some of those files Sam stole for you."

"That sounds like a plan." She reached out and touched his arm. "I've got the name of the man who—"

"Don't touch me." He moved away from her. "Not now. I'm feeling fairly explosive, and I'm trying to be civilized. You know I'm not real good at control."

"And you know I don't give a damn."

"But I do." He unlocked the door and let her precede him into the room. "Now sit down and talk to me."

"The man who helped Beth escape was Jessie William Newell. He's an orderly at the hospital." She pulled out her iPhone and accessed the file Sam had e-mailed to her. "Age twenty-eight, high-school ed-ucation at a school in Denver, served in the Marines for four years, worked as a trainer at a gym in Boulder for three years.

His mother still lives in Boulder. He's been working at the hospital for the last eighteen months." She looked up from the screen. "And he's been working principally on the third floor for the last year. No remarks on any unusual interaction with Beth Avery." She handed him her phone. "Here's his photo. Nice-looking guy. Very polite. And Kendra is very sure that he's been helping Beth."

"Why?"

Eve briefly filled him in on their encounter with Newell on the third floor of the hospital and the deductions Kendra had made from that meeting. "I didn't notice even a small percentage of the things that Kendra did, so I have to take her word for it."

"But you're willing to do it?"

She nodded slowly. "I trust her, and I trust the logic that she brings to the table."

His eyes were narrowed on her face. "But that's not all, is it?"

She smiled faintly. "You know me too well. Logic is all very well, but I've never been able to guide my life by it. I've been touched by too many totally illogical elements over the years." She paused. "Newell's middle name is William."

"I noticed. And you made the leap to the Billy of your dream?"

"Why not? He was in close association with Beth during those last months. It's not 'logical' that Beth would be able to be helped by someone not in that group." She added, "And that she would be thinking about him while she was escaping."

"Did you discuss this with Kendra?"

She grimaced. "No, I wanted to maintain my credibility with her. I'm not sure she'd understand why I'd rely on a dream to furnish me with vital information. It's definitely not her modus operandi."

"I don't know. We might be surprised." He was gazing down at Newell's dossier. "He lives at Sungate Apartments in the city. Apartment 2A. You said that you ran into him yesterday afternoon. That means he's probably working days at the hospital, and we can reach him at his apartment tonight."

Eve nodded. "That's what I thought. And we can work on checking out those other Beth Avery files today."

"Later." He didn't look up from the iPhone. "Go to bed and get some sleep."

She opened her mouth to protest, then

closed it again with the words unsaid. She was tired, and she would need to be alert when they met Newell. "You're right." She headed for the bathroom. "I'll shower, then take a nap."

She leaned back on the door after she had closed it. She hated this coolness between them. No, not coolness. That term could never describe what she and Joe felt for each other. Even though they were at odds for the moment, there was heat that made the hardness give off sparks.

But it was still disturbing to know everything was not serene with them. Oh, well, they'd work it out. If she didn't believe that, she'd be truly upset.

She stripped off her clothes and stepped under the shower. Relax. Sleep. Get on with the task of finding Beth.

And hope like hell that she hadn't damaged anything that couldn't be repaired in her relationship with Joe.

Apartment 2A.

Drogan glanced down at the address for the orderly Newell that Pierce had given him that morning, then started to climb the steps to the second-floor walkway.

Pierce hadn't wanted to give him the list. He'd been afraid that Drogan would cause an "awkward" incident that would reflect on him.

Screw him. Drogan was getting nowhere in the search for Beth Avery, and he needed to dig deeper. Someone had to have helped her to escape, and that meant someone knew where she'd go to hide. He had three other names that he was going to tap for information if Newell didn't pan out.

Including that little bitch Pierce was screwing. He almost hoped he would come up empty questioning the orderly so that he could take his time spoiling Pierce's lush little playground.

As he was going to take his time with Beth Avery. Every hour that passed, his anger was growing, his ego stinging from the memory of his failure that night.

He stopped at the door to 2A.

Locked.

No problem. He spent only a few minutes before the door swung open.

He stepped inside and closed the door. The apartment was empty, as Pierce had told him it would be. That was all right, he could wait. He went to the refrigerator and took out a beer before he dropped down in a chair facing the door.

Come on, Jessie Newell. I'm waiting to welcome you.

Joe was sitting in a chair across the room with his laptop on his lap when Eve opened her eyes. It must've been late afternoon because the rays of the sun pouring through the window were pale and slanted as they touched Joe's brown hair. "What time is it?"

"A little after four."

"I didn't want to sleep that long. Why didn't you wake me?"

"You evidently needed it." He raised his eyes from the computer to meet hers. "And I needed the time, too. I was feeling as if you owed me, and that was a very savage response."

She felt a flash of heat move through her. She held out her hand to him. "Come here."

He didn't move. "I'm over it. You don't owe me anything."

"The hell I don't. Oh, not because I closed you out from the action because I wanted to protect you. You have to deal with that because that's who I am. I'm not about to make love to you to make some kind of recompense." She tossed the sheet aside and pulled her T-shirt over her head and threw it aside. "Do you know what I owe you? The same thing you owe me. Now come here and give it to me."

He hesitated, then stood up. "You're sure?" Then he smiled recklessly and strode toward her, stripping off his clothes. "You'd better be sure because I've just gone beyond the point of no return."

"No, you haven't." She pulled him down on top of her, into her. "Not yet. Soon . . ."

Deep. Deeper.

Heat. Hardness. Rhythm.

She rolled over on top of him. "Joe . . ."

"Shh."

She threw her head back and bit down on her lip as his hips plunged upward.

Again.

Again.

Again.

It went on and on . . . and on.

When the explosion came, it was too much and yet not enough.

She was panting, her heart pounding

crazily as he drew her close. Neither of them could speak for a moment.

"We have to do it again," Joe said as his tongue teased her nipple. "And then again."

"Yes."

Joe parted her thighs, then came between them in one stroke.

"Aren't you going ask me why?"

"Obvious . . ."

"No . . . I didn't do it right."

"What?"

He smiled down at her as he slowly began to move. "Kendra wouldn't approve. I didn't concentrate."

The sun was going down when Eve and Joe got into the car and started for the Sungate Apartments. She gazed out the window at the sun streaking scarlet across the sea. "Beautiful . . . I keep thinking how many times Beth must have looked out her window at that hospital and seen this same view. The first time I saw that hospital on the hill, I thought of how free I am down here and what a prisoner she was. Do you know how small her suite was in that place?"

"You told me." He reached out and covered her hand with his own on the seat. "But now she's free, too."

"But for how long?" She moved her shoulders as if shrugging off a burden. "Sorry. Brooding isn't going to help. We've just got to find her." She glanced at him. "Did you find out anything from those computer files while I was sleeping?"

"I was mainly trying to access the physical records from her accident."

"And did you?"

"I found some forms with several complicated diagnoses and treatments. All under the supervision of Pierce." He paused. "But no record of any X-rays taken of the injury. Most unusual. You'd think the X-rays would have been sent with her from the clinic where she was first treated. I searched most of the afternoon in those computer banks and couldn't find a trace or cross-reference to them."

"Could they be entered in a separate file?"

"Possibly. Not likely. My bet is that Pierce destroyed them. It's difficult to forge an X-ray."

"You're saying that she probably didn't have a head injury."

"I'm saying that I can't find a record if she did." He pulled into the parking lot of the Sungate Apartments. It was a small, modest, two-story apartment complex with palm trees framing the entrance and the obligatory swimming pool. He parked and ran around to open her car door. "But maybe Newell can help us out. If he helped her get away, he must have believed that she shouldn't be in that hospital." He scanned the numbers on the apartment doors. "I think Newell's on the second floor." He headed for the staircase. "Let's go."

A few minutes later, they were standing before Apartment 2A. But Jessie Newell didn't answer the door when Eve and Joe rang the bell.

"Not at home?" Eve said. "Maybe he had to work late. We didn't really know his schedule."

"According to his personnel records, he drives a silver Honda." Joe was frowning. "And there's a silver Honda in the parking lot. I don't like it."

And neither did Eve. Joe's instincts were

near infallible. "Do you have his telephone number?"

"Yes." He rang the bell again. "I'll try it if he doesn't—shit."

She heard it, too.

A gasping groan, then steps inside the apartment.

But the steps were not coming toward the door.

"Step to the side." Joe reached for the doorknob. "I'm going in. Stay here."

"Hell no." Eve followed him into the apartment.

But she stopped in shock just inside the door. "Dear God."

Blood.

Blood spattered on the floor of the foyer.

Blood on the chair at the table in the kitchen.

Blood on the man tied to that chair.

Jessie Newell.

There was so much blood running from the two cuts on the face and clothing of the man in that chair that she could barely recognize him. He was gagged, and his eyes were wide with agony.

A knife was sticking out of his shoulder.

Joe was running toward the back of the

apartment. "I think whoever did it ran out the back way. I heard the door slam."

So had Eve, but it hadn't registered in the shock of seeing the carnage that was Jessie Newell.

She was across the room in seconds and jerking the gag from Newell's mouth. She was afraid to touch the knife sticking out of his shoulder for fear of damaging organs. "It's okay, we'll get you help."

"Bastard," Newell whispered. "Stop him. He took—he'll find her—"

"Quiet. Don't talk." She was untying the ropes binding his wrists. "Joe will stop him."

"I won't let him kill me. He's not going to win." He closed his eyes. "I'm losing blood. No time for EMTs. An intern lives in the apartment downstairs. Jensen. Go get him."

"I shouldn't leave you. You're bleeding . . ."

"If you don't get me help, you'll be staying with a dead man. I'll be okay. I don't think he cut any arteries. He wanted to keep me alive."

Make a decision.

"I'll be right back. I'll call 911 on the way down to get this Jensen." She ran out of the apartment and down the steps to the first level. Which apartment? She was talking to 911 as she went from door to door checking the caption beneath each doorbell.

There it was. K. D. Jensen.

Now pray that he was home.

Joe had come back to Newell's place by the time Eve and young Dr. Jensen entered the apartment. He was kneeling by Newell and applying pressure to a wound on his upper arm. Joe glanced at Eve. "I lost him. He had a car parked in the back."

"License plate?"

He nodded. "But Newell should know who he is." He turned to the doctor. "What can I do?"

"Go down and wait for the EMTs and bring them up here." He glanced at Eve. "You apply the pressure." Then he was examining the wound in Newell's arm. "What the hell have you been up to, Jessie? You into drugs?"

"I'm not stupid," Newell gasped. "Get— this thing out of my shoulder."

"In a minute." He was checking Newell over. "It might be better left in it for a little while. But you're lucky it's not buried in your heart."

"No . . . luck. I dodged to the side when I saw him coming to finish me off when the doorbell rang. The blade's mostly in the muscles of my shoulder. I knew he wouldn't have time for a second try at me." He was looking at Eve. "You were with that woman snooping around the third floor at Seahaven. Who are you?"

"Eve Duncan."

"Help me ease him out of the chair to the floor," the intern ordered Eve. "He appears stable enough, and I need to take a look at his kneecaps. There's blood on his jeans."

"There's blood all over him. So many cuts . . ." She carefully helped Jensen ease Newell to the floor, and resumed the pressure.

Newell flinched with pain and closed his eyes. "Why . . . Did Pierce send you to find out if I was the one? Did you send Drogan after me?"

"I don't know any Drogan. Is that who did this to you?"

"Drogan . . ." He opened his eyes. "I

didn't know his name, but he told me. Every time he cut me, he told me who was doing it. He was proud of the pain he was causing. Bad . . ."

"Why did he do this to you?" Eve asked.

"Beth. He wanted to know where she was . . ."

She stiffened. "But you didn't tell him?"

"Bastard . . ."

"Did you tell him?"

His gaze fastened on her face. "You know Beth?"

"No." She drew a shaky breath. "But I don't want her hurt. Believe me, I want to keep her safe."

Newell's gaze was searching her face. "You're with the man who ran through here and scared off Drogan. I saw him at the hospital. He's a detective."

"Yes, Detective Joe Quinn."

"He scared the shit out of Piltot and Pierce. I do—believe you."

"Stop asking him questions," the doctor said. "You can do that later."

Newell gave her a ghost of a smile. "If I'm still alive."

"Just yes or no," Eve said. "Tell me."

"No." His eyes closed again. "But he took— He may find her . . ."

"What did he take—"

"The EMTs are here." The intern lifted his head as he sat back on his heels. "I hear them on the steps."

So did Eve. It sounded like a herd of elephants running up the metal steps.

"Don't leave me," Newell whispered. "Stay with me at the emergency room until I get out of surgery. Don't let them check me into the hospital. Too easy. Doctors . . . Nurses . . ."

"Shut up, Jessie," Jensen said as he got to his feet as four EMTs poured into the room. "The police will find that scumbag. Nothing's going to happen to you now. We'll take good care of you."

Newell's gaze clung to Eve's. "Don't leave me."

Eve nodded as Joe reached down and helped her to her feet. "Don't worry, I'll hardly let you out of my sight." She added grimly, "We're going to talk."

"Soon," he said, as they carried him out of the apartment. "It doesn't matter that I didn't tell him. He'll find her . . ."

"Which hospital?" Joe asked Dr. Jensen as the intern hurried after the EMTs.

"Santa Barbara General." He tossed back over his shoulder, "Did I hear that you're a police detective? You'd better contact your headquarters. This has to be reported."

"Yes, it does." He took Eve's elbow and nudged her toward the door as Jensen left the apartment. He added in a low voice to Eve, "But not before we get a chance to talk to Newell."

"He told me that the name of the man who cut him is Drogan. While we're waiting for word on Newell, can you run a check and see if you can find anything about him on the database?"

"You bet I will. Drogan . . ."

Drogan's foot pressed hard on the accelerator, then lifted the pressure. He mustn't be caught speeding. That would be the stupidest thing he could do. It would be the crowning blow to a totally frustrating night.

Not that he hadn't enjoyed making the son of a bitch hurt. But Newell had been stubborn, and Drogan hadn't been able to squeeze the information about Beth Avery out of him before that detective Joe Quinn had broken into the apartment. It had to be Quinn. Pierce's description of the cop matched, and who else would be snooping around the hospital personnel?

Why the hell couldn't Pierce have managed to throw Quinn off the track? It was just one more example of the doctor's pitiful inadequacy and another wall for Drogan to overcome. The anger was searing through him, and he had to get a grip on himself so he could think clearly. He took a deep breath and tried to relax.

It was going to be all right. He had lost Newell as a source of information, but he had something else that might give him what he needed. He reached into his pocket and pulled out the cell phone he had taken from Newell.

Phones were magical instruments, and Drogan knew just how to pull that magic into the real world. First, go the simple route. Check and see just what calls Newell had received lately. Then check them all out until he hit pay dirt. Identify, locate the target, then execute.

But he had to hurry. He wasn't sure that

he'd managed to kill Newell, and he couldn't chance him calling and warning the woman.

He pulled over to the side of the road and began to go through Newell's call list.

Seventeen Mile Drive

Beth made a face as she switched the news channel off and leaned back in the chair. So much ugliness and corruption. Wars and dirty politics and unbelievable cruelty. Occasionally, there was a story that raised the heart, but they were rare. She had been tempted to turn the set off a dozen times and just stare out the window at the sea.

But she had promised Billy that she would take this time to learn about all the events of the years she had missed and try to grasp how the world was working. She had been studying the History Channel and Discovery as well as the news channels, and she preferred the past to the present. It was the violence of the present that was goading her to draw back into her shell and just look out the window at the sea.

Coward. She had done just that for all these years, and it was time for her to come alive. She had been drugged and manipulated into that false contentment, and she wouldn't do that to herself now that she was free. She was learning. She wouldn't be defenseless when she ventured out into the world. She just had to do as Billy told her and not try to hide her head.

She reluctantly reached out and turned the news channel back on. "Go ahead," she muttered to the slick-looking newscaster who was showing scenes from the latest Middle Eastern atrocity. "Give me another couple days, and maybe I'll get as callous as the rest of you. Though God knows I don't—" She broke off, stiffening, as her gaze flew to the desk across the room.

Her cell phone was ringing.

It was the first time the phone had rung since Billy had given it to her.

Billy?

She jumped to her feet and ran across the room. He had said he wouldn't contact her, but he was the only one who had her number.

Or it could be a wrong number.

She hesitated.

The phone rang again.

But what if it was Billy, and he needed to reach her?

Private number on the ID panel.

She slowly reached out and punched the access. "Billy?"

"No." The voice was crisp and business-like. "Santa Barbara Police Department. We're investigating the homicide of a Jessie Newell. Your number was on his phone. What is your name please?"

"Homicide?" Murder. He was talking about murder. Billy's murder. She couldn't breathe. "How? What—"

"He was stabbed to death. What did you say your name was?"

Stabbed. She closed her eyes. "Dear God."

"Your name." This time his voice was no longer crisp and businesslike. It was rough and ugly.

And she recognized it.

"Bitch."

A dark hospital room where she struggled for her life.

A man who cursed her and tried to inject her with that deadly hypodermic.

Panic.

Her heart leaped in her breast.

She hung up the phone.

He had found her.

She felt a wave of sickness wash over her.

And he had found Billy.

Stabbed him. Billy was dead.

He had died for her.

And now his killer would be coming to get her.

She steadied herself on the desk as the sadness and fear and anger attacked her.

Billy.

CHAPTER

9

Joe and Eve were in the waiting room for over three hours before Jensen gave them a report. "He'll be okay. The shoulder wound was only a glancing blow, and that was the worst of it," he said as he came out of the emergency room. "Thirty-two wounds, inflicted to give maximum pain. Whoever did it knew what he was doing." His face was tight. "Jessie could have bled to death if he'd been careless, or he might have gone unconscious from the trauma effect. Jessie's a good guy, he didn't deserve this. Do you know who did it?"

"No, did he tell you?"

Jensen shook his head. "I didn't ask him. That's not my job. But evidently it's your job. He's waiting for a room to be readied. You can go in and ask him a few questions, but I don't want him agitated."

"No problem."

Jensen frowned. "I mean it. Everyone likes Jessie Newell. The nurse on duty has been taking inquiries ever since we got here asking about him."

"Really? From whom?"

He shrugged. "People from the apartment. Coworkers from the hospital where he works. Look, I've no idea what he did, but I'd lay odds that Jessie is clean. That guy who did this must be a complete nut."

"Good chance. May we see him now?"

"Sure." He turned away. "Second door on the left."

"Coworkers," Eve murmured as she walked with him down the hall. "Pierce?"

"If he's the one who hired Drogan, the man who did this. Drogan might have called him with a report." He checked his phone. "No info on a Drogan yet. Maybe Newell will be able to tell us more."

"I didn't get the impression that he knew much more than his name, but I could be wrong."

When they entered the recovery room, Jessie Newell was lying in bed, swathed in bandages. "It's about time. You've got to get me out of here."

"I thought you'd changed your mind and were going to let them check you into the hospital," Eve said. "Your intern friend said you were waiting for the next available room."

"You can't argue with hospital personnel. I know that from experience. You just have to agree, then do your own thing." He struggled up in bed. "Get me something to wear. They stripped everything off me."

"They had no choice," Eve said dryly. "Your clothes were bloody and ripped in dozens of places."

"I have to get out of here. Now." He met Eve's gaze. "I'm vulnerable here. Doctors and nurses all belong to the same club. Pierce is well-known all over Santa Barbara. He or one of his cohorts could come in here, and they'd welcome him with open arms."

"You think he'd try to kill you?"

"Not if he could arrange for someone else to do it. But he's scared, and he might get desperate."

"Can you prove that he's behind this attack on you?"

"I can't prove shit. Why do you think that I was still hanging around the hospital after Beth got away?"

"I don't know. I don't know anything about you or your motives."

"Then get me out of here, and you might find out." He added firmly, "Clothes."

"Why should we help you?" Joe asked. "What if you split the minute we get you out of here?"

"You take the risk. Because if you don't, I'll find a way to get out of here on my own. I've wriggled my way out of tight places before."

"Not looking like a mummy from a grade-B movie." Joe hesitated, then turned away. "You'd better be worth the trouble. I'll see if I can float around the area and grab some scrubs."

"You expect us to smuggle you out of here?" Eve asked Newell as Joe left the room.

"Yes." He sat up in bed. "Because you

want me to talk about Beth Avery, and I won't do it until you spring me from this place. Why not do what I need? You must know that woman in the hospital they're calling Beth Avery is a phony. So you must know there's something nasty going on."

"I have suspicions," she said. "Were you the one who helped Beth hide the pills in her mattress?"

"You found out about that? Yes. I had to do it myself for the first couple weeks. After that, she had the clarity to help me hide them."

"Was it Drogan who tried to kill her that night?"

"I didn't know his name. Just that he was hired to do the job. But from things he said while he was working on me tonight, I'm sure that he was the one. He was angry with her. He expected a victim, and she was strong enough to fight him." He smiled. "Hell, she was strong enough to beat him."

And he was proud of her, Eve realized. It mattered to him that Beth was no longer the drugged, mindless creature she had been told about. The knowledge brought a rush of warmth toward him. "She was bedridden, wasn't she? I would have thought that her muscles would have been too weak to function after all those years."

"She wasn't in bed all that time. It depended on what doctor was on Pierce's favored list. From what I can glean from her medical history during most of her stay, the orders were to keep her fit and well exercised."

"That sounds like training a horse."

"Except they don't keep a horse drugged and under hypnosis for the majority of their waking hours."

"Hypnosis?"

"She had regular sessions with Pierce and an expert from Berlin from the moment she arrived here in Santa Barbara."

"Some kind of therapy?"

"You might call it that. I understand the expert from Berlin was a Dr. Hans Gelber who specialized in erasing the damaging memories of vets who suffered trauma during wartime. I thought it curious that Pierce thought that a skiing accident would cause that serious a trauma."

Memory erasure. She shuddered at the thought. Losing a part of your life as if it had never been. "How do you know all this?"

"I don't know nearly enough." His gaze narrowed on her face. "But evidently more than you. What are you doing nosing around here? What's Beth Avery to you? You said you didn't know her."

"I don't. I've never met her." She paused. "But she's my sister."

Newell went still. "I didn't know she had a sister. No one told me." He shook his head. "Beth would have told me."

Eve's lips twisted. "We appear to be in the same boat. No one told me either until she disappeared. My mother had to sign papers that Beth's birth was not to be disclosed. And I doubt if Beth knew about me. My mother kept her word. Beth belonged to the Averys and not to her."

"Interesting." His gaze focused on her face. "You don't look like her."

"No. But there's a slight family resemblance." Bonnie's curly hair that was so like that of Beth in the photo. "And I'm sure that she looks more like her father. He was very good-looking, wasn't he?"

"Yeah, I guess so. Beth said he was the handsomest man she'd ever seen. She only saw him a few times a year, but she loved him. She still loves him." He was carefully taking off the bandages on his face and neck. "The bastard never visited her since she came to that hospital."

"What are you doing with those bandages?"

"Quinn called me a mummy. The bandages attract too much attention. They'll stop me if I try to walk out of here with them on my face. I can cover the ones on my chest and arms." He frowned impatiently. "If Quinn gets a move on and brings me—"

"Shut up," Joe said as he came into the room. He tossed a bundle of blue-green scrubs on the bed. "It takes time to walk in and steal surgical garb from under the noses of everyone in the ER. We're just lucky it's a busy night. Tunic, pants, slippers. Do you need any help getting dressed?"

"I can manage." Newell swung his feet to the floor. "But I'll need to hurry. I can't take the chance of—" He inhaled sharply as he stood up. "Shit."

"Sure?" Joe asked.

Newell nodded and reached for the

tunic. "I'll slip out the door where the ambulance brings in the patients. Bring your car around and wait for me there."

Eve gazed at him skeptically. "You don't look very well. There's a good chance someone will stop you."

He shook his head. "Not if I do it right and look as if I know where I'm going. If I seem to have a purpose and appear a little impatient, no one is going to get in my way."

"Will they put out an alarm when they find this room empty?"

"No, they'll just assume someone else has come in and taken me to an available room. Hospitals aren't always efficient, and it may take them a few hours just to find out I'm not here. Believe me, I know." He was carefully working the tunic over his head. "Get out of here. I'm okay."

"If you say so." Eve turned away. "But if you go out another door and try to give us the slip, I'm coming after you, Newell."

"Don't worry. I'm not well enough to be deceptive. Though I might have tried that if I thought I could get away with it." He added grimly, "But I'm not the one who is going to suffer if I move too slow. Just have that car at the entrance. I'm not going to be able to do much for a few hours beyond getting to the front door."

"It will be there." Joe took Eve's arm as they left the room. "Tough. I believe we'd better look beyond the personnel record he gave to the hospital."

"I'm glad he's tough. He would never have been able to get Beth out of there if he weren't." She added as they walked out of the hospital and headed for the parking lot, "He told me that he'd found out that she was attended by all kinds of different doctors during the years. One of the first ones was a German doctor who specialized in memory erasure by hypnosis. It was the principal treatment during her first year at the mental hospital."

"Did you get his name?"

"Yes, Gelber, but won't it be in the records?"

"It depends on whether they wanted to have the details of that particular therapy documented." He opened the car door for her. "And what memory they were determined to erase."

"You mean the memory that someone tried to kill her on that ski slope?"

"I'm not sure they did." He shook his head. "I'm not sure of anything right now. We're only putting together the pieces one by one."

"And Newell should be able to give us a few more pieces to add to the puzzle." Eve's gaze was on the emergency door. "I think he cares about her, Joe."

"We'll see. When he first came around her, evidently she was almost a vegetable. It's difficult to develop any feeling for a woman in that condition." Joe's tone was noncommittal. "It could be that he just hates her enemies. It would have the same effect." He started the car. "There he is. Bold as brass. He's right. No one is going to stop him."

Newell's skin was pale against the blue-green scrubs, but his step was firm as he came toward their car as they pulled up before him. "It's about time." He opened the rear door and climbed into the car. "I told you it was an emergency." He sat up very straight on the seat until they had driven out of the hospital zone. "Okay." He slumped back on the seat and closed his eyes. "Give me a minute. Get on the highway and head north."

"Suppose we talk first," Joe said.

"I can't talk right now. And I can't wait for you to interrogate me." His hands closed into fists at his sides. "Drive, dammit. There's no time. Look, he got my cell phone. I tried to get one of those EMTs to let me use his phone to call Beth, but he wouldn't do it."

"I imagine they were too busy trying to save your life," Eve said dryly.

"I have to warn her, and they wouldn't listen to me. By the time I got to the hospital and persuaded the intern to let me use his phone, it was too late. She didn't answer."

Eve stiffened. "You think Drogan managed to find her?"

"I don't know, but there's a possibility. He could locate the nearest tower from her GPS if he has the right equipment." His lips twisted. "And he impresses me as a person who'd have the right equipment. He takes both pride and pleasure in his work. I learned that when he was cutting my flesh with such precision."

"Could he con her into telling him where she's located?" Joe asked.

Newell shook his head. "She's inexperienced, but she's not stupid. She'd see through him." He added half beneath his breath, "I hope."

"But you're not sure?" Eve asked.

"How can I be sure? Look, Beth has had years of being told she's a mental cripple and had to be cared for. They reinforced it with hypnosis and drugs. I've only had her for the last eighteen months. She'd grown accustomed to trusting everyone with whom she comes in contact. Do you know how hard it was for me to break that trust?"

"Tell us," Eve said. "And while you're at it, tell us why you bothered to do it."

He didn't answer for a moment. "I . . . like her. At first, I just felt sorry for her and pissed at those sons of bitches who were making her into a living corpse. She was like a little girl lying in that bed and smiling at me whenever I came into the room. She smiled at everyone, even Pierce's whore, Stella Lenslow, who liked to come in and taunt her. The bitch was even cutting her medication during the last six months. She was hoping that Beth would suffer withdrawal from the drugs." He shrugged. "She didn't realize that I'd begun weaning her off them nine months before that. But Stella's viciousness made Beth's increasing alertness more plausible, and since she was Beth's principal nurse, it worked into my plans. Toward the end, I had to make Beth pretend to be in pain a couple times when Stella was in the room to make Stella happy and not give away the fact that the decrease in dosage had little effect."

"We're on the freeway," Joe said as he entered the ramp. "Now where are we going?"

"Seventeen Mile Drive. Near Carmel."

"That's where she is?" Eve asked.

He nodded. "I used to work for a man who has a house there. He always spends this time of year in the south of France, and the house is vacant. I knew it would be safe for Beth."

"How? It's too close to Pierce and the hospital. I would have thought it would be safer for her to get out of California entirely."

"It was better if she was close enough so that I could help her if she needed me." He paused. "Besides, she wasn't ready."

"What do you mean?"

"What do you think I mean?" he asked harshly. "Beth's like someone from that fairy tale who's been asleep in a tower while the whole world grew up around her. There were hazards out there that she couldn't imagine. I tried to fill her in a little, but our time together was too damn limited, and my main objective had to be to get her out of that hospital. But I knew she had to catch up before she could fit in somewhere and hide out until we found a way to keep her safe."

"You've gone to a lot of risk to save Beth," Joe said. "Why? And don't tell me it was just because she was appealing and helpless. How did you know she had anything beyond that sweet smile to save? Most orderlies would have assumed that the doctors were right, and Beth Avery was a lost cause. Why didn't you? And why did you spend eighteen months as an orderly anyway? It's not exactly the kind of job a Marine with your record would embrace on a long-term basis."

Newell didn't answer.

"I'm not going to go any farther until I know," Joe said.

Newell shrugged. "Oh, what the hell, I guess it doesn't matter any longer. My uncle sent me here to check out what was going on with Beth Avery. He thought that she might have been railroaded in there, and he asked me to snoop around and find out."

"Your uncle?" Eve asked.

"Herman Dalker, he's a private detective."

"I know." Eve recognized the name. Sandra's "Hermie," whom she'd hired to find her daughter.

Newell's gaze shifted to narrow on her face. "How do you know?"

"Did your uncle tell you who hired him for the job? It was my mother, Sandra Duncan."

"You're really Beth's sister? I didn't know whether to believe you." His lips twisted. "You're a little late rushing to rescue her."

"I'm not making excuses to you. I'm here now. My mother told me that the detective she'd hired had told her that he'd keep an eye on Beth for her. It sounds to me as if he was doing a good deal more than that."

"He liked your mother. And he didn't like what he knew about the Avery family. There wasn't any evidence that they'd done anything wrong, but he didn't like the setup. So he thought it wouldn't hurt to send me out to look things over. I needed a break after my last deployment in Afghanistan, and it didn't seem much of a challenge."

She glanced at the wound on his neck. "Wrong."

He shrugged. "Some of the most innocent-looking fields are where the IEDs are planted. I expected to go in and work for a few months, make a report, then go on my way. It didn't work out that way. I didn't like the setup. I wanted to see what was happening."

"And did you?"

"Yes, but it took a hell of a long time. They watched Beth Avery as if she were a crown jewel. The people at the hospital had to get used to me and accept me as if I weren't there. So while I was waiting, I concentrated on checking out Pierce's computer records on her. My uncle had trained me on cyberespionage and I had plenty of opportunity to get to the records."

And if they'd been able to contact Newell, they might never have had to steal those records themselves, Eve thought. "And what else did you find?"

"Nothing incriminating. But her treatment was damn weird. She was drugged, and yet she had plenty of physical exercise. She swam and worked out in the gym. Once they even tried to take her skiing, but that required too much attention, and they were afraid she'd be damaged." He added bitterly, "That's the way they put it, 'damaged,' as if she were a piece of property they had to keep in mint condition."

"And not a person at all," Eve said dully.

"She wasn't a person to them," Newell said. "But she was damn important. There were notes by Pierce on the reports congratulating the different doctors and therapists who kept her in the pink of health in spite of the necessary sedatives. He said that it was important to keep her from disintegrating in case the family ever came to check on her. It was of the utmost urgency that they strike a balance until the Averys decided about her disposition."

"Do you mean whether they wanted her dead?" Joe asked bluntly.

"It was never spelled out, but the implication was there. I got the impression from those years of notes that there was some kind of conflict going on in the Avery family regarding Beth."

"Because they didn't just throw her into the hospital and forget about her?" Eve asked. "It seems to me that it came pretty damn close."

"They definitely didn't forget about her," Newell said. "She was a thorn in their existence even though they kept her in that place and tried to make her a zombie. But during the last months, I began to notice a difference in Pierce's attitude toward her. He cut out her exercise and made her stay in her room. It made me uneasy. I wondered if maybe the 'disposition' had been decided upon. I had to find out. So I had Uncle Hermie send me some hi-tech equipment and bugged Pierce's office."

"Did it work?"

"Partially. I never heard the call actually setting up the attack on Beth, so I didn't know who was going to do it or when it was going to take place. He must have made that call somewhere else. But I monitored a call from Pierce to Nelda Avery, and it was oblique but enough to raise a red flag. He said that he'd made the arrangement, and it would be handled soon. He said that he expected her to show her gratitude for his loyalty over the years in a generous manner."

"What did she say?"

"Nothing that would incriminate her. I believe she's too smart to make any statement on the phone that would endanger her in any way. She said that she'd always be generous to people who made that poor girl 'comfortable.' She said to let her know. Then she hung up."

"Cool. Very cool," Eve said thoughtfully. "So Nelda Avery is behind Drogan's attempt?"

"Presumably. At least she's the family member who's pulling the strings. Pierce was almost groveling when he was speaking to her. He must have been dancing on hot coals when he had to tell her that Beth had flown the coop. No wonder that Drogan is so frantic about finding Beth. Pierce is probably applying pressure." He frowned. "Or maybe it's personal. Drogan was pretty intense, but it was anger at Beth that was coming through, not worry about what Pierce was going to do. He made a couple of ugly mentions of what he was going to do to Beth when he found her."

Eve felt a chill. "And you think that he may have found her already?"

"I don't know. It could have happened." He looked at the GPS on the dashboard. "We should know soon. Another forty minutes."

"Drogan, what the hell are you doing?" Pierce's voice was shaking with anger as Drogan finally picked up. "I just had a call from the local police asking questions about Jessie Newell. I told you that any questioning had to be done discreetly. Just find out the information, then make the kill. You fumbled everything again."

"No, you did it. Everything would have gone off just as I planned if that Detective Quinn hadn't interfered. You were supposed to throw him off the trail."

"I tried." Pierce took a deep breath. "He's a cop. I couldn't just kick him out of the hospital. I thought that I might have convinced him that—" Why was he making excuses to this idiot, he thought impatiently. "Did you get a lead on Beth from Newell?"

"Yes, he's the one who helped her get away from the hospital. I took Newell's phone and talked to her on his cell."

Yes. Pierce's hand tightened on the phone. "So you know where she is?"

"No, she hung up on me before I could trace the call."

"You bungled that, too?"

"I'm getting very tired of your insults, Pierce. Be careful."

Pierce struggled to curb his tongue as well as his rage. Drogan was definitely unbalanced and unpredictable. Besides, the man was his only path to Beth at the moment. "You can hardly claim any great progress when you had a chance to trace her and lost her."

"I didn't lose her."

"What?"

"I'm going after her right now. You should be grateful I didn't kill Newell. He's going to lead me right to her. After I hung up from talking to Beth Avery, I headed for the hospital where they'd taken Newell. I knew that if I hadn't damaged him too much, he'd be on his way to her as soon as he could. He wouldn't tell me anything even though I hurt him bad. If she meant that much to him, he wouldn't stay in that hospital when he knew I'd be after her. So I staked out the hospital parking lot and waited."

"And?"

"Newell was picked up by Quinn and whisked away from the hospital."

"Quinn, again."

"And the woman who was with him at Newell's apartment. Find out who she is."

"I will." Quinn was displaying an odd intensity about Beth's case that was surely out of all proportion. He was reluctant to have to tell Nelda how badly the situation had deteriorated, but he might need her to do some discreet investigation into Detective Joe Quinn. "You think that they're going to Beth Avery now?"

"I'd bet on it. And I'm right behind them on the freeway. Quinn's taillights are only four car-lengths ahead." Drogan hung up.

"Drogan is following Jessie Newell. He thinks he may be on his way to Beth," Pierce said to Stella as he pressed the disconnect. "But Joe Quinn is with Newell. It could be bad if there's police interference."

"Maybe." She leaned on the corner of his desk. "But when I talked to the hospital inquiring about Newell's condition, I found out that it was the emergency room who notified the local police." She smiled. "Not Quinn, even though he was at the apartment. He seems to want to work alone. Now why would he want to do that? I think that we should find out."

His gaze narrowed on her face. "You don't like him."

"He didn't like me. He's either gay or a very cold fish."

Pierce chuckled. "He didn't respond, and your nose is out of joint. You want to punish him. Poor Stella."

"Shut up. I didn't really try. I only brushed up against him." She shrugged. "But that's usually enough. He's not normal."

"I agree. But we've got to find out just what he is." He grimaced. "And I have to call Nelda to help me do that. It won't be pleasant."

"But what comes afterward will be pleasant." She opened the top three buttons of her uniform, took his hand, and rubbed it against her breasts. "I like pretending to be Nelda for you. I like the pain and the fierceness. I even like kneeling naked for you because I know it's just a game and that I'm really the one in control. But if I was really Nelda, I'd be the one hurting you."

"But you're not Nelda." His hand closed on the fullness of her breast, and he squeezed with all his strength. "You're just a whore I use whenever it amuses me." He watched her expression for pain or weakness.

She only smiled and leaned forward and ran her tongue over his lips. "Or do I use you? Who is really the whore, Harry?" She stood up and buttoned her uniform. "Ask Nelda, why don't you?" She moved toward the door. "I'll be waiting for you in the apartment. I'll give you a particularly good time if you find a way to get her to take down that snooty Quinn."

He watched the door close behind her. He was as hard as a rock just the way she'd wanted him to be. Why could she do this to him? He'd taken her because he'd wanted a woman who was the perfect sex toy, but her sexual dominance over him seemed to be getting stronger every day. Even at this moment, when the situation was getting tense, she'd made him forget everything but her for that brief moment.

Forget her. Take what he wanted as he usually did and go about his business. But those taunts about Nelda's dominance had been particularly annoying when he knew that he was going to have to tell Nelda that he'd lied to her about Beth's being found and brought back to the hospital.

Dammit, just get it over with.

He reached for his phone and punched in Nelda Avery's number.

Stupid bastard.

Nelda hung up the phone and leaned back in her chair.

Keep calm. Smother the anger. She'd managed to maintain an icy control with Pierce, but it had been difficult. She'd let him make excuses and had assured him that she'd find about that troublesome police detective.

She hadn't let him know the fury and disgust that was tearing through her. Nor that he had forced her to make a decision she hadn't wanted to make.

"What's wrong?" George had come into her bedroom from his own suite. "Who's calling at this hour? It's almost midnight."

"Pierce." She pushed back from her Louis XV desk. "He's causing trouble. Nothing to bother you with. I'll take care of it."

"You don't want to talk about it?" He

shrugged. "I'm just as happy that you don't. I'd rather stay out of your dealings with Pierce."

"That's the problem. I believe I'm going to have to stop dealing through Pierce and handle the matter myself." She went to the closet and pulled out a Louis Vuitton suitcase. "I'm going out to the coast. I shouldn't be more than a few days."

He went still. "You're going to the hospital?"

"Of course not. That would attract far too much attention. I just need to be nearby to be more effective."

"My dear, you're always effective."

She glanced at him to see if he was being sarcastic, but he only looked very weary. "In this case, I have to be." She added softly, "For Rick's sake. There mustn't be any publicity that might take away the focus on what a fine president he'll be." She opened the case, which she always efficiently kept packed except for a few items she had to throw in at the last minute. "I'll keep you informed of developments. Tell everyone I went to a spa to relax after the whirl of town meetings in the past few days."

"I'll tell them, but they may not believe

me. Anyone who knows you would know that you thrive on pressure." He paused. "What am I going to tell Rick?"

"Nothing more than you tell the others. I'm going to call Lisa on the way to the airport and tell her to get her butt on a plane out of Miami and come here and make some appearances with Rick. She'll distract him enough to keep him from noticing that I'm not around."

"Do you think she'll come? She said when she left that she needed a long break."

"She'll come. She wants to be first lady, and its time she paid her dues." She slammed her suitcase shut. "You've always felt sorry for her. She knew what the situation with Rick was before she married him. She was ambitious. She said she could work it out."

"She didn't know she was going to fall in love with him, Nelda," he said quietly.

"That's her problem. If she loves him, she should fall into line and do what's necessary to give him what he wants." She called for the car to be brought around. "Damn, I forgot my night cream." She headed for the bathroom but paused at the door to glance at him over her shoulder. "I may need Spoder to come out to Santa Barbara if I find Pierce too difficult. It should be okay. Rick will behave himself if Lisa is with him." She shrugged. "If she stays at his side and watches him close enough. He does care about her."

"Which is very convenient considering they're married," he said dryly. "But you counted on that, too, didn't you?"

"I knew it was a distinct possibility. Everyone loves Rick once they get to know him." She went into the bathroom and closed the door. She quickly went to the jewelry armoire, unlocked the compartment above the drawers, and drew out a .22 revolver. She stared at it for a moment. She doubted if it would be necessary to use it, but she always believed in being prepared. So stop hesitating and get on the move. She slipped the gun into her tote. Then she relocked the compartment and shut the armoire.

She opened the bathroom door and smiled brilliantly at George. "I'm all ready. Don't worry. Everything is going to be fine. It's not as if I'm not aware of what's going on. I've made sure that what Pierce knows, I know." She moved toward the door. "I should have taken care of the problem myself from the beginning. But it's not too late to save the situation."

"If anyone can do it, you can."

That weariness in his tone again, she noticed; she'd have to address that attitude when she returned. It could hide signs of an underlying festering that would cause problems. "I'll call you when I reach California."

"Thanks." He turned back to the door leading to his suite. "Have a good flight."

She hesitated in the hall after she'd closed the door behind her. Should she go back to him and try to smooth away that disturbance?

No, it would be fine until she came back. She couldn't be everything to everyone. Rick was the important one at present. All the progress she'd attained from years of work could go down the drain if she didn't take care of this problem with Beth.

As she started down the stairs, her hand slipped into her tote and closed on the revolver. It felt cool and hard and sleek beneath her touch. She had studied a number of guns before choosing this one because it had reminded her of her own personality.

She could be just as dangerous and explosive as the weapon in her palm if she chose. She was a great problem solver, and so was a revolver.

Not that she was contemplating solving the problem of Beth with this weapon.

But one must have insurance, mustn't one?

CHAPTER
10

Seventeen Mile Drive

"Very impressive," Eve murmured as she got out of the car and looked up at the house towering above the crashing surf.

The house was English Tudor in design and resembled the castles Eve had seen in England. It would definitely have been more at home in the English countryside than on this lush California coast. "What did you say you did for the owner?"

"I didn't." Newell got out of the car. "I was Mr. Dendridge's bodyguard and personal trainer. He was a great guy. We became good friends before we parted company."

"I don't remember any mention of him in your personnel record."

"My uncle furnished me with that dossier and set up background records. If I'd given the hospital an authentic history, it would have led back to him." He was gazing up at the house. "God, I hope she's in there."

"And I hope she's still alive," Eve said grimly. "Let's find out. You have the security code, right?"

"Yes." He was moving toward the front door. "I gave it to Beth. It was the only way she could get into the—" He stopped and his gaze shifted to Eve's face. "I didn't tell you I had the code. Was that a guess?"

She ignored the question as she reached the door. "You'd better go in first. She must have heard the car drive up, but you're the only one she'd recognize. We don't want to scare her." She glanced back at the car. Joe had gotten out of the car but was standing there, his head lifted as he gazed around the courtyard. "Joe?"

"Go ahead. If the alarm is still set, it's probably safe enough inside. These mansions on the strip have state-of-the-art security. You have your gun?"

She nodded. "In my bag. Why aren't you coming?"

"I want to take a look around the property. Even if Drogan isn't inside, it doesn't mean he's not stalking out here. Call me if there's a problem." He started toward the steps that led to the beach. "It shouldn't take me more than ten or fifteen minutes."

Newell watched him until he disappeared. "Smart," he said "And careful."

"Always." Eve could feel the tension grip her as she watched Newell try the door, then punch in the security code. In a few minutes, she'd be face-to-face with Beth Avery. Relax. She was just a stranger. It shouldn't matter this much.

It did matter.

"It was locked. That's a good sign." Newell swung open the door and went into the foyer. "Beth!"

No answer.

Newell muttered a curse. "She might have gone on the run if she knew that Drogan was after her. He could have called and scared her. Hell, that would be the best scenario. Beth! It's okay. It's Billy."

"It's not safe to turn on the lights if there's a security guard monitoring these houses on the beach." Eve reached in her purse and pulled out her small flashlight. She moved forward across the foyer toward the staircase. "Keep calling her name." She shined her beam around the cherry stairs and mullioned windows on the landing. "I'm going upstairs."

"No, you aren't. Stay right where you are." The woman who had spoken was coming down the hall toward them. "Billy, that means you, too."

She had a gun.

The beam of Eve's flashlight fell on the Luger the woman was holding before her with both hands.

Eve froze.

"Beth?" Newell took a step toward her. "Don't be scared. It's me."

"Don't move. I don't want to hurt you, Billy. But I will if I have to do it to save myself. You told me that over and over, didn't you? Save yourself."

"Your hands are shaking on that gun. You're just as likely to shoot yourself."

"No, I won't. When I first saw that gun case in the library, I knew that I might have to break into it if it became necessary. I found some books in the library on gun usage and studied them." Her voice was quivering. "Remember? You told me I had to learn, to teach myself. It didn't take much studying to learn how to take off a safety and pull the trigger." She took another step closer. "But I don't want to pull the trigger, Billy. I don't want to hurt you. Tell me why you're here."

"For God's sake, I want to help you. Why else would I be here?"

"I don't know. I do know you told me not to trust you either. You said don't trust anyone. Not even me." She looked at Eve. "Who is she?"

"Eve Duncan. She wants to help you. *I* want to help you, Beth."

"He said you were dead."

"Who?"

"It was that man who had the hypodermic needle. He called me, using your phone, and said he was the police and that you were dead, stabbed to death. But I recognized his voice. It was the man who tried to kill me in the hospital room. He wasn't the police. I hung up."

"Then why in God's name didn't you run like hell?" Newell asked roughly. "There are ways that you could be tracked once you answered that call. You shouldn't have taken the chance of staying here."

"I was hoping that he'd lied, that you were still alive. I knew if he hadn't killed you, that you might come to help me. So I broke into the gun case and waited."

"And then pulled the gun on me."

"I'm afraid, Billy. I have to take care of myself. What if that murderer made you come here? How did he get your phone?"

"His name is Drogan. And he took it."

"How?"

Eve had enough. They had to break through this wall of fear and suspicion. "Show her, Newell." She took his arm and pulled him to stand before Beth. She jerked open his shirt and pulled it aside to reveal the bandages. "That's how Drogan managed to take his phone. Do you want me to take off the bandages and let you see the wounds? They're not pretty. Drogan wanted to inflict the maximum amount of pain. But Newell didn't tell him anything about you. Drogan located you through the cell phone."

"Billy?" Beth whispered. Her gaze was focused on the bandages, then lifted to the jagged stitches on his throat, where he'd torn off the bandages earlier. She flinched and reached out to touch the wound on the side of his neck. "He . . . hurt you."

"Yeah. Now will you put down the gun?"

"I'll take it." Eve reached out and her hand closed on the barrel of the gun. "Now let's talk reasonably and—"

Her head snapped back as Beth's fist connected with her jaw.

Pain.

Darkness.

"Beth!" Newell grabbed Beth and pulled her back. "What the hell are you doing?"

"Tell her to keep her hands off me." Beth pulled away from him, her hand tight on the gun, her voice fierce as she glared at Eve. "I don't know her. I guess I can still trust you, but I don't trust her. There's no way I want her here. Why did you bring her? Who the hell is she?"

"I told you," Newell said. "Eve Duncan. She's not going to hurt—"

"I'm your sister," Eve said baldly. "And I don't want to be here any more than you want me. But I have no choice. Therefore, you have no choice." She rubbed her jaw. "And if you ever do that again, I'll deck you. You won't catch me off guard again."

"Sister," Beth repeated blankly. "I don't have a sister."

"How do you know? I didn't. It appears that our relationship wasn't important to anyone in either of our lives." She turned away. "Until now. Now take us someplace where it's safe to turn on a light without its being seen from outside. I'm sure you must have checked that out since you've been here. Which room?"

She didn't answer for a moment. "The library. Heavy velvet drapes on all the windows. As long as the light wasn't too strong, it didn't show around the edge. I went outside just to be sure and checked it when I was watching TV and reading." She pushed past them and led the way down the hall. "I'm not doing this because you're telling me to do it. I just want Billy to have a chance to sit down and rest. He's paler than I've ever seen him."

"I'll accept that my wishes aren't of importance to you," Eve said. "And I don't give a damn. I just want to keep my promise and have this over." She followed Beth as she opened a tall, mahogany door and entered a large room lined with bookshelves. "Sit down, Newell. She's right, you're not looking so good." She moved toward a desk in the center of the room. "You don't want to end up back in the hospital."

"No, I don't." He dropped down in a leather easy chair. "And you might not help to spring me next time. After all, you've got what you want from me."

"I'm not that callous." Eve leaned forward and turned on the desk light. The library was suddenly flooded with soft light. "And I wouldn't want to set you up for Pierce. I've taken a great dislike for him."

"Not callous, tough." Newell turned to Beth, who was still in the shadows outside the pool of light. "Will you put that gun down now? Eve's not going to attack you."

"I couldn't be sure." She came forward to put the revolver on the desk. "She could have been fooling you."

"And I told you not to trust anyone." He made a face. "It was a good idea, but I'm beginning to rue the day I said it."

"You shouldn't," Beth said as she came toward him. "It's as bad out here as you told me. Look what that monster did to you." She gently touched the stitched wound on his cheek. "I'm sorry, Billy. Why didn't you run away when I did?"

"It wasn't the right time. I didn't know enough. I was trying to learn more about the bad guys." He shrugged. "But the bad guys found me instead. Or one bad guy, Drogan."

"And just who is Drogan?" Beth asked.

"I couldn't trace him. But we should know soon." He nodded at Eve. "Her significant other, Joe Quinn, is a detective and he's checking him out."

"Joe Quinn?" She whirled toward Eve. "If he's a detective, will they make him take me back to the hospital? Pierce knows all the police at— What are you staring at?"

"Nothing." Eve was staring at Beth Avery. The soft lamplight surrounded her sister, and Eve couldn't take her eyes off her. Her slender body was dressed in gray slacks and a cream blouse that she wore with simple elegance. Her dark hair resembled the curls and textures of Eve's Bonnie, and her face . . .

Beautiful? Yes, a fascinating face with large dark eyes set wide in a triangular-shaped skull with beautiful bone structure. The wonderful vitality Eve had noticed in the photograph was no longer there, and she felt a sudden anger that Beth had been robbed of that lust for life. Instead, there was a . . . watchfulness.

And Eve noticed something else.

Beth was two years older than Eve, but she looked much younger. Her face was perfectly smooth and glowing, as if she were a child who had only just woken from a nap. No wrinkles or lines that were the usual signs of emotional or physical stress.

Sleeping Beauty.

The words popped into Eve's mind out of nowhere. The fairy tale of the princess who had pricked her finger and fallen asleep while the world went on without her. A garden of thorns had grown up around her castle to make sure that no one got close enough to wake her, to save her.

"You're not telling me the truth," Beth said curtly. "I know when people lie to me. God knows, those doctors and nurses did that enough. I can tell the difference. I'm not stupid because they had me on all those drugs."

"I don't think you're stupid. You want the truth? I was thinking you look very young, like Sleeping Beauty coming out from behind the wall of thorns."

"That's silly." She frowned. "I don't belong in any fairy tale. I'm just trying to understand and survive."

Newell gave a low whistle. "I believe you've hit it, Eve." He touched the cut on his throat. "Right down to the sharp thorns."

"You can think what you wish," Eve told Beth. "You asked me, and I told you. Look in the mirror sometime and think about it." She took out her phone. "Now I'm going to call Joe and tell him that you're safe and ask if he's noticed anything suspicious while he was reconnoitering the grounds. If you want to be useful, you can find a first-aid kit in this place and rebandage any of Newell's cuts that need it."

She didn't move. "Joe Quinn? That detective Billy mentioned? He's here?"

"Yes, and you're lucky that he is. His presence ups your safety quotient about 70 percent." She saw that Beth wasn't moving, and she was suddenly impatient. "You can trust him, dammit. You can trust me. We're all here to help you."

"Are you?" She looked Eve directly in the eye. "Then why are you angry with me? Is it because I hit you when you tried to take my gun? I'd do it again. You don't care anything about me. I didn't know you even existed. I don't like you, and I don't want you here."

"I'm not angry." But she was lying, Eve realized. There had been a smoldering resentment connected with Beth since the moment Sandra had told her about her. Resentment, pity, shock, curiosity had all been there, and now there was this deep frustration that she had to bury all those feelings and just find a way to rescue Sleeping Beauty. And, added to that barrage of emotions, an instant antagonism between them had flared at their first encounter.

To hell with it, she thought recklessly. She would be honest and direct and forget about pity. It was the only way that she could deal with Beth Avery. She had an idea that Beth could take whatever she had to take. "Maybe I am angry. I don't need a sister, and I don't want one with all the baggage you're bringing into my life. But I promised our mother that I'd make sure you're safe, and I'll do it."

"My mother? I don't know anything about her. I never wanted to know. They told me she gave me up when I was a baby. She didn't care about me then. Why should I believe she does now?" She drew a deep breath. "So you can call your Joe Quinn and get him to take you out of here. I don't need you." She turned to Newell. "I'll be right back, Billy. There's a first-aid kit in the kitchen." She turned on her heel and strode out of the library.

"She does need you," Newell said quietly. "The cards are stacked against her. It has to be the Averys who gave the kill order. That's a hell of a lot of power for Beth to have to go up against. She can't even go to the police. Just the fact that she's been in a mental hospital all these years will make it difficult for anyone to believe her. She'd end up back in the hospital, and, in a year or two, they'd find a way to kill her."

"I'm not going to leave her." She shrugged. "Even if she tells me to do it. It's not totally my fault, you know. It appears that she's taken a dislike to me."

He smiled. "I noticed. It's a little strange. I actually think it's healthy. I've never seen her react like that toward anyone. She's always been sweet and docile. It could be that the drugs are totally out of her system now. Or it could be spending this period alone, she's had time to think, and her personality is beginning to assert itself."

"Or it could be a natural antipathy." She reached up and gingerly touched her jaw. "For any reason you choose to call it, her personality is definitely present and accounted for." She turned away and dialed Joe. "Everything is fine here. Drogan was in contact with Beth, but he hasn't shown up here. Anything suspicious out there?"

"No. How is Beth Avery taking all this?"

"Not tamely. Scared, but she's no timid rabbit."

"Do I detect an edge?"

"Probably. But I'm trying to work through it. Are you ready to come in? I'll unlock the front door."

"Not yet. I'll call you. I'm going to drive back the way we came and check to make sure we weren't followed."

"I didn't see anyone tailing us on the freeway."

"Neither did I. But Newell said Drogan was a professional who knew what he was doing. He might have been good enough so that we wouldn't have been able to notice him. It won't hurt to take a little time to be sure." He hung up.

"Okay?" Newell asked, as she hung up her cell.

She nodded as she turned back to face him. "He's going to backtrack in case we were followed. He'll call me."

"Smart move." He leaned wearily back in the chair. "Thorough."

"That's Joe." She gazed thoughtfully at him. "You look like you're ready to pass out."

"I've been worse." He smiled slightly. "But if I do pass out, you've got to promise that you'll take care of Beth for me. I promised Uncle Hermie that she'd come out of this okay."

"Is that the only reason?"

"No, I like her." He chuckled. "And I've no ambition to be the prince who battles through the thorns to save her."

"Yet you already have."

"Yeah, I guess so." He tilted his head. "But I feel more like she's my sister. I'd do it for a sister. Would you?"

She didn't answer. "She said that she didn't know anything about her mother. But your uncle told you about Sandra. You didn't mention it to Beth?"

He shook his head. "You have no idea how little time we had for small talk."

"Hardly small talk," Eve said dryly.

"It was for me. Everything I did, everything I said, was aimed at getting her off the drugs, clearing her mind so that she didn't stay in that damn fog they tried to keep blowing around her. It was all present and a little future, no past. You weren't important."

"I'm still not, but Sandra wouldn't agree." She thought of something else. "Beth calls you Billy. William is your middle name."

"And no one at the hospital would recognize it if she mumbled something by mistake during the time we were hiding those pills in the mattress. It protected both of us when she was still heavy into the sedatives."

"You thought of everything. She owes you a great deal, Newell. Does she realize that?"

"Of course I do." Beth was standing in the doorway with a bowl of water and a first-aid kit in her hands. "Why shouldn't I? I'm not on those drugs any longer. I can think, I can feel. Stop talking about me as if I was that woman at Seahaven—I'm not that person any longer." She came forward and set the bowl of water on the table beside Newell's chair. "I *won't* be her."

"Shh." Newell smiled at her. "You protest

too much. Of course, you're not her. I was just telling Eve how much you'd changed."

"You were?" Her expression cleared, and she suddenly smiled. "I thought that I was learning and changing in the past few days, but it's hard to know when there's no one around that you trust to ask if it's true." She dipped a cloth into the water. "Now be quiet, and I'll clean up these stitches and rebandage you."

"I could do it," Eve offered.

"Why? Because you think I can't?" Beth was carefully cleaning the blood from around the stitches. "I took a first-aid course when I was competing at a ski competition in Switzerland before . . . before they took me to the hospital."

"And you still remember?" Eve asked.

"I didn't. It was only a blur. But it's all been coming back to me for the past few days. Just bits and pieces, but the memories are as sharp as if it were yesterday." She dried the wound, then carefully rebandaged it. "This was nothing. I remember CPR lessons and laughing at—" She broke off and stepped back. "I remember laughing a lot. Then it stopped."

"Do you remember a Dr. Hans Gelber?" Newell asked.

"No. Why?"

"He was one of your first specialists at the hospital. I was just wondering if that was about the time that you forgot the laughter."

She shrugged. "I don't know. There were so many doctors. It doesn't matter. I'll know soon. It's all coming back now."

"You're wrong. I believe it may matter very much," Eve said slowly.

"I wasn't talking to you." Beth glanced at her. "And you're looking angry again."

"I am angry. But not at you."

I remember laughing a lot. And then it stopped.

Eve was finding those words incredibly moving. Her own life had not been filled with laughter, but her laughter had not been smothered by some doctor who had been ordered to destroy memories, and with it, a woman's laughter. "And I think that we should hurry the process along and track down that doctor Newell mentioned."

Joe slowed down to a crawl as he passed the long driveway of the estate next door to the Dendridge Tudor. It was dark, and there were several turns on the way up the hill. A good place to pull off and avoid possible scrutiny and yet be able to keep everything around him under surveillance.

Are you up there, Drogan?

If they'd been followed by Drogan, he could have pulled off at any of ten houses along this stretch.

And there was no proof that they had been followed.

No proof. But a nagging hunch that wouldn't go away. Joe believed in hunches. They had saved his life too many times for him to ignore them. And he had felt that strong whisper of instinct the moment he had gotten out of the car back at the Tudor. That sense of being watched . . .

He had thought it might be Drogan somewhere on the grounds, but that hadn't panned out. So he had decided to explore the road behind him.

Nothing.

Or nothing he could see.

He turned around and headed back toward the Tudor. He didn't like the idea of not being with Eve when he knew that bastard was somewhere around. He'd come back later on foot and scour the neighborhood.

He dialed Eve. "No luck. I'm on my way." He hung up, and his gaze once more traveled down the street of luxurious homes.

But I know you're out there, Drogan. You can't hide from me for long. I'll find you.

"Joe's on his way back." Eve hung up the phone and turned to Beth. "Newell doesn't look too good. Do you have any coffee in this place?"

"In the kitchen." Beth headed for the door. "I'll get it."

"I'll go with you." She said over her shoulder to Newell, "Stay where you are and rest. We'll be right back."

"I'm not moving." Newell closed his eyes. "It's been a rough night. I deserve to relax."

"Yes, you do," Beth said soberly. "I'm so sorry, Billy."

"No problem." He didn't open his eyes. "A little caffeine, and I'll be fine."

"Right away," Eve said as she followed Beth out of the room and down the hall. "I assume we can't turn on the kitchen lights?"

"No, but I always get the coffeemaker ready so I can have it in the evening."

Moonlight was streaming into the kitchen from a huge window over the sink, and Eve could see Beth hit the button on the coffeemaker and moved from the sink to the bronze thermal carafe sitting on the granite counter. "Caffeine is an essential for quality living for Joe and me. I suppose Newell is the same."

"I didn't like coffee at first. But I found it gave me a little zing and kept me awake while I was studying here. They never gave it to me at the hospital, and I only drank water and Gatorade before they took me there."

No, Pierce had probably not wanted to mix caffeine with her drug regimen, Eve thought bitterly. "I guess you were too young to develop an addiction to coffee. I keep forgetting that you were only a teen-ager when you had your accident." She paused. "What were you studying here?"

"Everything. Billy told me to catch up and learn how the world works these days." She made a face. "I don't like it very much. Maybe I didn't notice all the corruption and bad stuff that was going on when I was growing up, but it seems as if it must be worse now."

"Or maybe just more publicized. Media is all around us."

"And computers. I was surprised how easy it was to work the one in the library." She added, "Facebook. It's very . . . intimate."

"Only if you want it that way. Your choice. It can get in your way. It interferes with my work, so I usually ignore it."

"What is your work?"

"I'm a forensic sculptor."

"What's that?"

"I reconstruct skulls. You're not really interested in what I do, are you?"

"I suppose not." She took the coffee and poured it back into the carafe. "Or if I am, it's not because it has anything to do with you. I'm just curious. I'm curious about everything. At first, I was only doing what Billy told me to do, but the more I learned, the more I wanted to learn. It was like being . . . drunk."

"If you know how that feels, you must have been drinking more than water and Gatorade when you were a teenager."

"I went to parties." She frowned. "I had a friend . . . She laughed a lot . . ." She was silent, then shook her head. "I can't remember her name."

"I'm sure it will come back to you," Eve said gently.

"No, you're not sure. How could you be sure when I'm not? But I think it will. I hope it will." She took down cups from the cabinet. "It makes me angry that I can't remember everything. I feel cheated." She glanced at Eve. "You believe that this Dr. Gelber was responsible for making me forget things?"

Eve nodded.

"Drugs?"

"Maybe partially, but I'm leaning toward hypnosis."

She shook her head. "I don't know if I believe in hypnosis. Do you?"

"I don't know everything that it can accomplish, but I do believe that hypnosis can work. Gelber is evidently a very skilled practitioner, and he spent many sessions with you."

"Then wouldn't I remember him?" She shook her head. "Not if he didn't want me to, right? But why wouldn't he? And why would he want me to forget everything before I came to the hospital?"

"The reason on the chart was removal of psychological trauma."

"Billy says that I was injured in a ski accident. What kind of psychological trauma would I get from that? It doesn't make sense."

"I agree."

She gave Eve a disgusted look. "Is that all you're going to say? What help are you?"

"You said you didn't want my help."

"I don't. But you might as well be useful if you're going to stick around for a while."

"I'll keep that in mind." She added quietly, "But you have to come to terms with the fact that we've been thrown in this brouhaha together, and we have to cooperate. You appear to have some lingering resentment toward our mother because she abandoned you. Maybe you include me under that same umbrella. I should point out that since I had no idea you even existed, that's totally unreasonable."

"I don't have to be reasonable." Her lips tightened. "I'm mentally incompetent. Ask Pierce."

"Don't give me that excuse. You can't have it both ways, Beth."

"I can do whatever I want to do." She didn't speak for a moment as she screwed the top back on the carafe. "Okay, maybe you're right. I've just realized since I've been out of the hospital and free how alone I've been all these years. I could have used a friend to help me. What do they call it? To watch my back? But no one was there. I was alone. You may not be to blame, but it's hard for me to accept that there was no one there for me. Someone *should* have been there." She impatiently shook her head. "Listen to me. I'm whining. I've always hated whiners."

Eve smiled faintly. "I believe you have cause to complain. But suppose we strike a truce. We both have a motive to get you out of this mess. Let's work our way through it, then I'll go away and won't bother you again."

"I guess that would be okay." She picked up the carafe and turned toward the door. Then she turned back and gazed at Eve. "But what if I don't want you to go away then?"

Eve blinked. "What?"

"Never mind. That just came out. I don't know why." Her lips twisted. "It's probably my lack of 'reason' again. Sometimes my mind is just a jumble, and I wonder if Pierce was right about my being crazy."

"You're not crazy. And we all have moments of confusion and 'jumble.' Don't you remember that from the time before your accident?"

"I don't remember much about my thought processes. I don't remember much of anything except that I was happy most of the time. And that I always wanted to be first at everything."

"Competitiveness isn't bad. It can be very healthy. And, evidently, you were pretty good at everything you did."

"You bet I was." She started for the door. "But that's in the past. I mustn't think of that now."

"Why not? Why turn your back?"

"Because it's not healthy to—" She broke off. "It seems as if I've heard that before."

"You might have heard it. Posthypnotic suggestion?"

"Maybe. Or just something else that doesn't make sense." She added fiercely, "But it doesn't make sense for anyone to try to kill me either. Or to try to kill Billy. It shouldn't have happened. It wasn't right. And if you want to help me, I'll let you do it." She strode down the hall toward the library. "Why not?"

Eve heard her talking to Newell as she

followed her down the hall. Beth was such a combination of passion, bewilderment, and suppressed anger that it was like being next to a lightning rod during a thunderstorm. You never knew which strike was going to hit, but you were sure that one of them would. In that short conversation, Eve had learned a great deal about Beth. She had expected her to be vulnerable and weak, and she was neither. There was a fragility that was balanced by strength and intelligence. Though a few of her impulsive remarks might have been spoken by the teenager she had been before her normal life was cut short, that was to be expected. She'd had no mature experiences to hone away the rough edges and teach her discretion and diplomacy.

Not a bad thing, Eve thought ruefully. Discretion and diplomacy were only armor, and she'd be able to get to know Beth much faster if she didn't have them to hide behind.

And why did she want to get to know her? A truce would surely not require it.

It didn't matter. No matter what resentments and complexities made up their fledgling relationship, Eve knew that she was going to be driven to explore the person that Beth had been before and after Pierce had gotten his hands on her.

Her phone rang.

Joe.

"I'm parking the car down the street, so it won't be noticed. It will take me a few minutes to get to the front door."

"I'll be waiting there to unlock the door and turn off the alarm." She hung up and turned to see Beth standing in the library doorway. "It's only Joe. He's on his way here."

Beth followed her down the hall toward the front door. "Billy called him your significant other. That means you're not married, right?"

"That's right."

"But you sleep together and have sex?"

"That's right, too, but it's considered rude to describe exactly the nature of an intimate relationship."

"I didn't describe it exactly. If I had, it would have been pornographic, wouldn't it?" She stopped at the door and punched in the security code on the panel beside it. "And I didn't mean to be rude, I was just curious."

"You didn't offend me." She opened the front door. "I was just telling you what most people might think. You said that Billy told you that you had to catch up with what was going on in the world today."

"For God's sake, it's not as if I didn't know about sex before the accident. After all, I wasn't in a convent. I was just unfamiliar with the term and wanted to be sure that I had gotten it right."

Eve's gaze narrowed on her face. "And perhaps you wanted me to be a little uncomfortable?"

"Maybe." She met her gaze. "And maybe I was jealous."

"What?"

"Sex. I've never gone to bed with anyone. I was always into sports, and I never even dated. I thought there was plenty of time. But there wasn't, was there?"

Another important element of life the Beth had missed, Eve thought. "Not for the girl you were, but it's not as if you can't make it up. Sex isn't only for the very young." She grinned. "If it were, I'd be feeling pretty damn cheated myself."

"You like it?"

Eve caught sight of Joe, who had entered the far courtyard and was walking toward the house. "Oh, yes, I like it very much indeed."

"I can see that you do." Beth's gaze was focused on Eve's face before it shifted to Joe. "He's very . . . good-looking. No, he's just . . . I don't know, but I can see why you'd want to have sex with him."

"I'm glad that you approve of my choice," Eve said dryly. "Not that it matters."

"Would you mind if I had sex with him?"

Eve's eyes widened with shock. "I beg your pardon."

"You would mind." She shrugged. "I just thought that it might be okay. I think I'd like it with him, too. From what I've been watching on TV, people seem to be having sex with everyone these days, and no one seems too bothered about it."

"You've been watching the wrong programs. There is such a thing as fidelity, Beth."

"Forget it. It was just a thought. Sex is probably going to be awkward for me at first, and I didn't want to embarrass myself with a man I cared about. I thought I'd get it out of the way."

"Not with Joe," Eve said firmly. "And I'd

think you'd be thinking about how to keep alive instead of your first roll in the hay."

"I'm going to stay alive. But I can't close everything else away from me." Her voice vibrated with intensity. "You don't understand. Just staying alive isn't enough. I want to *live*. I want to drain the cup. I want to feel and know."

And who could blame her? That young Beth in the photograph, whom Eve had thought so vibrantly alive, had been imprisoned and was finally free and wanting to taste every morsel of life.

"You're wrong, I do understand."

"Do you?" Beth whispered. Then she smiled brilliantly. "I think you do."

Eve chuckled. "But you still can't have Joe." She turned to Joe, who was now only a few yards away, and said, "Come and meet my sister, Joe. This is Beth."

CHAPTER

11

It was the bitch!

Drogan focused his binoculars on the two women who stood in the doorway of the house as Quinn approached them. The first woman was the one he'd followed with Joe Quinn. The other was Beth Avery. He recognized her not only from the photo that Pierce had given him but also the glimpse he'd had of her in that hospital room. He would have known her anywhere. He had been thinking of her, lusting for too long after the moment he'd have her in his sights.

She was smiling faintly at Quinn as she

took a step back into the house. He lost sight of her.

Again.

But not for long, bitch. I'm not going to lose you again. You think that Quinn and those others can protect you? Now it's only a matter of time. When you least expect it, I'll be there. Did you see what I did to Newell? That's nothing to how I'll cut you. Pierce wants it to look like an accident, but that's not going to happen. I've waited too long for you. My dear Mama Zela taught me how to make death take a long time, and I've missed those nights in the bayou with only the fire and the prey and the Snake God.

He wriggled down the hill to the trees and stood up as soon as he had cover. He'd wait until they got settled, then start reconnoitering the property to see if he could find a way into the house that wouldn't set off the alarms. If that wasn't possible, he'd just stake it out until they left the place. Then he'd pounce and—

His phone was vibrating.

If it was Pierce, he wasn't about to answer. Not until the bitch had been put down in the way he wanted.

It wasn't Pierce. He looked at the ID in shock. What the hell?

He slowly pushed the access button. "Well, what a surprise. I wasn't expecting you."

"You were longer than I thought you'd be," Eve said as she closed the front door after Joe entered. "What's wrong?"

Joe shrugged. "Maybe nothing. I just decided to be extra careful. I needed to reassure myself that—" He stopped and glanced at Beth.

"It's okay," Eve said. "You're not going to have to worry about her crumbling away or crawling under the bed to shiver in terror because of Drogan. She met Newell and me in the hall with a Luger."

"Really?" He tilted his head. "Interesting."

"Not really," Beth said. "I knew enough to pull the trigger, but I wasn't sure I could hit anything."

"It's not difficult to hit a target if you're close enough," Joe said. "Just keep on shooting, and you'll have it covered."

Beth smiled. "I'll remember that. But I'm glad I didn't have to shoot at Eve and Billy."

Her smile faded. "What did you want to tell Eve that you were afraid would scare me?"

"Nothing concrete." He looked at Eve. "But Drogan's out there. I can feel it."

"But you didn't see him?" Beth asked.

"That doesn't matter," Eve said absently. "I'd trust Joe's instincts every time. So what do we do, Joe? I don't believe it's likely that Drogan will bring in the police or some help from the hospital."

"I don't either. I think he's a loner. But if he's a professional, then he'll have contacts and might decide to call in someone else that he knows he can dominate." He shrugged. "Which means that we can't stay here too long. My bet is that he'll try to find a way to get to her. We'll have to find another safe house."

"Newell needs rest," Eve said. "How much time do we have?"

"Your guess is as good as mine," Joe said. "I'll go out in an hour or so and see if I can track Drogan down."

"Don't do that," Beth said sharply. "I saw what he did to Billy. That's not going to happen again. I'm not going to be to blame for anyone else's being hurt because of me. Just find a way for me to leave here."

"I'll do what I can," Joe said. "In the meantime, I'll do what I think is right." He met her gaze. "Eve wants you safe. That means you *will* be safe. Back off."

Beth's hands clenched into fists as she stared at him for a moment. Then she turned on her heel and strode down the hall toward the library.

"Not what I expected," Joe murmured as he watched her disappear. "She won't be easy to manipulate."

"I don't want to manipulate her, dammit," Eve said through set teeth. "For years she's been stuffed in that hospital bed like a lifeless doll, with Pierce and his buddies trying to keep her quiet and not bother him and the Averys. She's been manipulated too much already."

"Shh." He brushed his lips across her cheek. "Wrong word. I didn't mean to stir you up. It seems she's arousing your sense of protectiveness. She may not need it. I notice that she has a mind of her own."

"That they tried to take away from her." She shook her head. "I can imagine how I would have felt in the same circumstances, and I wasn't like her. She was an athlete, and you could see from that photo how much she loved life." The anger was growing as she thought about it. "Hell, no, she's not going to be easy. She's only been out of that place for a few days, and she's already questioning, probing, trying to get back a little of what's been stolen from her." She suddenly smiled. "Actually, I think she's going to get back more than a little. She asked if she could go to bed with you, Joe."

"What?"

"She liked the look of you and thought that it would be better to have her first sex experience with someone she didn't really care about, in case she wasn't good at it."

"Okay," he said slowly. "Did you tell her that one glance doesn't guarantee a safe or happy experience?"

"No, I was flattered that she thought my choice of you guaranteed that for her."

"Oh, so you decided to give me to her for the experiment?"

She smiled. "No way in hell. Let her find her own man."

"Good." He kissed her. "And I'm sure she's not going to have any problem. She's exceptionally attractive."

She nodded. "Sleeping Beauty. Only very much awake and alive now." She

SLEEP NO MORE   321

started toward the library. "And we've got to keep her that way."

"You said you think Pierce's orders were to keep her quiet. I don't believe that was a slip of the tongue."

"No, don't you think the same thing? It's all too pat. A mysterious accident, and she's whisked thousands of miles away to a hospital where the Averys establish a connection with a rising young doctor who soars even higher under their patronage. She's kept there for years and virtually buried away from the Averys, the media, and everyone who has ever known her. Then there's the business with Dr. Gelber. Another layer in the attempt to silence her." She met Joe's gaze as they paused at the library door. "I think she saw something or found out something that made her presence in the Averys' lives very inconvenient."

"And they chose to send her to that hospital rather than kill her? If what she saw was that dangerous, wouldn't they have wanted a permanent solution?"

"She was an Avery. Family might have made a difference." She frowned. "I just don't know. And I don't know what changed that made Beth a luxury they couldn't afford. Why bring in a hired killer after all these years?"

"Then maybe we'd better ask Beth a few questions." Joe stepped aside to let Eve precede him into the room. "Not that I have much hope."

"You think I saw something I shouldn't have seen?" Beth asked blankly. "What?"

"If we knew that, then we wouldn't be asking you," Eve said dryly. "I know you said you had very little memory of the time before the hospital, but I was hoping if you tried . . . You did say that things were coming back to you."

"Not about the accident. I guess it was too traumatic for any memories to survive. Or maybe it was just that it was so quick that there isn't a memory."

"Of maybe it was that all of those, logical, fine reasons were suggested by Dr. Gelber," Newell said as he lifted his coffee cup to his lips. "What about before the accident? You were at a lodge skiing?"

"Yes. My roommate from school, Cara, and I were up in the mountains practicing for the big ski competition."

"Cara?" Joe repeated. "I didn't hear any

mention of a Cara when I was talking to the people at the lodge about your accident. Only about you, Beth."

"Then they must have made a mistake. After all, it was a long time ago. Cara was there with me." She stopped hesitating, then said firmly, "No, dammit, she was there. I know it. I won't doubt myself. I'm not that person I was in the hospital. Cara Sandler was there with me."

"Easy," Eve said. "We're not suggesting that you're having hallucinations because of the drugs. We're just trying to get to the bottom of this mess. Is that your friend you mentioned to me?"

"No, Cara wasn't a friend, just my roommate. Sometimes, I didn't even like her."

"Was Cara skiing with you that day?"

"No." She thought for a moment. "She said that her skis needed waxing, and she'd see me at lunch. I didn't care. I'd rather have skied alone anyway. I'm a better skier than Cara, and I'd have to wait for her."

"That must be annoying. You must like her more than you said to put up with it," Joe said.

"She's okay." She shrugged. "I liked her when she was first assigned to my room, but she was nosy, and she kept asking me questions. But I had to put up with it because the school wouldn't let me go anywhere alone. They said it wasn't safe."

"What kind of questions?" Eve asked.

"All kinds," she said vaguely. "About the places I'd visited, what I knew about Rick's mother, lots of questions about Rick."

"Rick Avery?" Eve paused. "Your father?"

Beth nodded. "Only he didn't seem like a father. Other girls' fathers were all boring. Rick was my best friend."

"Did your best friend ever visit you at the hospital?"

"No, I don't think he did." Then she shook her head. "I'd remember if he'd been there. Even if my head was messed up from the drugs, I'd remember Rick."

Because she loved him, Eve thought, as she saw Beth's glowing expression. That love couldn't have been more evident. What kind of man was this Rick Avery, who could charm Sandra and now his daughter, Beth, into forgiving whatever sins he committed?

"Stop looking at me like that." Beth's chin lifted defiantly. "I know what you're thinking. But if Rick didn't come to see me, he must have had a good reason. Maybe Pierce told him it would be bad for me. I could understand that. Rick would never want to hurt me."

"I'm not going to argue with you. I don't know Rick Avery," Eve said. "And it's natural for a daughter to defend her father. I'm just trying to put the pieces together. Rick Avery may be a very big piece." She paused. "You were raised by a Robert and Laura Avery until you went to school in Geneva. Did you always think that they were your parents?"

"No, they had the same name but they told me that I was to call them Aunt Laura and Uncle Robert since they'd only been hired to take care of me until I was old enough to go to school." She grimaced. "They said we should all be grateful to Nelda Avery for being so generous."

"Were they good to you?"

"They weren't bad to me. They did their duty. It was clear to me even as a little child that I mustn't expect any more than that." Beth shook her head. "And I always knew Rick was my father. He'd come to see me and bring me presents and take me to amusement parks. When I was old enough to understand, he told me that I was his little girl, but it had to be a special secret between us so that no one would say bad things about me."

"Or about him?"

"He loved me. He protected me. All the other kids at school had parents, but I didn't care. Every now and then, Rick would come, and it would be wonderful."

"Was Rick at the lodge that weekend?"

She frowned. "No, I told you I went there with Cara." She lifted her cup to her lips. "But that's all I remember."

"Except that she was always asking you questions."

"Not that day." She thought about it. "It's strange that it seems like yesterday. But I guess it was to me. All the other days were like shadows . . ."

"Cara didn't ask you questions that morning," Joe prompted.

"No, she seemed abstracted. She wasn't like me. She liked to have a lot of people around all the time. Maybe she was bored."

"It's possible."

"Why are you asking me all these questions about Cara?"

"Because she's the person who wasn't

there," Joe said. "Or no one remembers she was there. Intriguing."

"Are you going to call the lodge back?" Eve asked.

He nodded. "And see if I can find Cara Sandler and get a statement. What do you know about her background, Beth?"

"Not much. She was from Vancouver, Canada. Her mother was dead, and her father was an important politician. She never talked about either one."

"You didn't like Cara, but did you spend time with other people from school?" Eve asked.

"Of course I did." She lifted her chin. "I was smart, head of my class. And I was very good at sports. I won all kinds of awards in swimming and skiing. Everyone likes a winner."

"No, I mean someone you liked and who liked you because you just hit it off. Not because you were a star."

"Perhaps. I don't remember." She moistened her lips. "I guess you noticed that I'm a little— It wasn't that I didn't want to have friends. It was just safer to keep to myself."

Safe because she had been jerked away

from her foster parents when she was scarcely more than a toddler and been sent to one foreign school after another. It was no wonder that she had been afraid to form attachments. "Yes, I can see that." Eve smiled faintly. "I have a tendency in that direction, too."

"Do you?" Beth's expression was suddenly eager. "I wouldn't think that you'd—you seem to be so—" Her expression changed, became closed. "But what do I know? I don't know you at all, do I?"

Eve's brows rose. "And you don't appear to be too upset about that."

"I didn't say that I didn't want to know you," Beth said quickly. "Or maybe I did, but I—" She turned to Newell. "Do you want another cup of coffee, Billy?"

He shook his head. "I still have a bit." His brows rose. "And I don't appreciate your using me as a distraction when you get yourself into verbal jams."

"I wasn't doing that." She sighed. "Or maybe I was. I'm sorry, Billy."

"You're forgiven. I just wanted you to recognize that you have to face things head-on and not try to hide behind me." He added softly, "I know it's hard, but you've gone through tougher experiences. Remember when you were getting off the drugs and had to keep anyone from knowing that your body was being torn apart? I was very proud of you, Beth."

She glanced away from him. "And you should have been. I felt as if I were dying." She hesitated, then turned to Eve and met her gaze. "He's right. I was trying to hide from telling the truth. I can't do that again. Life is too short, and too much of it has already been taken away from me. I won't waste one word, one sentence, trying to protect or lie to myself or anyone else."

"Heaven help us," Eve said. "That could get all of us into bad trouble. I remember a Jim Carrey comedy that stressed the dangers of complete truth."

"Too bad. I'm not good at doing things halfway. You saw that when I started stuttering and running to Billy." She drew a deep breath. "Because I didn't want to admit that I . . . . might want to know what kind of person you are and if there's really any bond between sisters." She added in a rush, "I've told you I'm very curious. I know those kinds of stories about family closeness are probably bogus. After all, people are just people. But I've never had a family, so I'd just like to make sure that's true."

Eve was touched. Those words had been poignantly vulnerable, and it must have been difficult for Beth to open herself by speaking them. "Yes, people are just people. Sometimes outsiders become closer than blood relatives. I have an adopted daughter, Jane, who is my true daughter and best friend in everything but blood." She held up her cup in a half toast. "But I'm curious, too. It wouldn't hurt to explore our relationship a little."

Beth gave a sigh of relief. "Then that's settled." She turned to Joe. "So what's next? When can you get me out of here?"

"Not tonight. I'm going to do a little scouting. Then I'm going to go over some more of the records Pierce was keeping on you. I'll wait until tomorrow morning to call the lodge again."

"Tomorrow afternoon, then." She jumped to her feet. "Billy, you need to get some sleep. There's a maid's room at the end of the hall near the kitchen that has a bed and attached bathroom." She was pulling him to his feet and throwing his arm around her shoulders. "That way you won't have to climb the stairs. Eve, you and Joe can have the bedroom at the top of the stairs. I changed the sheets and got it ready to sleep in when I first got here. But then I found out I couldn't bear to curl up in a bed, so I came down and slept on the couch." She was half leading, half carrying Newell toward the door. "I guess it's because I practically lived in a bed at Seahaven. I wonder if I'll ever be able to sleep in a bed again."

"Beth, you don't need to help me," Newell said. "For God's sake, I can walk."

"You didn't need to help me, either," Beth said. "You could have turned your back and left me in that place. Instead, you got me away from Pierce and got yourself chopped up doing it. Now shut up and let me get you to that room. Lean on me. I'm strong, Billy."

"Yes, you are." He smiled down at her. "I knew it the moment I saw you. It was just waiting to come out."

"I'll help." Joe came and took his other arm. "It will be quicker."

"I didn't notice your being this solicitous after you got me away from the hospital," Newell said dryly. "I was on my own."

"That's what you wanted," Joe said. "And I wasn't sure how much of a victim you were." He looked over his shoulder at Eve. "Take my computer up to the bedroom, will you?"

Eve nodded. "Be careful out there, Joe."

"I doubt if Drogan is going to be on the attack unless I get lucky and locate him. His objective is Beth right now. He won't want to scare her off by slitting my throat."

"That's comforting," Eve said as she started up the stairs. "That's a pretty big 'unless' you just threw out. Good night, Beth, Newell."

"Good night." Beth's voice was surprised. Then repeated, "Good night, Eve."

"Why do you sound so startled?" Eve asked over her shoulder.

"They never said good night to me at the hospital. I guess they thought I was so hazy from the drugs that I wouldn't understand it. Or maybe they didn't really consider me a person. I guess I was just a job, or someone to—" She shook her head as she walked with Billy down the hall. "That sounds like whining again, and it's not really important. It's crazy that all the little things are bombarding me. They didn't say good night . . ."

Those little things were bombarding Eve, too, she thought as she watched Beth walk away from her. And the bombardment of small slights and sharp pinpricks were causing the anger to begin to build within her. The loneliness, the neglect, the careless disregard of humanity. She wanted to strike out.

Get a grip. As Beth said, this was a small thing in the big picture. Think about those years of captivity and subjugation. Focus the anger on Pierce or that monster Drogan or the Avery family, who seemed to be standing in the shadows, directing the action.

Her hand tightened on Joe's computer as she turned and started up the stairs.

Not for long.

We're going to bring you bastards down.

"Will you be okay?" Beth asked as she opened the door of the maid's bedroom. "Do you need me to do anything else, Billy?"

"Hell, no." His lips indented at the corners

with the faintest touch of amusement. "What would you do, undress me and put me to bed?"

"If that's what you need."

"It's not what I need." He reached out and touched her cheek. "I'm doing fine. Stop worrying. Tell her, Quinn."

"He can take it from this point," Joe said. "And you might damage his pride if you carry it any further. Marines tend to be a little touchy in that category."

Beth frowned. "Marines?"

"You didn't know Newell was in the Marines?"

"No, I didn't know. He didn't tell me."

"It wasn't important." Newell gave her a little push and went into the bedroom. "I'll see you in the morning. If you need me, come and get me. I'll be fine after a couple hours' sleep. Don't you go too far away from the house, Quinn. She's more important than taking down Drogan." The door closed behind him.

Beth hesitated, staring at the panels of the door.

"He'll be fine, Beth," Joe said. "You can't do anything more for him. Now go and get some rest yourself." He turned toward the door. "But first, walk with me to the door and give me the security code so that I don't have to disturb anyone when I need to come back in."

"It wouldn't disturb me." She turned and walked beside him toward the front door. "I don't sleep well anyway. Maybe I got too much rest during the last years."

"Somehow, I don't think that would have anything to do with it. You'll probably straighten out once your body adjusts to the new rhythm."

She shrugged. "It doesn't matter. I don't seem to be tired, and that means I can do more."

"More what?"

"Learning, absorbing," She paused. "Living." They had reached the door, and she swiftly punched in the security code. "It's a sequence of eight numbers starting with two and—"

"Continuing with three, six, eleven, four, nine, fourteen, one."

Her eyes widened. "You remember that from my entering it just one time?"

"No, I caught the last four numbers when

you set the code when I came into the house. I only had to concentrate on the first four."

"You have a good memory."

"Training." He smiled. "And concentration. Concentration is very valuable. Remind me to tell you someday about a lady who has recently reinforced just how valuable to both Eve and me." He opened the door. "Set the security panel behind me. Good night, Beth."

"I'll be awake when you come back." She moistened her lips. "I have a favor to ask of you."

"Oh?" His expression was suddenly wary. "Is that right?"

She suddenly realized what he was thinking. "Eve told you? I didn't think she'd do that." She threw back her head and laughed. "You shouldn't jump to conclusions, and there's no reason for you to be uneasy. It wasn't anything personal."

"I'd think that the proposition was intensely personal. At least to me." He tilted his head. "And I believe you and Eve have already discussed this. Why bring it up again?"

"I told you not to jump to conclusions."

She made a dismissing gesture. "I gave that idea up when it seemed to disturb her. I just thought it would save me time and trouble. From what I remember, everyone said most guys don't care who they screw."

"I'm not most guys," he said. "So what is this favor?"

"I want you to tell me about Eve," she said. "I want to know everything about her. I figure that you'd know more than anyone else since you're lovers."

"Why don't you ask her?"

"She wouldn't tell me everything. There are things she wouldn't consider important. A person looking from a distance sees a different picture." She paused, then said haltingly, "I've never had a family. Rick is more my friend than family. I kept telling myself when I was growing up that I didn't need anyone but myself. That I'd be just fine as long as I worked hard and made sure I was the best at everything."

"Everyone likes a winner?" Joe quoted her words.

"Yeah, but I'm beginning to feel . . . different. If I was wrong, then Eve could be important to me. I don't want to blow it. She's not like me, whose life just stopped.

She's been out in the world." She stopped, thinking about it. "And I think she's been hurt and has scars. I don't want to open wounds. She'd hate me."

"No, she wouldn't." Joe smiled. "But I'm surprised you've been able to sense that about her. Very perceptive, Beth."

"Not really. I keep stumbling and making mistakes, but I believe I'm not wrong about Eve. Maybe there's something about that family-bond thing." She looked him directly in the eye. "So will you help me, Joe?"

He studied her for a long moment. "As long as you don't demand any intimate details. I'm not comfortable about your idea of what's personal."

She gave a sigh of relief. "Okay, that would probably make me embarrassed anyway. It always did when my schoolmates described their sex with guys. I always wondered if some of the things they did weren't made up. They would have had to be acrobats."

"At that age, acrobatics are entirely possible. It gets more refined and satisfactory with time. Is that all? May I go now?"

She shook her head. "Billy. I didn't

know he was a Marine. I don't really know anything about him. It was always all about me."

"You were the prime objective. I'm certain Newell wasn't offended."

"But I should have asked. He made me talk about my life before I came to the hospital, and I never asked him any questions. How selfish could I be? He got me off those drugs. He saved my life, Joe."

"There's a good chance that's true. But if you want to know all about Newell, you may have to ask him yourself. I can only give you the bare bones, and I think some of his dossier was probably doctored to keep Pierce from knowing that he was being investigated."

"Then give me the bare bones. I'll work it out from there." She paused. "And I want to know about you, too, Joe. You're important to Eve." She frowned. "That didn't sound right. It's not that you're not important in your own right. You seem to be a very formidable—"

"Enough." He made a face. "I'm getting out of here before you add anyone else to the list."

"I don't know anyone else."

"You did it again. You managed to disarm me just when I was becoming pissed off at you." He started across the courtyard. "Go back to the library. I'll face your interrogation after I expend some energy trying to track Drogan."

Beth watched until he disappeared into the trees to the side of the courtyard before shutting the door. He was moving swiftly, and there was a sleek litheness to his carriage, a leashed eagerness.

A man on the hunt. No fear. No hesitation. He couldn't wait to track down Drogan. He was a police detective, but there was no cool, analytical demeanor. She suddenly shivered as she realized that he appeared more deadly and dangerous than Drogan. She was learning more about him by watching him during these moments than she probably would by anything he would tell her. He would be like Eve and not be able or willing to share the view from the horizon. She would just have to put the pieces together and figure out how she could deal with them.

But that instant when she'd realized how dangerous Joe Quinn could be had disconcerted her. If he was deadly toward

Drogan, could he also be a threat to Eve? How did Beth know who was bad or good? She had almost no practical experience, and there were so many dangers in this world.

She closed the door of the library and tucked herself in the leather chair in which Billy had been sitting. Her hand instinctively went to clasp the gold key at her throat. It always made her feel safe when she was most scared and confused. Rick had given the necklace to her on her sixteenth birthday and told her that she should wear it forever to remind her that he loved her.

She had been surprised that she'd still had it around her neck after the years on the sedatives. During the last few months, when she'd been totally drug-free, she'd noticed the nurses carefully put it back on her after they bathed her. Rick must have told them to do it. Which only proved that he still cared for her and had nothing to do with Pierce or that horrible Stella woman who had sometimes taken care of her.

But Eve and Joe had both been suspicious of Rick.

Forget it. Beth knew the truth about him. She would just have to explain and convince them of their mistake. Rick was the one good thing in that old life she could not do without. She had many changes she wanted to make in the way she lived her life. She wanted to reach out, instead of closing herself away from people.

She wanted to reach out to Eve.

One step at a time.

For the moment, she would sit there and wait for Joe Quinn to tell her how she could begin those steps.

Drogan had been in these trees.

Joe's hunch about Drogan's being in the long driveway of the house next door to the Tudor had paid off.

Joe knelt and shined his flashlight on the prints in the earth. One knee indentation, one foot bracing. Drogan had been kneeling there.

He would have had a good view of the courtyard from that spot.

Was he still around?

No car was parked in the trees. If there had been one there, he'd moved it.

Where?

Find out.

Fifteen minutes later, Joe found the car

in the driveway of the third estate around the curve of the road. A red Lamborghini was in the driveway, but in the trees to the left was parked a tan Toyota rental car with plates from a dealer in Santa Barbara.

He glided forward. No one in the driver's seat. Get inside the car and see if he could find any papers or evidence that would link—

The red Lamborghini roared to life and was barreling toward him!

A bullet creased Joe's cheek, and the car clipped his hip as he jumped to the side.

Pain.

Ignore it. He drew his .38 and fired off a shot that smashed the sports car's side mirror and ricocheted to hit Drogan's hand on the steering wheel.

Joe heard a spate of curses, then a bullet struck the ground next to him. He rolled to the passenger side behind the protection of the Toyota.

But Drogan had already reached the road, and the sports car was screeching around the bend.

And the lights were coming on in the house behind him, dammit. The last thing

Joe needed was to be found on the property and accused of being a car thief.

He got to his feet and limped into the trees. It wasn't likely that they'd be searching for the man who had stolen that Lamborghini to be on foot. But he had to get back to the house before there was an uproar in the neighborhood. The owners would report the theft to the police, and they'd be out to intercept Drogan.

But Drogan wouldn't risk being picked up. He'd abandon that car as soon as he could, and he no longer had his own rental to fall back on. Joe had come close to nailing the bastard, and he was mad as hell he'd blown it. But there were a few good results from a lousy evening. Drogan had a bullet in his hand, no car, and was in no position to go after Beth Avery at the moment.

And he'd bet that Drogan was going to be even more angry than Joe as he tried desperately to get away and cover his tracks.

He was going to *kill* Quinn.

Drogan clutched the steering wheel while he tried to wrap his handkerchief around his bloody thumb with the other. He'd probably lose the thumb if he couldn't get to a doctor in time. His teeth clenched as he tied the handkerchief above the wound.

Son of a bitch. Son of a bitch. Son of a bitch.

He had to get out of this car.

He couldn't risk driving it any longer. This was a high-security area, and Highway Patrol would be breathing down his neck within minutes. The Lamborghini would be as noticeable as a flashing red light.

Get rid of the car.

Find some schmuck and force him to take him to a doctor.

Then find a way to get back here before Quinn took off with Beth Avery.

And find the most painful way on the face of the earth to kill the bastard. Destroy everything and everyone he cared about before his eyes, then take his time killing Quinn himself. Before it had been just a question of eliminating a cop who had gotten in his way, annoying but not particularly important.

But now it was very important. Now it was almost as important as killing Beth Avery.

And the woman who had been with Quinn at the house? He'd taken a photo of her earlier in the evening and been going to transmit it to Pierce for him to attempt an ID.

Do you sleep with her, Quinn?

Too bad. You'd better get used to sleeping alone for the little time you have left.

CHAPTER

12

Beth straightened up in her chair as Joe came into the library. "What happened to you?"

"Drogan." He limped toward the TV and turned on the news station. "It's the second time I screwed up and let him get away. What the hell is wrong with me?"

"You're not perfect?" She glanced at the TV. "What are you trying to watch?"

"Drogan made off with a red Lamborghini. There's bound to be a pursuit by the local police." He began channel flipping. "With all these twenty-four/seven news stations, one of them should be covering it." He leaned closer to the set. "There!"

He was looking at the shot of a red Lamborghini parked in the driveway of a substantial brick home. There was a crowd of police and media personnel swarming around it.

"Abandoned?" Beth asked.

"Yes, and it was out of Seventeen Mile Drive. That may be good for us."

"How?"

"The search won't be as extensive in this area."

"There will be a search?"

"You bet your life. This area is pure money and political pull. They take care of their own." He glanced at the location where the sports car had been found and typed it into his phone. "But they'll grab the rental car that he left a few houses around the bend and check this area, too. Which means that we can't move too soon. There will be an alert out and probably media on every corner for a night or two."

"Will they search this house?"

"Not unless they think they have a reason. This house is supposed to be vacant and has a security guard checking it periodically. If we stay inside and keep a low profile, we'll probably be okay until it's safe to leave. In the meantime, I'll locate another safe house for you." He added grimly, "And do a little more-in-depth study about Drogan and the Averys."

"Should we wake Eve and Billy?"

"Not until we have to. What good would it do? I ran upstairs and checked on her, and Eve had managed to drift off."

"I'd want to know what was happening."

"And so will Eve. But she can find out after she gets a little rest." He frowned. "But Eve has my computer."

"There's one over there on the desk. Can you use it?"

He nodded. "I'd rather have my own, but I have the thumb drive." He moved across the room and sat down at the desk. "If you're going to curl up on that couch and go to sleep, do it. I can see by the screen, and I'm turning out the light."

"Why? I told you that you can't see through those drapes."

"I'm not taking a chance. There will be intense, not casual scrutiny." He took out the thumb drive. "But I want to get as much information as I can while we're having to wait to get moving. I have an idea that Drogan is going to be moving at full speed from now on. I glimpsed his face after I put a bullet in his hand."

"A bullet? You didn't mention you shot him." She was looking at the red streak on his cheek. "Was that caused by a bullet?"

"Yes." He inserted the thumb drive. "And I only shot him, I didn't kill him."

"So it wasn't worthwhile telling anyone. It wasn't important."

"It was important. It had the same effect as waving a red cape at a bull. And I didn't follow through and put the bastard down."

Violence, she thought with a shudder. Bullets and rage and Joe Quinn ready and willing to kill a man because he'd become involved in this hideous nightmare in which she'd become entangled.

"It's too late, Beth," Joe said quietly. He had looked up and seen her expression. "The game's begun, and we all have to play by the rules."

"I don't understand games like this. But you like them, don't you?"

He shrugged. "There's a certain amount of excitement involved. I admit to having a few savage impulses. In time, you might discover you have a few yourself. You're intensely competitive, and that's a likely sign." He smiled. "And you pulled a gun on Eve and Newell."

"And it scared me to death."

"The fear will go away, but the power remains. How do you feel right now? Are you angry with me?"

She was silent a moment. "I have no right to be angry. You could have been killed because of me. I should be grateful."

"And are you?"

She was silent again. "Yes, but I don't want you to do it again. I'd feel guilty that—"

"It's my choice. Remember that, Beth. No guilt. People make choices."

"Bullshit."

He chuckled. "I don't have time to argue with you now. Work it out for yourself."

"I will." She curled up on the leather couch and drew the throw over her. "But I'm tired of everyone's risking their necks and treating me as if I were still sedated and almost comatose in that hospital. I'm going to help myself, Joe."

"Fine." He was pulling up records on the computer. "When something comes up, I'll let you know."

"You don't mean that." She turned on her side on the couch to look at him. "But I do. There's so much I have to learn. I'm strong, but Drogan almost killed me that night at the hospital. You know all kinds of ways to fight people. Will you teach me?"

"If I have time," he said, his gaze on the computer screen.

"Make time," she said firmly. "I bet you taught Eve to protect herself. Well, she's like you, she's going to stay beside me and run risks no matter what I say. Wouldn't it be better if I knew how to protect both of us?"

He lifted his gaze. "You're very clever. You know exactly where to strike."

"It's easy. You love her. I don't know much about feelings like that, but I know that you want her safe. You wouldn't want me to die, but I don't really matter to you. Not compared to what you feel for her. Will you teach me so that she has a better chance of surviving if she stays with me?"

He smiled. "As I said, clever. Yes, I'd do that if we didn't have to move so fast."

"It wouldn't take much of your time to show me basics. I've always been a fast learner. And I'll have to learn even faster now. I have so much time to make up." She added quickly, "Don't answer me now. I know you'll do it if I pick the right time. I just thought I'd prepare you."

"Thank you."

"And I'll let you tell me about Eve later, too."

"Beth, go to sleep and let me work."

She was silent a moment. "I'm annoying you."

"Yes."

"Why? Tell me, and I'll stop."

"Because you're half-child, half-sage, and you have the drive of a bulldozer. It's a difficult combination for me to handle right now."

"But I think you like me, don't you?" She didn't wait for an answer. "And I've decided that I couldn't go to bed with you after all even if Eve didn't mind. Because I like you, too, and it would bother me if I thought I wasn't measuring up to what you'd want me to be."

"Well, I'm glad we've finally settled that problem," Joe said solemnly. "Though I thought that subject was already closed."

"You're laughing at me. That's all right. It might have been closed for you and Eve, but I have trouble letting go of anything." She changed the subject. "I'm not going to be able to sleep. How can I help you? Don't tell me no. Think about it."

He thought about it. "Keep the TV low so that it won't disturb me and monitor anything that might have to do with the theft of the Lamborghini or any police action in the area. Okay?"

"Okay." She reached for the remote and propped herself up on the couch. "I won't bother you any longer unless I see something you should know about."

"Excellent."

She didn't speak for a few minutes, then whispered, "I'm sorry he hurt you, Joe."

Joe didn't answer. He was frowning intently, and she didn't know if he heard her. And he might not care how she felt. Everything he did for Beth was because Eve wanted it to be done. What would it be like to have someone love you that much? She felt a sudden pang of loneliness that she instantly dismissed as soon as she identified it. She had been alone all her life, and she wasn't going to whine about it. Now that she was free, she was going to have a wonderful life and love and friendship might even be a part of it. She was difficult and obstinate, and it was hard for her to reach out. But maybe that could be overcome.

If she was lucky, if she didn't annoy everyone as much as she did Joe . . .

The green neon sign of the Immediate Care Medical Clinic blazed in the darkness.

TWENTY-FOUR HOUR SERVICE.

There were only two cars in the parking lot, Drogan noticed. That was good. They probably belonged to staff, and he wouldn't be forced to push ahead of any other patients and cause a disturbance. He had to be very unobtrusive until he got this damn wound treated.

"It's okay, pull in," he told the woman driving the car. What was her name? Hester something. Kippling, that was it. "Do you remember what you're supposed to do?"

Hester Kippling nodded jerkily. "I'll do whatever you say. Anything. Please don't hurt me." She parked the car in front of the building and shut off the engine. Her voice was strained as she tried to control herself. "I won't tell the police anything. Just let me go home to my granddaughter. Tiffany's only four years old. You can't be sure that she can breathe through that gag you stuffed in her mouth."

"Then you'd better get home to her right away before she suffocates. But it's more likely that you'll end up dead than the kid if you don't do exactly as I say. You wouldn't want her to end up an orphan." He tucked his gun back into his jacket and got out of the car. "I'll be watching you. One glance, one twitch of an eyebrow that tips off that doctor, and you're dead. Now get out and act like a loving wife who's so worried about me that you're shaking and about to collapse." He laughed. "It shouldn't be difficult. All you need to do is think about this gun in my pocket and the fact that if you cause trouble, I'll go back to your house and blow the kid's head off."

Hester Kippling. "No trouble. I promise." She hurried toward the front entrance. "Just don't hurt me or Tiffany. We didn't do anything to you."

No, and he probably wouldn't do anything to Tiffany Kippling. He didn't have time to go back and deal with the woman's granddaughter. He didn't like leaving witnesses, but a child wasn't really believable in a court of law. He had made sure she was terrified before he'd bound and gagged her. She wouldn't be able to even look at him without becoming hysterical. It was marginally safe leaving her alive.

And not at all safe permitting Hester Kippling to survive this night.

"Would I hurt that sweet little girl?" He opened the heavy glass doors and added softly, "Only if you force me, Hester, and I know you wouldn't do that."

It was over four hours later that Beth suddenly straightened on the couch. "I think this may be what you were talking about, Joe. It all connects."

Joe turned to look at her. "What connects?"

"Drogan." She pointed to the TV screen that showed an EMT van and several policemen milling around an Immediate Care Medical Clinic parking lot. "Triple murder. A middle-aged woman, Hester Kippling, a Dr. Dan Thomas, and Lynn Smith his nurse. Thomas and the nurse were on duty at this clinic about forty miles from here. Hester Kippling accompanied her supposed husband into the facility and insisted on

staying with him through the treatment."
She glanced at Joe. "He had a hand injury. His entire right hand was bandaged."

He nodded. "Drogan."

"Dr. Thomas evidently performed the
necessary surgery. But the doctor, nurse,
and Hester Kippling were found dead a
few hours later by another nurse who had
come in at a shift change. Shot to death.
There were video cameras in the reception area but none in the examining room.
No clear photos of the killer. He managed
to stay out of view." She looked at Joe.
"But it has to be Drogan, doesn't it?"

He nodded. "Otherwise, it's entirely too
coincidental." He smiled. "Good job, Beth."

She shivered. "Nothing good about it.
Three people dead because of me. It
could have been even worse. They found
a little girl tied up but alive at the Kippling
house." Her lips firmed. "But I won't think
like that. I have to keep telling myself that
I'm not guilty. It's Drogan. It's all because
of Drogan."

"That's right."

"But he has to be stopped, Joe. Did you
find anything else about him?"

"His photo." He pulled up Drogan's

photo on his phone to reveal dark hair, olive skin, and large brown eyes set in a narrow face. "He may not look quite the same. This was taken years ago. And I found out a few other things. I tapped the FBI database and found out that Drogan is the pseudonym of an ex–Army Ranger who was kicked out of the service after a friendly-fire incident that killed his commanding officer and was suspected of being far from friendly. His name is Carl Saglet, age forty-three, born in New Orleans. His mother, Zela Saglet, was a prostitute who was heavily into drugs and belonged to a voodoo cult that had monthly ceremonies at an abandoned plantation outside the city. There's no doubt that Drogan attended those ceremonies. He bragged about it at his school, and the welfare workers tried three times to take him away from his mother for child endangerment. But the police couldn't prove that there was anything criminal taking place at the ceremonies." He shook his head. "But years later they discovered a small graveyard near the swamp, in which seven bodies were buried. They couldn't identify all of them, but they were able to trace two who were known homeless vagrants on Bourbon Street." He paused. "And Drogan's mother, Zela. She was found in a makeshift coffin with the skeleton of a large water moccasin wrapped around her throat."

"Drogan?" Beth whispered.

"Probably. The FBI had records of three suspected kills years later with the same M.O."

"Suspected? Why haven't they been able to arrest him?"

"He's very careful, very smart. He became a contract killer a few years after he got out of the service, and he's been moving around the world and gaining a reputation for himself. He worked for the Italian Mafia for a while, then moved to Mexico. But he didn't do well down there; the drug cartels don't have any use for either caution or subtlety. They just hang their victim's heads on bridges as warnings. So the last word on him was that he'd moved to somewhere outside L.A. and was taking lucrative assignments from his base there."

"And Pierce found someone who put him in touch with Drogan?"

"It's logical. If he didn't want to get his hands dirty killing you himself."

"Why, dammit?" Beth asked. "Was I just in his way?"

"Not in his way," Joe said. "I imagine that Pierce would have been happy to continue with the arrangement for the foreseeable future. Why not? He was being paid a handsome fee, and you were no trouble."

"No trouble," Beth repeated bitterly. "I was like one of the zombies at Drogan's voodoo ceremonies. No wonder Pierce felt comfortable hiring him. It was entirely fitting, wasn't it?"

"Until you woke up. No one could call you a zombie now."

"No, I'm not," she said fiercely. "And I'll never be that way again. I won't let Drogan kill me or Pierce put me back in that stupor. I'll kill them first."

"Easy," Joe said. "There's no question of that's happening. We just have to work on catching Drogan so that we can get him to testify against Pierce." He paused. "And anyone else who's involved."

"Not Rick. It wasn't Rick. And I never

met my grandmother or grandfather Avery but there's no reason for them to want to hurt me. Why would they do that?"

"Maybe they don't want to hurt you. But they paid the bills for your stay at the hospital. Now, since we suspect that you should never have been there in the first place, wouldn't it be smart to dig a little deeper?"

She reached up and touched the golden key at her throat. "Maybe Pierce lied to them and said that I had an injury that was incurable. Maybe it wasn't their fault at all."

"And you'd rather believe Pierce was the villain than anyone else. I don't blame you. He's a bastard and should burn in hell." He met her gaze. "But unless we get to the bottom of this and prove he hired Drogan to kill you, there's a chance he'll be able to manipulate the system and put you back in that hospital."

"No!"

"You've been studying what's been going on in this wicked old world since you got out of the hospital. Truth can be twisted, and the good don't always come out on top."

She tried to smile. "But I've got you and Eve to help me."

"And your friend, Newell."

Her smile faded. "Billy's been hurt enough. I want you to find a way to send him somewhere where he'll be safe. Can you do that?"

"Possibly. If he'll agree to leave you."

"Make him do it." She moistened her lips. "I know neither you nor Eve will be persuaded to go away. I have to accept that you feel it your duty to help me because Eve is my sister. That's crazy, too, since I've been nothing but trouble. But Billy has no reason to run the risk."

"He thinks he has a reason." He shrugged. "I'll try to send him out of the line of fire. I can't guarantee anything." He got to his feet. "And now I'm going upstairs to tell Eve what's been going on." He glanced at the TV newscaster, who was repeating the story of Drogan's triple homicide. "Not a pleasant way to wake up."

"Ugly. I've known her for such a short time and yet brought so much ugliness into her life."

"She can handle ugliness. She can

handle anything that comes along." He turned and headed toward the door. "I never got around to telling you about her. Sometime, check her out on the Net. It won't tell you about the steel inside her, but it will give you an idea why she had to develop it." He glanced at his watch. "It's almost five in the morning. Why don't you try to take a nap? You were up all night staring at that TV."

She watched the door shut behind him and felt suddenly lonely. The hours of shared effort aimed at a common goal had been interesting and a little exciting. But now he was going to Eve, and Beth was alone again.

They would be together in that closeness and bonding that even Beth could recognize as being both rare and special. She felt a pang of envy. Oh, not of Joe or Eve but the relationship, the love itself, that she had never known.

And she might never know it. So just take life and drink every pleasure. She wouldn't behave like a hungry beggar at the gates. She'd make herself valuable to herself and become Eve's equal and maybe it would work out.

And maybe it wouldn't.

If it didn't, then she'd move on and open herself to other people, other experiences. But not now, when she could explore this tentative bond that was forging with Eve.

She tossed off the throw covering her and moved over to sit at the desk. She turned the computer back on and brought up the Net.

Find the steel and the reason behind it.

She typed in the name.

Eve Duncan.

Joe . . .

Eve rolled over in bed and went into his arms. Warmth, strength, love without end . . .

Then her lids flew open as she felt the cotton of his shirt press against her. He was still dressed.

Of course he was!

She lifted herself on one elbow and looked down at him. "Dammit, I fell asleep. One minute I was awake, then— Did you see anything that—" She stopped as she saw the red streak on his cheek. She reached out to touch it. "Joe?"

"It's nothing." He took her fingers and

brought them to his lips. "And, yes, I did see something."

"That's pretty obvious. It's almost dawn. You said that you were only going to do a preliminary scouting trip to the house next door, then come right back."

"I saw his footprints. One thing led to another. But I didn't get him, dammit."

"I knew I should have gone with you." She got out of bed and turned on the lamp. "What else did he do to you?" She shook her head as she saw the dirt on his shirt and pants. "You're a mess."

"A couple bruises on my hip. He tried to run me over with a Lamborghini." He smiled. "At least if he'd taken me out, it would have been done with class."

"That's not funny. If you weren't going to come right back, you should have let me go with you."

"No, it's not funny. But to be fair, I wasn't gone for more than an hour, and I did come upstairs to check in with you. I decided not to wake you."

"Bad decision."

He was silent a moment. "Not as bad as the one you made when you and Kendra went to get those records at the hospital and shut me out of the action." He held up his hand. "No, I didn't do it as some kind of revenge. I'm over that now . . . Well, almost."

She opened her mouth to argue, then shut it without speaking. He was right. She had opened herself to this action on his part. He would not have purposely lied to her. When you were dealing with a monster like Drogan, things happened that changed the situation minute by minute.

And she would not want Joe's self-will and independence threatened, even by her. It would be the quickest way to destroy what was between them. "Okay, but you should still have woken me when you came back. And why didn't you come to bed right away?"

He smiled slyly, "I was down in the library with Beth."

"What? Is she okay?"

He sighed. "That's not the response I was hoping for. I was enjoying the idea that you were a little possessive. I think you're taking me too much for granted."

"No, I'm not. And you'd be mad as hell if I didn't trust you. Now why were you with Beth?"

"I was using the computer in the library to see if I could check out background info on Drogan. I need to get to know everything I can about him." He met her gaze. "Because I believe that Beth isn't going to be his only target from now on. I made him very, very angry."

She slowly sat back down on the bed. "Why? Talk to me, Joe. Everything."

"I was about to do that. But I thought I'd take a shower and change first."

"No way."

"Whatever you say. But it will take a while. There have been developments." He leaned back on the headboard. "And then we're going to have to make a few decisions."

"Nasty." When Joe had finished speaking, Eve got to her feet and went over to the window to look down at the surf pounding against the beach. "Three innocent people, Joe?" She shook her head. "I guess I shouldn't be surprised after what he did to Beth and Newell, but I am. He's even worse than I imagined." She turned to look at him. "What decisions?"

"One, we have to leave here and find

somewhere safe for Beth. We probably won't be able to leave the area safely until evening. It's a break that the Lamborghini was ditched outside the drive, but they'll still do a cursory search since his rental car was found down the street. I'll have time to make some calls to contacts I have in Los Angeles and set up a safe house." He made a face. "But I guarantee it won't be as luxurious as this one Newell arranged for her."

"What else?"

"Dr. Hans Gelber."

She nodded. "The psychiatrist Pierce brought in to do the hypnosis on Beth when she first arrived at the hospital. But that was years ago. He may not even still be alive."

"He's alive. After I checked out Drogan, I went on the Net and verified Gelber. He moved from Germany the same year he was involved with Beth's therapy. Evidently he earned a nice fat fee from Pierce and was able to set up offices in Beverly Hills. We won't be able to squeeze any information out of Pierce, but Gelber may cave if we put some pressure on him. He's the only one besides Pierce who knows the story behind why Beth was supposedly so traumatized. If his job was to make her forget that episode, he must have known exactly what happened."

"That fat fee was probably supposed to guarantee Gelber's silence. And, if there was anything criminal behind it, he's not going to incriminate himself."

"Unless we can scare him. And I'm willing to do my damnedest." His lips tightened. "I hate the idea of anyone's circumventing a person's will, and for anyone to deliberately twist Beth's psyche pisses me off royally."

And she had no doubt Joe would be able to do it. He could be extraordinarily intimidating when he chose. And seeing his expression at that moment, she knew that he would choose. She wasn't going to try to dissuade him when she felt the same way. Pierce might have been the guiding hand behind his tool, Gelber, but the doctor had let himself be used and kept his silence for many years. Years when Beth was being held prisoner. "Do you have his address?"

"Oh, yes. I figured I'd pay him a visit once I got you and Beth settled again."

She shook her head. "Not this time. I'm going with you. Newell can stay with Beth."

He lifted his shoulders. "I thought that would be the way it would go." He was silent. "Shall we tell Beth?"

"Of course; it's her right to know what we're doing. She was that bastard's victim. Hell, she'll probably want to go with us."

"If she believes that he actually hypnotized her. It's all a blur to her. I think she's having trouble believing that there was any plot against her by the Averys. She'd rather think that Pierce was the sole guilty one who kept her at the hospital so he could milk the family for money."

"It's easier than having to believe Rick Avery had anything to do with it." She wrinkled her nose. "She clearly adores the man. I don't see how she could— Yes, I could. She didn't have anyone else. Everyone needs someone to love, and he evidently has a certain charisma." She added, "She can ignore the truth if she wishes, but we've still got to give her the opportunity to face her demons. Maybe she'll remember something from the therapy sessions if she sees him again."

"Perhaps." Joe got up from the bed and moved toward the bathroom. "And maybe she'll close her mind and refuse to see anything. I'm heading for the shower. I left Beth in the library. If you want to discuss this with her, I'm sure that she'll still be awake. I suggested that she take a nap, but I dangled the possibility of finding out more about you by tapping the Internet. Considering that she has a boundless curiosity about the world in general and you in particular, which suggestion do you think she'd choose?"

"You've learned a good deal about her."

"I like her. She's very human. And I can see similarities with you. That automatically puts me on her side."

"We're nothing alike."

"Wrong. You're both mentally and physically tough but have a certain vulnerability. Physically, there's little resemblance, but every now and then, I see her tilt her head in a certain way . . ." He smiled. "And I can see Bonnie in her."

She stiffened. "Her hair . . . it's curly like Bonnie's."

"No, that's not it. I can't put my finger on

it but it's there." The door of the bathroom shut behind him.

Crazy. Beth was really nothing like Bonnie. Beth was stubborn and wonderfully vital and as changeable as quicksilver.

But would there have been a character resemblance if Bonnie had grown up in the same environment as Beth? Bonnie had been taken from Eve when she was only seven, and she had been so special. But she had always been surrounded by love. Beth had not had that advantage and had grown wary. Would the years have changed Bonnie if she'd had to live a life like Beth's?

No, not Bonnie. Eve could not imagine Bonnie wary or afraid to give love.

And it was ridiculous standing there and mentally trying to compare them just because Joe had made that comment. She was already feeling the start of a fierce protectiveness toward Beth. Which was completely ridiculous. The woman had threatened to shoot her, been completely rude, then suggested that she would like to sleep with Joe.

Yet Beth had managed to touch her in a way that was completely mystifying.

They were approaching each other tentatively, half-afraid to commit, unsure of what they would find. Beth was surrounded by lies and terror and death, and Eve was beginning to feel as if she had entered into that suffocating cocoon with her.

Forget it. All this emotional fretting was getting her nowhere. Do what Joe suggested and go downstairs and discuss Hans Gelber with Beth and give her the chance to say yea or nay.

She threw on a robe and ran a comb through her hair. She'd shower later, when Joe was finished, but she wanted to get this talk over and done with. She ran down the stairs and down the hall to the library and threw open the door.

Joe was wrong.

Beth was not still awake.

But she was not curled up on the couch. She was sitting in front of the computer, her head cradled on her arm on the desk. Eve moved quietly across the room and looked at the computer screen.

A newspaper photo of a skull and Eve herself in her old blue work shirt, her hands caked with clay as she worked on a reconstruction. The skull had been that of little

Marty Brodwin, Eve remembered. She didn't like to give interviews, but the reporter had promised that if Eve cooperated, she'd see that photos of the completed reconstruction would be circulated throughout Ohio, where his body had been found in a shallow grave. It had been worth having her privacy invaded. Marty had been identified within a month after Eve had completed the reconstruction, and his murderer arrested six months later.

She looked down at the pad beside the computer. Web sites. Four of them crossed off, ones that Beth must have accessed before she dropped off to sleep.

But she'd be stiff as a board if she remained huddled in that office chair for much longer.

She reached out and touched Beth's hair. She received a tiny shock as she felt the soft texture of Beth's riot of curls against her palm. She remembered that last night before Bonnie had been taken from her, when her daughter had curled up in her lap while they sang together. The softness of Bonnie's hair against Eve's cheek had felt the same as Beth's curls did now beneath Eve's hand.

"Hey," she said softly as she gently stroked Beth's hair. "You can't sleep here. Go lie down."

"Eve?" Beth stirred drowsily, then went rigid. She sat bolt upright in her chair and hurriedly pushed her hair back from her face. "I thought I was dreaming." She grimaced as she glanced at the monitor. "Dreams? What you do is the stuff of nightmares." She added quickly, "I don't mean to offend you, I'm sure that it's all very worthwhile. But I'd never be able to do it."

"It's all in the mind-set and getting used to it. My job isn't as morbid as you might think, and you'll be surprised at what you'll find you can do." She smiled. "My nightmare would be going through what you've suffered all these years." She gestured to the couch. "Now go curl up and get some sleep." She turned off the computer. "Joe said you'd been up all night with him."

"I wanted to help." Beth got to her feet and moved toward the couch. "He told you all about Drogan?"

"Of course." She waited until Beth lay down before tucking her under the throw. "That's why I came down."

"Are you mad because I was looking

you up on the Net? Joe thought it would be all right."

"Why should I be angry? Everything on the Net is out there for all to see."

"But it's a violation of your privacy."

"Beth, I don't give a damn about my so-called privacy. I'd fight to the death if someone tried to invade my personal space, but if you're not ashamed of your past, there's no reason to try to hide it."

"That's good. I was afraid you'd resent my being curious."

Her lips quirked. "But you did it anyway."

"I decided I didn't have time to worry about whether you resented it or not." She yawned. "There's just no time, Eve . . ."

Because Beth had lost so much time already. "There's time for you to sleep." Eve turned off the desk lamp, and the room was suddenly plunged into darkness. "It's after five, but you have a few hours before you need to worry about anything else." She turned to leave. "I'll wake you by ten."

"Eve?"

"Yes?"

"Why did you come down to the library? You said Joe told you about Drogan, and that was why you came down to see me."

"It can wait."

"No, tell me now. I won't sleep if you don't."

"We've decided we have to go after Hans Gelber. I wondered if you'd want to go with us."

Beth didn't speak for a moment. "I'm a little afraid."

"Why? If Pierce is the only one involved, we still have to know what happened. If someone else was behind it, we have find out the details. You won't be safe until we do."

"It was Pierce. I know it was Pierce."

"Then why are you afraid?"

"What if Gelber was brought in because I really did have a trauma? What if I was being treated for some authentic mental disease? What if I still have it? Sometimes, I think I must be crazy." Her voice was shaking. "I get so scared, then I'm angry. I want to strike out and hurt someone. Maybe I belong in that room on the third floor."

"Bullshit," Eve said flatly. "Wanting to knock someone down and trample on them is the most normal response you could have after what you've been through. But I don't like that talk from you. I told Joe that I was going to give you a choice, but I'm not going to do it. You're going with us to see Gelber, and he's going tell us everything he knows. I'm going to let you see the weasel try to wriggle out of telling the truth; and then you'll know it's one big lie."

"You truly believe that?"

"Yes, and so would you if you were thinking straight. All this uncertainty is crap. Newell wouldn't have helped you if he hadn't been sure that you were a victim. Joe and I wouldn't waste our time. So it's up to you to straighten up, stop hiding, and start going after the bad guys. This is your life, and you have a right to live it."

Beth was silent, then suddenly chuckled. "I'm really not thinking straight, am I? You're damn right, I'm going to live my life. You want me to go with you to see Gelber? No problem. And if I think he's lying, I'll slap him around."

"Let's not get carried away." Eve headed for the door. "You may not need violence. Joe can usually accomplish the same effect just by being Joe."

"Yes, I've never known anyone like him. He's . . . larger-than-life."

"He just twists it to suit himself." She headed for the door. "I'll see you at ten."

"Eve, what's my . . ." She stopped. "What's my mother like?"

She turned to look back at Beth, but she was only a shadow in the darkness. Perhaps that was why she had waited until Eve had turned out the light. "I thought you weren't interested."

"I've changed my mind. I want to know. Is she like you?"

"No, Sandra is small and pretty and likes everything pretty around her."

"You call her Sandra?"

"From the time I was a child. She prefers it. It makes her feel younger."

"And that's important to her?"

"It's important, it's part of how she sees herself. She's really hard to describe. You should wait and judge yourself when you meet her."

"You don't want to talk about her. Don't you like her?"

"I love her."

"But do you like her?"

"She's . . . difficult for me. We're at different ends of the spectrum. She's never been able to understand the way I think. There have been times when we got along very well. She loved my daughter, Bonnie."

"But you still came out here to find me when she asked you."

"She loves you. I don't care what the Averys told you about her. She does love you, Beth. She loved my Bonnie, and she loves you. I couldn't say no to her."

"How can you say that she loved me? She gave me up."

"You can believe me or not. That's your choice. But if she could have, I think she would have kept you. She was a kid herself, and life was against her."

"Did she love me as much as she loved you?"

Eve was silent. "Some people don't have the capacity to . . . Love is rare for them. Maybe only a few people in a lifetime."

"You're saying she didn't love you."

"I think she tried. But she didn't have to try with you, Beth."

Beth was silent, then burst out, "She should have loved you. Look who you are. You deserve to—"

"Are you defending me, Beth?"

"Yes, why not? You came here to defend me. I don't want to talk about our mother any longer."

"Then we won't, but don't blame Sandra for something she couldn't help. Just accept her affection as a gift. When this is all over, I know she'd like to meet you."

"But I don't want to—"

"Don't make any hasty decisions." Eve opened the door. "Think about it. None of us can afford to reject love in any form. There's not enough of it around. Sleep well, Beth."

CHAPTER

13

5:45 P.M.

They were still there!

The car was exactly where Quinn had parked it when they'd arrived at the Tudor.

Drogan felt a surge of fierce pleasure as he lowered the binoculars. He'd guessed that he would have enough time to double back before they took off, but he hadn't been positive. Quinn was an unknown element, and he could have decided that he had to get Beth Avery out of the area immediately.

Quinn.

Smother the flare of rage. Now it was time to plan, to hunt, then to strike.

First, he had to get to Quinn's rental car and plant a bug to make sure he could track him. He wished he had a bomb to blow up the son of a bitch. Or, better still, bury him alive, as he had Mama Zela. The Snake God knew how to deal with Drogan's enemies. But he could wait for that final vengeance; he just had to be able to track him when he took off.

His thumb throbbed with pain as he started to wriggle up the side of sand dune on the north side of the house. That fool of a doctor had amputated the tip of it and given him pain pills, but he had not taken them. He couldn't afford not to have a clear head. Keep close, don't show himself. He'd like to wait until dark, but he couldn't risk it.

His phone vibrated in his jacket pocket.

Not now. Ignore it.

No, he couldn't do that. The prize was too big to risk the losing. He took out the phone and glanced at the ID. He froze where he lay on the dune. Then he picked up the call.

"Dammit, I can't do everything at one time. Leave me alone. I'll do what I promised, but it has to be on my schedule. And I can't talk now. I'll call you back." He hung up.

He had his list. He'd carry out his job. But he wouldn't put destroying Quinn on hold to do it.

He had his own private list now.

And the more he thought about it, the more he liked the idea of burying Eve Duncan in that coffin with the rattlesnake instead of Quinn. He had chosen a very special snake and begun to prepare it for duty. He had captured it near his house in the desert, and it was almost ready.

A very shallow grave.

So that Quinn could hear her screaming as the snake writhed around her body, striking and striking . . .

He would hold that thought close as he faced all the delays and was forced to creep forward at a snail's pace.

There was no question that he would kill Beth Avery, but she had suddenly taken on a minor importance. First, Eve Duncan, then Joe Quinn.

The Snake God was hungry.

• • •

Valencia, California

They did not arrive in the L.A. area until 11:40 that night. Joe had insisted that they stop at a rental-car agency to get a second car. He didn't like the idea of their movements being hampered by a lack of transportation. Newell gazed critically at the Spanish-style house, with its palm tree and row of plants dotting the front yard as he got out of the dark blue Toyota. "This isn't bad, but every house in the subdivision looks the same. It reminds me of the setting of those early Spielberg movies. My safe house was much better."

"Who knows? Maybe it was used by Spielberg. Don't be a snob," Eve said as she got out of the Mercedes. "It's very nice. Joe was lucky that he had contacts and was able to get this for Beth on short notice."

"All I cared about was that it had three bedrooms, and it's not that far from Beverly Hills." Joe slammed the car door and strode toward the front door. He located the house key underneath the decorative porch bench to the left of the entrance and unlocked the door. "I'm hoping to move fast enough that we won't have to be here long. If we can get Gelber to give us an affidavit that will incriminate Pierce and protect Beth from being thrown back into that hospital, we won't have to worry about keeping her under such tight security."

"The hell we won't," Newell growled. "What about Drogan? No one should know better than I how single-minded he is. He'd been paid for a job, and he'll do it. He's not going to care about what Gelber does."

Joe nodded. "But I may have managed to divert his attention from her."

Newell thought about it. "It's possible."

"That's not what I wanted," Beth said tightly as she walked past them into the foyer. "All I ever hoped was that I'd find a place to hide until I could figure out what was happening to me. Now you all seem to be targets. It's not right. I think I have to do something."

Eve's gaze narrowed on Beth's face. She didn't like that remark. Beth had been very quiet on the long trip down to L.A., and Eve could sense the fragile state of her emotions. Beth was feeling guilty and unsure . . . and afraid. She had put her fate in the hands of three people, two of whom she considered strangers. But then, everyone but Newell was a stranger to Beth, and that must be even more frightening. "What you can do is go with us to question Gelber. Maybe if he actually sees you as you are now, he'll get a few qualms of conscience, and we might cop a break."

"Appeal to his tender heart?" Joe asked sarcastically. "Not likely. Maybe an appeal to his wallet. I might try a bribe if we're not getting anywhere." He turned on the lights and illuminated a cozy living room-kitchen combination. "The bedrooms are supposed to be upstairs. I'll make a pot of coffee and we'll get settled." He turned to Eve. "I'd like to go pay our call on to Gelber tonight, but I have a little research to do on the security system in his residence. He has a house in Beverly Hills about three blocks from his office. I'll go out and take a look at it in case I decide we need to spring a surprise visit on him at home."

"Will he see us in the middle of the night?" Beth asked.

"No." Joe smiled. "But we could wake him up and persuade him. It would be more efficient to catch him off guard." He shrugged. "But if it's not a feasible option, then we'll go after him tomorrow morning after his autographing. He's signing his new book at ten tomorrow at Century Mall." He grimaced. "But I'd rather run him to ground where we don't risk an audience in a mall parking lot."

"You're worried about that security system?" Newell asked.

"I can manage to disarm most alarms," Joe said. "If it gets dicey, I'm probably going to regret not having Kendra's buddy, Sam, to help."

"I know a little about—"

"No," Beth said sharply. "You've done too much already, Billy. You're not going with us."

"The hell I'm not."

"I don't need you, Newell," Joe said quietly. "But if you want to be helpful, you can go in another direction. You can try your hand at breaking into Gelber's office and accessing his computer records on Beth. You said you managed to pull up most of Pierce's records on her. I'm hoping to drag Gelber over there and get him to hand them over himself, but a backup is always good. I could drop you off at his office on my way to his residence."

"I want Billy entirely out of it. You're not listening to me," Beth said, frustrated. "He could get into trouble."

"Have a little faith." Newell smiled at Beth. "I've been trained very well. This should be a piece of cake."

"Coffee," Eve said firmly as she saw Beth's expression. "Newell, go to the car and get the bags."

"I don't like this," Beth said between her teeth. "I feel like I'm being bulldozed."

"You are," Eve said. "But all done with the best of intentions. Newell would follow Joe if he left him behind. He might as well take a useful role off the front lines. That's all I can promise you." She checked her watch. "It will probably be a couple hours before Joe will know if he can breach the security at Gelber's residence. There's no use our going to bed, but we can wash up and have some of that coffee while we're waiting. We'll go out on the patio and try to relax. It's important not to let your nerves start playing tricks on you when you're waiting for the game to start."

"'Game'? You sound like Joe." She studied Eve's face. "But you don't think like him, do you? He actually does think of it as a game. That's what I was thinking when he left the house to hunt down Drogan."

"I guess we've been together so long that we do think alike in some things. And I had to become a hunter, too, during the years we searched for my daughter." She shook her head. "Do I enjoy it? No way. But I know what the elements are and how Joe and I can help each other toward a common goal. In a situation like this, that's crucial if you want to stay alive. You've got to have a plan, and there can't be any impulsive or emotional changes." She turned toward the kitchen. "Go upstairs and wash your face and choose a bedroom. Coffee will be ready in fifteen minutes, and when you come down, don't give Newell a hard time. You can't have it your way. He's made his choice."

Beth didn't speak for a moment, then turned on her heel and ran up the stairs.

"We'd be better off on our own," Joe said as he filled the coffeemaker. "You know that, don't you?"

"Yes." She took down cups from the

cabinet over the sink. "She says it's her battle, but she doesn't really realize what that means yet. If she sees Gelber try to lie his way out of the situation, it may hit home."

"Or he may be so plausible that she'll believe him when he tells her that she really needed all those years as a prisoner in that hospital." He glanced at Eve. "And that she still needs help and should go back and let those good, competent doctors take care of her."

"I don't think so."

"But you're afraid that it could happen."

"She's confused." She handed him the can of coffee. "But she's smart and tough. I'll bet on her."

He nodded. "But not too heavily. It could be dangerous." He suddenly smiled. "But what am I saying? It's not going to do any good to try to dissuade you. For someone who was so reluctant and wary to come to Beth's rescue, you've come almost full circle. I'll just have to do what I always do when I see your soft side coming to the forefront."

"And what is that?"

He turned on the coffeemaker, and

brushed his lips across the tip of her nose. "Why, watch your back, my love."

"I understand the problem, Pierce. But you're overreacting." Hans Gelber looked critically at his nails. He really did need a manicure before he went to the book signing at the mall tomorrow. "All you have to do is locate the woman, and the issue is resolved."

"Overreacting?" He could hear the barely controlled rage in Pierce's voice. "You can say that. You sit fat and happy in that office in Beverly Hills while I'm on the hot seat. My career could be ruined."

"Not to mention that you'd face criminal charges if Beth Avery could prove what you'd done to her."

"What we'd done to her," Pierce corrected.

"My part would be difficult to prove. I was very thorough in erasing her memories. She won't remember any of the details of our little get-togethers." He added, "And you told me that you'd not kept any in-depth records of the sessions. That was very clever of you, Pierce."

"But you didn't tell me that you'd

destroyed your own records. I don't trust you, Gelber."

"I'm shocked. We've been partners for a long time, and we've both prospered enormously from that single transaction. Why would I wish to hurt you?"

"To turn state's evidence against me and save your neck. But you'd be hurt as well. Your fine cars and that mansion paid for by your books, all those starlets standing in line to be hypnotized to keep those size-zero figures—your little bubble would burst."

"You don't have to threaten me, Pierce. I've no desire to make trouble for you." He couldn't quite keep the edge from his voice. "Even though it's entirely your fault we're having to have this discussion. You could have continued just to keep the woman as a patient, but you decided to take an action that was dangerous for both of us. Then you botched it and now you come to me frantically trying to plug every hole to save your skin."

"I won't be lectured by you, Gelber. What I did was necessary. It wasn't my choice, but now everything is coming unraveled. I just received a call from Nelda Avery with information regarding Joe Quinn. It's true he's a detective with Atlanta PD, but he was never assigned to Beth's case. And his live-in lover is Eve Duncan, Beth Avery's half sister. Duncan was here at the hospital day before yesterday. She found a way to attach herself to a music therapist touring the place, but she had to be snooping around. There's no telling what she found out."

"You're panicking for no reason. You've told me that Beth Avery's maternal family has never displayed an interest in her."

"Before she ran away from the hospital. Something has changed. I'll have to deal with Quinn and Eve Duncan as well as Beth. Now, will you cooperate or not?"

"I might consider it. What do you wish me to do?"

"Send me all the Beth Avery records."

"I believe you realize that is impossible. After all, they are confidential. You wouldn't want me to break my Hippocratic oath. They are quite safe with me. Anything else?"

Pierce was viciously cursing, and it took a moment for him to answer. "Leave town. Disappear. Go back to Germany for a while. Show off for the natives how well you've done."

"It's a global society. It wouldn't be long before I could be found."

"But it would take time, and I'd be able to finesse the problem out of existence before that time ran out."

"'Finesse'?" He chuckled. "What a word to describe the act I assume you mean. Very amusing."

"I'm not amused. Will you disappear until I tell you it's safe to come back?"

"I'll think about it. But it's not at all convenient. My new book just came out last week, and it has a chance to make the *New York Times* bestseller list with the right promotion. I have a signing at Century Mall tomorrow."

"Then leave right after the signing. I'll have Stella make the reservations for you. Just tell me where you want to go."

"Ah, the lovely Stella. If you'd lend me her company for a month or two, I might be persuaded to find a sunny beach in some out-of-the-way island chain."

"It can be arranged."

"But lust can't compare with the *Times* at my stage of life. Sad but true. Besides, I have no problem acquiring women. You've forgotten what a talented man I am."

"What do you want? I'll give it to you."

Desperation, Gelber recognized. It pleased him that he could make the arrogant son of a bitch dangle on his string. He would probably eventually give in to Pierce's demands. He had no desire to be caught up in the mess that appeared to be looming for Pierce if he didn't locate Beth Avery soon. He would do better to make himself scarce and be out of the range of the tornado. He would make a discreet exit and only return if he found that it was to his advantage.

"Let me think about it." Actually, it might make his new book sell even better if there were hints that he was involved in such a notorious case. Only hints, there had to be a balance. "Suppose we get together and discuss it before my signing tomorrow."

"You can call me."

"Breakfast is better. If I decide to accede to your request, I'd want to leave at once, directly after my autographing. I'd require that you bring a cashier's check for $800,000 to take care of expenses on my journey."

"What?"

"Don't squeal. I know how well you've

been doing all these years. It's time you shared. After all, I'm giving up a generous income to accommodate you."

"I'll think about it. Bring the records."

He ignored the demand. "It would probably be better if we met in private. There's a small motel north of Los Angeles where I occasionally go when I wish to have a discreet liaison with a client."

"You mean fuck your patient."

"Don't be crude. Be there at seven in the morning. It's the Twin Branch Arms and I'll be in Room 7 unless I call and tell you different."

"How do you expect me to get a cashier's check at that hour?"

"You're a man of influence in the community. Call one of your banker friends. You can arrange it."

"You actually think I'm going give you that money."

"I actually do. Good night, Pierce." He hung up.

He smiled with satisfaction as he stood up from his easy chair and went into the bedroom to shed his robe and get dressed. Not a bad deal. He might have saved his own ass by this move, and he'd managed to stick it to Pierce.

But he had to go to the office immediately to retrieve those Avery records and hide them. Pierce had been too insistent. He wouldn't give up easily after Gelber had held him up for that money. Perhaps he'd put the computer records in a safe-deposit box in his bank in Geneva. He'd known eventually those records would come in—

He froze.

A sound, soft, barely audible from the sitting room.

What the hell?

His gun in the nightstand. He had his hand on the cool metal when he heard another sound, closer, near the window.

Imagination?

Better be sure . . .

He moved toward the window.

"The son of a bitch is holding me up for eight hundred thousand." Pierce told Stella as he hung up the phone. "He doesn't give a damn what kind of trouble we could both be in."

"With Nelda?"

"Not only with Nelda."

Stella's eyes narrowed. "But it's Nelda who is pushing you. Why did you suddenly decide you had to send Gelber out of the way?"

"It wasn't suddenly. I always knew that he could be a problem. So did Nelda. But the problem didn't raise its head until Beth took off. Now Nelda wants every loose end tied up, and she's pressuring me. The bitch won't accept anything less."

"And Gelber won't cooperate without a fat bribe."

"He thinks he'll come out of this smelling like a rose."

"Is that possible?"

"Yes, if he decides to hand my head on a platter to the district attorney. He could make a deal."

"Then wouldn't it be safer just to give him the money?"

"Easy for you to say," he said harshly. "It's not your money."

"No, and I've been meaning to talk to you about that. You need to give me a bigger allowance. You don't like me to wear the uniform when we're alone, but how can I afford to buy anything decent on the money you give me?"

"I don't want you to be decent. That's the last thing in the world I intend for you." His gaze wandered over Stella as she sat with one naked leg over the arm of the black velvet easy chair. She was dressed in a gold silk robe that hugged her body and almost fully revealed the swelling of her breasts. Her red hair shone against the shimmering material, and she was totally and temptingly arousing. "But I like that gold thing you're wearing. Wear it tomorrow."

"Tomorrow?"

"I'm taking you with me when I meet Gelber at the motel tomorrow morning. In fact, I think we'll check into the motel before he gets there so that you can be ready for him. He thinks you're hot. He wants to screw you."

"Of course he does." She smiled as she pulled the robe down to totally bare her breasts. "Isn't he a man? But I thought you were mad at him. You want to give him a present?"

"Hell no, but I don't want to be robbed by the bastard either. There's a chance that I can bargain with him. I'll bring two cashier's checks for $400,000 each. I'll see if I can trade one of those checks for a few months with you and your promise to do any service he asks of you." His lips tightened. "And you'd better get him so hot that he can't think of doing anything else but screwing you. You can do it. You can drive him crazy."

"But only if I want to do it." She got to her feet and stretched like a cat. "Beg me."

"I don't have to beg you. You belong to me."

She took off the gold robe and dropped it on the floor. "Only when I choose. Haven't you found that out yet? I'm becoming stronger and stronger every time we do it and you're becoming weaker. You have more stamina than most men, or I would have left you before this." She tilted her head. "A few months is a long time to be another man's whore. Gelber isn't you. I could drive him crazy. He doesn't realize that I could break him in a few weeks." She moved toward him. "Do you want me to do that?"

"Maybe." His mouth was dry, and his

heart was beating painfully hard. She was all silken naked sexuality and every step she took toward him was giving him an electric, tingling jolt of pure lust. "I'll let you know."

"You do that." She slid onto his lap and wrapped her naked legs around his hips. "I think you'll tell me to do it." She rubbed her breasts against him as she made the adjustment. "Because you couldn't do without me for more than a week or two, could you?"

"Of course I could, you arrogant bitch. You're not—" His head went back, and he gasped as she started moving.

"Beg me," she whispered. "I want you to beg me, Pierce. Like I'm going to make Gelber beg for it."

"No, damn you."

She laughed, and her pace increased. "You will, Pierce. You will . . ."

"Shouldn't Joe have called by now?" Beth asked as she leaned back in the lawn chair and looked up at the night sky. "He and Billy have been gone over two hours."

"Unless he decided just to come back

and pick us up." Eve lifted her coffee to her lips. "Don't worry. Either way, I have a feeling it's okay."

"A feeling isn't knowing," Beth said. "And I can't believe you're taking this so calmly. They could be in trouble. Feelings don't mean anything. I need to have facts."

"Can't help you there," Eve said. "And I'm so close to Joe that I believe I'd know if anything had happened to him." She smiled faintly. "I'd *feel* it. Sometimes, you have to look beyond hard-and-fast reality to find answers."

Beth was silent a moment. "I . . . don't know how to do that. All I know is reality. The reality of the hospital, the reality of school and sports and competition." She paused. "Unless you mean when Rick asked me not to tell anyone I was his daughter. That wasn't real, that was pretense."

"No, that's not what I meant. It's not the same at all."

"Now you sound angry."

"Not at you."

"Rick, again. You shouldn't be angry with Rick. You wouldn't be angry if you knew him."

"It's better not to discuss him. We tend

not to agree. As I said, by looking beyond reality, I believe I'd sense it if Joe was in trouble."

"Would you? That's strange. Kind of spooky."

"I guess I believe in spooky stuff sometimes. I found it was the only way I could survive."

Beth didn't speak for a moment. "I read about what happened to your little girl when I looked you up on the Net. I'm sorry. It must have been pretty bad."

"Understatement of the century."

"I know," she said awkwardly. "I'm not very good with words. I don't even know what I am good at yet. I just wanted to tell—you've gone through so much. You've lost a child. You've had a career. You found the love of your life. You're still young, but you've lived through more than most people." She said haltingly, "That makes you a person who—it makes you . . . rich inside . . . and wonderful."

"Bullshit."

"No, it's true. Me, I'm still pretty much of a blank slate."

"That only means you have all the time in the world to write your own story on it."

She reached out and touched Beth's arm. "I hope your story will be a little happier than mine from this time forward. You deserve it. We'll have to see that it does."

"'We'll'? That sounds as if you're going to stick around after this is—I'm not asking you to—I know you're busy and you have Joe and Jane and your work—"

"That you find very spooky," Eve interrupted. "Stop stuttering. We'll just have to see how this plays out. You may want to walk away and never see me again."

"I don't think so. And I don't mind your being spooky. I've just never felt anything like that myself." Beth was silent. "Except maybe once. I had a dream about you, Eve."

"What? When?"

"A few nights ago. I dreamed you were at the hospital, running away, running down the road. It was crazy." She made a face. "Because I'd never met you. But I knew who you were. Oh, not that you were my sister. Just your name. I knew your name was Eve. I *knew* it. And when you showed up at the house, I recognized you. It kind of scared me. I guess that was one reason I reacted so . . . violently. Yeah, that was pretty weird."

Eve stiffened. More than weird. She touched her jaw. "Remind me not to scare you again."

"I'm sorry. I always seem to be saying that to you, don't I? But it's true, I just struck out without thinking." She looked away. "I was wondering . . . do you think my dreaming about you is a . . . sister thing? I was watching one of those paranormal shows on TV, and they said that sometimes dreams and stuff like that happen."

"Yes, it could happen."

"I thought maybe it was the drugs that could still be lingering in my system." She moistened her lips. "Unless you had the same kind of dream . . . But I suppose you didn't. That would be even more weird."

"No, I didn't have the same kind of dream."

"Oh," she said, clearly disappointed. "Of course you didn't."

"When I dreamed about you, I thought I was dreaming about myself. I was at our cottage in Atlanta, and it was before I knew anything about you or your history. But I swear, I was feeling what you were feeling. Only I didn't understand what I was thinking. It didn't make sense." She met Beth's gaze. "Because I kept thinking about a hospital and someone named Billy."

"Oh, my God," she whispered.

"I told you that sometimes you have to look beyond hard-and-fast reality for answers." Eve looked away from her and up at the stars. "So you're not alone in this particular weirdness. Does that make you feel better?"

Beth didn't speak for a moment. "It makes me feel . . . not alone. It's strange and warm and sad."

"Sad?"

"Maybe I should have said scared. Because it means that we're together in a special way and that if I don't do something wrong, you might . . . want to be with me sometimes." She lifted her chin. "Providing I want to be with you. I might not, you know."

"Beth, dammit, stop being so defensive." Because Beth's defiant, touching words were breaking her heart.

"I should be defensive," she said fiercely. "I *want* this. I like it so much, and what if it goes away? What if someone takes it away?"

Eve felt her throat tighten with emotion. What, indeed? Beth had had her entire life before her, and all those years had been stolen, taken away from her. Why wouldn't she doubt that it could happen again? She reached out and took Beth's hand. "Why, then we'll find a way to take it back. We're a team. No one can do that to us."

Beth looked down at their joined hands, and a brilliant smile suddenly lit her face. Her gaze lifted to Eve's. "You're right, no one can beat us, can they?" Her hand closed tightly on Eve's. "I knew that. I just wanted to hear you say it." She released her grasp and gave a sigh of relief as she leaned back in the lawn chair. "Do you ski, Eve?"

"What?" The abrupt change of subject took her off guard. "No, I tried once, but Joe had to pick me up out of a drift three times. I decided he was enjoying himself a little too much."

"I'll teach you. I'm very good. I have an entire wall of trophies." She stopped. "At least, I did have trophies. I wonder what happened to them . . ." She shrugged. "Oh, well, we'd have a great time on the slopes. You'll really like it once you learn how. And you can teach me to—" She frowned, lost for a moment.

Eve's lips quirked. "If this is supposed to be a reciprocal arrangement, you may be getting the short end. I hardly think you'd enjoy my teaching you how to reconstruct a skull."

"No, what else do you do?"

"Not much. I'm a workaholic. That eliminates a hell of a lot of potential hobbies."

Her frown vanished. "Then you need me. I'll save you from yourself."

"Heaven help me."

Beth threw back her head and laughed. "No, that's the point. *I'll* help you. We'll have such fun."

"If you say so," Eve said warily. "I'm not sure about all that snow, Beth."

"We could try swimming. I was thinking of trying out for the Olympic team. But it required taking time off from—"

Eve's phone rang. "It's Joe."

"Sorry I didn't call before. Gelber's home security system is state of the art and I was looking for a way to circumvent that damn alarm."

"Did you do it?"

"No way. We'll have to corner him to-morrow after the autographing. I'm head-ing for Gelber's office to see if Newell had any luck breaking in there. He called and told me the security system at the office is much less sophisticated, and we may have a chance. Everything okay there?"

"Fine. Except that I appear to be des-tined to spend a number of uncomfortable days fighting icy snow and my own lack of equilibrium."

"What?"

"Never mind." Her hand tightened on the phone. "Be careful, Joe."

"Always." He hung up.

"You lied to me." Beth's gaze was on Eve's face. "You are worried."

"I didn't lie. I don't have a bad feeling about this." Her lips tightened. "But some-times fate slips in a wild card. So distract me, Beth. Tell me about skiing and your competitions and all those trophies and your friends at school . . ."

"It's not bad at all," Joe murmured as he bent over the security alarm on the wall beside the door of Gelber's office. "It's clear he must have put more value on the things in his residence than here. Which doesn't bode well for his clients' confidentiality."

"We've got to hope that he was equally careless with his computer records," Newell said. "Hurry."

"That does it. Try the door."

Newell cautiously opened the door. "Jackpot. Are you this good at cracking safes?"

"I'm an amateur. But a good amateur." Joe moved into the office. "And I'm not nearly as good at bypassing codes to get into computer files." He jerked his head toward the paneled mahogany door beyond the reception area. "So get in there and see what you can find while I stay out here and act as lookout."

"Right." Newell glided toward the door. "It may take a while. I've no idea what the password might be, so I'll have to find a backdoor. And those records are old, and he may not have them in a current file."

"You're wasting time with all those explanations." He moved over to look out the window at the parking lot. "Just get in there and get busy."

The door closed behind Newell.

Forty minutes later, Newell still had not reappeared.

Another twenty minutes passed.

No Newell.

And he heard the faint sound of a siren in the distance.

"Shit!"

Joe strode toward the office and threw open the door. "I may not have been as good as I thought at disarming that alarm. I'm hearing sirens. We've got to get out of here."

"Give me one minute." Newell didn't look up. "I'm copying this file to disc."

"We don't have a minute, dammit." But Newell obviously wasn't going to be budged. "Wipe the prints off everything you've touched and exit the file. I'll do the same for the outer office."

"Right," he said absently.

Joe left the door open as he left the office and carefully wiped prints from the knob.

The siren was louder.

Joe wiped his prints off the windowsill and the door leading to the parking lot. "Newell! Now."

"Coming." Newell was running past Joe toward the car in the parking lot.

The siren was shrieking only blocks away.

Joe pulled out of the parking lot but didn't go to the cross street. Instead, he went left and turned the corner and parked a block away. "We'll wait until they pull into the parking lot, then we'll go to the cross street. We don't want to pass them on the—"

Two police cars, lights flashing, sirens blaring, had turned off the main street and were streaking toward the office building.

"What the hell?"

The police cars had gone past the entrance of the parking lot of the office and were driving straight down the street.

"What's happening?" Newell asked.

Joe wasn't sure but he had a good idea. "We'll know in a minute."

It was less than a minute when the sirens cut off abruptly.

"Gelber's residence," Joe said. "I didn't trip any alarms here at the office. They got a call to come to Gelber's residence." He started the car. "Now why would Gelber call them?" He pressed the accelerator. "Let's go see if we can find out."

"Do you think that's a good idea? I believe a low profile would be in order," Newell said dryly. "After all, we just robbed his office."

"We'll park a block away, walk to the house, and stay in the trees until we can see what's going on. Is that a low enough profile?"

"No, but I'm curious enough to go along with you." The house had just come into view. "Look, the house and entire area are lit up like a movie set. It was dark when we came— What are you doing?"

Joe had abruptly pulled over to the curb and turned off the headlights. "The second team is right behind us."

"Team?" Newell watched as two vans drove past them and parked in front of Gelber's house. "Who are they?"

"The first van is forensics." Joe's mouth tightened grimly. Questions were being answered, but it was looking as if he might not be able to get Gelber to answer the most important one. "The second is the L.A. Medical Examiner."

CHAPTER
14

"Gelber's dead," Joe said baldly to Eve when he strode out onto the patio, where she and Beth were still sitting an hour later. "I don't know all the details. It happened sometime between midnight and three this morning. Unknown perpetrator, stab wound to the heart, several other wounds on his body."

"Drogan?" Eve crossed her arms across her chest as a chill went through her. "Knives. He used a knife on Newell."

"That's my bet," Newell said as he came out on the patio. "Maybe he was trying to get the same information we were from Gelber."

"He didn't try too hard," Joe said. "That wasn't his main objective. I'd say it was only important to him to get rid of Gelber in the quickest manner possible. Otherwise, he would have spent more time on Gelber before he killed him. You said he enjoyed torturing you."

"Oh, yes, he did that," Newell said grimly. "Every little stinging wound. You're probably right. Drogan was going to leave any cleanup retrieval from his office for later."

"Dead," Beth repeated dazedly. She couldn't seem to take it in. "Gelber's dead? But we were going to see him." She shook her head as if to clear it. "Three people died yesterday. Now Gelber? Because of me?"

"No, because a son of a bitch is trying to cover his tracks," Eve said bluntly. "And he doesn't care whom he hurts to do it. Stop blaming yourself. All you're doing is trying to survive."

"I'm not blaming—" Beth lifted her shoulders as if to ease the tension. "Well, maybe I was, but it's difficult—" She took a deep breath. "So we won't be able to find out what Gelber knew about my accident and the therapy that—"

"I didn't say that," Joe said. "We managed to get into Gelber's office, and Newell was able to access the records and make a disc. That should tell us a lot. But it seems you had over six months of in-depth sessions with him. Newell has to go through it and try to organize the information and eliminate repetitions. Evidently Gelber drummed several points over and over into your mind." He paused. "One of them concerned Cara Sandler, Beth's friend who was with her at the ski lodge."

"Cara? Why?"

Newell raised his hand. "Don't ask me anything yet. I just noticed the repetition of the name when I located the records. I didn't have time to do anything but copy the record before we had to bolt out of there."

"We haven't had time to make any inquiries about Cara Sandler since you told us about her," Eve said. "I believe we'd better get moving on it." She turned to Joe. "I'll do that if you want to concentrate on the disc."

"Newell will be doing most of it, but I'd

like to be available to help." He glanced at his watch. "But we'd better get a little sleep before we go into high gear. Agreed?"

"Agreed," Eve said as she turned to Beth. "I think we all need to stop and get our breath, don't you?"

She smiled crookedly. "If that's possible. I feel like curling up in bed and pulling the covers over my head. I guess I shouldn't admit that. You all seem to be so cool and calm."

"You're doing fine, Beth," Newell said gently. "No one expects you to accept murder without flinching."

"I can't help what you expect of me." She turned and moved heavily toward the glass doors leading to the house. "I'm just trying to work my way through this. I know Hans Gelber was probably a scumbag and that he might have done terrible things to me, but it's too remote to me right now. It's not real. All that's clear is that he's dead. I'm going to bed. I'll see you all in the morning."

Eve frowned as she watched her go into the house. "We're throwing too much at her at once. I keep forgetting that she just woke up into a world that she can't possibly understand. Hell, even if she hadn't had that kind of experience, she might still be responding in the same way. Murder isn't exactly common."

"Understatement." Newell's gaze was on the glass doors. "But she's making a good adjustment. I admire her resilience. You can see how torn and confused she is about believing that any of this is real."

Eve nodded. "And we were just talking earlier about how you sometimes have to look beyond reality." She grimaced. "She can't quite understand 'spooky' stuff, but she's trying to be open to it."

Joe's brows rose. "Now I wonder how that subject came up."

"Not the way you'd assume. I didn't mention Bonnie." She picked up her empty cup to take into the kitchen. "I figured that would be too much of a test as to how open she could be."

"Bonnie?" Newell asked.

"My daughter, who died when she was seven." She left it at that as she moved toward the doors. "I'm going to hit the shower and go to bed. Do you suppose there's anything on TV about Gelber's murder yet?"

"I doubt it. I think they were caught flat-footed. There were no media trucks at the scene when we left," Joe said.

"Too bad. I'd like to know more."

"Me, too," Joe said thoughtfully. "There are a couple things I'm curious about."

Eve's gaze narrowed on his face. "Such as?"

"How did Drogan get in? I examined that alarm system, and it was state of the art. I'm not bad, and there was no way I could bypass it. He's either a positive Houdini with locks and alarms or there's something . . . funny."

"What do you mean? How else could he get in the house?"

Joe shrugged. "Maybe bribery to get the code from the alarm company? It's a possibility, but it would require either time or extensive funds to do it. I'm thinking it over . . ."

"Pierce has money, and he'd hired Drogan before."

"Yeah, like I said, I'm thinking about it."

"Anything else bothering you?"

"I overheard talk from two of the forensics guys about a note."

"What?" She frowned. "A suicide note?

With all those stab wounds. That doesn't make sense."

"No, it doesn't. That's why I want to see if the media was able to get a statement from the police about the note."

"Don't stay up all night waiting for the media to catch up. It's almost four, and you didn't get much sleep last night."

He nodded. "I'll only check one time before I turn in. You go on."

She hesitated, her gaze on his face. His tea-colored eyes were glittering, and there was the tension she knew well. He was wired. Even if he came to bed right now, he'd lie there, his brain moving at hyperspeed, going over possibilities. "Okay." She slid the glass doors open. "Let me know if you hear anything interesting."

"I will." He dropped down in the chair Eve had just vacated. "There should be news on the hour, and that's in twenty minutes."

"And five minutes later, I expect to see you," Eve said sternly. "Or I'll come down and get you."

He laughed but didn't answer her.

Eve stopped by Beth's room, knocked, and carefully opened the door. Beth was in bed but the light was still on. "Are you okay?"

Beth nodded, then smiled shakily. "You don't have to be so protective. I told you I was working my way through this."

"Sometimes it helps to talk it out. I'm here if you need me."

"I don't need you." Then, as Eve started to close the door, "Thank you. I'm . . . grateful."

"No gratitude necessary." She smiled. "After all, we're family."

Beth's smile became steadier. "That's right, I keep forgetting. That means you're stuck with me." She reached over and turned out the light on the nightstand. "Now get out of here and let me see if I can get to sleep in this bed. If I can't, you may find me downstairs sleeping on that couch in the living room."

"It looked pretty comfortable." She paused. "Aren't you the least bit curious about Gelber's disc Billy is trying to make sense of?"

"Yes." Eve couldn't see her expression in the darkness, but her voice was only a wisp of sound. "But I'm more scared than curious. If what you say is true about Gelber's manipulating my memories and giving me posthypnotic suggestions, maybe that's natural. Perhaps I was supposed to be too afraid to delve into what Gelber did. Do you suppose that's possible?"

Eve felt a surge of anger. "Yes, that's entirely possible." She turned. "So we'll just break through that wall he built around you, ignore what he did, and get what we need. There's nothing to be scared about."

"What if I did something . . . bad."

"Bullshit. You were a kid. What could you have done?" She started to pull the door shut. "Try to sleep." She paused a moment outside the door before she moved next door to her room. She had thought that Pierce was the principal villain of the piece, but the more she thought about Gelber, the more she was beginning to give him equal billing. Pierce had been her jailer, but Gelber had robbed her in a hideous way.

Murder was a terrible crime, but so was the crime that Gelber had committed against Beth. There was no way on earth Eve could regret Gelber's death.

Eve was still awake when Joe came to bed over an hour later. "So much for catching one newscast." She yawned and cuddled closer to him. "Well? Anything about Drogan?"

"No." His hand absently stroked her hair. "Nothing about Drogan. He's not a suspect."

"What?" she asked, startled.

"You heard me. A note was found on the coffee table in the living room written by a Paul Helmer, a director. He confessed to killing Gelber because he allegedly ruined his life by hypnotizing him, then threatening to tell his wife of his infidelities, which he'd confessed while under hypnosis. He stated Gelber was blackmailing him."

"It wasn't Drogan?"

"I didn't say that. I just told you about the note. The police think that since Paul Helmer was a patient, Gelber could have let him into the house. It's a pat explanation since the house was not broken into, and the alarm was so difficult to disarm. They checked out Helmer with Gelber's secretary and he'd definitely been undergoing therapy for the past two years."

"Have they picked up Helmer and gotten a statement yet?"

"Not yet. He wasn't at his apartment." He paused. "And they may not get a statement . . . in time. The note he left was a suicide note as well as a confession."

Eve was silent, trying to take it in. "All the ends neatly tied up. I suppose it could have been Helmer."

"If they find Helmer's body, then the police will close the case without any further investigation."

"Was the note handwritten?"

"No, computer, but it was signed by hand." He added dryly, "Much simpler to forge . . . or easier to persuade someone to scrawl."

"You're not buying it."

"I'm still betting on Drogan. Pierce knew we were getting too close to finding out what happened to Beth. It would be smart to get rid of one of the prime witnesses."

"You think he planned all this with Helmer?"

"It was clever, and I don't believe Drogan is that clever. According to his dossier, he's principally an assassin and good at what he does. But this is an elaborate cover-up, and he'd need someone to do that for him."

"But is Pierce that clever?"

"He's capable . . . and desperate. By using Helmer, no one would be looking at any connection to him. The killing is all spelled out for anyone to see. All he had to do was wait a few days until the police finished getting the info on Helmer out of his files, then send someone to get Beth's records." He shook his head. "I don't know . . . it's complicated."

"So what next?"

"We go through the disc we pulled tonight and see if we find evidence that will skewer that son of a bitch, Pierce."

"Can't we go to the police now?"

"We could, but not if you want to protect Beth. You prove that Helmer didn't kill Gelber and Beth was thirty minutes away, and you set her up. She's a mental patient who has a grudge against Gelber and wants revenge for an imagined crime against her."

"Dammit."

"Exactly. That mental-patient stigma is going to haunt her for the foreseeable future."

"I *hate* it."

"So do I," he said quietly. "She doesn't deserve it. But we have to accept the facts and deal with them."

"The fact is that Pierce put a major

stumbling block in our way when he got rid of Gelber."

"He got rid of Gelber, but we still have the disc. That could clear the path."

"Then what are we doing lying here when we could be working on that disc?" She sat up in bed and said fiercely, "Beth may be frightened of knowing what's in it, but I can't wait."

Joe chuckled and pulled her back down. "You'll have to wait. Newell has the disc, and you need to sleep." He kissed her. "Give it a few hours, Eve."

He was right. But she was still feeling a sense of sudden urgency. She put her cheek on his shoulder. "I just have a feeling that everything is moving too fast, and we need to keep up. We needed Gelber as a witness against Pierce, but now he's dead. Pierce is scared, and he's started eliminating everyone who knew what he did to Beth."

"If we can catch Drogan, he won't have a weapon to use," Joe said. "All we need to do is keep an eye out for him and pounce. There's no doubt that he'll stay close to us as he can get. Beth is the target, and I'm the lagniappe."

"'Lagniappe,'" she repeated. "That's the French word for a little something extra."

"And Drogan was born and raised in Cajun country, so he knows Cajun French. He's into voodoo. I've been thinking of that and wondering how we can use it . . ."

Eve shook her head and settled closer to him. Joe was thinking, planning, reaching out. She brushed her lips against the warm flesh of his shoulder. "You'd better not be the lagniappe. I won't have it."

He didn't answer and she felt a ripple of disquiet.

Voodoo.

A snake skeleton wound around the throat of a woman buried alive.

Her arms tightened protectively around him.

6:05 A.M.
Twin Branch Arms Motel

"I don't like this place." Stella wrinkled her nose as Pierce unlocked the door of Room 7. "It's cheap and looks like one of the places I took my johns when I was doing tricks."

"You're still doing tricks," Pierce said. "Only you're doing them when I tell you to do them." He threw open the door. "Now go change into that gold robe. Gelber should be here in about forty-five minutes."

"I'm not sure that I want to screw him if he's going to make me come to places like this." She opened her overnight bag and pulled out the gold robe. "I'll have to teach him to treat me as I deserve to be treated."

"I assure you that you wouldn't like that at all." He moved toward the TV across the room. "Be happy that I'm not going to—"

"Don't turn on the TV." She had stopped and was stripping and slipping on the gold robe. "I want music. Turn on Queen on the iPod."

"That's what you said in the car coming here." He turned to look at her. "Don't turn on the radio. Play the iPod. And what's this obsession with Queen?"

"I like that song, 'We Will Rock You.'" She fluffed her hair and took her discarded clothes back to the overnight bag on the bed. "I think it suits me. I can see myself rocking the whole damn world."

"I'm sure you can," he said dryly. "Just concentrate on rocking Gelber. In the end, that's all you're good for. You should be grateful I'm setting you up with a man who will be weak enough to let you control him. You'd be nothing if I hadn't taken you in hand and taught you. You'd still be a promiscuous two-bit whore putting out for any guy who would buy you a drink or a joint. The idea of your having any lasting effect on anyone is laughable." He switched on the TV. "And you can't have your iPod right now. I want to watch TV."

She smiled. "Then go ahead and watch it, Harry. It doesn't make any difference now. And I'm grateful for everything you taught me and everything I learned myself just from being with you. But you're wrong, you know. I will rock the world."

"Be quiet. I'm trying to watch the news." He could hear her moving behind him beside the bed. "And settle down."

"Wouldn't you like me to give you a quickie before Gelber gets here? I could make it exciting for you."

"Not now. I have to concentrate on what I'm going to say to Gelber to make accepting you a fair trade for that cashier's check. It's not going to be easy. There are some things more important than sex."

"No, there aren't. Not if you pick the right moment."

"That's your philosophy, a whore's philosophy."

"And one you embraced and developed since you met me." Her voice was soft and seductive. Though he was looking at the TV, he could smell the scent of her perfume as she came toward him. "This is the right moment, Harry."

"I told you that I—" He turned his head and she came into his line of vision. Shock jolted through him. Her gold robe was hanging open and every step revealed a flash of glowing skin and voluptuous body, but that wasn't what stunned him. It was her face, her eyes, the expression of total sensuality and power.

"You see it, don't you?" She sat on the arm of his chair, and one hand was rubbing his chest. "I can make your whole world go away." Her lips were only a heartbeat away. "Your heart is pounding. You want it." Her tongue touched his lower lip. "Tell me."

It was a surrender, but he didn't give a damn. There was something about her in this instant that was totally mind-blowing.

He was on fire. "I—want it. But hurry, dammit."

"Oh, yes. You're worried Gelber will interrupt us." She slid her other hand around his neck. "Don't you worry. I'll hurry, Harry."

A sharp jab in the back of his neck.

He jerked. "What the hell? You clawed me."

"But you like me to claw you sometimes. I've heard you pant and groan as I run my nails over you." She pulled back from him and smiled. "You thought you were the smart one, but I made you like everything I did to you." She got to her feet. "I wonder if you'll like what I did to you tonight."

"Shut up and come back here." His voice was hoarse and his throat was tight. He tried to clear it, but it just became tighter. "Stop teasing me."

"Actually, I'm tempted to see if I could keep you this hot until the very end. Kind of an experiment. But I'll get more pleasure out of just watching you." She stood before him. "Like you like to watch me all by myself sometimes."

He was beginning to feel . . . panic. Stupid. "I'm tired of games." He started to get out of the chair.

He couldn't move.

He tried again.

He was paralyzed!

His heart was suddenly exploding in his chest. Fear. Rage. Terror. "What did you—"

"A dose of medicine for what ails you." She smiled. "You taught me all about drugs, didn't you? Everything from Spanish fly to those sedatives you had me giving Beth Avery. You'd have been proud of my choice in this one, Harry. Even though it wasn't one that was on your recommended list. It's a little too exotic for your taste. You have no sense of adventure. In about three minutes, you'll have a massive heart attack, and no one will be able to trace the drug that caused it."

"No!" The terror was growing. "Antidote . . ."

She shook her head. "Too late. Relax. Just enjoy looking at me and remembering all the pleasure I gave you." She reached into his pocket and pulled out his wallet. "And think about all the pleasure this money is going to bring me. I need it if I'm going to rock the world."

"Please . . . stop it."

"Stop the drug? Stop your world from

ending? But why should I do that? I have no need for you any longer." She saw a flickering image on the TV screen from the corner of her eye. "Oh, look, there's your friend, Gelber. Dead, poor man. He doesn't appear to need my services any longer, so it's a good thing I'm here to take this money off your hands."

"You . . . knew."

"About Gelber?" She smiled. "It took a little doing to keep you in the dark about him until I could get you here. But you always underestimated me, and that helped." She turned his wrist and glanced at his watch. "One minute, Harry. It's almost over."

"Fool. You were always a fool. I—won't die. You probably got hold of the wrong . . . drug."

"You're underestimating me again. If I don't know, I get a man to serve me who does." Her smile became mocking. "Guess who taught me that?" She slipped the gold robe from her shoulders and dropped it to the floor. "I want to be the last thing you see when your heart explodes. I want you to take the vision of me to hell to burn you."

"You'll . . . join me."

"Not for a long time, and when I do, I'll

figure a way to rule in hell, too. Your face is flushing. Ah, it's coming, isn't it?"

Pain!

"No . . ."

"You're lying. I can always tell." Her gaze was on his face, greedily absorbing every hint of pain. "Yes, here we go . . ."

His heartbeat was a painful drumming . . .

Agony.

He screamed!

His heart exploded!

It hadn't lasted long enough.

Stella gazed at the slumped body of Pierce in profound disappointment. If she'd known that there would be no lingering pain or humiliating distress, she might have chosen a different drug. Oh well, it was supposed to be safe and foolproof as far as the actual death factor was concerned.

She turned away and picked up the gold robe and slipped it on again before she went toward the bed. She picked up her cell and dialed the number she'd programmed into the phone. "It's done. I'm ready for you." She hung up the phone.

She dropped down on the bed and settled back against the headboard. She might as well be comfortable though she doubted she'd have long to wait. She turned up the volume to watch the commentary from the TV hosts on the news story about Hans Gelber while she listened for the knock on the door.

Her cell phone was ringing, Eve realized drowsily. She'd better get it before it woke Joe.

But Joe was no longer beside her in bed. She sat up straight as the knowledge came home to her. Stop panicking. It was after eight in the morning. He'd probably just gone to the bathroom or downstairs to get breakfast. Or maybe it was him on the phone.

She grabbed the cell from the nightstand and punched the button. "Hello."

"Kendra Michaels. It took you a while to answer. Did I wake you?"

"Yes." She rubbed her eyes. "But it was time. I didn't mean to sleep this long. I haven't been getting a lot of rest lately. Why are you calling, Kendra?"

Kendra was silent a moment. "Curiosity. I don't like leaving anything undone. It nags at me. Did you find your sister?"

"Yes, she's with us now."

"And how is she?"

"How would you expect her to be? Bewildered, suspicious, scared, brave, angry. I keep thinking of Sleeping Beauty and what she must have faced when she woke. Even if I help Beth through this nightmare, she'll still have a hell of a lot with which to contend just coping with a life she's not prepared to face."

"Even if she gets through?" Kendra asked impatiently. "I thought that finding her would be the difficult part. Why the hell else did you make me come up there and help you? I gave her to you, now it's your job to straighten out the rest."

Eve smothered a smile. That rude demand was so typically Kendra. "I'm doing my best. There have been a few obstacles in the path." She quickly filled Kendra in on everything that had taken place since she had left, and ended with, "But as Beth says, we'll work our way through it."

"It doesn't sound as if you're doing very well."

After putting their scant progress into words, Eve could only agree with her. Every time they took a step forward, they were stopped in their tracks. "We have Gelber's disc. That may lead us somewhere." She changed the subject. "How is Justin?"

"Good. Breakthrough. I'm working with his parents on the follow-up."

"Fantastic."

"Yes, it is." She added, "Yes, I am."

Eve chuckled. "No doubt about it."

"And since I'm so fantastic, it would be very clever of you to try to persuade me to come and help wrap this up for you."

Eve's smile faded. "Clever isn't right. Four murders in the past couple days. You never bargained for that when you agreed to help us. Beth was just a missing person."

"Who turned out to be a victim of attempted homicide. I'm having problems turning my back on her."

"You shouldn't. Beth's my problem. Concentrate on Justin, Kendra."

"I am. He doesn't need me right now. You'd be a good fill-in."

Eve couldn't help but laugh. "You're impossible."

"I have that reputation." After a moment,

she added, "I don't like it that Drogan got so close to you. One bad break, and you might have been one of those victims."

"I don't need you to guard me. I'm not alone, Kendra."

"Shit happens."

"Not with Joe around."

"If you told Joe I'd offered to come, he wouldn't turn me away. He wouldn't worry about how right or moral it was to throw me into the mix if it would deflect attention from you."

"He'd worry." But she couldn't argue that Joe would do exactly as Kendra was guessing. "No, Kendra."

"Okay. Just tell him that I called," she said. "And say hello to Beth for me. I'd like to meet her sometime. I'm curious about the chemistry between you."

"You're curious, period. You remind me a little of Beth in that way. She has a voracious appetite for learning everything, seeing everything."

"Understandable. I was the same way after I gained my sight. I was no Sleeping Beauty, but I had my own garden of thorns to fight my way through. Just watch that she doesn't tear herself to pieces trying to do too much, too soon."

"That's the least of my worries right now. The next move is just keeping her safe from Drogan. Thanks for calling. Bye, Kendra." She hung up.

Too much, too soon.

She could see Beth racing through experiences as she had those downhill slopes, and crashing or burning.

But as she had said, preventing that was low on her priorities at the moment. Forget it. Kendra's call had made her even more uneasy, and she had to put it behind her.

She swung her feet to the floor as she called Joe's cell number. "Where are you?"

"Newell's room, working on the disc. I thought I'd let you sleep."

"I just woke up." She paused. "Kendra called and woke me. She didn't like the idea that Drogan was so close. She offered to come if we needed her. I told her we didn't need her."

Joe didn't answer.

"We can't put her in the line of fire, Joe."

"Do you hear me arguing?"

"No." But Kendra's prediction about his

response had been uncannily accurate. She changed the subject. "Anything more on the news about Gelber's murder?"

"Yes, Helmer was found dead in his car on Mulholland Drive with his wrists cut."

Eve inhaled sharply. "Another death."

"A dagger was found on the seat beside him, and you can bet it will be the one used on Gelber."

"So the police are going to close the case?"

"Not yet. But it's heading that way. Everything has been handed to them on a silver platter."

Clever. So clever. She didn't want to dwell right now on the timing and efficiency involved in Gelber's murder.

"Has Newell managed to do anything with Gelber's disc?"

"It's gradually coming together. At least some of the pieces."

She jumped to her feet. At last, something positive in this dark scenario. "I'll shower and be right there."

It was about time, Stella thought with annoyance, as she heard the knock on the door. She had been there for hours with nothing to do but look at Pierce and stare at that dumb TV set.

She jumped to her feet and moved toward the door. "I called you over three hours ago. I don't like being kept waiting." She threw open the door. "I did your dirty work for you, didn't I? I deserve a little consideration."

"Be quiet." Nelda Avery came into the room and slammed the door. "You deserve what I choose to give you. And what are you doing opening that door to anyone who knocks, dressed in that slut's outfit? Didn't it occur to you that you'd attract attention and be remembered?"

"That's not supposed to matter. You promised to get rid of the body. Did you take care of the check-in records?"

"No, do you think I'd handle that myself? It will disappear from the computer banks by noon, and the credit-card check-in will be gone as soon as opportunity presents itself. Drogan arranged to have one of his cohorts pretend to be a motel cleaner and remove Pierce in one of the laundry baskets."

"It sounds risky."

"It's efficient. I don't take chances."

"Don't you? Then why contact me to get rid of Pierce? Why not Drogan?"

"Drogan has his hands full right now. I've been keeping him very busy. I couldn't wait. Everything I've worked for is beginning to fall apart. Pierce was bungling the entire situation. I had to make sure that no one was left to talk." Her lips twisted. "According to my reports on you, I thought you might be willing and able to take care of Pierce." She moved across the room to stand before Harry Pierce. "He looks . . . distressed."

"What did you expect?" Stella raised her brows. "That's what happens when you die like he did. Did you expect him to be happy?"

"I wasn't complaining, merely commenting. Pierce gave me a good many headaches over the years and a positive migraine lately." She glanced coldly at Stella. "And I don't give a damn if it was a painful death. I just had to make sure you'd done what I told you to do. Every report I had on you indicated that you were something of a wild card. I'm pleasantly surprised. It appears that you're more intelligent than anyone gave you credit."

"It was probably a man who gave you your report," Stella said. "You should fire him. Men always think with their dicks and can't see beyond tits and asses." She smiled. "But you know that, don't you, Nelda? You've used men all your life. We're a lot alike."

"I didn't give you permission to call me Nelda." Her tone was icy. "And we're nothing alike. All you have to do is look in the mirror to realize how wrong you are."

"Of course, I'm young, and you're old." She gazed at her critically. "Though you look pretty good, considering. You must have had work done. It doesn't surprise me. You know that sex is a weapon."

"That just shows you how different we are," Nelda said with contempt. "You start off with sex, but you learn other ways of control."

"Maybe when you lose the edge. Sex is easier."

Nelda looked away from her. "Did you establish an alibi?"

"Of course, there's a young male nurse I've been sleeping with for the past two weeks. He'll do anything I ask him to do."

"Until you drop him."

Stella shook her head. "That would be dangerous. I figured that I'd let you take care of him when I'm ready to get rid of him. I know you'll be willing to tie up that little loose end for me. You wouldn't want to risk me becoming a suspect."

"No one is going to suspect you. Not if you did everything I told you to do."

"But you have to make sure that it's going to continue like that," Stella said softly. "Because you're such a careful woman, and the stakes are so high, aren't they?"

"They're high for you, too." Nelda took an envelope from her purse and threw it on the bed. "There's the proof of the electronic transfer I arranged into your bank in Grand Cayman, plus your airline tickets to Fiji. You have the very generous fee I gave you to rid me of Pierce together with those two cashier's checks you stole from him. That means you have close to $2 million to stash in an offshore bank." She paused. "Theft. And you've just killed a man."

Stella's gaze narrowed on Nelda's face. "You think that's a hold on me that will keep me quiet. It might, and it might not. I'm very smart, and there are ways to get around most crimes. You found that out, didn't you, Nelda?"

She stiffened. "I thought Pierce was too shrewd to talk to a bimbo like you. Are you telling me that I was wrong?"

"Oh, he didn't talk to me. He was too busy screwing me. But that doesn't mean I couldn't find out what I want to know," Stella said. "I like secrets, but only when they're mine. Beth Avery was the big secret that caused Pierce to jump through hoops. Of course, I had to find out what was so valuable that you'd give Pierce such a huge payoff all these years. Wouldn't you?"

Nelda didn't answer for a moment. "Yes."

Stella threw back her head and laughed. "Gotcha. I knew we were alike when I watched you pulling Pierce's strings." She dropped down on the bed and drew her leg beneath her. "I can't tell you how much I enjoyed him shaking in his shoes at the prospect of just talking to you. He liked to play domination games with me, pretending I was you."

Nelda's lips tightened. "Oh, did he?"

"But in the end, you and I always won,"

she said softly. "Because we were stronger. A man like him couldn't really touch us." Her hand was stroking the satin of her robe on her thigh. "No man could."

Nelda's gaze was fastened on the hand sliding over the satin. She jerked it away with an effort. "I told you to get dressed. I'm bored with chatting with you. You have to get out of here. You're taking a private jet out of Burbank at five thirty this afternoon."

"You're not bored. I'd never bore you." She tilted her head. "And there's a chance that you wouldn't bore me . . . at least for a little while. You're a beautiful woman, and you've taken good care of yourself. You're strong enough that I'd have to fight to keep you from making a slave of me."

"Go get dressed."

"Why? You like me like this. I see how you're looking at me. I knew the minute you walked in the room that I was right about you. You didn't have to come here. You could have sent someone. You were curious about me."

"I wanted to be sure you'd done what I'd told you to do."

"And you were curious to see if Pierce's toy was worth playing with for a while."

She smiled. "And you found that she is. I can make you very happy, Nelda. I'd be a challenge, and I know so many ways to please you."

"You're ridiculous. I didn't come here to audition a slut."

"Not until you found out how worthwhile I'd be in your life. Men are too easy for you. I'd never be easy." She got to her feet in one sinuous movement. "Now I'll go and get dressed. When I get back from Fiji, I'll come to you. I'd give you a demonstration. Right now, but you might be a little tense with Pierce staring at us. Personally, I think it would be a kick." She headed for the bathroom. "I could show you a lot of ways that you'd never—"

"Why?" Nelda's gaze was narrowed on her. "You have enough money to set yourself up very comfortably. You don't have to be anyone's whore. Certainly not mine."

"I don't have to do anything. It's always been my choice." She paused at the bathroom door. "Why? Because you'll always be worried that I might be caught, that I might talk if I walk away from you. That would mean I'd always be in danger. But if I walk toward you and become part of your life, then I become valuable." She smiled. "Oh, and I can make myself very valuable to you. You'd never want me to leave you."

The door shut behind her.

Stella leaned back against the doorway for an instant as waves of satisfaction surged through her.

Power.

It felt heady and wonderful, and in the past hours she had made great strides. But it was only the beginning. Nelda Avery would throw open new and dazzling doors.

She slipped out of the gold robe and began to dress, humming softly beneath her breath.

"We will rock you . . ."

CHAPTER

15

"I've got it," Newell said, when Eve answered her cell. His voice vibrated with intensity. "And it's pretty damn nasty. I'll meet you and Joe on the patio in fifteen minutes."

"Should I wake Beth and bring her with us?"

"Hell, no. It's going to cause big trouble, and she might split. We've got to handle this very delicately." He hung up.

Eve looked at Joe. "It's her right to know anything we know."

"Newell's not stupid. Listen, then tell her

later if that's your decision. You're being a little overprotective at the moment."

"She has a right to be protected." Then she shrugged impatiently and headed for the door. "But I'll wait and see what Newell has to say."

Newell was sitting on the deck chair when they reached the patio a few minutes later. He looked pale and tired, but Eve was aware of that same air of excitement and tension she'd noticed in his voice. "You didn't bring Beth. Good. I was afraid you'd ignore me."

"I would have done just that," Eve said. "Joe persuaded me to wait . . . for a while. I won't keep anything from Beth."

"Thanks, Quinn." Newell reached into a briefcase on the ground beside him and pulled out a thick sheaf of papers stapled together. "Beth's been through enough, and she doesn't need a shock. Let it come gently."

"Let what come?" Joe asked impatiently. "What was on that disc?"

"Nothing that could be clearly determined on most of them. Gelber took bits and pieces of her story, tore them apart, and concentrated on making Beth forget what he wanted her to block out. But there's one session that gives us the essence of what happened that weekend at the lodge. I printed out two copies." He handed the stapled documents to Eve and Joe. "I'm glad the son of a bitch is a corpse. I wish I'd done it myself."

Eve dropped down in a chair across from him. "That ugly?"

His lips twisted. "That ugly."

Eve hesitated and then started to read.

Gelber: "Now you have to stop resisting, Beth. Our last session didn't please me, and you know how important it is to please me. Say it."

Beth: "I—want to please you."

Gelber: "And you know that I'm the only one who tells you the truth. Someone has been telling you lies and making you believe them. You're confused, but I'm going to straighten it all out for you. But you mustn't resist me. It will hurt you. You know what happens. Every time you tell me one of the lies, your throat will tighten and your heart will pound and you won't be able to breathe."

Beth: "No! Please. It scares me."

Gelber: "It's not up to me. You're the one who tells the lies."

Beth: "I don't mean to lie. Keep it from hurting me."

Gelber: "I'll try. Let's go through it again. Open your mind. Trust me, Beth."

"Trust him?" Eve lifted her gaze from the page. "You're right, Newell. Gelber was a complete son of a bitch. He actually used torture?"

"He was a brilliant hypnotist. He used it as one of his tools. Diabolic. No evidence of what he'd done or marks on the body of the subject. But you can imagine the pain and panic of not being able to breathe."

"I can imagine," Joe said grimly. "And how eager that subject would be to avoid undergoing it after the first time."

"There were many, many times," Newell said. "I caught a glimpse of its use in several sessions. Beth was very stubborn. But they kept after her until they had what they wanted. She was almost there when she was in this session. Finish it."

Eve didn't want to finish it. It made her sick. But she had to go on. It wasn't fair to

Beth to avoid reading it if her sister had managed to survive it.

Beth: "But if I don't think about it, if I don't talk about it, then I won't lie. Won't that be good enough?"

Gelber: "You know it won't. You have to believe it, Beth. Now tell me about the night before your accident. That's where all the lies start."

Beth: "I don't remember that night."

Gelber: "That's not acceptable. Can't you feel the pain start?"

Beth: "Yes, I can't—I remember. I do remember. I was so happy. Rick had called to tell me that he'd rented a chalet for a week. It was only about ten miles from the lodge, and he said that he'd be able to see me the next day. Maybe we'd even go skiing. He laughed and said that I had to take it easy when we were on those slopes together. I was getting too good for him."

Gelber: "You're lying again."

Beth: "No, I'm not. I don't feel any pain yet. That must mean I'm telling the truth."

Gelber: "No, it only means that the lies have to hit home first. Stop being defiant. Go on."

Beth: "I was so excited. I hadn't seen Rick for over a year. I didn't want to wait until the next day. I wanted to see him right away. I decided to go to his chalet and surprise him. But I didn't have a car, and I had to ask Cara to take me."

Gelber: "Your friend, Cara Sandler."

Beth: "That's right. But she wasn't really my friend. She said she'd take me, but she wouldn't just drop me off at his chalet. She wanted to come in and meet him. She'd heard about Rick from me, but she was more impressed by the stories about how he was going to be the next senator from South Carolina."

Gelber: "And you agreed to her terms."

Beth: "I wanted to see him."

Gelber: "What time did you get to the chalet?"

Beth: "I'm not sure. A few hours later. Ten or ten thirty."

Gelber: "Tell me about it. You arrived at the chalet. What did you see?"

Beth: "Rick's car. He'd bought a new Mercedes the year before and took me for a ride in it." Pause. "And another car, a black Cadillac with rental plates. I was disappointed. I was hoping Rick would be alone.

But I was going to go knock on the door anyway. Cara parked down the road, a little distance from the chalet, and I unlocked my door."

Gelber: "But you didn't get out of the car."

Beth: "The front door opened, and a woman came out. She was older and dressed in a fur coat with a hood. She hurried down the steps and turned to call to the man behind her. 'Hurry, Rick. I have to get her to the hospital.' Then Rick came out of the chalet. He was carrying a girl wrapped in a green blanket. She had long black hair, and I think she was Asian. She had her eyes closed, and one bare arm was outside the blanket."

Gelber: "Dead."

Beth: "I didn't say that. I don't know. If the woman was going to take her to the hospital, then she wasn't dead. Right?"

Gelber: "But you were afraid she might be."

Beth: "I didn't know what to think. I was just confused and scared."

Gelber: "What happened next?"

Beth: "Rick put the girl in the backseat of the Cadillac. He looked scared, too. He slammed the door of the car and stepped back. He said, 'You shouldn't have done it, Mother. Why did you hit her with that statue? It wasn't her fault.' She said, 'No, it was yours. You know the rules. And it was only an accident, but I'll fix it. She'll be fine once I get her to the hospital. You just stay out of it.' He nodded. 'She's only a kid. You take good care of her.' She pulled away from the chalet. 'Don't I always take good care of everything? I'll call you later, Rick.' Then she started down the road."

Gelber: "That was when she saw you and Cara parked by the side of the road."

Beth: "Yes, her headlights were directly on us, and she saw us sitting there. I knew she saw us. She turned her head and stared at us as she passed. She looked . . . angry."

Gelber: "It was Rick's mother. Did she recognize you?"

Beth: "I don't know. I recognized her from photographs though I'd never met her. Rick said she thought it best for me not to be around the family. People might guess the truth about me, and that would be awkward."

Gelber: "Did it make you angry?"

Beth: "No, I think it hurt me, but I'd never be angry at Rick."

Gelber: "How fortunate. So did you go up to the chalet and ask for an explanation?"

Beth: "No, I was going to do it, but Cara started the car and turned it around. I tried to stop her, but she wouldn't listen. She said I should go back to the lodge and call Rick when I got there. He wouldn't want to talk to me right now. I was angry. What did Cara know about Rick? He'd never been angry with me about anything. But she just ignored me and drove back to the lodge. I went to my room."

Gelber: "And called Rick?"

Beth: "Yes, after I cooled down a little about the way Cara had whisked me back there."

Gelber: "Where was Cara?"

Beth: "I didn't know or care. She stayed in her car and was making phone calls."

Gelber: "To whom?"

Beth: "I don't know. I made her promise not to tell anyone about what had happened until I could talk to Rick. As long as she did that, it didn't matter to me."

Gelber: "What did Rick say when you reached him? Was he angry with you?"

Beth: "I told you that Rick was never angry with me. He loves me. He only said he wished I hadn't gone to the chalet. His mother had called and told him that the girl was going to be fine and that she saw us up there. I asked what had happened to the girl and who she was. He said it was complicated, and he'd explain when he saw me tomorrow. He was going to come over in the afternoon and take me to town for dinner."

Gelber: "But he didn't explain because you went skiing that morning and had an accident. You didn't see him again. You've never seen him since."

Beth: "Not yet. But he'll still come to see me. I know he will."

Gelber: "And what do you remember about the accident?"

Beth: "It . . . wasn't an accident. Some dumb kid played a trick and stretched a wire over the trail and tied it to two trees. I went flying face forward into the snow. Then something . . . the back of my head got hurt."

Gelber: "There was no wire, Beth."

Beth: "There was a wire. I saw it shining in the sunlight, but it was too late to stop."

Gelber: "No wire. You ran into a tree. You mustn't lie. It will hurt."

Beth: "No, I saw the— Oh, God, it's happening. I can't breathe. Make it stop. Make it stop."

Gelber: "I can't make it stop. You're the only one who can do that. You have to reject the lies and accept the truth. You never saw Rick that weekend, you never went to his chalet, you never talked to him on the phone. You made it all up because you're lonely and want his attention. Is your heart pounding hard?"

Beth: "Yes . . . hurts."

Gelber: "Soon you won't be able to breathe. The lies did it to you, but I can save you. We're going to go back over your story again and take lie by lie and turn it into truth."

Beth: "Can't breathe . . . dying."

Gelber: "No, you're not. But you could die, the lies could kill you. But I'll work with you and try to save you. Now start again, tell me about that night."

Beth: "Can't talk—hurt."

Gelber: "Nonsense. Start again. It's only going to get worse until you're healed. We'll take it sentence by sentence and purge the lies. Then you'll be able to breathe again. See, it's getting very painful already. I can tell."

Beth: "Can't—think—can't remember—scared."

Gelber: "Start again, Beth."

Eve had to wait a moment to speak after she'd flipped the pages closed, and even then, her voice was shaking. "He was a monster, and so is Pierce if he was responsible for those sessions. Torturing a helpless girl who was guilty of nothing but being at the wrong place at the wrong time."

"And then imprisoning her for over a decade." Joe flipped his copy shut. "Gelber, Pierce, Drogan. Very ugly. But they were only the tools. You have to look beyond them to find the real monsters."

"Nelda Avery," Newell said. "And perhaps Rick Avery. He was at least an accomplice."

"You won't convince Beth of that," Eve said. "He's the only person in the world she cares about."

"Then we may have to convince her," Joe said. "Because Rick Avery may have been responsible for everything that happened to Beth. Hell, that Asian girl may have been murdered at the chalet."

"But Nelda went to a great deal of trouble

to keep Beth alive all these years, when it would have been easier just to kill her. There had to be a reason why she did that. Maybe she knew Rick wouldn't go along with it, and it might damage her influence with him."

"Possibly."

"And from the conversation between Nelda and Rick, it would indicate Nelda was primarily guilty of whatever happened to that kid." She shrugged. "But it may not be murder. We'll have to run a check of the local hospitals and see if there are any records."

"You won't find anything," Newell said. "Nothing near that lodge. It was a small hospital in Toronto, Canada."

"What?"

"Gelber was evidently curious about whether the girl died, too. There were records attached to the Avery file about an investigation he did after he was brought into Beth's case. Su Kim, a twelve-year-old Chinese girl, was taken into the emergency room at St. John's Hospital in Toronto a day after the incident at the chalet. Nelda clearly didn't want any local scrutiny about what happened at the chalet. However, she eventually permitted the girl to be taken to the Canadian hospital by her father. The emergency-room hospital bill was paid through one of the Avery corporations."

"What was the diagnosis?" Eve asked.

"Concussion. Serious stuff. She'd been struck by a sharp, heavy object."

"But she survived?"

"I doubt it. No one but her father or Nelda Avery knows for certain. The girl's father insisted on taking her away from the hospital after the doctors told him she'd either die or end up as a vegetable. The doctors said he appeared very angry with her."

Eve stared at him in disbelief. "For being a victim?"

Newell shrugged. "Put it together. Rick Avery likes very young girls. Not easy to satisfy an appetite like that when you're being groomed for high office in this country. The girl had Chinese documents, and so did her father. In China, it's possible to obtain anything for a price, and it's far enough away to be able to avoid media attention. Maybe that's how he managed to get what he wanted and still be safe. But it wasn't safe to bring the girl back to the U.S. My guess is that Su Kim was a prostitute and her father her pimp. Nelda turned the kid over to her father and sent them both out of the country."

"Rick told Beth that the girl was all right."

"That may be what Nelda told him," Joe said. "Or it may be that he was just lying to protect himself and his mother. Evidently, she was the one who struck the blow."

"Why would she do that?" Eve shook her head in bewilderment. "A child he was using. I can see her being angry with him, but the girl . . ."

"Unless Su Kim got scared and tried to fight her when Nelda was trying to jerk her out of there," Newell said. "Nelda could have picked up some object and struck out at her. Who knows?"

"There are too many things we don't know," Eve said wearily. "What about Cara Sandler? She left the lodge the morning of Beth's supposed accident. She knew what happened at Rick Avery's chalet."

"And she was on the phone when she and Beth got back to the lodge. Who was she calling? Nelda?" He turned to Joe. "You were checking on what happened to her. Did you find out anything?"

"Only that she went back to Canada and took a job at a newspaper. She apparently did very well. She got lucky with a lot of tips and managed to uncover some fairly hot stories." He paused. "And she was equally lucky on the stock market. She acquired quite a fortune over the years."

"Blackmail?" Eve murmured.

"A giant payoff to get her to leave the country, then a constant flow of favors and cash to keep her happy. Her father was a very prominent politician, so it would have been dangerous to try to get rid of her any other way. It's possible."

"Where is she now?"

"Still in Vancouver, I think," Joe said. "I've been trying to get a cell number to phone her. I should be getting a call with the info anytime now."

"We probably don't have a chance that she'll talk to us," Eve said. "Her lips have been sealed about what happened at that chalet all these years. Nelda has been very careful to make sure that there have been no leaks."

"But the situation is changed," Joe said. "Nelda was content to pay for silence as long as she could keep the status quo, but Beth blew that to hell. Now Nelda's scrambling for damage control. When we tell Cara about Gelber's death and Drogan's killings, she might be uneasy enough to turn her back on Nelda. She must know by now how ruthless Nelda can be."

It made sense, Eve realized, and the thought brought a ripple of hope. "Then we might get a statement from her that would substantiate the fact that Beth was railroaded into that hospital. It would help keep the authorities from throwing her back in there and ask questions later. We both know that would be their first reaction. Ever since I realized that threat was hovering over her, I've been worrying about it."

"I know you have." Joe reached out and gently touched her cheek. "And I can't say that there's no basis for worry. A history of mental illness is an easy out for law enforcement. I have to admit it would influence me."

"But Cara Sandler could help. Keep on her Joe." She got to her feet. "Now I'm going upstairs to give my copy of this session to Beth. It's time she read it."

"It may not do any good," Newell said. "She doesn't remember any of its happening. Gelber saw to that."

"I don't care. It could trigger something. She deserves us letting her be part of this. It's her past, her life." She added fiercely, "We've been sitting here trying to puzzle everything out as if Beth was the mental incompetent they tried to convince everyone she was. She's *not* incompetent. She's smart and she's able to—" She broke off. "Sorry. You know that without my preaching at you. It's just that I feel as if everything is closing in on us, on her. Nelda is weaving a giant web and blocking every way for Beth to get out." She headed for the sliding glass doors. "And I'm not even sure that I want Beth to remember those sessions with Gelber. That trigger I was talking about could be the one that causes her to go through that damn torture. Gelber was very thorough and efficient about making sure that it was firmly in place. I don't know what the hell kind of damage is still lingering after all those years. What if her breathing shuts down, and I can't stop its happening the way Gelber did?"

"You could opt out of letting her read it," Newell said. "I would."

"No, I'd want to know everything, whatever the risk. I think she would, too." She went into the house and up the stairs to Beth's bedroom.

She hesitated at the door, then knocked. "Beth."

"Hi." Beth threw open the door. "I slept longer than I thought, and I just got out of the shower. I couldn't sleep in that bed, so I moved to the rocking chair and—" She stopped, her gaze on Eve's face. "What's wrong?"

"Do you want a list? Present or past?" Eve handed her Gelber's notes. "Gelber's interview with you regarding that last night at the lodge before your accident. It's very revealing . . . and horrible. I want you to read it."

"Of course. I want to read it." She frowned. "You read it? Why didn't you let me read it first?"

"Newell said that you'd have a problem with it." She sat down in the rocking chair.

"I agree with him, but I'm not sure what kind of problem, so I'm going to stay here until you're finished. Then we'll talk."

Beth sat down on the bed, leaned back against the headboard, and curled her feet beneath her. "You're very grim."

"It's the way I feel at the moment. Why not? The situation is grim and getting grimmer." She leaned back in the rocking chair. "Just read those pages, Beth."

"Don't tell me to hurry," Drogan said harshly, his gaze on the Spanish-style house down the block. "Dammit, I can't get to Beth Avery right now. I'm working on it, but she has Quinn, Eve Duncan, and Newell practically on top of her. It's going to take a little time."

"I don't have time, Drogan," Nelda said coldly. "And neither do you. I told you when I contacted you that if I upped the stakes, I'd expect you to perform accordingly. So far, I've had no problem with you except for a certain rudeness and a lack of alacrity in obeying my orders. Because of your slowness, I had to enlist other help to speed things along. But I can accept that if we can bring this to a swift close."

"It's not as if I'm not doing even more than you could expect of me. I gave you Gelber. I'll give you Beth Avery, too, if you can find a way for me to get her away from Quinn and the others. Of course, I could blow that whole damn house to hell and gone and get rid of all of them, but you said no publicity where she was concerned."

"No, that would be totally unacceptable. I've paid you a good deal of money. It's really not my job to make it easy for you, Drogan."

"But you will. Because you'll do anything to have this over quickly. It's too inconvenient for you."

"You have monumental nerve to believe you can judge what I will or will not do." She was silent for a moment, thinking. "There may be a way. I don't want to do it, but I may be able to make it work. I have both Quinn's and Duncan's telephone numbers. But do you have a way to contact Beth directly?"

"No, she got rid of the phone Newell gave her after I called her that first time."

"We may still be able to work through Duncan. I'll have to think about it. It's all in the positioning. Don't make a move. I'll get back to you." She hung up.

"Did you hear that?" Drogan murmured as he looked down at the small metal container on the seat beside him. "It's all in the positioning, Mama Zela. You know about positioning, don't you?"

He smiled as he heard the familiar slither within the case. He had chosen well. This Mama Zela was restless and eager to strike. It was his habit to call all the snake gods by his mother's name whenever he decided a death deserved the proper ritual. Sometimes, as he watched with fascination a snake writhe and strike, he wondered if his mother had come back to earth and could truly be one of the snakes he used to kill. It wouldn't surprise him. His mother had been as vicious and full of poison as a rattlesnake until the day he had shoved the bitch into that coffin and given her the snake to keep her company. The idea of her coming back as a serpent amused him; he liked the idea of being able to keep her caged up and made to do his bidding. "Don't be impatient, Mama. I'll have plenty of work for you soon," he whispered. "Everything is ready. We only have to wait until that other bitch comes through with what I need. We don't get the chance of doing kills the way we want them very often, do we? But this is worth a little time and risk." His hand stroked the smooth metal of the case. "You're going to like Eve Duncan, dear Mama Zela."

"What am I supposed to say?" Beth asked as she closed the last page. "You're looking at me as if you think I'm going to explode or something."

"I didn't know what you were going to do," Eve said. "But I thought there would be more response than this. I was more upset than you are."

"I'm upset. I think it's terrible. But it's as if it happened to someone else. I can't *remember* it, Eve." She moistened her lips. "And how can I believe it if I don't remember it?"

"You don't believe it happened?"

"I think some of it might have been true."

"Why not all of it?"

"The part about Rick and that young girl. It's . . . ugly. I won't believe he'd do that kind of thing. Rick isn't like that."

"Isn't he? You must have noticed that he

was attracted to young girls. What about your friends? Didn't he ever comment on them? Didn't you notice that he liked to be around them?"

"No!" Beth's eyes were suddenly blazing. "Stop saying things like that. It's natural that he'd like to be around my friends. He knew I was lonely because he couldn't be with me. He told me that he wanted me to have lots of friends around me to make up for it. Of course he liked all of my school friends. And they liked him, everyone likes Rick."

"I'm sure they did. He seems to be a charmer." Eve added quietly, "But a charmer with a terrible flaw, Beth. We think the Asian girl you saw that night was a Chinese prostitute who was only twelve years old. And there's a good chance she died because Rick's mother thought she was a danger to her son's career."

"If it did happen, it was his mother's fault. Rick had nothing to do with it." Her hand reached up and desperately clutched the golden key on the chain at her throat. "He would never hurt anyone."

"There are many ways to hurt besides the physical." Her gaze was on the golden key. "I've noticed you grab that pendant whenever you're upset. Did he give it to you?"

"Yes, when I was sixteen." Her voice was uneven. "He told me to wear it forever, and I'd know that I had the key to his heart. No matter how far apart we were, we'd still be together." She stared at Eve defiantly. "It was on my neck all the time I was in the hospital. He must have told them to make sure it was never taken from me."

"Very sentimental. It would have been better if he'd dropped the sentiment and tried to find a way to get you out of that place."

"I'm sure he would have done it if he could. They must have lied to him. He wasn't to blame. He loves me."

Eve gazed at her helplessly. Beth wasn't going to believe anything against her father, and, since he was the center of what happened that night at the chalet, she was looking at the entire report skeptically. How was Eve going to reach her?

"Beth, I believe that Gelber told the exact truth in those notes. Why would he lie?"

"How do I know?" she said jerkily. "I've been surrounded by violence and lies since

Billy helped me escape from that hospital. Black is white. But I have to hold on to something. The only person I believe in is Rick. I won't give him up because of some scribbling of that idiot doctor."

"Beth . . ."

"No, Eve." She shook her head forcefully. "Don't talk about it anymore."

"I *will* talk about it," Eve said. "Cling to Rick if you have to do it, but believe that what happened that night was the reason that you lost all those years. You saw something you shouldn't have seen, and Nelda Avery had to be sure that you didn't talk. You may be right that Rick did love you and that—"

"Of course—and he still loves me."

"Let me finish. If Nelda Avery wanted to keep her hold over her son, she couldn't risk killing you. Even an accidental death would appear entirely too 'convenient' to him under the circumstances. But a tragic skiing accident in which your injury required permanent care and restraint would fit the bill. It actually must have been very satisfying for her on several levels. Your very existence must have been a constant thorn in her flesh since her son insisted on keeping in touch with you. It was much safer to have you under strict control. Will you accept that as being reasonable?"

"Maybe." She went on in a rush of words, "I know that you think I'm being foolish. But what if that report was twisted and not true? All that about me not being able to breathe . . . Wouldn't that posthypnotic suggestion have some kind of an effect on me now if it wasn't pure bull? I'm fine, Eve."

"Because in your heart you're still believing what Gelber told you to believe, that you never went to that chalet. Because you're afraid it's going to hurt too much if you believe what really happened. You'd take the physical pain but not the emotional."

"Think what you like." She tossed the pages on Eve's lap. "Everyone has gone to a lot of trouble to try to help me, and I appreciate that you—" She had to stop, her eyes glittering with tears. "I'm sorry, Eve," she whispered. "It hurts me to have you believe I'm not grateful for all you've done. I want to think what you think, do what you think is best, but I can't. I have to go my own way. Please forgive me."

Eve could feel her throat tighten as she

looked at her. In a way, she had tortured Beth as much as that bastard Gelber by bringing her face-to-face with her father's sins and his involvement in her imprisonment in that hospital. How could she expect her to be willing to accept it? It might take a long time for her even to come close.

But they didn't have a long time, she thought desperately. Things were moving at light speed.

Maybe they could work around Beth in some way, Eve thought wearily as she got to her feet. They seemed to have no choice at the moment. "There's nothing to forgive." She put the notes back on the bed. "I only ask you to read it again and see if—just read it again." She turned toward the door. "I'll see you later. I'm going to check with Joe and see if he's been able to contact Cara Sandler. We're trying to verify Gelber's notes. I know you didn't like or trust her, but we have to do what we can to—"

"Eve."

Eve looked back at her.

"I . . . have to tell you something."

"So tell me."

"This is . . . difficult for me. I think I— I

don't know much about affection and stuff like that except with Rick. But I think I like—" She lifted her chin. "No, I think I . . . care for you. After all, we're sisters. I guess that's not weird or anything. You don't have to feel the same way about me. That's okay. We've barely gotten to know each other. I just wanted to let you know. Things happen, and if you don't say the words, then they might get lost, and I wouldn't—"

"Hush, Beth." Eve smiled at her. "It's difficult for me, too. We seem to be alike in more than blood. I think I care for you as well. But we're as different as night and day in most things, and it's going to take some doing to bridge those differences. We'll have to take our time."

Beth's eyes were bright with eagerness. "But we'll get there, won't we?"

"We'll get there." She closed the door behind her and stood in the hall for an instant, trying to smother the emotion Beth's words had ignited. Beth was part child, part woman, and her eagerness, vulnerability, and strength were impossible to resist.

And Eve didn't want to resist, dammit. She had fought against letting Beth into her life in a meaningful way, but that was in the past. But as she had said, they were two individuals who would have to walk carefully not to damage one another.

"Eve?" Joe was walking toward her down the hall. "You're upset. How did she take it?"

"The way we thought she would," Eve said as she went toward him. "She won't believe anything bad about Rick Avery. And she's leaning toward not even believing much of Gelber's notes because she's in defense mode about her father. I asked her to read the notes again and think about them."

"Will she do it?"

"Maybe. I don't know. She doesn't want to do it. Her first impulse is to reject." She made a face. "But she has an intrinsic honesty that keeps her from being completely blind about it. I'm hoping that she'll be able to begin to accept that it might be true the longer she lives with the knowledge." She added soberly, "But time seems to be running out, doesn't it?" She didn't wait for an answer but changed the subject. "Did you get Cara Sandler's number and manage to contact her?"

"Yes, I got her cell number." His lips

twisted. "But no I didn't contact her. The call was picked up by the Vancouver police, and I got bombarded by questions."

"The police?"

"Cara Sandler's car went off the highway and down a gorge yesterday evening. She was killed on impact."

"Damn," Eve whispered. "How?"

"That's what the police are trying to determine. They think the brake lines were cut."

"Nelda Avery?"

Joe nodded. "Probably through one of Drogan's contacts. Or maybe she's had a plan in mind for Sandler for a long time and just set it in motion. She appears to be very efficiently tying up all the loose ends she left dangling all those years ago."

"Hans Gelber, now Cara Sandler. So much for having a witness that could keep Beth from being tossed back in that hospital." She leaned her head on Joe's chest. "Hell, Joe, Cara Sandler was in Canada. Nelda is reaching out like a scorpion and stinging—" She drew a deep breath. "Maybe if we tell Beth about Cara Sandler, it will have some effect and she'll be able to see the pattern."

"We can hope it will—" His phone rang and he glanced at the ID. "Newell? Why would he call from—" He accessed the call. "What's happening?"

He listened for a moment. "See what you can find out from your friends at the hospital." He hung up and took Eve's arm. "Come on, let's go downstairs and watch the news on TV. Harry Pierce has been reported missing."

"Pierce?"

He nodded as he nudged her down the stairs. "He had a meeting with an important donor at noon today and he didn't show. He took out $800,000 in cashier's checks early this morning. Stella Lenslow was with him last night and presumably this morning."

"Then maybe Pierce lost his nerve, and he and his lady friend took off for some South Sea island."

"Maybe. He didn't impress me as being very brave but he was greedy. Less than a million dollars? I think he'd want more than that to set up his own Shangri-la." His lips tightened. "Newell is seeing what he can find out at the hospital. We'll have to watch for more news and try to put a picture together."

"When are you coming home, Nelda?" George asked as soon as he picked up the phone. "I can't stall the media much longer, and Rick is asking questions, too. What's happening?"

"I've called Rick and told him that I'm fine. Let the campaign people handle the media." She didn't want to deal with George just then, but it wasn't smart not to keep him calm and think he was still in the loop. She was too far away to influence him on a physical basis, and verbal reassurance was the best she could do. "I just wanted to let you know that everything is going well, and I should be able to come back in a few days."

"You didn't answer me," George said. "What's happening? Have you found Beth?"

"No. Not yet. But I'm getting close. It shouldn't take much longer."

"If you're that close, then leave it up to Pierce."

Pierce. It was going to cause a problem

when George learned about Pierce's death. Maybe prepare him a little? "I'm having trouble getting in touch with him. He may have decided to take the money we've been paying him and head for sunnier pastures."

"Bullshit," George said bluntly. "He's been under your thumb too long. He hasn't the guts to double-cross you."

George was too sharp. She'd just have to deal with the Pierce problem when it developed. "I hope you're right. I just want to have Beth back in that hospital and be on my way home to you." She added quickly, "I have to go now. Take care. I'll let you know if there's any progress."

"There doesn't appear to be much chance of that happening."

"Don't be pessimistic. Trust me. Things are working out very well. Definitely progress." She hung up.

It was true. There had been progress once she had gathered the reins into her own hands. Not the kind with which George would be happy, but it was the only kind she could make and still protect herself. She had taken the weapons she had found and made them her own. Drogan had been a particularly valuable tool, with his lethal mind-set, contacts with other equally efficient killers around the globe, plus a total lack of loyalty to Pierce. She'd needed only to furnish the money, and he had provided the means to start eliminating all the troublesome people who had been a danger to her for years. It had been almost a relief to know that she could break those chains she'd been forced to wear because of that night at the chalet. She was going to be *free*. She should probably have made this move before, but Rick had always been in her way. Now she had no choice since Pierce had failed so miserably to erase Beth from the scene.

But the list of the people who had been dragging her down and keeping Rick from reaching for the heights was dwindling. All she had to do was control Drogan after he cornered Beth and made the kill. It shouldn't be too difficult. She was far more clever than Drogan.

And far more clever than Stella Lenslow.

She had a sudden memory of Stella sitting on the bed that morning. She couldn't deny that the slut had stirred her. It had been a long time since she had felt that intensity of lust, and it had been even stronger

because she knew Stella was so dangerous. It might have been interesting to take
a few chances and enjoy the skills Stella
was offering to show her.

Interesting and exciting . . .

CHAPTER
16

Stella had never liked mountains.

She gazed out the window of the plane at the darkness of the Rocky Mountains below her.

Beaches and surf had always been more flattering backgrounds to show her off to advantage. Heat and undulating rhythms and sensuous breezes suited her very well. What could you do with mountains but climb them and smile when someone said how inspiring they were?

Boring.

As boring as the trip had been so far. It had been bad enough during the daylight hours when she had first boarded the plane, but now that it was dark, all you could see were the red lights on the wings and the shape of the mountains below. She was ready to land, but it was at least another hour until they reached Vancouver, where she would change planes.

The only thing that made the trip bearable was the fact that she was on a private business jet. Well, not totally private. There was a Korean businessman toward the back of the Learjet who looked promising but seemed too involved with his wife sitting beside him to be worth bothering about. She had flown with Pierce a few times on private aircraft, and she liked them. They made her feel rather special, and this corporation jet of Nelda's was particularly luxurious: soft lights, leather seats, and burl wood accents.

"More champagne?"

She looked up at the smiling male flight attendant, Mark Telfer, who was standing beside her seat. Good-looking but probably gay. He hadn't paid her more than polite attention.

"Why not?" She gestured to her empty glass. "It's very good."

"The best." He refilled her glass. "If you'd like anything else, all you have to do is call me. I received a note from Mrs. Avery right before we took off, and she said to make sure that I fulfilled your every wish. She specified the year for the champagne and sent a box of after-dinner chocolates for me to serve you."

That was good news. Not that she doubted her effect on Nelda was anything but a success. She was always able to gauge her power over people. She lifted her glass. "I'll keep that in mind. I can see how you'd want to please the boss. How long have you worked for the Averys?"

His brows rose. "Oh, I don't work for them. This jet is leased to New China Porcelain. We have no direct connection with the Averys." He shrugged. "Though occasionally we're hired to do a discreet run for them. But then they always have their own crews and insist that their names are never listed on any record. They just show up at flight time and board the plane. Like you, Ms. Lenslow."

"Discreet?"

He grinned and winked. "Top secret."

"How interesting." Her eyes narrowed.

"Don't you find it curious enough to explore?"

"No, I like my job just fine, and they're only one client among dozens. Not really important."

It might be important to Stella. Another weapon to use against Nelda? She would have to keep her eyes open to make sure that she was always one step ahead of her. "Perhaps we could talk about it later." She smiled. "Do you get to Fiji very often?"

His smile remained, but he looked suddenly wary. "Now and then." He turned away. "Be sure and buzz if you need anything. I'm at your service." He hurried back down the aisle.

Definitely gay. She took another sip of champagne. But she might still be able to use him. She would have to think about it and see who he—

"I almost forgot to give this to you." Mark was standing beside her chair again with an envelope. He glanced at his watch. "But I'm right on time—7:27. Mrs. Avery said it had to be right on the nose. Please tell her that I obeyed instructions."

"Mrs. Avery?" She looked at the envelope as she took it from him. Heavy, rich, stationery, faintly scented. The same scent she'd smelled when Nelda had been in the motel room that morning. "She sent it to you?"

He nodded. "Together with my personal letter and instructions." He started back down the aisle. "Nice perfume, isn't it?"

She stared down at the envelope. She didn't like this. It gave her an uneasy feeling. She slowly tore open the envelope. Nelda's handwriting was bold and clear and struck with the force of a hammer blow.

> **Stella—**
>
> **Did you really think that I'd let you dominate me? Your arrogance is incredible. Yes, I found you desirable, but as you grow older, you learn to pick and choose what you will allow yourself and how to say no to alluring toys. You wish to follow in my footsteps and perhaps supplant me someday, but you would never have learned that, Stella.**
>
> **So good-bye, temptation.**
>
> **Two minutes, Stella. Enjoy them.**
>
> **Nelda**

Stella's heart jerked in her chest as panic struck.

Two minutes. In two minutes, it would be seven thirty.

What was going to happen at seven thirty?

They . . . insist their names are never listed on any record.

Like you, Ms. Lenslow.

The airline company has no direct connection with the Averys.

She sent a box of "after-dinner chocolates."

The mountains below looming dark and hard . . . and waiting.

"No!" She threw her champagne glass to the floor and jumped to her feet. "No, you bitch. It's not going to happen."

She ran to the door of the cockpit. She was aware of the Korean couple staring at her with startled expressions. Mark Telfer, the flight attendant, was running down the aisle toward her as she tried to jerk open the cockpit door.

"You've got to land!" she screamed as she pounded on the door. "Let me in. This can't happen to *me*."

"Go back to your seat," the flight attendant said soothingly. "Have some more champagne. I'll ask the pilot to come out and talk to you."

"Too late. You fool, it's too late. Those damn chocolates. It has to be—"

She screamed.

Because precisely at seven thirty, the Learjet exploded into flaming shards of metal and hurtled into the Rocky Mountains below.

"I've talked to everyone at the hospital who could have any access to special info," Newell said several hours later as he poured coffee into Beth's cup. "As far as anyone knows, Pierce has done a flit with his luscious lady."

"He's gone?" Beth shook her head in wonder. "I can't believe it. Those last months at the hospital I'd watch him whenever he was anywhere around me. Before that, the drugs made him only a hazy figure to me. He *liked* what he did. He liked the power and everyone's deferring to him. I don't think he'd walk away from it."

"I don't, either," Joe said. "But where the hell is he?"

"But I was told one other interesting thing

when I was checking," Newell said. "The woman who was impersonating Beth is no longer occupying the room where she was quarantined. Before they left the hospital, Stella Lenslow gave an order, supposedly from Pierce, that the woman be moved back to the ward where she evidently was before Pierce pulled the switch."

"Why didn't Pierce give the order?"

Newell shrugged. "He'd already gone to the car. It didn't ring true to me, either."

"I don't like it," Joe said flatly. "Even if he was going to leave the area, why pull the phony patient and leave the suspicion that Beth was still on the loose?" He was channel flipping through the news channels. "They've checked the local airports for his car and didn't find it. No Pierce. No Stella Lenslow."

"Maybe not Stella." Eve came into the kitchen from the living room where she'd been monitoring the other set. "But they've just found Harry Pierce. Turn on Fox."

Joe switched to the station to see a shot of a BMW wrapped around a telephone pole. Police and ambulance trucks surrounded the vehicle. "Pierce? Where is this supposed to be?"

"A northern suburb," Eve said. "He's dead."

"Suspects?"

"They don't even know if it's murder. It may take days for the medical examiner to determine it," Eve said. "No obvious lethal wounds." She paused. "But also no broken bones that they can determine."

"Dead," Beth said dully. "Another one."

"Be happy," Newell said. "No, don't be happy. It would have been better if they'd stuffed him into a prison to rot like he did you."

"Dammit, I wanted him *alive.*" Joe got to his feet. "Hell, everyone who could testify to Beth's sanity is being sent to the morgue." He headed for the door. "I'm going out there to see if I can find out anything more."

"Like what?" Eve asked.

"Like where's Stella Lenslow and does she have any evidence that can help." His lips tightened. "And if there's anything in that wreck of a car that could prove what a lying son of a bitch Pierce is to the Santa Barbara Police, even though he had them in his pocket. We need *something* fast."

"Why? What's suddenly put you on edge?"

"The deaths are piling up, and we have to stop worrying about Beth's being thrown back into the hospital and start worrying about her being arrested for murder. It's a little too convenient that a mental patient's two doctors have shown up dead when she's still wandering around loose."

My God, he was right. First Gelber, now Pierce, Eve thought. Not only convenient, but chilling.

"I'll see if I can find anything to use to deflect attention from her and gather any clues out there." Joe turned at the door. "Newell, you stay here with Beth and Eve. I should be back in an hour or two." He looked at Eve. "I'll call you from the accident scene and let you know what's happening."

"You'd better." She made a face. "I'm not all pleased at staying here and holding down the fort. I believe that position is vastly overrated."

"But you'll do it." He glanced at Beth. "You have a reason to hold down this particular fort. Keep safe, Eve." The door shut behind him, and he strode toward the car parked at the curb. He paused before he opened the driver's door to look up and down the street.

Nothing.

Yet he was still uneasy even though he had no reason to be. There had been no sign that Drogan had been able to follow them to L.A. from the Seventeen Mile Drive. He had even checked the car for bugs before they left the Strip and found nothing. However, there were all kinds of devices available these days that weren't detectable except with equally sophisticated equipment.

But Drogan had been very busy if he'd managed to kill both Gelber and Pierce in the span of such a short time. It wasn't likely he'd have also been able to stake out Beth in Valencia.

Not likely. But possible.

He glanced back at the glowing windows of the house he'd just left as he backed out of the driveway. It appeared warm and cozy and safe. It would be okay, he told himself. Newell was there, and he would be on guard.

His cell phone rang as he drove toward the subdivision entrance.

Kendra.

"You persisted in telling us how busy you are, Kendra," he said when he picked up the call. "But you seem to have plenty of time to harass us."

"What a treasure is gratitude," Kendra said sarcastically. "And you don't know anything about harassment. It's an art form. I'll have to teach you someday."

"I am grateful," Joe said quietly. "And Eve is even more grateful than I am. But she wants to keep you out of this. Things are a bit dicey."

"You mean like Pierce's ending up smashed into a telephone pole?"

"You saw the news story."

"Why else would I be calling you? It's all over the news channels. Look, I know how Eve feels, and I've been trying to respect it. On the surface, Pierce's getting killed could actually seem to make it safer for Beth and Eve. If you tell me that's true, then I'll reconsider my plans."

"What plans?" he asked warily.

She ignored the question. "Is the fact that Pierce bought it going to make Drogan less of a danger to you?"

She wasn't going to give up until she

had the answer. What the hell. Talk to her. That uneasiness was still with him, and he wanted to surround Eve and Beth with every barrier he could find. Kendra could be one hell of a valuable barrier. "No, someone else has entered into the mix."

"Nelda Avery. Rick Avery. Which one?" Kendra asked. "I was wondering whether they'd come out of their golden shells and take over the action. Pierce seems to have been a royal screwup."

"I think Nelda Avery is tired of hiding in the shadows and paying hush money. She wants a new deck and is determined to get it. But the stakes are very high for her as well as her son." He paused. "She committed the murder that started all this business rolling."

Kendra gave a low whistle. "Yeah, that would give her a giant stake. Should I know anything else before I get there?"

"You're coming here?"

"I'm on my way. I just got on the San Diego Freeway. Where am I going?"

He chuckled. "Yes, that would be a good thing to know. Valencia. You know that Eve's not going to be pleased with either one of us."

"She'll get over it. Are you going to the site of Pierce's smashup?"

"I just left the house. I thought I'd see if I could find out anything from examining the wreckage."

"I'd have a better chance. But I can go to the impound lot later and take a look if you don't see anything."

"Which you don't think I will?" he asked dryly, with a mixture of annoyance and amusement. Kendra was moving with her usual full head of steam. "I'll try to prove you wrong. How soon will you be here?"

"About an hour, maybe less. Keep me informed."

"Why, Kendra? Why are you being so determined about this?"

"As I told Eve, I hate leaving anything unfinished. It bothered me that I had to leave without having everything wrapped up."

"And?"

"Stop pushing me, Quinn. Why should there be anything else?" She was silent a moment. "Except that I like Eve. I've never had that many friends. When I was blind, I was always defensive and working hard at overcoming my handicap. Then, after I gained my sight, I'd get impatient when others who'd had their vision all their lives couldn't see what was right before them. I wanted to shake them. Not exactly an attitude that endears people to you."

"No, and Eve certainly wasn't enamored of you in the beginning."

"But we worked our way through it. I felt close to her. And, when I found out about her daughter, Bonnie, I kept thinking about it. I wanted to help her to find something or someone to replace her."

"Not possible, Kendra."

"Oh, I know that, and she'd hate it if she knew I felt . . . but I thought that if I could give her Beth, it might help a little."

"*Give* her Beth. Good God."

"Too arrogant? Okay, you're right. Besides, I didn't get the chance. But now maybe I can do something to help her keep her." She paused. "If it's worthwhile. How does she feel about Beth? Was she a disappointment?"

"Eve had no preconceived ideas of what her sister would be or what she wanted from the relationship. But, no, Beth wasn't a disappointment. I'm not exactly sure what Eve feels for Beth, but she wouldn't want to give her up."

"Good, then it's settled. I'll see you soon." She hung up.

Joe was smiling as he pressed the disconnect. That last remark had been typical Kendra, full of confidence and decision. It was her previous words that had surprised him. She had always shown him only her toughness and keen intelligence. Evidently, Eve had managed to reach down and touch another side of her. But, then, Eve was able to touch most people just by being Eve.

His smile faded as he thought about how much Eve had touched and changed him through the years. God, he loved her.

And everything might be settled in Kendra's eyes, but there was a darkness looming. He just hoped he could keep it from enveloping Eve as well as Beth.

His foot instinctively pressed the accelerator at the thought. Check out that accident scene, then get back to the house.

Keep Eve safe. Keep Eve close to him.

"You've been very quiet since Joe left." Eve dropped into the lawn chair beside Beth and handed her a cup of tea. "It's going to be okay, Beth."

"You keep saying that." Beth smiled. "You treat me the way Billy does, as if I'm a little girl. By the way, where is he?"

"Making his rounds. He took Joe's order about watching out for us seriously."

"He takes everything seriously." She lifted the tea to her lips. "He's a good man, Eve. He doesn't deserve all that's happened to him."

"He's not complaining. Stop having all these guilt feelings. Though I know everything seems confusing, and it was a shock to realize that Pierce is dead."

"It is a shock." Beth looked down into the amber depths of her cup. "But then I seem to be dizzy with shocks. Every time I turn around, something else happens." She made a face. "But it's not as if I cared anything about Pierce. If what everyone tells me is true, he was a monster to me. I can't be sorry he's dead."

"Which is an entirely healthy response."

Beth smiled. "From a woman who everyone was sure was loony as a hoot owl."

"Are hoot owls loony? I wonder where that saying came from. At any rate, no one will say that about you for long. We'll make sure they don't."

"I can almost believe you."

She looked her in the eye. "No almost. Believe me, Beth."

She nodded. "I do believe you, Eve. It's just that it's—"

Eve's cell phone rang. "That must be Joe. I wouldn't have thought he'd have been able to make it to the accident scene by—" She frowned. "It's not Joe. No ID." She accessed the call. "Eve Duncan."

"Rick Avery, Ms. Duncan."

She stiffened, stunned. "What?"

"I know this must be a surprise to you, but I've been told you're with my daughter. I need to talk to her."

"Go to hell. You're the last person she needs to talk to."

"You have a right to be angry. You've been told lies, and you only want to help my daughter. I've heard you're a fine woman, but you don't understand. Let me help you to understand."

"Your daughter? Where have you been for Beth all these years?"

Beth suddenly sat up straight in her

chair, her eyes wide. "Rick?" she whispered. "He wants to speak to me, Eve?"

"Yes. Don't talk to him, Beth." But she could see she was talking to the wind. Of course she was going to talk to her father. "I'm pressing the speaker. I need to hear what he says."

"I don't care." Beth snatched the phone from her. "Rick? It's been so long. I've missed you."

"Do you think I haven't missed you?" His voice was a little husky. "My best friend, my little girl? They told me that it was better for you if I didn't see you, that I'd disturb you and make you sad when I had to leave."

"I wouldn't have cared."

"I cared for you. I told them everything had to be just right for you after you got hurt. You had to be treated like a princess, and nothing must hurt you. They did what I told them, didn't they?"

"Yes, no one hurt me."

Eve's nails dug into her palms. No, nothing hurt Beth because of the drugs that kept her from feeling. She wanted to scream that out at him. Beth's face was radiant with love and joy, and she was believing every word he said.

And heaven help her, Eve was beginning to believe him, too. Rick Avery's voice was deep with feeling, and his words utterly sincere. Maybe he did believe that what he was saying was true. Maybe Nelda had been so convincing that he had believed her without question. Why not? It would have been easy to believe that Beth didn't need him, and he should go on with his life.

What was she thinking? This man preyed on young girls. He was indirectly responsible for the death of that twelve-year-old at the chalet. "Don't listen to him, Beth."

But it was Eve Beth wasn't hearing. Beth was totally focused, totally absorbed in her father. She was paying no attention to Eve. "I knew that you weren't to blame. I still have my key, Rick. When I saw it, I knew that you hadn't stopped caring about me."

"Of course I care about you. Nelda gave me reports about you every month." He paused. "But I've been so worried about you since you left the hospital. Why did you do that? Everyone wants to do what's best for you. Nelda said it was some young orderly who filled your head with lies and caused you to run away." He added harshly, "I wanted to break his neck for putting you in danger like that. You weren't prepared to face life outside of the hospital. Anything could have happened. Everyone was searching for you, even the police. Did you know that?"

"Yes, and Billy is my friend. He wanted to help me. He could see that I wasn't really sick."

"You *are* sick," Rick said gently. "All the doctors say that's true. You have to believe it, so that we can try to get you well."

"And keep me there another ten years or more?" Beth asked jerkily. "I'm not sick. I'm not crazy. Eve says that it was all a plot."

"Do you know how paranoid that sounds?"

"Rick, you have to believe me. Please."

"I want to believe you. Do you think I wouldn't be over the moon if I thought you were getting well after all this time? But Dr. Pierce says that you haven't altered the—"

"Pierce is dead."

"What?"

"You didn't know? A car accident here

in L.A. At least the police think it's an accident. Joe and Eve aren't sure it's not murder."

"Good God, it's no wonder you're paranoid with them pouring poison like that in your ears. Dr. Pierce took care of you for years, and your half sister appears on the scene, and you forget everything he did for you."

Eve couldn't let that go by without a response. "Imprisonment, drug addiction, theft of everything that made life worth living." She was speaking loud enough so that he could hear her. "That's what Pierce did for her, Avery."

"You're mistaken," Rick said. "And I'm sorry that you feel that way. It's clear that you wish to help Beth and I'm grateful. But you couldn't be more wrong. You don't believe her, do you, Beth?"

Beth looked at Eve. "I think I do, Rick. Things have . . . happened."

Silence. "Then we have to talk this out. I was just going to ask you to come back to the hospital with me, but I want to be fair. If there's any possibility that you're right, I'll be there for you. We'll get everything straightened out, and I'll take you home with me. But if you can't convince me, then you'll go back to therapy. Maybe a new doctor at a facility close to me, so I can visit you. It's what I always wanted anyway."

"Close to you?" Beth repeated. "I *will* convince you, Rick. I swear there's nothing wrong with me."

"You're already convincing me." He chuckled. "Now you remind me of my tough, beautiful girl who put all those other girls in your school in the shade."

"You're the only one who ever called me beautiful." Her hand reached up and clasped the key pendant. "They say . . . something happened at the chalet that night. I don't remember, but I know it wasn't your fault."

"You don't remember?" He sounded suddenly relieved. "Then it's better forgotten. We'll start new and bright after we get all this straightened out." He added crisply, "I'd come to you, but we couldn't really talk with you surrounded by all those people who think I'm not doing what's best for you. It's better if you come to me."

Beth frowned. "South Carolina?"

"No, I'm in Los Angeles. Nelda said that no one could find you but that I might be able to help. As soon as I knew you needed me, I hopped a plane and came here."

"A little late," Eve said. But she had little hope that it would have any effect. "And, of course, Nelda had no ulterior motive."

"I won't let you malign my mother. She wants me to be happy and Beth to get well. That's her only agenda. Beth, will you come to me so that we can talk?"

"No!" Eve said.

"Where are you?" Beth asked.

"I had to keep away from the big hotels. The media are always after me these days. I'm at a small beach house near Malibu. As soon as you get on the way, I'll give you the address."

"She's not going," Eve said. "I don't trust you or your mother or whatever slime-balls you might have waiting for Beth."

"I'll be alone. I promise, Beth." He paused. "But you'll have to be alone, too. Don't bring Quinn or your friend, Billy. They would only get in the way. I love you. I've always loved you. Will you trust me?"

Beth spoke without even a hesitation. "I trust you. I'm coming, Rick." She hung up.

"Don't be crazy, Beth," Eve said. "It's a trap."

"It's not a trap. Couldn't you tell? Rick meant every word he said. He's never lied to me." She met her gaze as she got to her feet. "He cares about me."

She couldn't argue with Rick Avery's sincerity. It was no wonder Beth had believed him. Eve had tried to punch holes in his words, but she couldn't fault that part of his story. She could see how Sandra, and now Beth, had been caught and held by him all these years. If he was a liar, he was the greatest one she had ever met. "So he appeared to be telling the truth. It doesn't mean that he's not being used."

"What if he's not? We're not sure if his mother is to blame for what happened. I can't remember anything. Maybe it was all Pierce's fault, his plan." Her eyes were glittering in her taut face, and her expression was alight with excitement. "I have to go to Rick. He wants to talk to me. We may be able to go home together."

"You've never had a home with him," she said in despair.

"Not because he didn't want to give me a home. It was just . . . difficult." She gazed at Eve pleadingly. "It's my chance, Eve. I don't want to turn my back on it."

"It's a trap."

"No. Rick wouldn't do that." She turned and started toward the garden gate. "I'm going. Don't try to stop me."

She meant it, and there was no way to argue her out of it.

"Okay, I won't." She jumped to her feet and strode toward the gate. "But I'm going with you. Don't argue. You're not going alone. I'll drive you."

"Rick told me not to bring—"

"Then Rick will have to change his mind," she said grimly. "You can leave Newell and Joe out of the mix, but you're not going to leave this house without me. I'm going with you, I'm taking my gun, and I'm going to search that beach house before you take a step inside it."

"It's going to be all right, Eve," Beth said. "I feel it. Whatever you believe about his mother, I know Rick is a good guy. I just have to show him that I'm not a mental case, then we'll put our heads together to try to find out what happened to me."

"We're already trying to do that." Eve made an impatient gesture. "And we've come pretty damn close without Rick Avery's help. But I can't convince you of that, can I?" She didn't wait for an answer as she pulled the garden gate closed behind her and headed around the house toward the car in the driveway. "So we'll do it your way and hope that you're right. But there's no way that I'll bank on it. If your father wants to get cozy with you, then he'll have to take me with the package." She got into the driver's seat of the Toyota and started the car. "Get in. Faith is a wonderful thing, but I'm sadly lacking in it at the moment. Let's get this over."

"You don't have to have faith," Beth said. "I have it. You'll realize when you meet him how—"

"Eve!" Newell was running out the front door. "What the hell is happening? Where—"

"I'll call you," Eve called to him as she drove off down the street. "I promise." She turned the corner and headed for the entrance of the subdivision. Her hands tightened on the steering wheel. "I don't like leaving Newell in the dark. I don't like anything about this."

"Then let me take you back, and I'll drive myself," Beth said quietly. "You've done enough for me. Let me take over now."

"I can't do that." She drew a deep breath

and tried to release the frustration that was both useless and emotionally wearing. "I have to see it through to the end. I understand that sisters do that for each other. Give me my phone. I'm calling Newell. Although it's probably too late to stop him from calling Joe." She dialed Newell's number. "I'm sorry, Newell. Rick Avery called Beth, and she insisted on going to him when he said he needed to see her."

Newell cursed long and emphatically. "Are you nuts, Eve? Do you want to set her up? It has to be a trap."

"She won't believe it, and I couldn't let her go alone. I had no choice."

"I would have had a choice. I'd have knocked her out, then given her a shot to keep her that way."

"No, you wouldn't. You'd be doing the same thing I'm doing. Trying to keep her safe. I'm not going to take any chances. I have my .38 and I'm not going to go in blind."

"But you're going in alone. And Joe is going to go ballistic. I'm calling him as soon as I hang up. Where are you going?"

"Malibu somewhere." She saw Beth shaking her head. "I can't tell you exactly where. He's going to give us an address as soon as we get in the general area." She added, for Beth's benefit, "He didn't want anyone but Beth, but that's not an option. He'll put up with me. And I'll give you and Joe the address when I pull up to the house. That should give you both a chance to get here within a reasonable length of time and still let Rick have his opportunity to convince Beth that he's only misunderstood. Tell Joe that I'm not answering my phone. I'll talk to him at Avery's place."

"Coward."

"You bet. I know how stupid this is. I just have to do it." She hung up.

"Rick's not going to like not having much time alone with me," Beth said reproachfully.

"Compromise." Eve turned onto the freeway. "He gets what he wants. We get what we want."

It sounded good, but it might be a shallow victory. Was Drogan behind her on the freeway?

Or was he waiting at that house in Malibu?

"You're worried," Beth said. "You have a right to worry considering all you've been through for me. You think I'm foolish. But don't we have to trust the people we love? Isn't that what you're supposed to do?"

She opened her mouth to tell her that Rick didn't deserve trust. But she glanced at Beth and sighed resignedly. Her expression was no longer luminous and excited, but the wonder and wistfulness was just as touching. God, she was hoping Beth's trust wouldn't be betrayed in any brutal way. She reached out and gave her sister's hand a quick squeeze. "So they tell me. We're certainly giving it a good try." She took her hand away. "Now do a return on Rick's call, tell him we're on our way, and get an address from him."

"She did what?" Joe tried to keep his voice even when he wanted to shout at Newell. "I told you to keep watch over—" He broke off. This wasn't Newell's fault. Eve had made the decision.

And that decision was scaring him shitless.

"I thought I was watching to keep the bad guys from coming in and attacking,"

Newell said. "I didn't think they'd be running away to meet them."

"I know." He strode away from the flashing lights of Pierce's accident scene toward his car. "And Eve wouldn't have done it if she'd had any way to persuade Beth."

"At least Eve's on guard. She's not all dewy-eyed like Beth," Newell said. "She said Avery is in Malibu, and she'd call us with the address. I've called a taxi to take me to the nearest rental-car place to pick up a car, but you'll probably get to Malibu before I do."

"Maybe. I'm a good hour away."

And a second could mean the difference between life and death.

Kendra.

"Look, don't go to the rental agency. I'll call you right back." He hung up and dialed Kendra. "How close are you to Valencia now?"

"About twenty minutes."

"Try to make it sooner." He rattled off the address. "Pick up Newell. I'm across town, and he has to move fast."

"Problems?"

"Mega problems. Newell will explain." He hung up and called Newell back. "Kendra

Michaels will pick you up. Get out there to Malibu." He hung up and called Eve.

No answer. He didn't expect one, but he'd had to try. Eve had made her decision and wouldn't permit any interference. She'd committed to Beth and was attempting to walk a fine line to keep Beth safe and let them have their chance if she was in danger. She was trying to be all things to all people, dammit.

And she could get herself killed.

CHAPTER
17

The cottage in Malibu was very modest, but it was not crowded on top of its neighbors. It was on one of the back streets, not on the beach, and the neighboring cottages were a good hundred yards away.

Rick Avery came out on the wraparound deck as they pulled up in the driveway. He smiled, a beautiful smile that lit his face. "Beth. Come up here and let me hold you. It's been too long."

"Rick." Beth jumped out of the car and tore up the steps toward him.

"Shit," Eve muttered as she ran after her, her hand closing on the gun in her jacket pocket. All her plans of searching the house before she let Beth meet with her father were out the window in the first minute. But that didn't mean she couldn't still try to make it as secure as possible. As she reached the deck, she stopped to look at Beth and Rick Avery a few yards away. Rick was holding Beth close, and she was clinging desperately to him.

Love.

Eve had known that Beth loved her father but had doubted that the feeling was returned. She had been wrong. Gentleness, sadness, love were all in his expression at that moment.

And, good heavens, the man was wonderful looking. There were a few threads of gray in his hair, but she could that see he still exuded charisma and magnetism and, yes, youth. You wanted to walk closer to him, speak to him, have him look at you with that beautiful smile.

I understand now, Sandra.

Rick lifted his head and saw Eve. "You're Sandra's daughter? You don't look like her."

"We're very different." She pulled her gaze away and looked around the deck, then to the sliding glass doors. "How many rooms are there in this house?"

His brows rose. Evidently, he wasn't accustomed to anyone's dismissing him. "It's quite tiny. Two bedrooms, a bath, living room, and kitchenette."

She slipped her gun out of her pocket and headed for the glass doors. "You'll probably not have more than twenty or thirty minutes before Joe and Newell get here. If you're going to talk to Beth, you'd better not waste time."

"A gun?" He was smiling as he shook his head. "I'm sure you have the best of intentions, but it's not necessary. This is all a misunderstanding. No one is going to hurt my daughter."

"You're right, you've already done that. It's not going to happen again."

"That's not fair," Beth said as she stepped back from Rick. "I know it wasn't Rick's fault."

"Yes, it was his fault. You were his daughter, he had a duty to protect you." She ignored Beth's exclamation of protest and went inside the house. The lights were all on, and the floor plan allowed her to see from one end of the cottage to the other. It took only a few minutes to go through the rest of the house. No one lurking. Nothing suspicious.

Except the entire concept that Rick Avery had suddenly been called upon to lure his daughter to meet with him.

It had to be a trap.

Yet, if it was, she was beginning to believe that Rick didn't realize that it was a trap.

She came back on the deck to see Rick and Beth talking quietly, their hands clasped. How beautiful they were together, she thought suddenly. The resemblance was striking, silky dark hair, wonderful features, that eager smile.

He turned to Eve as she came out of the house. "Satisfied?"

"No, but there's no one in the house. That doesn't mean your mother hasn't arranged something else to surprise us."

He frowned. "Don't accuse my mother of anything. You can talk about me, but leave her alone. She only wants what's best for Beth."

"Is that why she kept Beth drugged and

in that prison of a hospital for over a decade?"

"Beth was ill."

"Look at her, Avery." Eve gestured to
Beth. "You've seen her, talked to her.
There's nothing wrong with her. There was
never anything wrong with Beth. Putting
her away was just a convenient way for
your mother to protect herself and still not
let you know she was even more of a monster than you were."

"She wouldn't do that. You're being ridiculous. She's not a monster. She couldn't
be more loving or protective of me."

"She protected you a little too much. All
your life, Avery. But it became more difficult for her when you developed a passion
for young girls. It was a dark passion and
not acceptable for the career Nelda was
planning for you. I'd bet she provided you
with safe amusement in Asia to keep you
from staining your reputation here in the
States. But you decided to bring one of the
girls here. That girl you had at your chalet
that night was only twelve years old. The
chalet was secluded, and you thought it
would be safe to have the girl there. But

your mother found out about it and came to tell you that you had to get rid of her."

"I don't want to discuss this." Rick glanced at Beth. "Beth, she's making it all sound ugly. It wasn't like that. You know me. I would never hurt anyone. Tell her what kind of person I am."

"I've already told her. Why do you think I'm here, Rick?" Beth looked from Eve to Rick, her expression torn. "I told you, I don't remember anything, Eve. Rick believes in his mother. How do I know that she's not everything he thinks she is?" She took a step closer to him. "Doesn't she have a right to defend herself?"

"Beth, she *is* defending herself. Every-thing she's done has been to defend her-self and strike out at any danger to her family and position. Including killing that child at the chalet."

"No," Rick said quickly. "Su Kim didn't die. She was fine. Her father took her back to Macao. I sent a generous bonus to him a few months later."

"That little girl probably died in Toronto, Canada. It was too late to treat her by the time they got her out of the country to a place Nelda considered safe."

"That's a lie," Rick said. "That's not what happened."

"Tell her what did happen, Rick," Beth said. "I know it's some terrible mistake about that girl." She gazed at Eve defiantly. "Why do you keep talking about her? Gelber's report was probably nothing but lies."

"But it bothers you, doesn't it?" Eve asked. "And you were particularly resistant when I asked you about Rick's attitude toward your young friends."

"Because it was nasty. Rick's not—"

"Didn't you hear him just now?" It was proving almost impossible to break through Beth's loyalty to her father. "Everything in Gelber's notes was true. Your father isn't denying it, Beth. That girl was at the chalet. She was hurt, and he thought she'd recovered." She whirled back to Rick. "And do you know why Beth didn't remember anything about what happened at that chalet? Because those wonderful doctors your mother turned loose on her tortured her every time that memory popped up. There's still so much trauma that she won't let it surface."

His eyes widened in shock. "Now that's

a complete falsehood. My mother wouldn't do—"

"She did it," Eve said coldly. "It's clear she'd do anything to protect herself. She probably considered it a fair exchange. You'd made her commit murder by your self-indulgence with that Asian girl. So she took away your daughter, whom she considered a major inconvenience anyway."

"That's not true. My mother wouldn't do anything like that."

Eve gave him a skeptical glance. "You couldn't have gone through all these years with her without seeing that side of her. I'm sure she tried her best to hide it from you, but you're not stupid. Though I can see you accepting whatever she told you because it was more comfortable for you."

"You think it was comfortable for me to know that Beth was in a mental hospital?" His arm tightened around Beth's shoulders. "I love my daughter. You don't believe any of this, do you, Beth?"

"No, of course not." Beth was shaking her head dazedly. "Didn't you hear me? I told Eve that it was all wrong." She lifted her hand to her temple. "But I don't remember—I don't understand. She said terrible things about you, Rick. About you and that young girl—and you're saying that she was there, too. But you wouldn't do that, Rick. You wouldn't hurt a twelve-year-old girl."

"No, of course I wouldn't."

"But she was there. You said she was there."

"Because she wanted to be. I've never forced a girl in my life." His hands closed on Beth's shoulders, and he turned her to face him. "Listen, Beth." His voice was soft, urgent. "If she hadn't wanted me, I'd have sent her away. I spent time with her, making sure. She liked me. She even said she loved me."

Beth was looking at him with an expression of growing horror. "She was twelve years old."

"She had a hard life, I gave her enough money so that she'd have a choice whether she wanted to go with any other man again. I wanted to make sure that our time together was only good for her." His hand stroked her cheek. "So stop looking at me like that, Beth. It hurts me."

"I don't want to hurt you," she said dully. "But twelve years old, Rick. Why?"

He didn't speak.

"Why?"

"It's hard to explain." He shrugged. "It's just . . . preference. Why not? I told you that I didn't hurt anyone. I made them feel good, not bad."

"And . . . how did you feel, Rick?"

"I loved them," he said simply. "They were fresh and sweet and like the first breath of spring. Nothing complicated, just bright and happy and wanting to make me happy."

Beth looked as if he'd struck her. "I feel sick." She closed her eyes. "So wrong, Rick. You're so wrong." Her eyes opened, and she whispered, "And if you're that wrong about those girls, how can I be sure you're not wrong about your mother's putting me in that . . . place?" She stepped back away from him, and her voice broke. "And that Eve's not right about your turning your back on me because it was more comfortable for you."

"Because I love you," he said harshly. "You're my little girl, my daughter, and I love you more than anyone in the world." He shot a tormented glance at Eve. "You see what you've done? She believes those lies you've been telling her."

Eve ignored him. "I think you're done here, Beth. It will be at least fifteen minutes before Joe or Newell get here, and I don't think it's safe to stick around. Shall we go?"

Beth nodded jerkily and turned toward the steps.

"Wait." Rick was suddenly standing before Beth, and he smiled the beautiful smile that he'd given Beth when she'd first arrived. "You're upset right now," he said coaxingly. "But you'll think about everything I've said, and you'll realize that I'm still the father you've always known. Perhaps there have been mistakes made, but we can make everything right."

"How?" Her voice was shaking. "By putting me back in that hospital?"

He flinched. "No, you're well now. My mother must not have realized that you'd made such progress. We'll start out fresh."

"You still believe her," Beth said wonderingly. "And that scares me more than anything that's happened." She turned to Eve. "We'd better go. You were right. Coming here may have been a terrible mistake. They could have used him to bait the trap."

"Don't be silly," Rick said. "There's no

trap. No force. I was only supposed to persuade you that it would be better to go
back to the hospital to continue your treatment. But it's clear that's not necessary
now." He reached out and gently touched
her cheek. "Do you know how happy I am
to see you so well? It's like a dream come
true. But you'd better give me your address, so we can straighten all of this out
with the police."

"I don't think you'll need our address,"
Eve said grimly as she followed Beth
down the stairs. "Your mother has probably taken care of seeing that she'll know
where we are." She unlocked the driver's
door and got into the car. "But we'll work
on changing that as soon as I meet with
Joe and—"

The scent of sulfur.

It smells of sulfur.

Kendra's words in Beth's hospital room
came back to her.

And Eve had caught that scent again
the moment they had gotten into the car.

"Eve?" Beth was looking at her, puzzled.

"It's okay." She reached into her pocket
and drew out her .38. "Just . . . get out of

the car, Beth. I forgot to tell Avery something."

"What?"

"Get out of the car!" she said sharply. "Now!"

Beth instinctively threw open the door and started to scramble out.

"Close that door. Get back in the car." The muzzle of a gun was pressed to Eve's head as a man's arm slid around her neck from where he was kneeling on the floor of the backseat. At the same time, the edge of his other hand came down on Eve's gun hand, numbing it. He took her .38. "Unless you want to see her brains spattering on that windshield."

"Drogan?" Eve said. "God, I was stupid. I should have searched the car and not counted on just locking it."

"It took me a good five minutes to open it. I was in full view of you for a couple of those minutes," he murmured. "But you were very absorbed with each other. I was counting on that since I couldn't be waiting for you in the house. I cased it before Avery came today but there was no decent place to hide. And she said that her precious boy mustn't be involved. Now start the car and back out of the driveway."

"Let Eve go," Beth said. "It's me you want, isn't it?"

"Actually, you've taken second place of late. Start the car, Duncan."

"Beth?" Rick Avery was coming down the steps, his eyes squinting against the glare of the security lights from the garage. "What's happening? I saw you start to get out of the car. Did you change your mind? Come back into the house, and we'll talk about it."

Drogan muttered a curse. "Keep him away. Tell him anything, but keep him *away*."

Beth was frantically rolling down the window. "Rick, stop."

Rick had reached the bottom of the steps. "I won't stop. This is too important to both of us."

"Keep the bastard away," Drogan snarled. "This wasn't supposed to—"

But Rick was beside the passenger side of the car. He was smiling. "Beth, I knew you wouldn't let our—"

A pop of sound.

A hole appeared in the center of Rick Avery's forehead.

Beth screamed.

"Start the damn car," Drogan said through his teeth to Eve. "Or I'll put another hole in *her* head. Everything's gone wrong. It wasn't supposed to happen this way."

Eve started to back out of the drive.

"No, I've got to go to him," Beth was struggling to get her door open, tears running down her cheeks. "Maybe I can—"

"He's dead, Beth," Eve said.

"Quiet her down," Drogan said. "I don't really care whether I kill her now or later. It's up to you."

"Beth," Eve said. "You can't help Rick. But you can help me. Just don't lose it. Calm down, okay?" She didn't wait for an answer but continued to back out of the driveway with a screech of tires. She had to get Beth away from the sight of Rick's crumpled body. She couldn't count on anything from Beth after she had just seen the murder of the only person in the world she loved. "Where, Drogan?"

"Just around the corner and two blocks up. We need to ditch this car and take my truck. Quinn will be able to track this car too easily. He won't know what I'm driving." He pocketed the gun he'd taken from Eve before pointing to an old Chevy truck parked next to the curb. "Get out. Both of you."

"Why not just let us go?" Eve asked. "Nelda Avery is paying your blood money, isn't she? You just said that you'd blown your deal by killing Rick Avery."

"That was your fault. If you'd driven out of the driveway right away, I wouldn't have had to kill him. He was going to cause trouble. I had both of you where I wanted you, and I wasn't about to let him ruin everything."

"And you panicked."

"I don't panic, bitch."

"You killed him, didn't you? Now you're not going to get any more cash from her. Let us go."

"I might still be able to negotiate with her. It depends if her love for her son is greater than her love for herself. I'd bet on her loving herself more." He shrugged. "And, if I'm wrong, there are other satisfactions. You're a rare prize, Eve Duncan. I was hoping to have Quinn present to participate, and that might still be an option. That would be the best scenario."

She heard a sudden rustling, slithering sound.

Drogan chuckled. "Mama Zela agrees with me." He held up a small cage. "She likes to perform to an audience."

A snake. He had a snake in that cage.

Eve had a sudden memory of that part of his dossier.

His mother's skeleton was found years later buried in a coffin with a snake wrapped around her throat.

Mama Zela was his mother's name. And he called this snake Mama Zela. It seemed hideous that he'd name a snake after the mother he'd murdered.

She was shuddering. The idea filled her with horror. Don't let him see it. He would feed on her fear as that snake had fed on his mother.

But he'd already sensed it. "You'll be braver than my mother," he said softly as he opened the car door and gestured with the gun for them to get out. "She couldn't believe that it could happen to her, that I'd actually do it. She kept screaming for me to let her out."

That brought a picture to mind that was even more vivid. She didn't answer him.

He didn't like that response. "But everyone breaks in the end. When they realize no one is going to save them. You'll beg me just as she did."

"Go to hell."

He laughed. "Oh, you'll pay for that." He glanced at Beth, who was sitting frozen, her eyes fixed straight ahead in shock. "Or she will. I'm still annoyed with her. Quinn's interference just managed to shift the principal emphasis."

"You killed Rick," Beth said numbly. "How could you do that?"

He didn't answer.

Eve reached out and took Beth's hand in silent support.

"How touching," Drogan said. "You've obviously become very close. Maybe I should put both of you in the same coffin. I'll have to think about it . . ."

Kendra was kneeling in the driveway beside the crumpled figure of a man when Joe's car screeched to a stop in front of the Malibu cottage. She looked up as he jumped out and ran toward her. "Eve?"

She shook her head. "Not here. Neither is Beth. I got here ten minutes ago, and all I found was him." She nodded at the dead man. "It's Rick Avery."

Joe nodded jerkily. "Evidently, the trap didn't go as planned." Keep cool. Keep calm. He wouldn't get anywhere if he panicked. "But he didn't kill either Eve or Beth. Maybe Drogan had plans, too. He was angry as hell when he phoned me yesterday." Better not to think of that vicious malice toward Eve now. "Where's Newell?"

"He took off to check out the houses in the neighborhood and see if he could find any trace of Drogan. I wanted to stay here and look around."

"What did you find out?"

She shook her head.

"Don't tell me that," he said through set teeth. "I know what you can do. This is Eve. You've got to—"

"Shut up, Joe," she said curtly. "I know you're hurting. But I'm not perfect, and I can't pull something out of the air if it's not there. Do you think I don't want to—"

"Sorry." He cut her off and reached for his phone. "I'll call the local police and report Avery's murder. We can at least set them moving on his trail." He talked briefly to 911 and hung up. "You said you'd been here ten minutes? There aren't any neighbors or curiosity seekers around. That bullet in his skull must have come from a gun with a silencer."

Kendra nodded. "Possibly. But I think he may have improvised this time. Maybe wrapped his gun in rags or a towel to muffle the sound."

"How do you figure that?"

Kendra knelt at the edge of the driveway and picked up two small, charred, cloth fragments in the tall grass.

Joe took the fragments. They both showed evidence of flash burns and gunpowder residue. "You're right. But that's not the kind of information I need, Kendra."

"I've found the car." Newell was striding down the street toward them. "Drogan made Eve abandon that rental car she was driving. It's parked down the block and around the corner."

Joe was already running in the direction Newell was indicating. The Toyota was unlocked, and he jerked the driver's door open.

Nothing. What had he expected? A miracle? A sign from Eve that would have told them something, anything.

"Nothing here." He turned to Kendra who was now beside him. "Not a damn thing."

"That may not be true," Kendra said slowly, her head lifted. "Not in the front seat. But maybe in the rear . . ." She opened the rear door of the car. "Yes . . ."

"For God's sake, what?"

"A combination, I think." She turned on her purse flashlight and shined the beam on the carpet. "And one that could come only from Drogan . . . or someone with similar interests." She brushed her hand across the floor, and tiny black grains stuck to her fingers. She sniffed her hand. "I think this is . . ." She held it out to Joe. "Taste it."

He tentatively touched it with his tongue.

"For God's sake, I'm not trying to poison you," she said in disgust.

"You never know." He tasted it again. "Salt?"

She nodded. "Black salt. Voodoo practitioners use black salt for protection. You said that Drogan believed in that stuff, didn't you?"

Joe nodded.

Kendra rubbed her thumb and forefinger together. "It's mixed with the oil I've been smelling. Sulfur, again . . . I smelled it in Beth's hospital room, too, but it didn't strike me as too unusual then since sulfur is also used in medicines. It didn't really click until I was driving here tonight and thinking about what you and Eve told me about Drogan's being into voodoo. They use various oils in their ceremonies, and sulfur is one of the most-frequently-used ingredients."

"Ceremonies? In the backseat of the car?"

"Don't talk. Just let me concentrate for a minute and see how many ingredients I can identify."

"What difference does it make?"

"Drogan has to get his oils from someplace. We might be able to locate him through his source."

"Maybe he makes it himself."

She shook her head. "Not likely. Among other things, the oils are supposed to protect against negative energy. The cults have strict recipes and procedures, and most practitioners only trust holy men to create them."

"How do you know all this?"

"I spent a summer working in a club on Bourbon Street. You don't hang around

New Orleans long without becoming a little familiar with voodoo lore."

"And with you, it would be more than a little familiar."

"It's fascinating . . . and dark. It . . . drew me."

"And how would you be able to trace Drogan through his voodoo oil?"

"They're not all the same. The various holy men prefer different ingredients. It's like a signature. This one is . . . unusual."

"Where are you supposed to find a voodoo holy man in the middle of California?"

"You think voodoo is limited to Louisiana and the islands? No way. It's just not as frequently practiced."

"I stand corrected," Joe said. "If you can find a voodoo holy man who will lead us to Drogan, for God's sake do it."

"There are tire tracks on the edge of this grass, Quinn," Newell called from where he was kneeling on the side of the curb.

"I'll be right there." He glanced at Kendra before he turned away. "Why is it unusual?"

"I've smelled this oil before, but now there's something else here. The oil is interacting with something else."

"What?"

"It smells like . . . cucumbers."

"Is that part of the recipe?"

"No . . . it means . . ." Kendra looked up. "There was a snake in here, Joe."

He stiffened. "What?"

"He had a snake in this car. Some snakes' musk glands can give off an odor that's similar to cucumber. I know that smell." She gave him a level glance. "And the way the odors blend and interact . . . I think he may have oiled it."

"The snake?" He stared at her. "Totally bizarre."

"Particularly if he spread the oil on the snake with his own hands. That would really be weird." She made an impatient gesture. "Go check out those tire tracks. You can't help me with this. I'll be with you as soon as I'm through here."

Newell looked up at him. "I think he was driving a truck. There are two treads, close together."

"Which won't do us much good." Joe was tensing with frustration. Time was passing, and they were running into blank walls. "We don't have time to run those tire prints and identify the usual trucks who use them."

"I'm done." Kendra was beside them. She examined the tire tracks. "Not much help here, is there? Not on an immediate basis." She went a little farther down the curb. "But here's a footprint . . ." She knelt and shined her beam. "Men's size eleven or twelve, fairly common hiking boot . . ."

Sirens in the distance.

She lifted her head. "There's the police you called, Joe."

"Then let's get out of here." Joe turned and strode back toward the beach cottage. "I did my duty by calling them. But I can't be stuck here answering questions and filling out reports. You think you can find the source of that voodoo oil? Let's do it. Hurry."

Kendra almost ran to keep up with him. "I am hurrying. I know that you— Who is that?" She had stopped in the street and was staring at the driveway of the Malibu cottage.

A woman was kneeling on the driveway beside Rick Avery, cradling him in her arms and rocking back in forth in an agony of sorrow.

Joe muttered a curse. "Nelda Avery." He was striding up the driveway. "We may have just gotten lucky." He stopped before Nelda. "Where is Drogan?"

She didn't seem to hear the question. "My son is dead." Tears were running down her cheeks. "My Rick is dead."

"And Beth and Eve may end up that way before the night is over if I don't get Drogan. I don't give a damn about your son. Tell me where I can find Drogan."

"It wasn't supposed to be this way." She was gently stroking the hair back from her son's forehead. "I told him to be careful, not to hurt my Rick. He didn't listen. Now look at him . . ." She was sobbing. "I made Rick promise to call me right after he talked to Beth, and he didn't do it. Rick always kept his promises to me. I called him, and he didn't answer. I had a terrible feeling . . ."

"Where is Drogan?"

She was rocking Rick back and forth again. "Go away."

Joe bent toward her and his voice was low and fierce. "Listen to me. You tell me where he is. Quick. I'm not having those police decide you're some pitiful victim and taking you away. I don't care if you're the mother of this poor, half-witted bastard. You're responsible for getting Eve here. Now tell me where Drogan took her. Or, by God, I'll break your neck."

Kendra took a step forward. "Joe."

He ignored her. "Where? Stop protecting him."

"Protecting him?" Nelda looked up at him, her face ravaged by pain. "Do you think I'd protect Drogan? He killed my son. He's ruined my life. I want him dead."

"Where is he? I'll be glad to oblige."

"I don't know. He didn't trust me. I've always contacted him by phone, and he was always telling me that he'd do things his way." She looked down at her son. "This is his way," she said bitterly. "Go find him. Go kill him. I'd like to do it myself."

"There must be something you can—"

"I tell you that I don't know where that bastard is," she said hoarsely. "Now go away and leave me with my son."

"She doesn't know, Joe," Kendra said. "Can't you see? She's telling the truth."

Joe gazed at Nelda for an instant longer, then whirled on his heel and stalked down the driveway toward his car. Newell straightened from where he was leaning on the front bumper. "I know how you feel, Quinn," he said quietly. "I'm not sure I wouldn't have broken her neck anyway. Drogan was the weapon, but she was the one who wielded it." He got into the backseat of the car. "So we struck out, Kendra. Can you pull any rabbits out of your hat?"

"How the hell do I know?" She got into the front passenger seat and took out her phone. "Get us away from this subdivision before the police get here, Joe. Those sirens sound pretty close. I'll see what I can find out about that voodoo oil."

"How?" Joe asked as he pulled away from the curb. "We don't have time for you to—" His phone rang. His heart leaped as he saw Eve's ID. His finger jammed the access button. "Eve? For God's sake, where are you?"

"With me. Drogan. I couldn't resist talking to you. I hoped to have you present when I got rid of your woman, but that might not be wise. So I thought that I'd let your imagination help me."

"If you touch her or Beth, I'll butcher you the way you deserve, you son of a bitch."

Drogan chuckled. "No, I'm on top now. All you have are empty words. You won our first encounter, but I'll win the last. I'll get you eventually, but now I have Eve Duncan.

Do you know what I'm going to do with her?"

"I'm sure you're going to tell me," Joe said hoarsely.

"I've decided she deserves a ceremonial end. You're a good cop, aren't you, Joe Quinn? I'm sure you were able to research my somewhat colorful background. Your Eve reminds me of my mother." He added softly, "Do you know what I did to my mother?" He hung up.

Joe's right fist crashed down on the steering wheel. "Bastard. Bastard."

"Joe?" Kendra tentatively touched his shoulder.

He drew a harsh breath. "Well I definitely know what he's planning for that snake." He turned to her. "And I won't let him do it. We're going to find him. Help me, dammit. He may toy with her for a while, but he's—"

"I'll try. Calm down. I'll make a phone call," she interrupted as she dialed. "Dave Kramer. He's an old friend who owns a head shop in San Ysidro. He also sells a lot of this Goth and occult stuff. He might be able to give me a lead on Drogan's source."

"Who may have a delivery address?" Newell asked.

She shrugged. "We just have to follow the dots." She put the phone on speaker as the call was accessed, "Dave, Kendra Michaels. I need—"

"Do you know what time it is?"

"Did I wake you?"

"No, but you interrupted me." He added sourly, "Never mind. What do you want?"

"Voodoo oil. I need the name and address of a holy man who sells black arts oil in California."

Kramer made a disgusted sound. "Kendra, don't tell me you believe in that crap. The only reason I carry this stuff is that—"

"I don't want to buy it. There's a certain oil I need to trace back to the maker. Can you help?"

"I can name four people right off the top of my head. Some of those college kids in Burbank have been fooling around with the cult since there have been all those movies and zombie shows."

"This isn't a college kid. He's the real thing and very nasty. I have to find him fast, Dave."

He was silent. "Okay. Bring it in, and I'm pretty sure we can—"

"No time for that. I'm in Malibu. But I

think I can tell you most of the ingredients."

"Why make it easy for me, huh?"

"I identified several of them. Probably
not all." She began to reel off the scents
she'd detected in the car.

Joe shook his head. Kendra always
amazed him—a few minutes of concentration, and she had been able to separate
and identify at least ten elements.

"Wait a minute." Dave stopped her.
"Cola?"

"That's what it smelled like. Am I wrong?"

"Yeah, that's cinnamon bark you're smelling. Give me a minute to look through my
catalog." He came back on the line. "There's
only one person in the area who deals with
a black oil made with cinnamon bark. It's
Nancy Geronimo and the cinnamon bark is
kind of her trademark. She's an elderly Na-
tive American woman, and she claims that
the cinnamon bark soothes sacrificial ani-
mals used in the rituals."

"Snakes?"

"I never heard of its being used on
snakes. I guess it's possible. But they're
not usually one of the sacrifices. They tend
to embody a god or something."

"Drogan may be establishing his own rules. Where does she live?"

"Mojave."

"The desert?"

"The town. It's in the desert."

"Can you give me a phone and address?"

He paused, checking, then rattled off the information. "Is that all? Now may I go back to bed?"

"Yes, thanks, Dave."

"Well, it wasn't my pleasure, but you've done me a couple favors, Kendra. Come and see me next time you're down my way." He hung up.

Kendra immediately dialed the phone number for Nancy Geronimo.

No answer.

No voice mail.

Joe muttered a curse.

She dialed again.

No answer.

Kendra hung up and turned to Joe. "We can go bang on her door. But Mojave is over an hour away. When we get there, the old woman may not know anything about Drogan. Or she might be mailing his order somewhere. However you look at it, it's risky. It's your call, Joe."

"Yes, it is." If this turned out to be a wasted trip, then Eve and Beth could be killed before he found them. By shooting Rick Avery, Drogan had burned his bridges, and he was not going to wait too long to get at least a little satisfaction.

But what the hell else could he do? He had no other clues at all.

His foot pressed the accelerator.

"We go to Mojave."

"Inside." Drogan threw open the wooden door and pushed Eve inside the shack. He gestured to Beth, and she stumbled after Eve over the threshold.

"Here we are all together." He lit the oil lamp on the table. "Cozy."

Eve was immediately assaulted by the scent of peppercorn and sulfur again. She could now detect some other ingredients: mustard, patchouli . . . and the potent burning oil was pervading the air of the shack. No wonder it had clung to Drogan . . . and the snake. "It stinks in here. Is that some kind of voodoo brew?"

"Black arts," he corrected. "There are many oils, but I prefer this one. It brings back memories of childhood."

"And you actually believe in voodoo?"

"Sometimes. When I wish. I rule it, it doesn't rule me. Those memories were very exciting. My bitch of a mother liked to frighten me at those voodoo ceremonies when I was a child, but I learned to beat her at her own game. Occasionally, I feel a tug of nostalgia, and I have to go back to my roots." He set the cage down on the dirt floor and opened it. "Come out, Mama, we're home."

Eve stiffened. "You're letting the snake out?"

"If she chooses. I like to give her freedom before she's confined again. I take very good care of her. I feed her, I stroke her down with special oil to protect her." His gaze was narrowed on her face. "You don't like snakes?"

"It depends. What kind of snake?"

A rattle came from the cage.

"Does that answer you?" He smiled. "Yes, I thought so. As a boy, I used coral and water moccasins, but rattlers are easier in the desert. This one is very aggressive."

Eve couldn't keep her gaze off the door

to the cage. Why wasn't the snake coming out? She moistened her lips. "Where is this coffin you were bragging about?"

"It's near the grave I dug out back in the trees. Do you think I wouldn't be prepared for you?"

"I don't think about you at all. You're not worth—" She inhaled sharply. The rattlesnake had slid out of the cage and was coiled in the middle of the floor. Stop freezing, she told herself. Think about how she could kill the snake before it killed her.

Or Beth.

The snake was sliding across the room toward her sister.

"No!" Without thinking, she grabbed the oil lamp and hurled it at the snake. It struck the rattler but then glanced off and broke on the floor. "Get out of the way, Beth."

Beth shook her head, as if to clear it, and was staring at the burning puddle of oil and the snake that was undulating away from it. "What—"

Opportunity. Move.

Drogan was cursing as Eve leaped for him.

But his gun instantly swung to cover

Beth. "Back. Or I'll put a bullet in exactly the same spot between the eyes as I did to her father."

Eve froze. "I'm not moving."

"You bet you're not. And it's time I put you in the ground."

"No, you can't do that," Beth said, her gaze on the snake. "I won't let you hurt her."

"As if you could do anything about it. You're nothing, a weakling. I knew it was a fluke that you got away from me in that hospital room." He turned away, keeping the gun ready and on Eve. "Now be still while I put Mama Zela back in her cage to take her with us." He was moving swiftly, catching and handling the snake with an amazing deftness. In a matter of minutes, the snake was back in the cage, and he was closing the cage door. "There you are, Mama. You didn't like her doing that to you, did you? Don't worry, you'll be able to teach her a lesson soon. It will be a pleasure that—"

He screamed.

Beth had picked up a jagged shard of glass from the broken lamp on the floor and thrown it at his face. Blood spurted from his left eye.

"Bitch." Drogan leaped forward and hit Beth with the barrel of his gun. He hit her again as she was falling to the floor. "I'll break your head, you—" He whirled back to face Eve as she took a step toward him. "Out that back door." He grabbed the snake cage. "Now."

She didn't argue. At least she had managed to distract him from Beth. Though she wasn't sure that the intervention wasn't too late. Beth was lying very still; the blows had been vicious.

"Move." Drogan was wiping the blood from the corner of his eye. "I've had enough of you. Let's see how you deal with Mama."

The white house where Nancy Geronimo lived was small but neat. The baskets of fake geraniums hanging from the posts on the long porch were the only spots of color.

"It doesn't look like the house of a woman who makes voodoo oil," Newell murmured. "Maybe cookies for the PTA."

"You can't label people." Kendra was knocking on the door. "Maybe she does both."

"No answer," Joe said tightly. "But there's

a car in the driveway. Wake her up, dammit."

"I'll do my best. But she may be taking some of her own potions." She banged harder on the door. "But one way or the other, we'll—"

"Get away from my door." The front door had swung open to reveal a tall, thin, elderly woman, dark hair pulled back from her face. She was dressed in a pink flowered robe that was completely incongruous to both her grim expression and the shotgun she was leveling at them. "And then get in your car and take off before I blow you away."

Kendra held up her hands and backed away. "We're no threat to you. We just want information."

"That is a threat to me," she said grimly. "In my business, you can get your throat cut for giving out information. Go away."

"This is a police investigation." Joe stepped forward and showed her his badge. "A kidnapping. Trust me. You don't want to get involved, Ms. Geronimo."

She glanced at his credentials. "This is an Atlanta badge. You can't have authority out here."

Sharp. And probably very familiar with police procedure.

"I could still get a court order. It would just take me time. I don't have time. And if the kidnap victims are murdered in the meantime, you'll be in a world of trouble."

She moistened her lips. "I'm not involved in any kidnapping. I just sell herbs."

"And black arts oil."

"Which doesn't hurt anyone. It's just a game some of my clients play."

"We're looking for a man who bought your oil."

"I sell a lot of oil. I wouldn't remember. I have clients who come to me from four other states. Sometimes on weekends, my front yard is bumper-to-bumper with cars and trucks."

"This would be a truck," Kendra said. "A tall man, large feet, probably usually wears Timberland hiking boots. The footprint I saw had an imprint of cross-pattern lugs sole. That's pretty distinctive of Timberland."

Nancy Geronimo was gazing blankly at her. "I don't pay much attention to boots."

Kendra shrugged. "Not many people do. Sometimes it strikes a bell." She turned to Joe. "Wait, do you have a photo?"

"I thought you'd never ask," Joe said dryly. He pulled up a photo on his phone. "This is Drogan."

The woman looked at the photo. "Maybe I've seen him."

"Yes or no?" Joe added softly, "If you lie, I'll make your life hell."

"I've seen hell before. But I'm not going to stick my neck out for someone who doesn't mean a damn to me." She looked again at the photo. "Yeah, I've sold oil to him. Several canisters in the last month. Surly son of a bitch."

"Does he live near here? Or does he drive in from another state?"

"He's local, I think. I was driving out in the desert gathering supplies a few weeks ago, and I saw his truck. It was near a beat-up old shack with a broken door."

He straightened. "What color was the truck? Where? Which direction?"

"Red truck. Sort of rust red. The shack is . . . East." She waved a vague hand. "And I don't know where. I told you, I was driving around, trying to locate some of my ingredients."

"Eye of newt?" Newell murmured.

The woman gave him an ugly glance. "I

think maybe it was southeast. That's all I can tell you." She started to close the door, then stopped. "He's . . . kind of creepy. He carries a snake around with him. I've heard it rattle in the cage."

"And you're not accustomed to creepy clients?" Kendra asked her, as Joe turned and headed back to the car.

"Yeah, but he's in a class by himself. Don't tell him I told you where to find him."

She slammed the door.

"But she didn't tell us," Joe said tightly. "It's going to be like looking for a needle in a haystack." He started the car. "Southeast. Dammit, but *where*?"

CHAPTER

18

The moonlight was bright and the ground soft and giving beneath Eve's feet as she went ahead of Drogan out the back door of the shack and across the sand.

"Here," Drogan said roughly.

She had almost stumbled into the grave Drogan had dug. She stared down at the open coffin in the three-foot-deep hole.

"Are you afraid?" Drogan asked.

"No."

"You're lying."

"No, I'm not afraid of facing what's beyond. There are times when I'd welcome it." Because Bonnie was there and would welcome her. "But you should be afraid, Drogan. I think you are. I think that's what all this voodoo business is all about."

He was cursing beneath his breath. "Jump down in the coffin and lie down."

Should she do it? The death he had planned for her was hideous. She could make a move on him now and she might get lucky.

And she might not.

Joe could be near. God, she hoped he was near.

She jumped down into the coffin and lay down. It was narrow and barely held her slender frame. She tensed, waiting.

She didn't have long to wait.

Drogan dropped the snake on her chest. The rattler was striking in all directions.

Don't move. Don't breathe. Don't give the snake any reason to strike at her body.

Darkness.

Drogan had dragged the lid over the coffin.

She could feel the snake slowly move up her body toward her throat.

Barren desert, cactus, moonlight stark on shadowy dunes.

No shack.

No truck.

No Drogan.

"Try farther east," Newell said. "It's got to be near here somewhere."

"No, it doesn't." Joe's hands gripped the steering wheel with a white-knuckled grip. "Not if she lied."

"She wouldn't have a reason to lie," Kendra said quietly. "She didn't like the idea of being involved. You're not thinking clearly."

That was without question, Joe thought. The only clarity to his thinking was of Eve with Drogan. It was making him sick to his stomach with fear.

"East," Newell said.

Joe nodded jerkily. "I'm changing direction. For God's sake, keep an eye out for that truck."

The snake was lying across her throat, and Eve was afraid that the pounding pulse beat in the hollow would cause the rattler to strike out. There was nothing but darkness and the heavy scent of the oil coating the snake's body.

Don't swallow.

Breathe shallow so that her neck would not move.

The triangular head of the rattler was in her hair, and it was still.

Why wasn't it moving?

Because it's as scared as you are, Mama.
Bonnie?
Yes, I'm with you.
Eve could not see her, but she could feel her there in the darkness. Why? Is this the end, baby?
I don't know, you're doing all the right things, but sometimes that's not enough. I didn't want you to be alone.
I'm not really afraid. I'd be happy to be with you. It's just that it's a natural instinct to feel like this. And Joe . . .
Yes, Joe.
And I don't like snakes.
They're just creatures like the rest of us. It's afraid, too.
Drogan thinks the snake's a she and may be his mother. Isn't that crazy?
Pretty silly. Bonnie was silent. Mama, I'm going to leave you for a little while. That snake is too terrified for me to reach, but I may be able to do something

inside the shack. Don't move. Just keep on doing what you're doing. I'll be back soon.

Bonnie was gone.

Eve felt a ripple of panic, and she must have swallowed, because the snake draped across her throat suddenly stirred.

She froze.

Keep on doing what you're doing.

Which was absolutely nothing, dammit. If she was going to die, she desperately wanted Bonnie back with her for these final minutes. What was she doing in that shack anyway?

"I think we're going around in circles," Newell said.

"No, we're not," Joe said. "That much I know. It just seems as if—"

"Smoke." Kendra grabbed Joe's arm. "I smell smoke."

"I don't smell anything."

"You will soon. It's faint. The wind is blowing it from that hollow over there to the west."

It was over a minute before Joe caught a whiff of the smoke. "Yes."

"It could be nothing," Newell said.

"Or something." He could only pray it was something. They had come up with zilch, and time was running out. Joe was already gunning the car toward the hollow. He inhaled sharply as they crested the hollow.

A shack, flames blazing, fire devouring it.

"Truck?" He bit out.

"There. To the left of the shack," Newell said. "I can't tell what color. It's dark . . . could be red."

"Close enough. We're going in."

"There's someone near that stand of trees," Kendra said. "Do you see him, Joe?"

Just a vague shadow, but the man was tall and slim.

Drogan was said to be tall and slim.

Joe stomped on the accelerator for the remaining distance separating them from the shack. He screeched to a stop as they came near the burning house. "Both of you get out. See if you can get into the shack and check and see if there's anyone inside."

Kendra and Newell were already out of

the car and running toward the burning shack.

Joe turned the car and headed toward the stand of trees.

Drogan.

The headlights picked up Drogan in the beam. His eyes were wide, his expression vicious, and he was raising his gun.

Joe ducked as a bullet shattered the windshield. He jammed on the brakes, opened the driver's door, and rolled out of the car. Drogan was coming toward him, firing.

"Welcome, Quinn," Drogan said. "My plans were all disrupted, but here you are anyway. It must be fate."

"Where's Eve?" From his vantage point all he could see were Drogan's legs on the other side of the car. "I may let you live if you tell me—"

A bullet hit the hubcap of the car next to Joe's head.

"No, you wouldn't let me live if I told you where she is," Drogan said. "You'd be very angry with me. People seem to have a particular horror of the death I've planned for your Eve . . . and you. I hope I can keep you alive long enough to have you join her in her coffin."

Coffin. It was what Joe had feared most. "Where did you bury her?"

Drogan laughed. "Guess. Either she'll suffocate, or the snake I gave her for company will get her. I'll leave it to your imagination."

And Joe's imagination was scaring him to death. If Eve was already in a coffin, he might have only minutes, seconds. He had to put an end to this. He took careful aim under the car. "I'd rather imagine you writhing in hell, Drogan." He shot out both of Drogan's kneecaps.

Drogan screamed, and his legs gave away.

Joe was on him before he touched the ground. His hands clutched Drogan's neck. "You like the idea of suffocating? Let's try it on you, Drogan." His thumbs cut off Drogan's air. "Where is she?"

Drogan gasped, his eyes bulging as he struggled to breathe.

"Talk."

"Dead." His eyes burned with malice. "I haven't heard anything from her for almost ten minutes. She's dead. Mama . . . Zela took . . . her." He suddenly rolled to the side, breaking Joe's hold. He grabbed a knife from the holster on his leg and lunged toward him.

The knife nicked Joe's upper arm before he twisted Drogan's arm and managed to jerk the knife away from his body. "Where is Eve?"

"I told you. I'm not saying anything more."

"No?" Joe's hands closed on his throat again. "You say you killed her. Then you're of no use to me, and you're wasting my time. One last chance?"

"You're a cop. You won't do anything to me."

"You're wrong, you know," Joe said softly. "Good-bye, Drogan."

His hands tightened, jerked, and he broke Drogan's neck.

He jumped to his feet and didn't look back as he moved toward the trees.

Newell was running toward him. "Quinn, did you find Eve?"

"No. She wasn't in the shack, was she?"

"No."

That would have been too much for

which to hope. Drogan had been far too sure, too malicious.

"But Beth was in the shack, still alive," Newell said. "She was crawling out the door when we got there. She's hurt, but Kendra's with her. Did Drogan tell you where—"

"No. She may be somewhere in this stand of trees. You go to the left. I'll go to the right."

Drogan had said he hadn't heard anything from Eve for ten minutes. That meant she must be close.

Find her.

And pray Drogan had been lying or wrong.

"Eve!"

Footsteps.

Frantic cursing.

Joe's voice.

Eve's heart leaped into her throat, but she couldn't even scream to him because it would have caused vocal-cord vibration.

"Eve." The lid was torn off the coffin and thrown aside.

Joe. The bright beam of a flashlight. "Oh, my God." He drew a long, ragged breath. "Stay perfectly still. I can't shoot it. I have to grab the snake quick and throw it out of the coffin and away from you."

He bent closer and moved with painstaking slowness. "He's lifting his head out of your hair. I think he senses me."

And would strike at him . . . or her, as soon as he was sure there was a threat, Eve thought.

Be careful, Joe.

Of course he would be careful. Joe would be careful, and sure and fast.

But things could go wrong, Bonnie had said.

Joe pounced, grabbing the snake behind the head. The next moment he had flung it far away from the coffin and across the yard. He grabbed Eve out of the coffin and up into his arms. "Shoot it, Newell."

"No, let it go. Bonnie wouldn't—" She was clinging desperately to him. He felt so good. Safety. Strength. Joe. "She said the snake was only scared, like me."

"Bonnie," he repeated. He was cupping the back of her head and rocking her back and forth in an agony of relief. "Hallucinations, Eve?"

"Maybe. I was scared enough. I desperately wanted her there. No, I don't think so." She looked beyond his shoulder to see the flames devouring the shack. "Beth! We have to get her out."

"She's out. She was crawling out the door when we got here. Kendra dragged her away from the house and is checking her over. Newell said she was hurt."

"Drogan hit her with the butt of his gun." She looked at Drogan's body a few yards away. "He would probably have let Beth burn to death. It must have been the oil lamp. I didn't think the fire was that bad."

"Bad enough." He held her closer. "Or good enough. The fire led us to the shack. It might have taken us a good deal longer if we hadn't seen it blazing in the distance."

"Drogan killed Rick Avery. I guess you know that."

"Yes." His hand was probing her side. "Are you bleeding?"

"I don't think that—" She had a sudden memory of the instant when Drogan had thrown the snake down into the coffin. The faintest sting . . . "It may be a snakebite from the first couple minutes. It's probably nothing. I didn't even notice that it had gotten me."

"It got you all right." He was examining

the two tears in her shirt. "Looks like a superficial bite, but we'll take you to the hospital to have it treated." He lifted her to her feet and shouted to Newell. "We're heading for the nearest hospital. Tell Kendra to bring Beth."

"I'll tell her. I need to see her." Eve was running toward the shack. "Drogan hit her twice, and it was—" She stopped beside Beth and Kendra, who were a few yards from the burning house. "How is she, Kendra?"

"Not great." Kendra was bathing the deep cut on Beth's temple. "But she comes in and out of consciousness. She asked about you a minute ago." Kendra's gaze raked Eve's face. "And how are you?"

"Okay." She fell to her knees beside Beth. "I have to go to the hospital to have a bite checked out. Beth's in much worse shape than I am. When she threw that glass into Drogan's eye, I thought he'd kill her. We have to get a doctor to look at—"

"No . . . hospital." Beth had opened her eyes and was staring up at Eve. "Not again."

Eve's hand closed tightly on Beth's. "This time it will be different. I'll be there with you, and I won't leave until you go with me."

"Promise?"

"Yes, believe me, Beth. I'll never let anything happen to you again."

Her eyes closed. "I do believe you. Is the little girl . . . safe?"

Eve stiffened. "Little girl?"

"The little girl in the shack. When she came, the fire kept growing and leaping and she was right in the middle of it. It was swirling around her . . . She kept telling me to crawl, to get out the door. Is she safe?"

Eve looked back at the blazing shack.

I may be able to do something inside the shack.

Evidently, Bonnie had found a good deal she could do in the shack.

"You're not answering me." Beth's eyes were open again. "She's just a little girl. If she's not safe, we have to help her."

Eve smiled as she brushed the hair back from Beth's forehead. "It's okay, don't worry," she said softly. "She's not in danger any longer. The little girl couldn't be more safe now."

"Get out of here, Eve. The doctor said Beth's going to be fine," Kendra said as she came into Beth's hospital room. "You've been hanging out here for the last thirty-six hours. You should go to a hotel and get a good night's sleep. I'll stay with her if you like."

Eve shook her head. "I promised I wouldn't leave until she did."

"I should have expected that." Kendra smiled. "I did, really. And, of course, Joe won't leave you."

"He's busy anyway. He's trying to get a permanent release for Beth from the mental hospital. It's not easy. The board is all in a turmoil because of Pierce's death, and they hate the idea of saying they were criminally negligent."

"In this age of lawsuits, you can't blame them."

"I do blame them," she said fiercely. "I blame everyone for not paying attention to what was happening to her. They just drifted along, and time passed. There should have been tests and reviews of Pierce and his staff."

"Hindsight." Kendra put up her hand to stop her protest. "I agree. I'd feel the same if I were you."

"Eve . . ."

Eve's gaze flew down to Beth's face.

Her sister's eyes were open, and she was looking up at Eve. "Back with us? How do you feel?"

"As if I've been hit by a gun butt," she said hoarsely. "And most of the time, I haven't been sleeping. I've just been lying here thinking. I'm sorry, Eve. I'm to blame for everything. And I wasn't much help to you."

"What are you talking about? You al-most took Drogan's eye out. If I'd been faster, we'd have stopped him in his tracks."

"I should have done something before that. It was just that I felt as if I was in some kind of terrible fog." She drew a deep breath. "But that's an excuse, and I don't have the right to try to excuse myself when I should have been there for you." Her gaze fell on Kendra. "You were at the shack. You helped me."

Kendra nodded. "I'm Kendra Michaels. I'm glad you're better." She smiled and turned toward the door. "And now I'll go try to find Joe and see if I can help him. My mother is wonderful at cutting bureaucratic red tape. She gets a vicious pleasure doing it. We'll have you out of here in no time."

Beth looked at Eve when the door closed

behind Kendra. "Red tape?" She moistened her lips. "Trouble, Eve?"

"Nothing we can't handle."

"I won't go back there."

"I'd never let you go back." She smiled as she clasped Beth's hand. "So stop worrying and start thinking about what you want to do with the rest of your life."

"Live." Her face was suddenly lit with an emotion that was amazing in its intensity. "I want to do everything, see everything. There's not one experience I don't want to explore. I told you that the first night I met you."

"Yes, you did." She looked down at their joined hands. "But I wondered if Rick's death had made a difference. It may be a while before you can come to terms with it."

"I may never come to terms with it." Beth's eyes were glittering with tears. "I think I'm trying to hold it at bay. I loved him so much, Eve."

"I know you did." She was silent. "And I think he loved you, Beth."

"That was hard for you to say." Her lips twisted. "But he did love me. I know it. But not as much as I loved him. If the situation had been reversed, I would never have accepted what they told me. I would have fought for him. I would never have stopped. He wasn't what I thought he was, but maybe there was a way I could have helped him, changed him. You don't give up on people because they're not what you want them to be. Not if you love them."

"That's right," Eve said. "Not if you love them." She leaned back in her chair. "Now see if you can go back to sleep until they bring you your lunch."

She shook her head. "I've slept enough. I want to—"

"May I come in? I had to see how you were, Beth." Nelda Avery was standing in the doorway. She was dressed in a gray designer suit, and her makeup and hair were perfection. She didn't wait for an answer. "The nurses said that you weren't seeing visitors, but I told them that family was different." She came toward the bed. "After all, I'm your grandmother, Beth."

Beth was staring at her, stunned. "What?"

"This is Rick's mother, Nelda Avery," Eve said. "I've never met her myself, but I've seen photos. I'm sure you have, too, Beth."

"Yes."

"But we've never seen each other in

person, have we, Beth?" Nelda said. "You don't recognize me?"

"No, I've never seen you, but Rick talked about you. He loved you very much." Beth was still gazing at her. "You look so young and beautiful."

"It's not natural, I assure you. I go to the very best people."

"Why are you here?" Eve asked bluntly.

Nelda smiled. "You're Eve Duncan. You've caused me a great deal of trouble." For a moment the smile faltered. "I understand you were there when my son was killed by that maniac. I don't know if I can forgive you for not preventing that from happening."

"Are you mad?" Eve asked. "If anyone is to blame, it's you. You're the one who persuaded him to be the bait in the trap to lure Beth."

"I have no idea what you mean," she said. "But if I did, then I'd tell you that everything would have been fine if you hadn't been with Beth. It should have been a smooth transaction. My son shouldn't have died."

"No, Beth should have died," Eve said bitterly. "Wasn't that the plan?"

She didn't answer directly. "No one died but my son and the maniac who killed him. Drogan obviously had some grudge against Rick and took the opportunity to have his revenge."

"You know that's not true," Eve said. "You were behind this entire horror. How on earth do you think you can get away with a story like that?"

"Can you prove that it's not true?" Nelda looked her in the eye, and said coolly, "Try it. I have money and power. I've built a reputation that can withstand almost any attack. Besides, nothing can be traced to me."

"What about the money you gave Pierce for keeping Beth at that hospital all those years?"

"I was only a compassionate grand-mother trying to save her grandchild. Look at all the money I poured into getting her cured. My son begged me to do all I could for her, and I did it."

"You lied to him about me," Beth said. "Didn't you?"

"Perhaps." Nelda lifted her chin defiantly. "He couldn't expect to have everything. I had to protect myself. I had to protect him."

"But mostly yourself," Eve said. "Joe told me you were a broken woman the night that Rick was murdered, but it didn't last long, did it? You bounced back, and you're on the attack."

"What do you know?" Nelda said harshly. "Rick was the center of my life, and he was taken. But I won't let the rest of my life be trashed. I deserve the chance to build again."

"You're not going to get it," Eve said flatly. "There will be a way to connect you to Drogan and the murders."

"Find it. And I'll have a battery of lawyers and investigators working to disprove it. I had a reason once to avoid publicity, but that died with Rick. The litigation will go on and on until you finally drop it." She took a step closer to the bed. "Don't listen to her. You wouldn't want to waste your time like that, Beth." Her voice was soft, persuasive. "The whole world is opening for you. Did you know you're going to be a very rich woman? Rick inherited a trust fund from my husband's mother. It's a very large trust and actually makes you a bit richer than even my husband. I was surprised to find out that Rick had left it to you in his will. He never told me."

"Perhaps because he thought you'd try to talk him out of it," Eve said. "You effectively erased Beth from his life."

"It was necessary," Nelda said. "But now we'll make it up to her."

"If I don't cause you any trouble?" Beth asked. "Tell me, did you provide those young girls to Rick?"

She didn't answer for a moment, then shrugged. "Why not? It made him happy and content, and I could keep control of his little affairs. I never understood why he couldn't have more normal relationships, but it was just an adjustment I had to make." She turned. "Now that we've had our discussion, I'll go and let you rest, Beth. You know you only have to call me, and I'll be there to help. After all, we are family."

"Wait," Beth said. "Why did you really come to see me?"

"I told you, the situation has changed, and we have to change with it."

"That's not it." Eve's eyes were narrowed on that smooth, perfect face. "You had to be sure."

Nelda's brows lifted. "I don't know what you mean."

"You had to be sure that Beth still didn't remember anything about that night at the chalet. You had to reassure yourself that Gelber's therapy was still holding firm. The only way you could be certain was to breeze in here and show yourself and look for a reaction."

Nelda smiled. "There was no reaction. I was never at the chalet. Neither was Beth. If there are any records to say that was false, then they're obviously in error. Who would believe that anyone could be hypnotized into forgetting such a traumatic event?"

Eve stared at her with horror. It was possible that Nelda might actually get away with her part in those murders. A combination of almost unlimited money and power would be nearly impossible to fight and, if Nelda had truly been careful in covering her tracks, it could become a nightmare. "And what if Beth starts to remember?"

"And change her story? It wouldn't hold up in court. Of course she could lie and say she did remember, but there are polygraph tests. She wouldn't want to go through that." She glanced at Beth again.

"Look at how delicate she is and what she's suffered through the years. Let her enjoy her life and spend that money Rick left her. She doesn't want to waste one minute trying to punish me when she knows I loved Rick as much as she did."

"Don't I?" Beth was gazing steadily at Nelda. "I think you destroyed Rick. You could have stopped him, taught him, instead of giving him whatever he wanted. I *hate* what you did to him. And I hate what you did to me. You tried your best to destroy me. I'm not sure you still wouldn't do it if you thought you could get away with it. After all, I'm a witness against you."

Nelda shook her head. "Not a credible witness. You're a mental patient, for God's sake. A defense attorney would tear your testimony apart."

"Perhaps. But I'm still a threat to you."

"A threat? Don't be absurd. You're nothing, you've always been nothing."

"Don't underestimate me." Beth added softly, "Because I won't underestimate you, Nelda. I'll watch you and search out your weaknesses, and when I find one, I'll destroy you."

For an instant, Nelda appeared shaken,

but she quickly recovered. "And spend the rest of your life hounding me? Is that what you want to do?"

"No, because that would mean I'd be a sacrifice on your altar." She smiled faintly. "But I can live my life and still go after you. Look over your shoulder, and I'll be there. I can delegate. Rick left me the money to do it."

"It won't work," Nelda said. "I'll win, I always win."

Beth silently shook her head.

Nelda's hands clenched at her sides. "You're pitiful. You can't even see how overmatched you are. I've had years of experience at getting exactly what I want. Who do you think you are?"

"The one person who's qualified to take you down. Look at me, and you'll see yourself. I may have things to learn, but I learn very fast. After all, I'm your granddaughter, Nelda."

Nelda gazed at her for a long moment, a myriad of expressions chasing across her face. Then she made a low exclamation, whirled, and left the room.

Beth drew a long shaky breath and closed her eyes.

Eve gave a low whistle. "Interesting . . ."

"Not for me." Beth's eyes opened. "It was terrifying."

"You were afraid of her? You didn't show it."

"I wasn't afraid of her. I'm afraid to *be* her." She paused. "And I could be her if I let myself. I could feel the power and the will . . ." She swallowed. "I won't let that happen to me. Then she would win, just as she said. And I won't let her win. It may take me a long time, but I'm going to find a way to take her down." She closed her eyes again. "If you don't mind, I think I'll rest now. You go somewhere and rest, too. You don't have to stay with me."

All the energy had drained away from Beth, yet Eve was still aware of a strength and endurance that hadn't been there before. She had suffered and made mistakes and fought her way through the wall of thorns that had held her prisoner, and it had taken a terrible toll. Beth was changing, growing, becoming what she would have been if she hadn't been caught and held for those nightmare years.

And Eve couldn't wait to see what that change would bring.

"Oh, I'll stay with you." Eve once more took her hand. "It will be my privilege."

"Good news?" Eve looked up from her magazine as Joe came into the hospital room four hours later. She smiled as she read the answer in his expression. "Very good news."

"I convinced the board they wanted to get rid of Beth as soon as possible." He crossed the room and kissed her. "And that keeping her in that hospital was more legally risky than letting her go. It was all about protecting the hospital and their positions on the board." He glanced around the room. "Where's Beth?"

"She's at the atrium down the hall with Kendra. She was getting restless cooped up in this room."

"And a little nervous?"

She shook her head. "She's . . . not the same, Joe. You'll see." She paused. "I want to take her home with us. Is that all right with you?"

"Of course, it is. She's walking wounded right now. She needs us."

"That's what I thought." She stood up and went into his arms. Lord, that felt good.

They had not had more than a few minutes together since the horror at Drogan's shack. "But I had to check with you. You've gone through a hell of a lot for Beth since we came here."

"And you haven't?"

"She's my sister."

He chuckled. "I'm fully aware of that fact. I believe that's what this has all been about." He gave her a quick, hard kiss. "Are you afraid I'm feeling imposed upon?"

"Yes."

"Don't. She's part of you, blood kin. That's enough for me." He kissed her again. "Now go down the hall and tell Beth that she's a free woman and is going to be our guest for a while."

She started to turn away, then looked back at him. "Truly free, Joe? I called you and told you what Nelda Avery said to her. Is there any way the police can find a way to arrest her? She seemed so confident."

"She has a right to be confident," he said grimly. "Nelda Avery is holding a strong hand. I think she's been planning on getting rid of everyone who has been a threat to her for a number of years and had everything in place for when it became necessary. She used some of the tools that Pierce had in place but probably also some of her own. But we'll keep gnawing away until we get a break. There's no way we're going to let her get away with murder. Right now, she's playing her son's death as a murder committed by a maniac who wanted to kill him because he was going to be the next president. The media are going along with it. After she secures her position, will she go after Beth?" He shook his head. "I don't know. I admit I'm afraid for Beth."

"Don't be." She smiled. "Beth's not afraid. She may even look forward to it."

She was still smiling as she walked down the hospital corridor toward the atrium. She could see how Joe would be wary of Nelda Avery, but he hadn't seen the confrontation between Nelda and Beth. Both Eve and Joe were more worried than Beth. She was right about being a mirror of Nelda Avery. She had strength and endurance and even a little of the ruthlessness that Beth, herself, feared would come to the forefront.

She might be Sandra's daughter, but Eve could only see Nelda's strength and not her mother's weakness in Beth.

Sandra.

She had to call Sandra and tell her that Beth was fine now that the situation had stabilized.

"I saw Joe going into my room." Beth turned away from Kendra as Eve came into the atrium. "What news?"

"You're free to go anywhere you wish to go. You're a free woman." She held up her hand as Beth gave a cry. "I imagine you'll not get an apology or admission of misdiagnosis. That would be a confession of guilt. But the hospital is officially releasing you."

"*Yes.*" Beth's face was flushed and luminous, her eyes glittering. "I don't care about confessions or punishments. All I want is to be done with that place." She gave Eve a hug. "Thank you, thank you, thank you."

Eve returned her hug and laughed. "I think you're happy."

"And I'm going to stay that way. No one's going to bring me down again."

Beth's glowing expression made her look as young as the teenager she'd been when the nightmare had started, Eve thought. It was strange that Beth, though appearing grown, seemed younger than her years, while Bonnie, though appearing young, seemed older than her physical body. And where was Eve? Somewhere between and loving both of them with all her heart.

"They wouldn't dare try to bring you down," Eve said. "Joe and I would like you to come home with us for a while. We'll form a united front to repel all invaders."

Beth's smile faded. "And I'll be safe and comfortable and protected by both of you."

"Yes." There was something in Beth's expression that caused Eve to stiffen. "Is something wrong, Beth?"

"What could be wrong? You're two wonderful people who care about me. I'd be foolish not to snatch what you're offering me."

"Yes, you would." Kendra spoke for the first time, her gaze on Beth's face. "But maybe you have a right to be foolish." She turned and moved away from them. "Not my business. I'll keep my mouth shut."

Eve's gaze had not left Beth. "I don't understand. You don't want to go with us?"

"I do want to go with you," Beth said passionately. "I want to be safe. I want to be with you, to get to know you even better, to be part of your life." She paused. "I want that so much that I know that it's wrong."

"Explain."

"I don't have the right to be safe. I haven't taken any chances, I haven't experimented, I haven't made terrible mistakes, I haven't conquered Mt. Everest, I haven't learned how to make friends and keep them. For God's sake, I'm still a virgin."

Eve had to smile. "I believe we've addressed that particular problem before. We have no intention of keeping you from doing any of those things, Beth. We just want to be there to support you."

"And I'm grateful. You can't know how grateful I am. But there's a part of me that wants desperately to go back to that life I lived at the hospital. I don't know if that was part of the posthypnotic suggestion or if I just became accustomed to the routine and care. All I know is that if I want to be free, I can't have supports to prop me up. I might lean on them too much." She smiled shakily. "Please. It's not because I don't care. I'd love to be with you. Maybe someday I'll be able to take what you want to give me. You and Joe are very strong.

You're generous, and you'd want to keep me from getting hurt. But that's not the way I'll learn to be a complete person, is it? You have your own lives, your own careers. I have to find mine, Eve."

Eve could feel her eyes sting as she gazed at her. "It's not because I'm being generous that I want you to come home with us. I'm being selfish. I don't want to worry about you." She swallowed. "But I'll just have to get over it, won't I?" She drew a deep breath. "Okay, you don't have to come live with us. But there are a couple things that you should do. Come to the cottage for a couple days, then I'll let you walk away. I want you to meet Sandra."

Beth stiffened. "I don't know if I want to meet her. I can't understand how she wouldn't care about you."

"You're being defensive. Perhaps she does care about me in her way. But I know that she loves you. Remember what you said to me? You don't give up on people because they're not what you want them to be."

"But I don't love her."

"Give her a chance. I would never have

known about you, never come to help you, if she hadn't loved you enough to tell me about you."

"I'll think about it."

Eve looked at her.

"Oh, all right." She was suddenly smiling again. "See, if I lived with you and Joe, I'd always be doing the right thing and not what I want to do." She gave Eve another hug. "And now I'm going to call Billy and tell him the news. I think we should all go somewhere and celebrate, don't you?"

"Excellent idea." She watched her take her phone out of the pocket of her robe and go to the atrium rail and start to dial. Beth was glowing, eyes sparkling, expression as vivacious as that of the teenage girl she had been all those years ago. Eve felt a pang of emotion that was a mixture of joy and sadness.

No, banish any hint of sadness, embrace the joy. New life. New opportunities for her sister.

And a new set of anxieties for Eve.

"She sent you packing?" Kendra had come to stand beside her. "I could have told you, Eve."

"She was very polite about sending me on my way." She glanced at Kendra. "How did you know?"

"Because I looked at her and saw myself. When I regained my sight, I couldn't stand the thought of being sheltered any longer. I had to break free."

"And, from what you've told me, when you broke loose, it was like a nuclear bomb exploding." She shook her head. "That's not very comforting, Kendra. I'm worried enough about Beth."

"She'll get through it." She smiled. "With a little help from her friends."

"She doesn't want to take my help. She didn't want to come to Atlanta at all."

"Then send her back here. Beth wants to live? California has everything: sin, purity, corruption, glamour. She can pick and choose."

"It's too big a choice."

"No, it's not." Kendra's gaze went to Beth. "Not if she has someone who's been there and can tell her what's waiting on the other side."

Eve's gaze flew to Kendra's face. "Are you saying you'd be willing to keep an eye on her?"

She shrugged. "I can't think of anyone who could do it better. And I wouldn't make it a full-time job, like you would, Eve. I'd let her make her mistakes and just be there to pull her out in an emergency. And I can't see Newell not being around for a backup."

"Why would you do that, Kendra? You've told me from the moment we met how busy you are with your kids."

She was silent a moment. "She's your sister, and, besides, I like her. She has a chance of becoming someone special. I don't want her to blow it." She added, "So suppose I talk to her and try to persuade her that life in the Golden State is the life for her. Maybe she'll tell me to go to hell."

"I don't think so," Eve said. "In your way, you can be very persuasive." She paused. "Thank you, Kendra."

"I'm not doing it for you. Well, maybe I am . . . a little. But I told you, I don't like to leave anything unfinished. Beth is still in that category. We saved her life; now, we've got to make it worth saving." She looked away from Eve. "When we were talking before you came, she asked me about the little girl she saw in the shack again."

"What did you say?"

"I told her that there was no little girl, that she was a figment of Drogan's beating. She didn't want to believe me. She was sure the little girl had been there." She paused. "A little red-haired girl in a Bugs Bunny T-shirt."

And Kendra had researched Eve's story and probably run across references to Bonnie's clothing on that final day. Perhaps Beth had also accessed those same stories. Yet Eve was grateful neither one seemed to want to confront her about Bonnie just then. "But Beth finally did believe you?"

"You'll have to ask Beth. At least, she didn't seem to be worrying about her any longer. She said something about having trouble learning to look beyond reality." She met Eve's gaze. "But you probably won't ask Beth, will you?"

Eve shook her head. "It's one of the things she'll have to come to terms with on her own." She added quietly, "If she comes to me and asks, I'll answer her. But I don't think she'll do that." She glanced at Beth. "She's finished her conversation with Jessie Newell. It's time we got her checked out of this hospital. The doctor's already given her a release. She wants us all to go out on the town and celebrate her not having to go back to Seahaven."

"That sounds like a plan." Kendra smiled. "Champagne, good friends, family, and a bright new life. I can handle a celebration like that."

Eve nodded as she started across the atrium toward Beth.

A bright new life.

Eve could see those words reflected in Beth's glowing face. Eve was still worried about her, and that would probably continue. But that was part of any relationship, wasn't it? If you cared, you accepted everything that went with it.

"Billy's coming right over." Beth was laughing. "He told me that it was only right that he plan out our party tonight since he'd been the one to teach me everything since he woke me up in that hospital. He said that one of the things he hadn't had a chance to teach me were the fine points of celebration. There didn't seem to be anything to celebrate." Her eyes were shining with excitement and eagerness. "But that's all changed now, hasn't it?"

"You bet it has." Eve found herself returning Beth's smile with a joy and eagerness that was almost equal to Beth's. She gave her an affectionate hug before releasing her and taking her arm to lead her down the hall toward her room. "As Kendra said, good friends, family, and a bright new life. That's what celebrations should be about."